What began as a holiday escape to Turkey....

PARADISE
also has its
PRICE

A novel by
THOMAS LAWRENCE

*If anything Connie's Achilles' heel
lay in her incurable romanticism in this hardened age*

ISBN
978-1-957378-03-9 (Paperback)
978-1-957378-02-2 (eBook)

*My sincerest thanks to Maureen and all the others for
their research and help in writing this novel*

*And many thanks to Cynthia Chase for her dedication, patience,
and times of general help from my wife Helga and myself*

And in memory of Tom Lewiston

Table of Contents

TURKEY A LAND FOR LOVERS AND DREAMERS
Author's preface

Turkey can be many things to many people. For archaeologists it is a dream come true as major universities around the western world and Japan continue to send teams of PhDs and graduate students in Archaeology to dig through the Turkish earth in order to recover our common history.

To sun lovers and worshippers Turkey offers a different kind of panacea as each summer tourists from western Europe and England flock to Turkish beaches to enjoy the sun, a warm sea so blue, and yes, oftentimes sex. I journeyed to Turkey in 2000 to see Troy but wound up staying sixteen years in a pretty little Turkish seaport called Fethiye which I made the setting for this novel since *love* is what its story is about.

I observed while living in Fethiye that middle-aged and even elderly English women fly there and oftentimes wind up staying as expatriates. Now as all who have even a rudimentary knowledge of history know, the English have been for centuries a seafaring people. Yet many of the English don't know how to swim and are afraid of water which is something I discovered while living in Fethiye where roughly ten percent of the population were English expatriates. Helga and I became close friends with many of the Brits. I was asked by several if I would teach them how to swim. Of course I said *yes,* and I developed a method which is rather unique.

At Calis (pronounced 'Chalish') Beach the water's depth increases slowly and the area close to shore is usually crowded with English and sometimes Dutch or German bathers (myself being the only American living in Fethiye) and to give swimming lessons to those who had asked, I had first to take them through that crowd treading water and talking, out to where the sea became clear, cool, the bluest of blues, and oh so, so refreshing in the intense heat of the Turkish summer.

To take them out that far, I quite literally floated them like you would a child in your arms, with their lives quite literally in your hands. To distract them I would start them talking about themselves so that they would lose track of how far I was actually taking them.

Occasionally, upon discovering they were in water over their heads, they would demand to be taken back in close to the shore. But they had enjoyed the experience and would ask to be taken out again, and again, until finally they lost their fear of that lovely, lovely water and were ready for swimming lessons. And now I will describe how I was able to make them safe and comfortable swimming in the deeper water.

Having floated them out a sufficient distance, I would have them first learn to float on their backs as I remained beside them, and at first quite literally held them. Then, when they had accustomed themselves to floating, I would swim a few feet away and have them come to me swimming on their backs, promising to catch them. They enjoyed that, and gradually I increased the distance between us until they had no problem swimming on their backs. Then I introduced them to the breast stroke. It was in that period when they were still getting used to floating on their backs that one of my students—Maureen (she was in her early forties and a high school teacher in Manchester) said as she looked up into my face, "You should write something about this!

CONNIE
KAHRAMANLAR

Chapter 1

WITH ITS SURF THE COLOUR of jade, Oludeniz lies situated where the Aegean Sea meets the Mediterranean. Its backdrop of rugged mountains descending steeply into the turquoise blue water makes it the most photographed shoreline in Turkey. Beside the main beach which faces the open sea and tucked a little behind it lies the picturesque Blue Lagoon perfect for swimming: or at least that was Connie Cullingsworth's first thought upon being introduced to this idyllic setting by her new Turkish friend, Omer, who had promised to teach her to swim.

Once, as a child, she had nearly drowned and had been trying to overcome her fear of water ever since, first in that swimming pool in Manchester where she had been told by her instructor that she must learn to breathe through her mouth as she worked her way slowly along the sides of the pool, like a goldfish following the confines of its bowl, the instructor walking beside her at the same tortured slow pace, just above her head. Omer had told her the opposite, "Breathe through your nose. Forget that instructor and listen to *me!*" I've spent half my life in the water and was a diver. So forget everything that silly woman ever told you. And when I've taught you to swim, we go diving!" he said beside her there in the water of the warm Mediterranean that as a girl in Scotland and being incurably romantic, she had dreamt of someday escaping just like a Lord Byron.

"Do you like it here?" Omer beside her asked, gesturing at the sky. Floating, she could see above them: a soft blue filled with the tiny shapes of paragliders floating so effortlessly, drifting or sometimes spiraling downward against the backdrop of hazy steep mountainsides and she *did* she knew she did every bit as much as s he detested cold rainy Manchester. A part of her even wanted to stay once she had realized that she was not going to drown, that Omer would not let her go under.

She was comfortable in fact talking, revealing to him parts of her life using him as a release perhaps, just as she had once used Joyce as her confidante, and her conspirator too in their teenage rebellion.

"And you've never even been in Turkey before according to Alice. This is your first holiday here," said Omer.

She nodded. Except it wasn't intended to be her holiday, it was really Alice's. Alice was her daughter and if she had not gotten into difficulty, had not needed rescuing, then Connie would not be lying on her back now in a sea so blue, being held there by Omer. "Why did it take you so long to come, Connie? I know why!" said her new Turkish swimming instructor gazing down at her through playfully warm eyes her own would stray up to.

"Tell me why," she said.

"Because you didn't know I was waiting—is that the reason?" His black eyes in which she could see sparks of joy looked down at her teasingly. But she liked being teased this way. "When will you go back to England?" he then asked.

"I told you, ten days," she answered and something in those eyes, their disappointment, made her add, "Sorry."

"And Omer will never see you again. Because you don't *want* to come back?" he said, holding her close beside him in the water.

"I can't, Omer. I have my job. Besides, my husband detests it here," she answered truthfully.

"Why?"

"It's hot. *Dirty,* he thinks." From where Omer held her close they could spot Charles lying upon his sunbed at the water's edge immersed in his book on computer science. To her inner embarrassment he stood out always as the only English tourist who insisted on wearing socks and shoes to the beach.

"Charles according to his daughter, is a computer genius and has an important job with the Manchester schools. At least that is what Alice said when I let her stay on the diving boat right after the robbery."

"She hasn't told me that part. Alice isn't really his daughter however—she's mine. I've been married twice. But Alice is right, Charles is a computer programmer and, as such, responsible for all the school computers. He's highly respected," Connie added for no reason—she wished to conclude the subject.

"Who was your first husband?"

"Cliff? Just some salesman. I was young—too young, and too impressionable. We lived with this religious aunt and I suppose I wanted to escape. Anyway Joyce, a girlfriend I had— she pretended to be a hippie— introduced us and I...got pregnant," Connie revealed feeling those intense dark eyes move appraisingly over her body as she lay like a patient on an examining table stretched before him to see. She had been married two times too many, she thought as she met those warm flirtatious eyes, and certainly was not looking for anyone else in her life!

"Do you like being a schoolteacher, Connie?"

"As I haven't much choice, yes," she said feeling his eyes upon her *that way.*

"Can I ask you a sort of personal question?"

"Of course," she said, his intense gaze starting to make her uneasy.

"How old are you?"

She already knew his age. "Thirty-five," she heard herself say. She couldn't help it and now it was too late: the lie had slipped out before she could retract it.

Chapter 2

WHAT SHE HAD TOLD OMER about having almost drowned was not a lie. It had happened in Scotland where she lived as a child—her father being from Glasgow.

Summers Connie had spent growing up beside Loch Fyne with her Scottish aunts and uncles who were elderly. Looking back, she saw herself alone, wandering through hallways, or in high- ceilinged rooms of that rambling two-storied house belonging to her eldest uncle on her father's side: Jim, whom Connie who had no real grandfather thought of as being like one, gruff, cantankerous, who ruled his tiny domain and those trapped in it including her father, like a feudal lord his fiefdom. "Quiet!" he would order, "I can't hear the wireless. Weather's coming on." Connie could remember how he would point the finger at her father then, "Alan, I said quiet! If we want to take the boat out we have to know the weather."

Uncle Jim's wireless had been almost her only contact to the outside world on weekdays when work kept her father in Glasgow. With little else to occupy herself on rainy days since Uncle Jim refused to allow television, Connie would find herself half listening to her aunts' constant complaints of aching joints and high blood pressure, or other signs of age which Connie found repetitious and uninteresting. But sometimes, if her mother were not present, Connie would overhear parts of conversations: things said in secret about her mother and their English past. When the aunts discovered Connie listening, conversation abruptly ceased. There were things Connie knew she was not meant to hear. She believed that they had to do not only with her mother and the fact that she was English but with things before that that were being kept secret.

And that that was also why her Scottish aunts and uncles looked down on both of Connie's parents, not just because the two had met in a Glasgow pub and within a week were married without Connie's father having first sought the family's approval. No, there was a part Connie was not being allowed to know, and that had to do with improprieties on her English side. Whatever had happened, they looked down on her also she believed—at least the aunts did. Connie herself was never sure which she was, English or Scottish. She belonged to neither and that was perhaps why she so quickly attached herself to Joyce later.

But as a child growing up beside Loch Fyne it was boredom she felt mostly, especially on those rain-drenched days where she was forced to wander through rooms. Why was her uncle so set against allowing her to watch television? Once, mustering her courage, she even suggested that on days when she couldn't go outside, watching television would give her something to do. "I donna want to see any niece of mine fill her head with filth! If it's entertainment you're wanting, lass, you just march yourself right up those stairs to my library."

It was there, in her grandfather-uncle's library, and with nowhere to go on those rainy grey mist-filled days, that Connie first discovered her love for reading. Even before the drowning accident she knew practically by heart Sir Walter Scott and Robert Louis Stevenson. Uncle Jim's library even held copies of Homer in expensive leather. One summer she managed to read the entire *Odyssey* and even parts of the *Iliad* when she could find nothing more interesting. Connie tried picturing in her mind the face of Helen. How she wished she could look like Helen! But she didn't, she was plain and ordinary; a face boys wouldn't look twice at.

But not all days were rainy on Loch Fyne and when the sun shone Connie would go off on long walks by herself over the yellow gorse or up hillsides purple with heather that looked down upon the black ominous water of the loch. Sometimes, passing through the clustered red berries of Rowan trees, she would emerge at the crest of a hill, and from it gaze out at the distant mountains just as Helen had, from the windy towers of Troy, handsome Prince Paris beside her. Had there been a real Paris? If so, what did he look like? Like her handsome cousin John, Uncle Jim's son, who was so good looking she thought. She tried to picture Paris as John: picturing herself beside him, the Greek army below. Or perhaps he had been wounded by a Greek arrow or spear. She pictured herself caring for him there in the failing light. It would be dark soon she realized she must turn back.

"What do you find to do out there by yourself all day long, child?" her Aunt Jean who was more her grandmother would ask if it were very late.

"I'm not a child and don't treat me like one!" Connie would half whisper, knowing Jean to be practically deaf.

Connie did not much like her elderly aunt and, after the events of one afternoon in particular, she found good reason. Despite her loss of hearing Aunt Jean conducted the affairs of Jim's household with authoritarian rule from the highbacked rocker where she would sit rigid in her laced black shoes wearing always the same shapeless black dress as she observed them all through steel-rimmed spectacles that made her eyes appear as depthless glassy reflections. Her brother would pour the ladies a bit of sherry from the decanter he kept on the bar in the front parlour while the men, of course, were offered their choice of whisky.

This afternoon, however, Uncle Jim was not present—Connie could not recall why: only that Jean did not offer them their normal glass of whisky or sherry. She remained instead upright and silent transfixed in her gaze, Connie saw. One of her father's weaknesses, she knew, had always been whisky and she watched as her father rose finally and made his way to the bar before all eyes. Connie remembered seeing him reach for the decanter, and a glass, and it was then her aunt suddenly spoke:

"Alan, I don't think our brother puts his whisky there for anyone who walks in and decides to just help himself without Jim first offering. Especially you, Alan, considering your weakness."

Connie watched in utter humiliation as her father was forced to set the decanter back. How she had hated Aunt Jean at that moment! She glanced through the room to find her mother, search her face for support and at tea which followed Connie would poke at her food and fidget only half listening to her aunts, not hearing the actual words—listening instead to the dreariness of the rain beating against the window.

But there were sunny days too when her spirits lifted, when she could look forward to going out on Uncle Jim's boat. "Constance, if you want to go out fishing with the men this evening, you had better clean your plate better than that!" Aunt Jean would warn. She preferred being with her uncles and looked forward to nothing so much as going with them in Jim's small boat. Powered by an outboard motor, it roared across the loch to find little coves and bays where the fishing was best.

Loch Fyne was itself dark and deep, no one knew how deep, and often fog-like mists would hang over its surface. Yet she never thought of it as dangerous—she supposed because of her father's presence which made her feel safe. Being the only child left in the family, and a girl, her uncles would dote over her as they taught her how to bait her hook then drop it till it touched bottom before drawing the line up taut. Then she must be patient and wait. And don't jerk the line up when you feel the first little nibble. Let the fish take the bait, then strike! And whatever happened, they warned her not to get excited and stand up or change places in the boat too quickly.

On the evening of the accident her cousin John, home on leave from the army, had decided to come fishing with them. Lucky for her! because, of all those in the boat that evening, only her Cousin John knew how to swim.

John was Uncle Jim's only son; and though he was nine years her senior, Connie had always known she was in love with him.

It was a secret she shared with no one. Well almost no one: there were two exceptions. The first was her girlfriend at school, the only one Connie had that she dared trust with such a secret! Second was a diary which contained her most hidden thoughts and even here John remained disguised as a darkly handsome prince with whom she would ride off to her own private moor like a Kathy with her Heathcliff. Then two years ago her child's world, which had never been very secure, shattered when her cousin married suddenly and though she had nothing against John's wife personally—in fact, when she compared herself with her future cousin, Connie was forced to admit that Dorothy might even be the prettier!—she found herself picturing Dorothy in some terrible accident. And she would see herself rushing then to John who would fold her into his arms as their lips met.

Nothing of that sort happened of course, and nor would she have wished it. The wedding took place without hitch and, surprisingly, Connie was even picked as one of the bridesmaids. Just before the newlyweds left Loch Fyne, John had presented her with a pretty little pendent of gold filigree with an amber coloured cairngorm stone he had purchased just for her in India he said.

That had been two years before and now he was back looking ever so handsome with his neatly trimmed moustache and tall military bearing, sitting beside her in the boat as it bobbed. It had been smooth crossing the loch but a wind had come up and now there was a chop which cause the boat to rock slightly. They were fishing near the shore. Even so, the water was very deep here. How deep caused a tremor to pass over her each time she reflected back those twenty-seven years.

"Everyone be quiet!" her Uncle Jim had ordered, "or you'll scare away the fish."

As she sat beside her cousin holding the fishing rod with one hand lightly, its reel secured between her closed thighs, she gazed across at his handsome face, his pellucid gray-green eyes with just a suggestion of sadness, Connie thought, and the fine, slightly aquiline nose and prominent chin with its faint dimple. She could still make out the white scar from something that had happened to him in childhood, a prank that had left his right eyebrow slightly split. Connie wondered what Dorothy thought and felt when she gazed into John's face. *Were they feelings much like her own?* She was envious of her female cousin, and curious to know what they did when they were alone. If John should just suddenly look at her *now*, at this very moment, would he read from her face those thoughts? A part of Connie wanted him to!

Suddenly the tip of John's rod bent. It bent again, almost to the water. "I've got a big one!" he hollered.

In her joy for him Connie completely forgot her own fishing rod and stood up to see better. The boat rocked sharply. She felt the rod slip from her loose grasp and she turned just in time to glimpse it disappear. As she grabbed after it the boat tipped, and she could feel herself falling, see in that split instant the murky- dark water rush frighteningly at her.

The next minutes—it could not have been more than two or three, she thought—had seemed an eternity to her, one filled with the sensations of drowning. There was the frigid blackness of the loch itself, and the taste of salt in her mouth. It burned in her throat as she swallowed it, and in her nose as she tried not to breathe it in. She had gone down thrashing, she was near the surface again—she knew because she saw the cold blackness turn a luminescent green. Then everything was black again and she knew she was drowning. Then John's arm found her.

He pulled her to the surface finally and they dragged her back in the boat feeling more dead than alive. She was numb with cold and must have swallowed a good deal of water because she started vomiting it up. She retched all the way back to shore, to the big white house where Aunt Jean ordered her to bed and forced her to drink hot sweet tea—her cure for all recognizable ills.

That next day, when Aunt Jean and her mother both insisted that she must continue to convalesce after her harrowing ordeal, she was visited by all and made to feel like a little princess, even by Aunt Jean. But it was her cousin she really was waiting for and at tea that evening she could hardly keep her eyes from looking his direction. Dorothy, who sat next to him, must surely be aware and she did not want it to appear to her Scottish aunts and uncles, or to her mother and father, that she was in any way a flirt. So she would risk only occasional glances at John. Once, when their eyes met, he had returned her smile with his own which had sent tingles through her.

It had been an exceptional August, for Scotland especially, she remembered, the rain for now was gone, and there were days on end when the sun shone in a cloudless blue sky. Normally she would have resumed her solitary walks along the hillsides above the loch. But this August she didn't because it was the last week of John's leave, *and what if she shouldn't see him again!* she thought.

Most of his remaining time John spent doing bits of work about the property, things too strenuous for his father at seventy. Connie was wearing the special pendent her cousin had bought just for her that day she came upon him cutting up logs near the shed at the side of the house. It was an unusually warm afternoon and she worn only her swimsuit above a pair of shorts which left her legs entirely bare, and the pendent in full view as it lay above the cleavage of her breasts which she had always wished could be larger.

His back to her, she watched him work. Watched the muscles of his powerful shoulders and forearms flex and unflex as he rhythmically raised then swing the axe. What a lovely figure John had. What a beautiful back! And she became aware of a warm sensation travelling down through her insides as she crept up behind him. He still had not discovered her.

They were alone she believed as she reached to stroke his shoulders. Perhaps he had thought it was Dorothy; he didn't look around but just lowered the axe, relaxing his back for her. Impulsively she pulled the straps of her swimsuit down and began rubbing her breasts against him softly.

He turned then and she saw the look of astonishment come over his face. And then she became aware of someone else standing just beyond them on the path and she knew by the laced- up shoes *who!*

"Constance!"

Her full name. Nobody ever used it unless it was for something serious.

"Get into that house this minute!"

As she turned to run pulling up the straps of her swimsuit, her fingers caught the gold chain of her pendent. It broke and the pendent flew off somewhere in the grass. She dared not even stop to look for it, and in her room behind the locked door she cried inconsolably. She hated her aunt! Hated Scotland!

Connie did not know exactly how long she had lain there. Through the lace window curtains she watched the light of the summer evening fade. Twice she heard taps at her door which she ignored. Then her mother's soft voice:

"Won't you let me in?"

Connie did, and her mother sat on the bed beside her. "You should come down to eat."

"I'm not hungry!"

Her mother paused to look at her then for a long, uncomfortable moment. "So you've done a silly thing. We all do silly things occasionally. By tomorrow it will all be forgotten, Connie. So why don't you come down?"

"Because I don't even want to see their faces tell Aunt Jean!" Again she felt her mother's soft appealing eyes fix on her:

"Connie, so you made a mistake. It's already forgotten. Now come have your tea."

"Tell Aunt Jean I don't want it!"

"Connie, your aunt didn't send me up here."

"Then who did?"

"Somebody else you know."

Then she discovered the envelope her mother was holding out for her. "Who!

What's in it?" she said angrily.

The pendent. John found it. He wants you to have it back." She tried to push her mother's hand with the envelope away.

"Tell him I don't want it!" But she knew she did.

Chapter 3

IN THE AUTUMN OF 1973 when she was just thirteen, following the closure of her father's shipyard on the River Clyde, they left Scotland. *Forever,* Connie thought, squeezed into the rear seat of the family car with their clothing and whatever household possessions could be fitted in.

Her father who, besides his classical music, liked history, drove, stopping only long enough as they crossed the border for him to show her Hadrian's Wall through a downpour of rain, driving toward Aunt Isabel's house in Manchester where Connie would spend the next seven years in that narrow attic room Aunt Isabel had especially prepared for her, and with a window that faced out onto the branches of an apple tree which after a time she would learn to climb down in the dark: escaping from her aunt's once, briefly, through her unhappy first marriage (though she could not have known that either).

Originally a *Council house,* the Victorian structure her aunt resided in was one of many identically joined housefronts: cheerless brick facades dulled as though from the leaching effects of incessant rain, and before which the car now drew up. Aunt Isabel was waiting in the door.

Connie, who had not seen her English aunt in perhaps seven years and was no longer sure what she would even look like, found herself being hugged, then kissed by the aged mouth around which she could make out a faint dark moustache and withered face of Aunt Isabel. "Haven't you gotten tall, Connie! My, but so thin—you don't get that from your English side, does she, Elizabeth?" It was true. Her father's side of the family were tall mostly while they were all shorter and tended to be stout on Connie's English side. Her aunt then drew back as if to see her better. But Connie saw the aunt's eyes look past her, "And I see you've come. Welcome to my house, Alan!" *Only she didn't mean it* thought Connie: her aunt's voice had instantly changed, become formal. Underneath her aunt disapproved of her father Connie sensed. Because of his Scottishness? *Yes,* and that was why she had turned against her aunt Connie later thought.

But there were other reasons: her wanting to wear lipstick.

"I'm sorry, young lady: girls your age might get away with that in Scotland, but in my house they don't! Do you know what our minister would say if he could see you now?"

Minister? Her Scottish family had been religious too, so religion had always been present. Being non-religious like her father, Connie had had to accept it as part of everyday existence much like you would the furniture in a room because it was there. But, copying her father, she had always kept a safe distance from it so that, until now, it had posed no actual threat. Her childhood memories of her English aunt had not included this as several mornings later Isabel showed her and her mother the way to *Queen Elizabeth Grammar School for Girls* where the aunt already had Connie enrolled. It was the school her minister recommended she told them, since the children of Pakistanis or Jamaicans; children who were not even of their race or colour, did not go there. Then the following morning Connie was taken by her aunt to the clothing outlet to purchase the required school uniform. Just seeing it made her wish she were back in Scotland. The jacket and skirt were of unfashionable navy blue and worn with gray stockings while the shoes were ugly black oxfords. Worse still was the childish-looking velour hat that together with the shoes made her look like a kid! She could just picture herself forced to hide her face each time she passed a boy her age on his way to the school she should be attending!

Queen Elizabeth Grammar School for Girls she found was a cold and drafty place with high echoey corridors where the steam radiators hissed and made *clanky* noises. At first, she felt alone. Many of her classmates chose to snub her. But because she loved to read, English became her best subject and soon she rose to the top of her class, 'Teacher's pet' some of her classmates who had taken an immediate dislike to her, would say.

Not all of her classes were easy. Math certainly wasn't, and there were those she disliked, such as Latin. Why must she study Latin when there were so many languages she wanted to learn, like Italian which was a beautiful language, so full of love and tragedy she knew from lying curled in her father's lap listening to Puccini on his *lp's.* If she could learn Italian, then she could live in Rome! She pictured herself jumping wildly some warm night into the *Tivoli Fountain,* like Sophia Loren or *somebody* had, she thought. Or if she could learn Spanish! She loved to listen with her father to the Toreador Song from Carmen and picture herself sitting at a table in an outdoor café, then meeting a romantic bull fighter!

Latin wasn't the only class she disliked. *Games* she loathed: being forced to play netball and hockey—what possible value could they have for her and, anyway, she wasn't good at games. Above all she hated gym and being herded afterward into the showers and forced to stand naked before the teachers, to be inspected. They were all older women, and spinsters like her aunt. They wore identical suits of grey tweed like uniforms, flat black shoes with laces, and all had short-cut hair. She felt exposed and degraded as she was forced to stand uncomfortably before them.

"It makes you wonder what that old bitch—the one in front of us—is thinking about when she looks us over, like *now!*"

Turning in surprise, Connie discovered a dark-haired girl beside her.

"She's a dyke!" whispered the girl.

Connie tried to hold back a giggle.

"It's true," the girl whispered close to her ear and Connie saw her flash the end of her tongue at the teacher whose eyes had been looking her up and down.

"*You there,* have you got a problem?" said another teacher who had seen the tongue flick.

"No, Miss Jensen."

"Then go about your business. And you two girls separate!"

"Meet me after school in front of the cafeteria," the girl said in her ear as they parted.

Her name was Joyce. Connie had been watching her for some time already in class: a dark-haired pretty girl with alert hazel eyes that took in and understood everything with just a glance, her attitude at once critical if not contemptuous: *standoffish* Connie thought from the way the girl looked upon the rest of her classmates so that, though curious, Connie had kept her safe distance also. "I've been watching you in class," said the girl to her, "and could tell right away you don't like it here, do you? Parents make you come?"

And when Connie nodded back:

"Unfortunately for me, so did mine. Both want me to have the best education, quote unquote. I know you're not from Manchester. Where do you live at, man?"

And when Connie told her and briefly described for her the aunt's house, Joyce had said:

"Bummer! You want me to show you where I live? It's not so far. My parents both work so we have the house to ourselves. Want to? I can show you my collection of psychedelic posters that are far out, man!"

It was hippie-sounding expressions like that, and words like 'petti-bourgeoisie' that had made Connie want to draw close to this enigmatic new classmate as free-sounding as Connie knew she was restricted, and who would soon become her ally and friend. As they walked Connie had described to Joyce the school she attended in Glasgow and her classmates. Save for one girl whom she had been close to, Connie had never felt comfortable with them, never part of the group. Connie then briefly described her summers spent in her elderly uncle's library on Loch Fyne. But it was her father who had been the lone sheep of the family and often ridiculed that she felt sorriest for; made redundant when the shipyard closed, now he was forced to look for work at his age and that was why they were staying temporarily with the aunt.

"There's my house now," announced Joyce.

It was a bright red brick house, detached, in a cul-de-sac with a trimmed lawn, driveway, and a garage large enough for two cars. It even had a burglar alarm system which Joyce had to first disarm before Connie could enter.

After raiding the refrigerator, Joyce led Connie up to her bedroom off the second-floor landing. Inside, lining the walls, were posters of all their favourite rock stars—and that was only the beginning as Joyce next led Connie across to her closet: "Want to see my latest purchase, man?"

Stilettos!

She hadn't even worn them yet but would this weekend if she decided to try getting into the discotheque Joyce told her, showing Connie her clothes next starting at one end of the rail and moving from her mini-skirts and tops to her dresses. They were beautiful dresses in the latest mod fashions! Envious, how Connie had wished she could have clothes like that as Joyce said to her, "I figured myself out finally and a part of me is definitely materialistic. I don't know about you, but I could never really be a hippie because I like nice things. I'm like split. Maybe a half of me wants to be hippie and my parents, who are totally square, would never understand that part.

But that's alright. It's okay to be a little bourgeoisie if you don't allow it to trap you—know what I mean?" Connie hadn't— she had never tried to think herself out in ways like that before and so remained, she knew, the sum of her own unthought-out values. But the one common value she knew they both shared was their resentment of the place and time in which both lived— the chief difference between them being, Connie reflected, that Joyce's parents were comfortably well off and so could afford being generous.

Chapter 4

JULY OF 1976 WAS A magical date for both girls, now sixteen. It meant they were free of *Queen Elizabeth School for Girls* at last. Yet neither had any real idea of what they wanted from life— only what they did not. Life was too short and too precious, said Joyce, to squander it away working at some meaningless nine- to-five job in Manchester; she knew they were destined for something higher than just *that* her friend proclaimed. Then, as a kind of graduation present to her, Joyce's parents booked a family holiday at a hotel in Salo, Spain and two weeks later Joyce returned with wild stories of all-night discotheques practically on the beach, beaches that were entirely topless, and swarming with boys. The place to "definitely be, man!" was on the Costa del Sol announced Joyce as she showed Connie photos of herself lying topless in the sand.

Two events that brought change occurred as result of Joyce's glowing report: one, with her friend's persuasive help Connie talked her parents into allowing her to work after school and with the money she earned Connie bought herself clothes which she first kept in her attic closet since the aunt did not come there because of the narrow steep staircase. Then on Fridays and Saturdays, dressed up in the sexy new attire she had bought days before, she would sneak quietly out to meet Joyce, until one evening when she came downstairs wearing her latest purchase: a mini-dress and fishnet stockings. Connie had walked with quiet quickness past the door to the living room not really concerned because she could hear the loud blare coming from the television inside which meant that Isabel, who was practically deaf, must be watching TV. Connie had all but reached the front door when she heard the voice behind her: "Constance!"

Her aunt! She froze.

"Stop! Stop right there.–Elizabeth, you better come out here, see what your daughter is up to."

She saw her mother's face then, its look of shocked surprise:

"Where are you going dressed like that, Connie?"

"To Joyce's, like you said I could—remember?"

"Not wearing something like that you're not!" said Aunt Isabel:

"Do you know what you look like, child?"

She searched for some answer. "...no."

"Like a tramp. Like some streetwalker is exactly what you look like. Now get upstairs and take those ridiculous clothes off!" Her father who had found work driving a taxi was not there. There was no one she could appeal to for support as Connie felt herself explode and lash back, "Does that mean I'm going to turn out like your sister, Aunty? Like my English grandmother who wasn't even married when she had Mum! And who isn't even Scottish like me? Who was English like you, Aunty!"

The words like tracers struck their mark. It was her aunt's face now that showed loss and confusion as her mother rushed forward: "Connie, you don't mean that. Apologize to Aunt Isabel!"

"You heard me, I meant it!" Connie said as she turned and fled upstairs to her room where she fell face down on the bed and cried, *I hate you all!*

After that Connie left her sexy new clothes in a suitcase with Joyce. Then on Saturday nights Connie would leave, if forced to by climbing down the apple tree in the dark, and the two would meet at a bus stop, Joyce carrying the suitcase with her sexy attire which Connie would change into, up on the top deck of a city-bound bus, undressing and dressing before the startled faces of mostly men huddled over their cigarettes in the dank cold English dark, just to spend those next few hours beneath strobe lights like a carriageless Cinderella at her heavy rock ball—except that, no matter how hard she might wish, and though she soon discovered that she was a very good dancer, Connie found no romantic prince.

That was the second thing her friend made happen. She and Joyce were determined to leave Manchester and that autumn Joyce talked her into enrolling at the Commercial College where both signed up for beginning Spanish. Juan Garcia was the instructor's name. He was young—twenty-six, and with a degree in English from Madrid University he told her— singling her out from all the other female students in the hallway her second day of class with flashing dark eyes that held her in their warmth, and a smile she found she could not turn down when he invited her to attend his class in conversational Spanish which met three evenings a week, after which the instructor would adjourn to a pub near the campus for his nightly pint of bitter, and of course his students were invited. Joyce's evenings were taken up now, mostly with her new boyfriend. So Connie would accompany others of her class across to the pub. Or sometimes she would go by herself. One evening, after the rest of her classmates one-by-one had left the pub, Juan offered to drive Connie home and that was how their relationship had started, with their first goodnight kiss.

Then, one night as he neared the spot where he always dropped her off, she felt his hand reach under her dress. He was from Madrid and described it for her: the Plaza Mayor with its quaint bars beneath the street where you drank cold sangria from small earthen pitchers, and where the *tunas* serenaded you. She did not know what 'tunas' or 'sangria' were. The tunas were university students Juan explained, and they came dressed like troubadours back in the Middle Ages, strumming their medieval instruments as they sang love ballads at your table. As for the sangria, she could try that herself here in Manchester, at a Spanish restaurant where he often dined. "Do you want to, Constancita?" he said, calling her by that pet name he had coined for just her, "Si?"

"Where and when?" she asked.

The restaurant was called the Grado he said, "Saturday night then, let us say at eight o'clock. Si, *guapa?*"

She found she could not turn him down. "Mum, is it okay if I stay with Joyce Saturday night? It will just be girls—she's having one of her sleep-in's?" Connie asked her mother the next morning.

"So I take it you intend to spend the night at his pad?" said Joyce when Connie told her. She had been unprepared for the direct question. "Guess I haven't decided...He may not ask me."

"Oh he *will*. Do you know if he's married?"

"He's not wearing a ring."

"Did you expect him to?" said Joyce, "And even if he is she's not here, she's in Spain. So what difference can it make? If I were in your place and wanted to, I wouldn't think twice."

"I think I'm in love with him!" said Connie unable to hold the thought back. She saw Joyce's surprise turn to instant cynicism:

"Oh Man, don't be *operatic!* Stay real." Joyce looked at her.

"So you like him—okay. And since it has to happen with somebody sooner or later, *why not him?* Look, it's bound to be messy because you've never done it—right? Personally I'd rather go to bed with someone who knows what he's doing the first time (and I think Juan has had his share of women, don't you?). So you going to let him?"

"I don't know."

Thinking back on it, it was as if she had known all along what she would do and had merely failed to tell herself—even before Joyce had discovered it and had told her. Otherwise, why would she have agreed to meet him at the Spanish restaurant to begin with? It wasn't for the food, or even the sangria, she thought—though she had drunk plenty of that! Enough so that he had had to almost carry her to his car. Then at his apartment help her into and out of the lift, his voice all the time whispering to her words that sent tingles of pleasure through her. "Guapacita!

Mi amor!" he whispered again as he opened the door to his apartment and drew her inside. She remembered seeing the bottle of red wine and watching him open it. Then he had put some Spanish guitar on and had tried to show her some dance steps. But she kept falling into him.

"So you're saying he got you thoroughly pissed," said Joyce: "How much can you remember?"

She had fallen backwards onto the bed. Then he began undressing her. Had she wanted to stop him at that point, she could not have. But she hadn't wanted him to stop. "Constancita. Mi amor!" he kept whispering.

"Did it hurt much?" Joyce asked.

Hurt? It was difficult to disentangle and separate the rush of feelings and sensations she felt flood through her. "Just a little."

"So that part is over with," said Joyce after an interrogative pause. "Are you going to continue seeing him?"

"He wants me to. He wants me to come home with him after classes."
"And?"

There was no doubt in Connie's mind that she loved Juan and would do so forever. "I said I would. I'll just have to go on using you. I told Mum I stayed at your house last night, just so you know."

And that was how her affair had begun in earnest; how it had continued up to the very end, with Joyce covering for her. It was during this period that she became such a convincing little liar because for the first time in her life she was in love and, being in love, would have done anything to hold fast to her joy, those pleasures without the least regard for where they led. It was Joyce who first raised the possibility of Juan leaving her, going back to Spain. "Just how long is this *Don Juan* of yours going to be the Spanish teacher? Do you know anything about his contract? Or if he plans to renew it?"

"I don't know," Connie said: "I haven't asked him...I just never thought of it, I suppose." —which was not entirely true. Juan was here because of his job. Surely he must return to Madrid sooner or later she knew, *forever, or would he come back to her?* Though she feared his answer, the question now raised by Joyce could no longer be avoided and one grey wet Manchester afternoon as she lay next to him on the bed half watching the rain run down their window, she asked:

"When will you go back to Madrid?" The question had taken him by surprise and when he answered there was a faint uneasiness to his voice.

"Why do you ask, Amor?"

"Curious. I don't want you to is all."

"And I don't want to either, *guapa*. I have my contract to finish here."

"But you'll go someday—?"

"Claro."

She felt his fingers explore her nipple, then start slowly down—how she loved being touched by those fingers! "...Do you miss Madrid?"

"It is my home, Amor. Si."

"More than you would me?"

"It is a long time yet. Don't let us think about it, Amor."

"You mean that we won't see each other again?"

He remained silent. And when he resumed there was again that uneasiness she could sense:

"When that happens, Amor, if it does, but you can come with me! To Madrid! I take you to all those places you like. Plaza Major where we drink sangria, *si?* And the tunas will sing *only for you!*"

She had just turned seventeen with little or no money. How could he expect her to follow him to Madrid? He was not being honest! The discovery made her intensely unhappy. She considered dropping the class.

But despite her vow to do so—break his hold over her that way—she continued to meet him in secret.

Then came his sudden change of attitude. It had happened quite literally overnight. He had always greeted her entrance into class with that flashing warm smile that she sensed was only for her, often followed by the momentary touch of his hand upon her arm, or sometimes the small of her back, or her buttocks. But then one afternoon when she had entered class the smile was no longer there. If anything, she sensed his deliberate avoidance of her which even Joyce had noticed; and as they left the classroom, her friend said, "Connie, what ever did you do to Juan?"

The following afternoon's Spanish class was cancelled, and when it resumed two days later Connie was startled to discover a new face before the class. He identified himself as a substitute teacher, explaining that Senor Garcia had had to return unexpectedly to Madrid because of his wife who was seriously ill. "When will he be back?" one of the students asked and with sinking suddenness she had known.

She felt worthless. "He never loved me for even an instant!" said Connie to her only friend as they sat down in the school cafeteria and she felt two wet tears slide down her face.

"And you did him—?"

"Yes." sensing Joyce's eyes study her. She could not bring herself to face her friend directly. "He even talked about me following him to Madrid...I never believed him."

"I want to say don't be operatic! But you really did dig the bloke or you wouldn't have kept going back, and I'm not blaming you—I probably would have done the same, okay? But I told you he might be married.

Look, either way the affair would have had to end just as it did since it was always only a question of time before he did go back and *okay,* so he like manipulated you. So what. I think you're even lucky!"

"*Lucky*—how?"

"As previously stated, it had to happen. Good looking bloke?

In your place I'd have done exactly the same. But I wasn't the one who turned him on. So why let it upset you? *Okay* so your Don Juan flew.

You'll forget him. You're starting to now (though you're not aware of it yet). It was an adventure! There are other fish in the sea besides Juan. So go catch yourself one. Just this time don't get yourself caught."

She was accustomed to Joyce's cynicism, but even it failed to buoy her. She dropped her Spanish class as a period of depression followed in which she walked around feeling dead to herself. She was just seventeen and had lived all her life without sex, with only the curiosity, and now she felt suddenly so directionless. A terrible half year in which she struggled with herself!

But worse was to come. Shortly afterward Connie received a phone call from her mother: "Your father has been taken to the hospital, you had better go!" When Connie ran into the doctor in the hospital corridor she knew at once from his face the direness of their situation. Her father had been a heavy smoker and now a malignant tumour had been found in his left lung. Its location made it inoperable, said the doctor to her there in the corridor.

Less than a week later he was dead, his body cremated and for months afterward Connie dreamed always the same dream. She was standing in a bare cold room, before a threatening door which she watched slowly open. But behind it there would be nothing and she would wake then in terror.

Chapter 5

NOT QUITE A YEAR LATER, pregnant, Joyce announced her marriage to the child-to-be's father, Ron, who was a promising young salesman. Connie was at once happy for her best friend, and perhaps not a little envious. At the rushed engagement party which followed, Joyce introduced Connie to Ron's friend and fellow salesman, Cliff Rafinelli. Cliff was known in the circle of friends Ron and Joyce, and now Connie, partied with not just for the powder-blue Porsche he famously drove, but he also had the reputation of being very much a ladies' man. After her own sudden engagement was announced, Connie let it be known to that same circle that hers had not been love at first sight, but rather love at first *dance!* Almost the very first thing she had noticed about Cliff was how marvelously he danced. Joyce had said later, "What a perfect pair the two of you make!" He, tall and handsome like a Spanish bull fighter, led while she, willowy in her trailing auburn hair had followed almost in a trance with her slender body keyed to his every caress.

She had had more than enough alcohol to loosen her up, make her forget fear because she'd heard about it later through the friends of friends: her *dirty dancing* that night.

Joyce and Ron were married that February in a simple ceremony after which they set off with Connie and Cliff, a foursome for three joyous days at Blackpool where they had gotten totally drunk, especially Connie—too drunk to think about taking a tiny white pill. After missing her first, and then her second period, she told Joyce. Her fear had been that Cliff would refuse to marry her. "He's Italian, isn't he? He will! But I think I'd fix him a nice dinner first," said Joyce "and have the champagne already poured before I tell him. Oh and don't forget to remind him just *who* got you so pissed that night!"

She followed Joyce's advice. Cliff's first response had been: "But why didn't you tell me this before!"

"Because I've always had that problem—been irregular. But I was at the doctor's this afternoon and he confirmed it." She could see him thinking, perhaps he did not want the child!

"I guess I will just have to squeeze enough time out of my schedule to apply for the special license," he said finally.

But it was not the decision he had wanted to make she sensed as their marriage, a hastily arranged civil one, took place that April with just Ron and Joyce, Aunt Isabel and her mother who had distrusted Cliff from the start, attending.

At first, just possessing him—feeling his body through hers— alone had mattered. But with marriage Connie's life changed, and what followed was hardly less than a revelation as she began seeing his shortcomings which she must have known of before. There were crack-like faults which she watched widen to become a gulf—separating them. Politics over which they fought was one such gulf. Like his father, also a top salesman, Cliff was *Tory* through and through and his one serious failing Connie who came from a socialist working-class background found was in his anti-labour attitude. Cliff had come from money—how much Connie still did not know: but enough to have provided him with a public school education which gave him that urbane charm women found so attractive and which he honed to attract new clients.

But, married to him, Connie was no longer like a client. For the entire time she carried Alice she had suffered from severe morning sickness and, though he rarely complained aloud, she knew by his silence that he had little tolerance for people when they were sick. It was only afterward, when Alice cried at night that the anger surfaced and he would say, lying in bed beside her, "Can't you keep that baby quiet? If I should lose this sale—!"

Sometimes she told Joyce about it and it was interesting to note how Joyce could switch alliances. "Just *what is it* about Cliff apart from having been spoiled rotten?" Joyce would say, "He's vain, we've already established that much." Yet when they were a foursome together, partying, or off on their weekend adventures, in Cliff's presence Joyce showed her other face. She would turn flirtatious and find ways to catch his attention. During her first trimester, and even into her second, she would insist Cliff dance with her—that was one way. Of course, it was all in fun and after they'd had enough to drink, before she became so big. When she had and could no longer dance, she would say to him, "Do you think I drink too much, Cliff? Carrying this baby, I know I shouldn't. And nor should you, Connie—should she, Cliff?"

With enough alcohol she often became aggressive. During those last two months when her expanding size made dancing impossible, she would show off her ungainly stomach by lifting her loose-fitting top to show her stretch marks, saying, "This is why Marilyn Monroe didn't let herself get pregnant. Can you blame her? And it's as uncomfortable as it looks." Then, turning to Cliff, "Touch me, love. It's hard as a rock!"

Connie was to see much less of her friend after that. She still lived in Cliff's increasingly cramped apartment, and something had to be done. Cliff arrived home early one afternoon to announce that he would forego his golf Saturday because a close customer friend had just told him of a house at Knutsford up in Cheshire that was about to go on the market. A split-level affair with four bedrooms and three baths up, while down on the lower level there was a recreation room with bar just perfect for clients and friends! Moreover, if Cliff liked the place half as much as the customer thought he might, don't hesitate to mention the Rafinelli name! Also Tory and a Freemason, the owner had apparently known Clifford Senior and it was the customer's belief that for as little as seventy-five thousand pounds and a hefty amount down, the owner would sell. At least Cliff should try by using his charm!

That next day Connie and Cliff went to look and the house turned out to be all the customer had said it was. Set upon a rise overlooking pastureland and trees, it had been fully landscaped with a lawn, flower gardens, and a patio perfect for summer parties. At a final price of seventy-eight thousand pounds, twelve of it down, the owner had even agreed to leave before Christmas so that the Rafinellis could get settled in before the baby arrived. It was more than she could ever hope for! Connie acknowledged when asked by Cliff if she would be happy living in a place like Knutsford? So far she had seen it only in its wintry gloom but she could picture their lives here in summer: the lawn green again for their baby and Joyce's toddler to play on; the manicured flower beds a blaze of colour from the rose and dahlia bushes; and drinks in the patio protected by the leafy cool of the grape arbour never once thinking that she could ever get lonely out here—not in a beautiful house like this, she thought as Cliff mobilized their friends.

With that many helping the move took only a day and at their home-warming party that Christmas Cliff had raised his glass before her, "To my beautiful (if very pregnant) goddess. Our happiness!" He had been in Christmas form, entertaining to his friends and associates as he danced his way through their women while Connie, big and awkward, could only watch. In another month she would look streamlined and attractive again and it would be her he wanted to dance with just as before.

But it did not happen.

Due to their location so far from the hospital or their friends, and with Cliff often coming home late, it was decided that Connie's mother would stay at Knutsford with her. If on time (and indications pointed to a normal delivery said the doctor who had examined her during that first week in January) the baby, a girl, could come as early as next week. So Connie had driven to Manchester that next morning, in the small sub-compact Cliff had bought her to get about in, to bring her mother back and four afternoons later, as they sat facing each other on opposite couches, her mother crocheting booties for the baby, Connie noticed suddenly that her underwear felt wet. Her mother had known at once what it was and phoned the doctor who ordered her to bring Connie to delivery and come *now*! While her mother went upstairs for the suitcase they had packed, Connie placed a call to Cliff's secretary who said he was out of the office and gave her a second number where he might be. But there was no answer. Connie had already started to have pains and on the drive in they intensified. "See if you can't get a hold of Cliff. He'll want to know!" Connie said to her mother as the last thing before she was put to bed. Alice was born at 1:15 *a.m.* and it was her mother's face Connie discovered first, smiling down at her as she cast her eyes searchingly about for Cliff: "Where's my husband?"

Cliff arrived about ten that morning, apologetic and carrying freshly cut roses. His secretary had failed to tell him he said. He had been dining with an important client and had not arrived home until quite late to find Connie gone of course. He knew there was only one place she could be. But it was already past midnight, so he had decided to wait until morning he said. Much of Cliff's time was taken up with clients so it was impossible to know if he was telling them the truth or not. "When my secretary phoned me the news this morning I rushed right down here of course," said Cliff as he bent to kiss her. "I assume everything went like it was supposed to—you look happy, Sweetie. And, since no one yet officially has told me, it is a girl?"

"*It* is your daughter, Cliff, and *yes* there were no difficulties— if that's what you're asking," said Liz sarcastically. From the beginning only Connie's aunt had liked Cliff because of his perfect English ways, and because she believed that, unlike Alan, he had money. Her mother, suspicious of those *too* polished manners and *too* perfect diction, had tried to dissuade Connie from marrying him from the start. "How much older than you is Cliff exactly?" she would ask.

"Why should I care about that, Mum, if I love him!"

The hospital released mother and daughter in the morning on the sixth day and Liz drove them back to Knutsford in the sub- compact, Connie and baby Alice—the name having been picked by Cliff after Connie and her mother could not decide—squeezed into the back. Liz had decided to stay on with her daughter at least for the next few days, to help get the house back in some sort of order to please Cliff and to assist with the baby until Connie was physically able, or instruct Cliff to, since both women had expected him to help out somewhat. But he hadn't, or very little, especially where changing Alice's nappy was concerned. "Cliff, take this. Just take it!" Liz would say to him. "It's your baby's *bm!* I can't let go of this child so just take it and put it in the garbage. What is your problem?!"

Housekeeping chores had always fallen to her from practically the first day of their marriage. Cliff demanded a clean house with everything in its assigned place in case he should decide at the last moment to bring home a customer. That responsibility was her part of the marriage and at first it seemed reasonable, especially while they had lived in that small flat. But keeping up a house this size required both time and labour; then add to that the work of tending to a baby, answering her needs. So she was more than pleased when, at the end of the first week, her mother announced she would stay longer. However irritating Cliff might find her presence, Connie found her mother's support indispensable. It would be her mother who did the last-minute tidying up of the house and tended to Alice while

Connie was busy upstairs getting herself dressed—particularly on those days when Cliff would phone to announce he was bringing someone home with him. Even when he hadn't, Connie still liked to dress and make herself attractive just for him. Cliff liked her best when her hair fell loosely about her shoulders and when she wore one of her short dresses, especially before his customers, or when he wanted to really impress a colleague. So, finishing her face and hair, she would join her mother on the couch and, reaching for her knitting needles, resume making clothes for Alice while they awaited Cliff's arrival.

Sometimes they would not hear him enter. His face would just appear and, seeing the two of them knitting together, he would stop. Setting aside her needles, Connie would rise to kiss him while her mother would say, "Hello, Cliff" while keeping her focus on her pair of needles which had not stopped. Then Cliff would move past them and into the party room, only to reappear moments after with his whiskey glass and go straight to the TV remote, and they would continue their knitting while Cliff sat facing the television set which he would gradually turn up until the noise became disturbing. Then he would throw up both hands suddenly:

"Do you have to do that each time I feel like watching the telly? All I ever hear is that *click click click click!* It'd drive any decent man to distraction!"

"Come on, Mum, you can help me in the kitchen. We need to get started with Cliff's tea."

Chapter 6

CLIENTS FORMED THE NUCLEI OF Cliff's crowded life and were the cause of his frequent delays coming home at night. When her mother returned to Manchester to attend the aunt who was close to eighty and needed caring for, life again changed for Connie. In the lead-up to and excitement of at last having her own baby to care for and love, it had never occurred to her that she could become lonely living in such a beautiful setting, in a house that until now she could only have dreamt of one day owning. Sometimes, after putting Alice down for her afternoon nap, Connie would wander the house from room to empty room, waiting for the phone to ring and Cliff to say that he was coming home, that he would only be a little late. Dressed the way she knew Cliff liked and made up, looking as he wanted her to look each time he brought home a client, she would wait for the sound of his Porsche in the driveway.

Sometimes he would arrive very late. One night she had waited and waited, listening for the Porsche. At about midnight Alice began to cry at her feeding time. Connie managed to get her fed and quieted down by rocking her, and softly singing her favourite song from *Porgy and Bess* which as a child she would listen to with her father, curled up beside him, her face resting in his lap. *"Summertime, and the living is easy. O your daddy is rich, and your mummy's good looking. So sleep little babyee..."* When at last Alice was asleep in her arms, Connie gently put her back into the crib careful not to wake her, and she resumed her wait.

She could sense that something of fundamental value had changed. She felt increasingly isolated. Her existence was now a measured set of routines: changing and feeding and bathing Alice, putting her down to nap, then cleaning the house, vacuuming carpets, doing the washing, and finally preparing her face for Cliff's anticipated return. When he did not, she knew he would say he was with a customer, and there was nothing intrinsically false in that either. Cliff was like an actor comfortable with his lines. He would tell her how he loved her not because it was true (or untrue for that matter)—but because he was offering her something to believe in, and the believing not the truth was what was of concern. Or, to take the thought a final step: truth, if it could even be determined, was irrelevant and what mattered most was only the sales pitch.

As Alice began to crawl, then take her first steps, Joyce would sometimes bring Johnny out so that Alice could have a playmate while the two women enjoyed having an afternoon together.

"So how do you like living out here?" Joyce would ask as she glanced appreciatively about the room, "Of the two houses, I would say you definitely got the best...So how is Cliff? Behaving?"

"How should I know. He doesn't tell me that part," Connie would say and add, "I've missed you. I feel so far away from everything living out here."

"I know, and wish we lived closer."

There was a small lending library in Knutsford and when the weather turned terrible, or when Joyce was unable to bring Johnny out for Alice to play with, to pass her days Connie took up reading again. One evening as she sat with her book Cliff arrived home, early for once.

"What's that you're reading?"

"You're home!" she announced looking up in surprise. "A novel by Virginia Woolf." She handed it up, watched him glance over both sides of the dust jacket.

"I've heard of her, haven't I? From that movie *Who's Afraid of Virginia*—"

"That wasn't about her."

"No, then who is Virginia Woolf?"

"Novelist. Short story writer. She wrote about women's problems. In the end she killed herself in a horrible manner."

"How?"

"Loaded her pockets with rocks and walked into a river."

"She did that! She must have been not right *up here!*" said Cliff and dropped the book onto her lap as he turned and disappeared into the party room to make himself a drink.

The problem was, she thought, they had been two totally different people occupying such different space, and with different views. Cliff and his circle were staunch Thatcher supporters and Masonic brothers belonging all to the same lodge, with identical Tory wives, Tory beliefs. Saturday was the one day that Cliff, freed from his business responsibilities, spent his time together with her and if it did not rain they would pack Alice's pram into the company Audi along with baby food and drive to the aunt's house in Manchester, to leave Alice with Connie's mother for the day. Then it would be on to the Brookvale Club green for Cliff's day of golf.

Called the *Nineteenth Hole*, the course clubhouse was the meeting point for all Cliff's friends and their wives. Spacious, it served multiple purposes. Her favourite part was the dining area with its oak-paneled walls upon which aged photographs and portraits were hung of former members, dignitaries and socialites, some now dead, she thought. At one end there was a small stage just big enough to hold a dance combo or other musical groups, before a dance floor surrounded by tables which, on weekends, were always filled. Connie loved nothing more than to have dinner there Saturdays, then dance away the night following Cliff's afternoon round of golf from which the wives were excluded because there was more than golf at stake on the greens: there were potential business deals.

During the day the restaurant itself remained closed. Club members and their guests would pass through the empty tables to the club's bar at the rear where ladies were now allowed and it was here that Connie would spend her afternoons beside the other waiting wives, sipping gin or vodka tonics mostly while she listened to their conversations but carefully avoided having to voice her opinion since, being Conservatives, Cliff and his friends all were against trade unions. So Connie would be forced to sip her drink in silence.

At Christmas the standing member of Parliament from their district had been killed in an automobile accident and a bye election for his successor had been called for late that spring. Henry Marshall-Taylor was one of the candidates. A Conservative, and also a member of Brookvale, he was the huge favourite among Cliff's friends and associates. The Socialist opposing him was Geoff Smith, a name on not just Connie's tongue suddenly, but the wagging tongues of all in the clubhouse bar that evening following a tabloid article alleging the Chair of the local Council Planning Committee had close ties with both Smith and to a building firm that had been handed a certain highly lucrative building contract, and that the money was rumoured to have been passed from the said builder to Smith for future favours should he win. It was a charge in serious need of investigation according to Henry Marshall-Taylor during an interview on the local news. Geoff Smith, in response, was threatening legal proceedings according to the tabloids.

"So who are we to believe—not the Socialist surely!" said one of the Tory wives to Connie's right. "Oh my heavens, no!" another said. "But what's the bloke's name who's lining Smith's pockets is what I want to know."

"Higgens," Connie heard Cliff say, "and there's something else I heard about him having ties to the Socialist Workers Party."

"Bloody hell!" said someone along the bar. "No wonder this Smith bloke never likes to talk about himself," said another whom Connie recognized as one of Cliff's associates. "I hear he comes from the pits."

"Did he even go to public school?"

Connie listened in anger.

"He certainly won't get my vote."

"Nor, I daresay, the vote of anyone in this club."

"He'll get mine and you're right. I didn't go to public school either and I am a Socialist just like my father! I am for unions and you make me sick with your bloated self-righteousness!"

She stopped. The entire bar had gone silent and she was at its centre as she looked about, saw upon their gaping faces expressions of amazed disbelief: Cliff's among them and she could see his rage as he pushed his drink aside and rose.

She watched him pay, then stop to offer a few goodbyes, here, there. "We're leaving," he ordered as he walked by. Her anger past, astonished at herself, what she had just said and done, she rose and meekly followed him out, past tables being set now for dinner.

"You do know what you just did, don't you?" he said as they walked to the car, his voice hardly above a whisper—seething. She had an idea. But it was not until Monday and the full gravity of it began to sink in that she realized how complete her exile now was. The next day when she phoned Joyce. Her friend's first comment had been, "I heard all about how you wrecked Cliff's golf game!" the voice sounding amused, cynical— perhaps a bit cool.

"Who told you, Ron?"

"I have ears. And I think if I were in your place I would forego my pride and sue for peace."

It was not long afterward that the mysterious phone calls began. After the *Nineteenth Hole* debacle he did not speak to her for two days. Sunday he just left not saying where he was going, or when he would return, and she knew better than to ask. Monday evening when she still had not heard from him by seven, she made herself tea. Alice, missing her *daddy*, and perhaps sensing something was wrong, cried and Connie had a difficult time getting her to sleep. Finally, she had and undressed for bed thinking *This cannot go on.* She felt at least partly to blame since had she just thought first she would never have shot her mouth off, and the next evening when he at last came home she met him wearing the miniskirt she knew he liked. With an arm laid about his shoulders to prevent his escape she began moving her hand downward to his fly which she slowly opened. "Is ihm still so angry at his Connie?" she said in her most coaxing voice.

He made only a half-hearted effort to free himself: "You might have cost me my reputation," he said.

In the beginning Joyce would still drive out for the occasional afternoon. Johnny was six months older than Alice and when the weather warmed enough to dry the grass, they would turn both tots loose on the lawn where they could easily be watched while the two women enjoyed drinks on the nearby patio chairs. Or there was Brandon Park with the usual children's slides and swings not far from the house where they sometimes went, since Johnny was capable enough on his feet to use them. Seeing Johnny climb the ladder and go down the slide made Alice want to do the same, "Mummy, I slide!"

"No, sweetheart, you'll have to wait till you're a bit older."

"But, Mummy, I want!"

Then Joyce came up with an idea. "Connie, why can't you carry Alice up the ladder and put her on the slide while I wait at the bottom to catch her?"

So they had done that, repeating it several times, Alice squealing with cries of delight as she rushed down the slide into Joyce's arms.

But when it was time for them to leave Alice put up resistance. "Again, Mummy!"

"No, sweet, Auntie Joyce has to go home to make Uncle Ron his tea. And Daddy will be coming."

When she returned home, Connie checked the phone as she always did for messages. A Susan had called and had left her number for Cliff to call back.

"I don't know any Susan," Cliff had said. He reached for the phone and dialed nonetheless. "No answer," he said finally and put the phone down. "It can't have been very important."

But two days later the phone rang. Connie, who had been lying beside Alice on the carpet helping her colour in her new colouring book, reached for the receiver: "Hello…hello?" She knew there was someone at the other end because she heard a click and the line went dead. She had barely hung up when the phone rang a second time: "Is Cliff there?"

It was a woman's voice. "He's at work. Who is this? If you'd care to leave your name—"

But the caller had hung up.

"—and you say this woman asked for *me*?" Cliff said when Connie told him of the two unexplained calls. "Sure it wasn't a wrong number? I'm not the only Cliff in the book."

Curious, Connie checked. There were two other listings. Three days later the phone again rang and Connie answered: "Rafinelli residence."

"Can I speak with Cliff?"

"Who *are* you!"

"For me again! A female?" said Cliff when she told him that evening. "I honestly can't think who it could be, Sweetie. Was it an older woman's voice?"

"Why?"

"Because the only person I can think of who may have my home phone is Judy Campbell. Judy is the buyer for Melon Graphics. I'll find out."

Perhaps Cliff forgot. The subject was forgotten until several mornings later as Connie was preparing Alice's bottle. The phone rang and this time when she answered it went dead. Who was making all these calls! She had just sat Alice into the high chair and snapped the tray into place when the phone rang a second time. She grabbed for it: "Just who are you!"

"Who am *I?*"

"Oh, Cliff!" She felt relief. "I just now had another of those calls."

"I think somebody is having what they think is a bit of harmless fun, Sweetie. I mean, I've asked all around the office and I think I told you that it's not Judy Campbell. I'll keep asking but the problem is, Connie, there may be a hundred people out there who have our home phone. Think of how many business cards I must pass out in just the course of a week. But, if it's not as I suspect—a harmless crank—whoever it is, is bound to surface. Oh, and Connie—"

"Yes?"

"Don't wait up for me. I happen to be with a buyer tonight." Connie hung up, thought for a moment, then called Joyce. "I just had another of those disturbing calls, Joyce."

"The same woman?"

"I don't know for sure, Joyce, she hung up."

"And Cliff knows?"

"Of course. He doesn't know who it is, he says. I was thinking maybe we ought to get a new number."

"—if they continue, you mean? That is something I would certainly want to discuss with Cliff first...otherwise how are you getting on by yourself out there?"

"Oh, Alice and I are just sitting here feeling a bit...down, I guess. Why don't you pack up Johnny and come out?"

"Connie, I'd love nothing better. But Johnny for one thing has been under the weather. And I've got a visitor."

"Then I'll let you go. Cheers." To Alice she said as she hung up: "We don't need anybody else, do we!"

June had been a bumper month for Cliff with three hefty contracts signed and delivered. He had been picked 'Salesman of the Month' and there had even been a full-page article highlighting his achievements in the company's bimonthly magazine. The result of all the new acclaim was that Connie would see even less of him.

When it did not rain Connie would take little Alice to Brandon Park where she would push her back and forth in the baby swing, and where Alice could play in the sandbox beside other tots her age. It was here before the sandbox one afternoon that she met Mandy whom she instantly liked.

A rather small, dark-complexioned girl with alert grey eyes and a face Connie felt drawn to, Mandy taught the sixth form after having put herself through teachers' college entirely on her own following her divorce, and so now lived totally on her own, she told Connie.

"And you manage okay by yourself?" said Connie: "You don't miss having a husband?"

"I certainly don't miss *him!* Thank you, I do quite well on my own."

That interested her just the way Mandy had said it. She supposed that she would want another man if the right one showed, Mandy said, but she wasn't looking for him. Teaching kept her quite busy she said, and there were plenty of women's causes she could become active in if she had the time and wanted to donate it.

The two began meeting on the playground after school was out; and while Alice played with Mandy's little boy who was a year older the two women got to know each other better. Connie was especially curious about why Mandy had decided to be a teacher. Simply, after the break-up of her marriage, she knew she had to do something with her life, Mandy told her. In exchange, Connie revealed that she had considered at times doing something like that even though it probably would never happen—their circumstances being so different. For one thing, Cliff made top money—so she really didn't need to work. Secondly, if she were to do so, the small amount she would make in comparison could hardly be worth the friction it would create. "Cliff thinks he's the best salesman the firm has (and he may be). Anyway, that's why he wants me at home. He thinks if I were to go out and work, his colleagues would get the idea that he was forcing me to. Or that he was incapable of controlling me. And *that* might spoil his future chances."

"Chances for *what?*" asked Mandy.

"He thinks if he keeps going like he is they may make him a vice president."

"And for that he keeps you as a personal maid almost, to trot out for his customers—? Fuck him!" said Mandy.

In the weeks that followed Mandy became Joyce's replacement. It was Mandy's boy, Michael, who now played with Alice in the sandbox while the two women kept each other company close-by. Connie discovered she had more in common with Mandy than a desire to teach. Both had voted Socialist and were Thatcher haters. It had been a warm rainless afternoon, the sun pleasantly overhead, on the day they made that discovery. Connie had been in the middle of describing her husband's business partners and affiliates, mentioning their rightwing and Masonic ties telling Mandy about how she had shot her mouth off at the golf club. Engrossed as they sat together on a playground bench, they had taken their eyes off the two children when Mandy glanced over and instantly gripped Connie's arm.

"What?"

Mandy's little boy had climbed to the top of the slide and Alice was trying to follow him. But there were other children on the ladder with the inevitable pushing and crowding.

"Alice, *no!*" screamed Connie. Both women had risen; they rushed toward the slide. There were several three or perhaps four-year old's crowding the top of the ladder and Connie watched helplessly as Alice tried to push her way through them. Suddenly one of the toddlers was falling.

Alice! Connie saw her falling head first. Saw her hit and lie there not crying.

She had heard from someone—her mother perhaps—that if a child cried after its fall, it was probably not hurt. But if it did not, that could be serious! Connie could see Alice's bruised, scraped forehead where she had landed and reached carefully for her baby. "Mummy's here, it's all right, my sweet," said Connie cradling her through her tears while Mandy rushed about collecting their things and throwing them into her car.

The closest hospital was in nearby Chester; Mandy drove. Clutching Alice, Connie waited frantically before Reception while Mandy explained to the receptionist what had happened. Soon a doctor in green appeared, listened while he examined Alice's injured face, then told Connie to come along. To where? X-ray, he explained as she followed to find out first if anything was fractured or broken. Afterward, Alice again in her arms, she was led to the lift. "Where are we going?" she asked the nurse accompanying her.

"Intensive Care, love."

In the children's *IC* ward Alice was taken from her and put into a bed with high-slatted sides. One of the nurses brought a chair. Connie waited and waited. Finally, a doctor appeared with some good news: the x-rays failed to show anything. Did that mean Alice was free to go home? Connie's mind was forming the unsaid question.

"But she's got a concussion, definitely. So we're going to keep her here."

"For how long?"

"Probably just overnight. But we'll know tomorrow."

Downstairs in Reception Mandy was trying to devise ways of keeping her three-year-old occupied. Connie apologized for the delay as her friend drove her back to the playground where her own car remained parked. "Are you fit to drive?" Mandy asked her.

She was, she told Mandy, and would know right where to find Cliff who was attending a two-day conference at the Hotel Britannia in Northenden, which was the side exactly opposite to where her mother and aunt lived in Manchester, but was not all that far from where Joyce and Ron had purchased their house.

It was two as Connie pulled into her own driveway. Perhaps the conference would break up early since it was on its last day, Cliff said. She had the hotel's phone number upstairs somewhere, she thought she knew right where... *Yes*: Connie reached for the phone.

"Hotel Britannia. How can I help you?"

"There's a conference going on there and I need to contact my husband!"

"One minute, Madam."

She heard hotel music: *I'd love to get you/On a slow boat to China. All by myse*—the music abruptly stopped. "Now how can we help you, Madam?"

"I need to contact Mr Rafinelli. He's in the conference."

"One moment."

She waited.

"They don't seem to be answering," said the voice, "They might be on a break. I suggest you try again, Madam."

Impatient suddenly, she dropped the phone and grabbed for her car keys. There was no way to avoid the centre of Manchester. It took her the better part of two hours to locate the hotel and park. She entered the lobby and walked quickly to the reception desk: "There's a conference going on—"

"Yes, Madam, the Civil Engineers," said a desk clerk.

"No, not them, the Association of Manufacturers I need."

"No, Madam, afraid that ended yesterday."

"En—but it can't have!"

"Sorry, Madam, it did. The Civil Engineers started this morning."

Confused, not knowing what to do, Connie had retreated across the lobby to one of the settees where she sank down. So the conference was over but where was her husband? Marlene would know! Marlene was the office secretary and the slip with her phone number was somewhere in Connie's purse. She began rifling through it, then dumped its contents out beside her. Something had happened to the slip of paper!

She could see the face of her watch: 3:30! If she drove fast, she could arrive at the office before it closed. If Alice had sustained serious injuries, Cliff would never forgive her! Or even if the injury weren't threatening, he was her father and would want to know! As she reassembled the contents of her purse, Connie had another thought: Joyce! She would still have the number—unless she had thrown it away by now? It was certainly worth a try, she thought as she got back into her car: it would only take her a half hour to drive to Joyce's.

Less! She had needed only twenty-five minutes to reach Joyce's house. She could see it ahead at the end of the street and she remembered how envious of Joyce she had been just for having a house like that. She had always been envious of Joyce, and not just for her friend's brains—but for her looks too! She could see little Johnny playing at the side of the house as she parked; see him running to meet her.

"Auntie Connie, Uncle Cliff!"

She bent to hug him. "What about Uncle Cliff?"

"Cliff come."

Here? But his car wasn't. Connie hurried up the walk to the door and pushed on the button. She could hear it chime inside and she waited. Then she pushed again:

Joyce had to be home!

Finally, she heard someone approach. The door was being pulled open then and she saw Joyce's startled face; saw Joyce freeze in the act of opening. "Connie, what a surprise!" said her friend as she stood transfixed in the open crack of the door.

"Can I come in?" said Connie.

"Sorry, love." Opening, Joyce stepped aside to watch as Connie entered and started toward the living room, her feet carrying her mechanically. "So what brought you?" said Joyce as she followed.

"Alice. She's had a fall."

"Fall! Not serious?"

"Don't know yet." Her eyes automatically took in the room, its objects. Johnny's toys she saw were strewn about. "She fell from the top of the slide, in that park we used to go to. And now they're keeping her at least till tomorrow, in the intensive care."

"Oh my god!"

"So I need to find Cliff." She could see hanging from a chair in the dining room one of Joyce's bra's and not far from it, in a heap on the carpet, was a man's long-sleeved shirt. It looked familiar. "Ron's at work, I suppose. You don't have his old office number, you know, when he still worked with Cliff?"

"No, Connie, I never keep things."

She was aware of her friend's nervousness as they sat at opposite ends of the couch, and how Joyce's eyes followed hers as they inspected the room. "So now you see it, the lair," said Joyce, "I never was much of a housekeeper—Ron constantly complains. How about a cup of tea? Then you can tell me exactly what happened."

Without awaiting any reply, Joyce jumped up. Connie watched her dart about snatching up first the shirt, then her bra, and disappear with them toward the kitchen leaving her to wait, immobile. She thought of sneaking upstairs but knew her legs would lack the courage. She realized too that to stay here any longer was pointless.

Joyce returned with the tea, and as she set the cups before them Connie thought her hands might have trembled. Also, her friend's hair appeared to have been hastily brushed. "Now tell me in detail what happened."

Connie had, explaining how she had driven to the Hotel Britannia first, expecting to find Cliff.

"So he lied to you, you're saying."

"What else would you call it?"

Joyce nodded. "Well, he's not been here today."

"But when I arrived Johnny said something like, 'Uncle Cliff come.'"

He did yesterday."

"Yesterday?"

"Briefly. He stopped to talk about something with Ron though I have no idea what."

But as Connie left she had a sudden thought. On pure hunch she began to drive slowly through those streets closest to Joyce's. She had not gone three blocks before she spotted the powder- blue Porsche. It must be Cliff's! As she came closer all doubt vanished. She stopped briefly to copy the license number though it hardly seemed necessary, before continuing home. She had decided to skip Cliff's office, afraid that she would be unable to control her emotions, afraid she might breakdown in tears.

When Connie arrived home, the house looked exactly the same. She saw dishes still lying about from morning—they ought to be put in the dishwasher. But she found she didn't care—she felt centerless as if she had lost something of immense value and without which all the other things she had collected and assembled so painstakingly, and that together were her life, now were also valueless. Except for Alice.

She phoned the hospital, asked for Intensive Care. The nurse on duty said her baby was sleeping comfortably and would probably be released sometime tomorrow. No sooner had she hung up when Mandy phoned, concerned about Alice. "And were you able to get hold of your husband?"

"No, I missed him. He must have gone for drinks somewhere right after the conference ended. He left word he'd be home later. I'll call you tomorrow." What would she say when Cliff did decide to come home? Connie thought as she set the phone aside.

Then at quarter to nine she saw the headlights of the Porsche turn into the drive, and she waited.

Heard the door and saw Cliff's face enter. Discovering her he stopped, and she thought from his eyes that he might have been drinking. "Sorry I'm so late, Connie."

She said nothing.

"I was with Joe Morgan who's a buyer. You don't know him." He seemed for a moment confused; then, swaying slightly, came to her:

"So how's my pretty Sweet!"

But when he tried to kiss her, she pushed him away: "Is that *his* shirt you're wearing?"

He looked briefly down at himself. "It's Joe's and you'll never guess what happened. We were in this restaurant, Joe and I, when a waiter—"

"Why didn't you tell me the conference ended yesterday?"

"Well, I didn't know myself. What did you do—phone?"

"Drove when I couldn't get through. So why did you lie to me? And just where were you today?"

"I was starting to tell you. Joe and I—Joe's the buyer for Nexall—"

"Your daughter is in the hospital, as I'm sure Joyce told you."

"Alice in the hospital!"

"Don't lie to me, Cliff. I know you know. You spent the day with Joyce! What happened to the shirt you left here with this morning and later dropped on Joyce's carpet?"

"Connie, now just listen. You're imagining…I don't know what. Joe's wife said she would launder it for me and lent me one of Joe's (and we'll have to get it dry-cleaned by the way—I promised I would), and how it all came about is, we were in this restaurant in Didsbury and I'm trying to close a deal, when this waiter spills a tray of food over the both of us—talk about a mess! So anyway, we drove to Joe's which was closest but how is Alice—shouldn't we go find out?"

"Tomorrow. So you're saying you didn't spend the day with Joyce?"

"I'm telling the God's honest truth and Rafinellis don't lie— where you going?"

Her legs were shaking as she crossed the room. "Get my purse." She returned with it and dug inside, searching for the scrap of paper.

"And you still haven't told me how our daughter is."

"Alice has a concussion they think," she answered him almost rudely. She had found the piece of paper. "Cliff, you said you were nowhere near Joyce's today?"

"I told you, I was in Didsbury."

"Then how is it your car was parked two blocks from Joyce's house? Or a Porsche exactly like it. With exactly the same license number." She thrust the scrap of paper at him: "This is your number, isn't it!"

Silence: he drew a step back and she could feel his rising temper.

"I haven't seen Joyce in two months and that's the God's honest! But okay, if you won't believe your own husband, maybe you'll believe *him!*"

She watched Cliff rifle through his wallet in search of something. A business card: she saw him draw it out:

"Joe Morgan's. He's the buyer for Nexall. Phone and ask him, he's there. And he'll be glad to tell you. Say who you are—my wife—and ask where I was today." Cliff picked up the phone and forced it into her hand: "Now phone!"

Chapter 7

THERE HAD BEEN LITTLE CHOICE other than to leave him Connie revealed there in the water of the Blue Lagoon, allowing her new swimming instructor, Omer, yet another glimpse into her life, one that stopped just short of revealing the hurt she had felt, and the shame, as she sat in the taxi with Alice on her lap and watched the road unravel: rush up into her vision like a broken ticker tape of white lines that drew her as if with them, back to that dreadful Victorian house, a scene of so much painful memory. Her father's unexpected death and her mother placing the urn with his ashes on the mantle where they would stay until, with her mother's second stroke, the responsibility for them became hers.

"When my daddy coming?" Alice asked looking up at her.

"He's not, Sweet. We're going to be staying with your grand- mother and Auntie Isabel. Everything is fine."

But *it* wasn't. She had been in love with the wrong man and now she must pay. She could well imagine what things all her friends would be saying already! Former friends. She did not wish to see them and be forced to admit her mistake.

She retreated with the help of the *Valium* supplied her by their family doctor, and each time she passed a pretty young woman in the street, Connie could not stop herself from wondering if Cliff had not shagged her also. Each time he phoned, Connie would simply hang up.

But one evening her mother picked up the phone first. "Connie, it's your husband and this time maybe you'd better speak with him yourself."

"Tell him I'm not here. What does he want?"

"Can he see Alice Sunday, he wants me to say."

It flashed across her mind: This would be a way to hurt him back! "Why this sudden interest in Alice ask him. He never cared before—not even when she fell off the slide!"

"I think she said *no.*" Her mother listened another moment, then lowered the receiver onto its cradle. "He said he'll contact his solicitor."

"He can do what he pleases!"

"Connie, you're going to need a solicitor yourself," said her mother, "so listen to me for a change. If you no longer care what happens to you, at least think about Alice!"

She had, finally. Fears for her daughter's well-being combined with her mother's plea had prompted her to enroll in the teacher training college following her messy divorce from Cliff and now, fifteen years later, continued worries for her daughter's future brought Connie to Turkey. Alice had no business malingering in a place like Turkey where she might wind up forced in the end to marry some Turk and ruin her life that way. She ought to be back in Manchester right now preparing for the start of her freshman year at Leeds! Connie had told Mandy. But Alice had always been a difficult child to manage; independent-minded and head-strong. That had been all her great aunt's fault; Isabel had catered to her every whim, every desire, no matter how self-destructive. It was Aunt Isabel who had spoiled the child rather than try to instill in her any sense of responsibility.

Isabel had lived until age eighty-eight and up until the last six months of her life she had retained enough of her faculties so that she now became babysitter for Alice during those years when Connie was again in school and her mother worked to help out financially. Liz now lived upstairs in Connie's old attic room while she and Alice occupied the large front bedroom, and her aunt the smaller one to the rear. At eighty-one she was still able to take care of not just the house, but Alice, thus freeing Liz, while Connie attended classes for those next three years until her graduation in 1987. With advanced age, the aunt had lost much of the vituperation shown toward Connie's father, and now doted over Alice as if she were her own daughter *who never had been* perhaps more a mother to Alice than was Connie herself whose time had been completely taken up by classes and schoolwork, save for those weekends on which she still had Alice.

Because every other Saturday Cliff's Porsche appeared again in front of the house. He had been given permission to keep Alice on odd weekends by the court. The aunt would dress her in her best and march her through the door into Cliff's waiting arms while Connie would watch from the window. Alice was starting to lose her chubbiness. As a teenager she would become like her mother, slender, but with her father's complexion and dark, inviting eyes. Already she was a precocious child: pretty, and who liked to flirt Connie saw.

Sundays Alice would return usually wearing a pretty new dress, often carrying home a doll or some other toy Cliff had bought for her. One Sunday afternoon for her third birthday she walked through the door carrying a new CD player: CDs had just come onto the market and afterward, as they sat over tea, Connie had asked, "Do you like your father, Alice?" feeling her resentment just behind the words.

"Of course, Mummy, he likes to buy me things!" And as they washed and put away the dishes that evening her daughter had asked, "Mummy, why don't you like Daddy? Daddy still likes you he told me to say. Said tell you he can explain."

"I don't want his explanations tell him. Tell him to go tell it to his girl friend!" she said, and could feel pain still, just beneath the surface. At the beginning she had tried to block Cliff from being allowed to see his daughter. He would snatch Alice from her too, just as he had everything else she had wanted to hold tightly to, and leave her stripped, feeling naked and ugly. So she had run to the one place she thought herself safe from him. But he had followed her even here, to threaten her fragile peace by that letter from his attorney. Then that court decree. And it was her mother who finally made the appointment for her, with a solicitor their family doctor knew of. "Do I have to go, Mum?"

But she knew she had to. *This is all your making, no one else's!* her inner voice reminded her. She rose to go upstairs. You were warned but you rushed ahead anyway and got yourself pregnant. So what else had you expected? she thought to herself. *I know that* said the voice.

John Hardy of Hardy and Harding had been perhaps fifty, jowly, balding, and with an immediate friendliness that belied his somewhat seedy appearance. But time was money and behind the cordial exterior was an alert legal mind practiced in the art of extracting answers from carefully placed questions. After coaxing from Connie a history of her marriage and subsequent separation, and glancing through the court document and letter from Cliff's attorney, Hardy turned to Connie with a question: "Does your husband own a blue Porsche?"

Did all of Manchester know Cliff by his Porsche! "Yes."

"And he's a member of the Brookdale Golf Club? I met him." She felt a mute surprise.

"More importantly I also know his solicitor, Dave Cartwright. We golf together. I'll give him a call the minute you leave. Now here's what I think we should ask for," said the lawyer as he swiveled around to half face the window: "Infidelity. You can also charge him with mental cruelty." Swiveling his chair he again faced her, "In the terms of the divorce we'll claim child support of course. Financial assistance—you will be needing that. And of course there's the matter of the house...Do you know what your husband's income was last year, Connie?"

And when she hadn't, he said, "That's okay, I'll find out. I think your husband will accept the divorce."

Just as John Hardy had predicted he would, Cliff agreed to the terms of the settlement. The only concession Connie had been forced to make, if she was to avoid having to confront him openly in court, was to extend Cliff's visitation rights to allow him overnight custody of Alice on alternate weekends.

That he would want to keep Alice overnight puzzled Connie. Perhaps it was because Alice was starting to grow into a pretty little girl—someone he could show off to his associates just as He had showed her, *Connie,* off! At their parties when he brought clients home, Connie remembered, he had urged her to wear mini dresses that showed as much of her as possible. Perhaps all men were the same and when they said love they meant only the sex. Her father had not been like that! How Connie wished he could be here and she could again cuddle close. What bothered her most in the settlement was being forced to share Alice overnight. Alice liked her father but what was less clear was why Cliff wanted to keep her overnight now when he had cared so little for her before—unless it was to get back at herself!

The part of the divorce proceedings Connie had dreaded was having to face Cliff, who was so good at twisting words, in court. But John Hardy managed to prevent that by having Cliff agree to sign the necessary papers out of court and while Connie could not receive alimony until the terms of the divorce had been finalized, perhaps due to his solicitor's urging Cliff had put the house on the market within days. The timing could not have been better: just in the past ten months alone property values had climbed by almost ten percent in choice locations like Knutsford.

The house remained on the market for less than a week before her lawyer phoned her: someone had snatched it up! Three weeks later he again called. The bank check was waiting for her! Though the house had sold for a hundred thousand pounds, they'd had so little equity in it that the check when she saw it was for less than three thousand; just enough for her to buy a three-year-old Ford Fiesta, and to pay for her school tuition.

That car had been her salvation. It allowed her to regain control over her life again in the months that immediately followed, since she no longer need fear running into one of Cliff's likely girlfriends and being forced to display a friendly face, and in that respect the Fiesta was like a protection even as it gave her that much desired freedom.

Once back in school, Connie's days began by taking Alice to kindergarten at a quarter to eight then driving on to Manchester Teacher Training College in the city centre for two morning classes plus one in the afternoon: History, which was her major. She loved going to lectures again, loved immersing herself in school and study: they become the principle means of her escape from herself, and that part of her life she wished to avoid. In work she found oblivion. Then something else happened.

It was at the beginning of her sophomore year and Alice was now in first grade, a pretty child of six with long strands of dark hair and instantly warm, flirtatious eyes. Connie would drop her off and proceed on to her own classes that lasted the full day, except on Fridays. Friday, she had only one class in the morning, after which she was free for the day.

As she approached Tesco on her way home one Friday, Connie remembered some items she needed and so decided to stop. She had just pulled into the parking lot, just gotten out and was closing her car door, when she chanced to look up in the direction of the street. It was one of the busiest in Manchester with multiple lanes of traffic, and at its busy time of day. Connie could see cars, perhaps five or six in a group, approach then one caught her attention. She saw it pull out of traffic and slow as if to stop. Connie watched it ease toward the curb and she thought *Why is it stopping?*

But it didn't, it just slowed, and she saw its rear door open. She saw a small dog suddenly being thrown from it. Saw the door slam closed and the car pull back into traffic. For an instant, the dog appeared disoriented, confused as it looked around. Searching for the car that had just dumped it, Connie thought seeing it start to run. She watched helplessly as it ran out into traffic. *It's going to get hit!* She flung her purse back inside the car and ran, fast as she could out into the traffic amid honking car horns, chasing after the dog. But there was something wrong with one of its front legs and it couldn't run.

She was almost on top of it. Without slowing hardly she reached down and scooped the animal up and twisting right, ran for the safety of the sidewalk where a small crowd had formed. She heard voices, talking.

"That car just dumped it."

"Lucky she didn't get hit."

"Are you taking it to the R.S.P.C.A., dearie?" a voice beside her ear said.

She turned to discover the wrinkled face of an old woman and she clutched the poor animal to her even more tightly.

It was only when she was safe in her car that Connie looked closely at the dog she held still cradled in her arms. It had long hair, white and black mostly, but with patches of light chocolate here and there, and it looked up at her through frightened brown eyes. She could feel it shaking in her arms and she was aware then that her hand and a wrist felt wet. The dog was a male and the poor little thing must have peed all over itself!

"You're a pretty little dog, aren't you? Connie's not going to hurt you, no-o." She remembered then it had a bad front paw and she reached for one and felt. Then the second, which she gently squeezed. With a yelp the little dog pulled it from her. "Connie's sorry," she said and knew then what she must do. "What a poor scraggly thing! But don't you worry, Connie's not taking you to any old R.S.P.C.A. She's finding you a vet!"

The dog was mostly terrier thought the veterinarian, between two and three the lack of wear on its teeth—and very neglected. Whenever the poor thing stood Connie saw, it would hold the right front paw raised to avoid having to put weight on it.

"Did he sprain it?" she asked.

"I won't know until I x-ray," said the vet.

Connie had waited. Finally, the vet returned with the X-ray. "It's a greenstick fracture right *here*," he said, pointing to a spot in the x-ray."

"And that happened when the dog was tossed out of the car?" asked Connie.

"Or somebody may have stepped on it. The leg has to be put in a cast, which means keeping it overnight. Also, it may need worming and I doubt if it's had its shots. What do you intend to do with the animal, Mrs—?"

She had almost used Cliff's name: "McKnight—Connie. –I haven't thought about it."

But had she not already fallen in love with this little dog that had been so badly abused? "Keep it. My daughter I know will want him!"

"I think this dog would make a good child's pet, Mrs— Connie. He cringes," observed the doctor: "but that might be because he's been hit in the past or kicked. What he needs right now is just love."

The vet started to turn away with the dog tucked under his arm, but stopped: "Oh and do you want to have the tail shortened? Now would be the best time. And, for the medical file, do you know what you're going to call him?" asked the vet.

He had looked so abused to Connie with his fur all knotted and scraggly. "Scraggles!" she said.

It was a different looking Scraggles the nurse carried into the waiting room for them that next day. The knotted hair was gone and his fir brushed clean. Besides the fresh plaster cast over his right front leg, his tail, now a stub, wore a white protective bandage. Seeing the little dog, Alice had skipped with delight.

"Oh, Mummy, please can I carry Scraggles to the car?"

"No, Sweet. He's still too weak from the anesthetic. See, he doesn't know who we are yet, or what is happening to him."

"Tell you what, Alice," said Connie's mother who had come along to assist. "If you're very careful, you can hold Scraggles on your lap until we get back." So with Liz and Alice tending to a still drowsy little dog in the rear seat, Connie started home. There was a Tesco en route. Leaving her mother to guard over Scraggles, Connie hurried inside. In finding her way to the pet food aisle, she had to pass the fresh meat counter where she remembered someone saying that pork was good for a dog's coat. So she stopped, having decided to buy a small pork roast the more she thought about it. And while here, why not some beef stew meat—Scraggles would like that!

Aunt Isabel was standing in the open door waiting to see the newest family member which she instantly began fussing over. Although she had become unsteady on her legs, Isabel insisted on getting the pillow and blanket for Scraggles' bed herself, putting them first in the kitchen beside food and water bowls, until Alice objected:

"Mummy, why can't Scraggles be with us!"

So they had relocated Scraggles' bed and water dish to the living room for all to keep watch over him as he lay still glassy- eyed from the anesthetic and scarcely aware of Alice's face just inches from his on the carpet, and at ten when they rose to go up to bed the little dog still had not woken. Connie knelt and touched his nose. It felt dry and hot. Was there something wrong with Scraggles?

But the next day the dog seemed normal as his appetite returned. He lapped at the beef broth and practically swallowed half whole the cubes of pork fed to him by hand. They watched him stump about the house on his front leg bound up in a cast exploring behind furniture and in all the corners. That night when they moved his bed into the kitchen Scraggles cried, and his pitiful cries which they could hear upstairs kept them awake.

"Mummy, why can't Scraggles sleep with us?" said Alice.

"That's something we don't want to start," Connie told her. But she too disliked having to hear the dog cry all night and brought its bed upstairs. So long as Scraggles had the greenstick fracture, an exception could be made, she told her daughter as she placed Scraggles' bed beside their dresser. But Scraggles next wanted to sleep with someone and would whine beside the bed asking to be lifted up.

"Why can't he come with me, Mummy?"

While Scraggles' leg was still in its cast, Connie said absolutely *not!* "What if you should roll onto him in your sleep, Alice? Or accidently knock him onto the floor?"

But one night Connie had woken to discover Scraggles' eyes looking balefully up at her, and in her weakness she had lifted him onto the bed. Connie's was a queen-sized mattress and in her sleepy state she had expected the invalid dog to crawl over to the unoccupied side of the bed and simply go to sleep. Instead, Scraggles tried to burrow with his nose down inside the bed covers.

"Oh, all right this once," she whisperingly gave in and lifted the top sheet, feeling Scraggles crawl down beside her until, settling himself, he went to sleep against her leg. That had been in 1986 and she had kept Scraggles safe from harm's way for the next eight years, she counted. Today her Scraggles would be at least fifteen, if still alive. *Was he?* How they had loved that little dog! Alice, her mother. Even Aunt Isabel. All in fact had but Charles. Charles disliked dogs to come even close.

Chapter 8

IN 1989 ALL CONNIE'S DETERMINATION and hard work had finally paid off as she graduated in the top ten percent of her class and was hired almost immediately to teach the fifth form at Claremont that autumn. 1989 was also the year that the National Curriculum was established, with far reaching effects. No longer was what teachers taught a matter of teacher choice or even discretion. Daily lesson plans had to be submitted and approved in advance, forced targets met; and the progress of each student tracked, and the outcome published nationally. If that weren't enough to keep Connie in a constant state of near anxiety, add to it the arrival of the school's first classroom computer.

It was an ungainly slow contraption and as its lights would flicker to life one by one and wink back at her, they somehow made Connie think of old Frankenstein movies. She began calling it her *Frankenstein Monster.* "Today's our day to get the Frankenstein Monster, class," she would announce as she wheeled it into the room on a trolley. Her class was allowed to use it three afternoons a week and with the class size thirty, each student got one turn on it once every second week which created new problems for Connie, since she must now split her time between those at the computer and the remainder of the class. So it was difficult even on those afternoons when the *monster* was cooperative. When it chose not to be, all class activity came to an abrupt stop as Connie was forced to run frantically through the halls trying to locate Margaret Worsley, the teacher picked to troubleshoot the problem. "Margaret, it's Frankenstein! He's down again!"

Because the school had anticipated just this problem, the assistant headmaster had selected Ms. Worsley, one of the most capable teachers, to make herself computer literate. But even with Margaret now available to dash about the school and reboot the monster each time it crashed, there remained the problem of classes being disrupted and time lost. That was why Connie had been forced to attend night classes because someone in the upper echelons of authority had decided that the only permanent fix was to make each teacher computer literate. There were rumours that the Local Education Authority had hired a former teacher to head up its new computer department and take responsibility for the entire program from the instillation of the software to instructing the teachers and already talk circulated about him. Apparently, he had been a science teacher but hadn't liked teaching—or had encountered problems. But those who had attended his class all agreed he certainly knew his subject! But he had one disturbing habit. When standing in front of the class fielding their questions, he would unconsciously reach for his right ear, which was noticeably larger, and pull at its lobe. His name was Charles Cullingsworth and he was thought to be a computer *genius!* Also, a "nerd". Connie checked immediately with the dictionary and decided she probably would dislike him. Due to the limited number of available computers the Education Authority was forced to divide up its teachers into groups. Connie found herself in the second group and scheduled to attend class on Tuesdays and Thursdays. Her class started at seven. How pleasant it had felt to return once more to the place where she had spent the last four years of her life and if they had not been exciting years, they had not been unhappy ones since here at least she had been provided with a place to go where she might start to rebuild her badly damaged ego.

The room was already filling with teachers as Connie arrived. She located an empty chair and sat down to face, on the table before her, a computer. Directly beside it was a booklet-sized manual rubber-stamped **Property of the Manchester Education Authority** and beneath its title she read 'by Charles Cullingsworth'.

Punctually at seven the instructor entered. *Fortyish,* Connie thought as she watched him pass. He was on the tall side but walked with slightly stooped shoulders, she observed. "Good evening, class. My name, as you've probably noticed printed on the blackboard behind, is Charles Cullingsworth and I will be conducting this seminar on how to use your new *1600 series* IBM desktop computer. On each of your tables there should also be *this* manual." Charles held one up. "Does anyone not have it? Raise your hands…No hands? Good! And now to start off, I would suppose you're wondering about me—who I am. Well, like all of you here I'm a teacher and um..taught high school science until someone gave me aah…compiler to play with and well aah..you see what happened."

Like his computers did, he seemed to deliver his words erratically, sometimes in clumps she observed: observing his cleanly shaven round cheeks, reddened in places. *Was it shaving rash?* she wondered as she waited for him to pull at his ear. But he hadn't—not then. The introduction over, Charles ordered them to turn on their IBMs. "And you'll have to be a little patient, class, it takes a minute and a half for the machine to uhm..warm up before the screen lights up. This evening we'll start out by ahm…practicing how to do 'command prompts.' Now I want you to start out by typing *a c, full colon,* then *back slash* followed by the queen arrow"—Charles indicating with his pointer: "*here.* That wakes the computer up. Now it's ready to receive its first command. Perhaps, let's say, you want to begin with a spreadsheet. So we type *ms word* in lower case."

She'd had no trouble performing the simpler tasks. It was not until she was told to turn to page eighteen in her manual and, following the instructions, format her screen that the screen went dark. She raised her hand but had to wait as there had been a flurry of hands. Charles started through the room to answer each of their questions in order, and as Connie waited her him pull at the ear, amused.

"So what happened here?" he asked sympathetically when he reached her desk finally.

The words were spoken softly, each enunciated with slow care—and so precisely. "It crashed like it always does. I'm afraid computers just don't like me!" she answered looking up at him.

"Oh, I would doubt that's the reason," he mused, regarding her a moment. His eyes were a cold, intense blue. She could feel their blueness as she said:

"They don't! The one at my school for sure doesn't. I even gave it a name: my Frankenstein Monster."

"Really!?"

She sensed he was interested. "You're probably thinking because I don't like it. And I do see it as something a mad scientist might want to assemble like in the Frankenstein film."

"Which version? The Boris Karloff classic, I hope." He smiled—it was not a warm full smile but something more tenuous, something *in between* she thought. "Well, I'll tell you what we'll do, Misses, Miss—?"

"Connie—and I'm not married."

"*Connie ?...I see.*"

While they waited for the machine to restart, she had examined his face. Save for those faint red splotches, it was totally drained of colour. "You don't spend any time in the sun, I think."

"No." He looked taken by surprise: "Why do you ask?"

"Because you're so white."

"That's something my ex used to say to me!"

The scorn she felt in his admission told her something of immediate interest about the School Authority's choice for department head as she mulled it over in her thoughts later, before the voice changed and became playful, solicitous even. "Anyway, this is Manchester. *Sun?* I didn't know there was one." he'd said.

His dry humour carried in it a certain appeal and she found herself defending him against snide remarks some of the other teachers were making behind his back. He was thirty-eight, or would be in a matter of days, he told her the following Thursday in the hallway where the students gathered for their break. It was a ten minute one, exactly the time required to smoke a cigarette down to its filter. With smoking inside the classroom banned, those who had to smoke were in a rush to light up, Charles among them. Connie watched him move slowly in her direction, pausing to exchange words here, there, with his students. "So how do you like the class by now?" he asked stopping before her, displaying that tentative smile.

She smiled back: "I suppose that...once I memorize each procedure— what to push when *this* or *this* happens—I'll be okay. But I will never be comfortable on one of them—not like you."

"You say that now, but wait. It is really a marvelous piece of technical engineering once you get to understand it as I do. Don't you agree?"

"Not at the moment I'm afraid," she said but stopped, hesitating, "Do you care if I call you Charley? Or Charles?"

"I prefer Charles."

"And I prefer 'Connie.' When I was a child and misbehaved, the grown-ups would register their disapproval by addressing me as *Constance!*" Again she saw the smile appear and sensed in it, tentativeness.

"Tell me what made you decide you didn't want to be a teacher?" she asked.

"Unruly misbehaved teenagers who liked nothing better than to break into my lab and contaminate my samples. I'd spend hours carefully preparing an experiment to do in class the next day, and they'd sneak in and purposely wreck it."

"How awful!" said Connie. "So you couldn't handle them?"

"I preferred not to."

Was it authoritativeness? A certain perhaps *rigidity* she thought she sensed behind his words? Curious, she wanted to find out, but their smoking break was over and students were already returning to the classroom.

That had been on Thursday. Then at the end of class Tuesday, and as she started to file out, Charles asked her to stay for a minute. There were a few students still gathered around him at the lectern and she had to wait until the last one had left and he was free. "*Yes?*" she said.

"I aah…was wondering. There's a pub not far from here and I thought if maybe you wanted to join me for something…for my birthday yesterday. Tea?"

"For your birthday?" She was thoroughly amused. "You feel like having a cup of tea?"

"No, I'm ordering wine for myself. I'm saying, you can have something different. I'll pay for it."

The pub he led them to was close-by; she knew it from having had lunch there. They located a table in one of the small dining rooms off the main bar and what started as a one-time belated birthday celebration became a repeated habit as she discovered just how lonely and isolated she was; how starved for, very simply, someone to talk to, a release.

She supposed it must have been the same for Charles. Like her he had been unhappily married to a dental hygienist who, he was to discover four years later, had been having an affair with the dentist for whom she worked he told her. "And I gave Marilyn—which was her name—all the rope in the world to hang herself with too, and that, it turned out, was a good part of the problem to begin with."

"In which way?" asked Connie, pleased too to discover they did have things in common!

"We rarely saw each other—except in passing," said Charles: "She'd be coming and I'd be going, usually to class. I was teaching daytime and studying computer programming at night."

"So was she unhappy with the arrangement you think?"

"Well, if she was, she didn't tell me," said Charles dryly. "The first I knew about it was when she asked for the divorce. I mean, I wasn't the one playing around—it never even crossed my mind until one day out of a clear blue sky, she announced she was leaving me. I watched her pack up and she moved out. Phoned her *Sheik* as I called him because he was East Indian, or something. 'Your *Sheik of Araby!*' I'd say just to see if I could get a rise out of her: 'I hope you're keeping his teeth clean for him!' Anyway, he arrived and took them both with him and that was that—not even goodbye."

"Both?"

"I neglected to mention, I have a daughter."

"You too! How old?"

"Aah..thirteen. Her name is Sylvia."

"Alice, mine, is nine.—Do you see much of her?" Connie asked and saw the slow emphatic headshake.

"I don't see any of them. My ex and I weren't exactly on speaking terms at the end. I've since heard through one of my sisters living in Derbyshire (she's the only one I still stay in contact with) that Marilyn and her Sheik moved to America but where I don't know."

"You don't sound like you care," observed Connie. "I don't."

"Is that the extent of your family—one sister?"

"No. Both parents are deceased, but I have three sisters and a brother living there still, not to mention cousins, aunts and uncles. We're a huge, extended Catholic family."

"I didn't know you were Catholic."

"I'm not. And as an outspoken atheist, I'm regarded by the rest of my family as the black sheep."

"My father was a nonbeliever," Connie remarked: "So you were raised strictly Catholic?"

"You can't get more Catholic than the Saint Boniface School for Boys where I spent ten years of my life. Ten *brutal* years I might add."

The night classes designed to make Connie computer literate lasted four weeks, at the end of which she had joined the rest of her colleagues before Charles' lectern to express thanks and say their goodbyes. "Can you wait, Connie?" he said.

She had, standing to one side as the rest of the class filed out and he was free at last. "I'm much afraid this wraps it up. As we may not cross paths again, why not have a final glass of wine with me?"

She had wondered if he would ask. "Is that a formal invitation?"

"As formal as I can get it. I'll pay of course, and you can give me your thoughts on my class. I'm always open to criticism."

But their final night together had turned out very much a disappointment. Charles really had talked about his class and the teaching methods he used before moving on to the topic he loved most, computers. Then computer software which led him to the rising star of Bill Gates whom he described with an eagerness that verged on hero-worship. "You know all about computers, but it's late and I still have papers to correct," she said, gathering up her things.

"Look Connie, uhm—"

She saw him reach for his ear. "It is late," she reminded him. "If you still have problems, you can always reach me." She watched him draw his pen. "You can call me either at Central Computing or at *this* number, which is private."

She thanked him a second time and rose. "Connie—"

She stopped.

"Would it be alright if I called you at home?"

"Yes," she said and wrote out her number. But when after a time he still hadn't, she slowly lost interest—remembering him when she did not as that man with the distended ear—but with a fondness for all the kind help he had given her in class: the patience, the consideration he had shown, until one afternoon as she sat in the teacher's lounge he suddenly appeared. She jumped up. Charles, I'm here! How unexpected a surprise! What brings you to Claremont?"

"*Windows Three*" he told her. Then, shifting, he apologized for not having phoned but he had been terribly occupied getting the system up and running while still teaching that night class. She saw his hand edge inside his suit coat. Had she not told him she liked classical music? he said as the hand emerged holding an envelope. "Do you know anything about Gustav Mahler? Because somebody gave me these. Open the envelope and look." A pair of tickets to the BBC Symphony which had come to Manchester and was doing an all Mahler program. Symphony Number One Tuesday at *8pm*. She could have hugged him!

Because it was a school night they decided to meet at the concert. Of all the music she and her father had enjoyed listening to, Mahler's had been her father's favourite. His was also the music her aunt for whom there was no music worthy of even the name after Bing Crosby objected to most, because of Mahler's lack of religious faith, and "because of those horrid songs he wrote about dying children!" Isabel charged before her father as if he were somehow implicated. Where the aunt had picked up her misinformation Connie could only guess—perhaps from the back of *lp* jackets but Mahler and the bottle of sherry her father one day set out in plain sight before her were a source of much enmity between the two and how she had mourned his passing, Connie whispered over as the house lights dimmed.

Her fear was that Charles would dislike the Mahler First Symphony. "I didn't dislike it, put it that way," he said when they stopped for something to drink and a bite of something sweet before going their separate ways.

"It was a bit long, but I've suffered through much worse." She was relieved, "What kind of music do you like? Jazz?"

"Somewhat. Rock and Roll—though *Grunge* I don't like. Do you want to take in a gig with me, Connie?"

Somehow she had not expected that. "Sure. Do you like to dance? "Afraid I never learned. That isn't the sort of thing you're taught in a Catholic school."

"I do. My ex just loved to! I bet I could teach you!"

"Oh I really don't think I want to learn...but I'll look around for some tickets if you want."

Two evenings later he phoned. He had located a pair for Saturday. There was just one catch he told her: the price. She was used to paying her own way: "How much?"

"Thirty five pounds," he said.

Thirty five! "Even the BBC Symphony didn't cost that!" she objected.

"It's up to you. But these are the *Sex Pistols*."

She was used to going *Dutch treat* anyway and not one time since her separation and divorce had she gone out to dinner and somewhere afterward. The gig started at ten. It was agreed that Charles should pick her up from her house, which would mean introducing him. As her friend? No, a colleague. Someone of importance like a department head—which she knew he was as she meticulously did her face before the mirror. Then selected her most attractive skirt and blouse combination. "Mummy," said Alice: "you haven't looked like that since Daddy!"

So you still remember thought Connie, conscious of three pair of curious eyes all looking at her interrogatively. Then Charles arrived and she ushered him inside to meet her family, conscious of his uneasiness. Scraggles was the first to rush forward. Seeing the dog, Charles froze.

"Don't you jump up on that nice man! Alice, catch Scraggles!" she ordered.

They left after that for the restaurant: Chinese not far from the hall where the gig was to be and all you could eat for four pounds, but well worth the price! Charles assured her. The restaurant resembled more a cafeteria with plain tables and hard, metal frame chairs, she found. But the food turned out quite good!

There were endless varieties of all her favourites: sweet and sour pork; deep fried prawns; crab in black bean sauce. They each picked up a plate and started down the row of steam trays where the spring rolls caught her eye. "Charles, *these* look good—they have tiny shrimp."

"No, I prefer those others—the straight cabbage variety."

They moved on to the crab in black bean sauce. "Aren't you going to have some, Charles?" she asked.

"No, I'm going to have *those*." He pointed to the next tray. "It tastes exactly the same and it's made with soy."

That was when she first discovered that he was a vegetarian. "Were you always?" she had asked once they were seated and had started to eat. "No."

"So what made you decide to become one?"

"Did you ever watch an animal being slaughtered? It's not a pretty sight. And they do feel pain you know!"

It seemed an odd thing to say. "Was your wife also vegetarian?"

"No, she was very much the carnivore," Charles responded, and she saw the trace of a smile involuntarily form.

As they waited to pay, she said to him, "This is the first time I've gone out with anyone since I split up with Cliff. We used to do this: go out to dinner, then dance the night away. My ex was a lovely dancer!"

"Afraid I can't help you there," said Charles.

Her mother who had sensed Charles' discomfort said the next morning at breakfast, "He's not comfortable meeting people I notice."

"Why does he pull on his ear, Mummy?" Alice asked.

"It's a habit, Sweet, and habits are hard to stop. Like you when you wiggle you foot under the table."

"Well, if that's your boyfriend, he's hardly Mister Sex!" her daughter said next.

Connie was first to recover, "Where did you bring that home from?"

"Elsie's. It's something Louise, her mother, says after her boyfriends leave."

"Are you sure you should be spending all that much time at Elsie's— because I certainly am not!" And it was true, she had become entirely too lax with her daughter, thought Connie with a pinch of guilt. She had heard rumours before of Elsie's mother entertaining a constant stream of men and she knew she should be keeping a closer watch over Alice—why did she not! But she knew the answer. It was because of her own childhood: her aunt's disciplinarian control. She did not want to risk her daughter's rejection of her by repeating Isabel's mistakes.

Besides, she had her own life to lead did she not and Alice, though the most important piece of it, was not her only consideration. Surely her mother would have stepped down by now if Alice were in any real danger, Connie reasoned without wishing to pursue the thought further. At least Alice had stopped seeing her father—remarried, Cliff had ceased asking for her but mother and daughter conversed very little, in part because of Connie's busy schedule. And because Alice had become such a moody child, Connie thought—distant, and each time she tried to come closer, she was rudely pushed away. *Mother, why do you want to know!* In the end it was easier to simply give Alice her space. "He's your Mum's friend, Alice. Just somebody at school."

For the next half year that had remained the case. Weekends they began spending together just for the companionship having discovered in each other similar tastes, and histories.

Charles was not against going to the theatre when there was a play one wanted to see and in that way she introduced him to a few of her favourite plays and films. He liked things old, she discovered: movies from the thirties or forties with actors who to her were just names. Also, unlike her former husband, he was not adverse to reading and would even express interest in some of her novels from time to time. They soon had a list or restaurants they went to. Steak houses were, by their title alone, to be avoided, as were Indian restaurants where you were never entirely sure what you were being tricked into eating. You could sift through Indian food with your fork all day long and still not know, he said. Chinese restaurants were safe, as were some pubs they made a practice of patronizing. Also Vince's, which was Mediterranean. The one other thing that in the end had drawn them together was their shared fondness for wine. With wine Connie could watch his tongue loosen. She was curious about his ex, Marilyn.

They met while students, he said. What was she like? Blond. Connie saw him stop. Looked at her and she saw that creep of his smile, "Meatier than you I'd say."

She'd had enough herself to drink to find his drollery amusing, "Would you want me meatier?"

"No, I prefer you as you are."

"I'm passable, you mean? How did you meet her— Marilyn?"

In the biology lab he told her. They had been forced to share the same dissecting table. He detested having to pith frogs; to dissect a tiny living creature was more than he could bring himself to do. Observing him struggle, Marilyn had finally done the cutting and dissecting part of the experiment for him and in that way, they became friends. Then *more than friends* he told her.

"You took her to bed?" said Connie, "*Cheers!* by the way."

"Cheers! She wanted sex. If anything, she took me to bed!

All that part would change of course, and in hindsight I should have suspected all along that she was up to things, but I didn't. I know now that she never loved me for even a day. People like that are incapable of being faithful. But at the time I didn't know.

"Trusting her was my biggest mistake."

"Then we made the same mistake!" said Connie and immediately raised her wine glass. "Cheers!"

"Cheers!" he said back as they clinked glasses.

He had gotten drunk enough that night to become interesting to her Connie realized the next day as she recalled other things Charles had revealed, or partially revealed. Marilyn's plan from the day they met and hopped into bed, he said, had been to work her way through medical school and then become a dentist. "She was always a very clean person anyway," he let drop as an afterthought.

"And that was what turned you on?" Connie asked.

"I was aware of it—put it that way...and she knew I had plans to teach high school. So we just combined spreadsheets you might say. It was a perfectly good spreadsheet: it worked for ten years and—who knows—it still would be good except for other things we hadn't taken into account nibbling like so many vermin at the edges."

She was beginning to appreciate his occult humour: "Like your students, you mean?"

"They were little gangsters! But they were the least of my worries. By far the biggest unplanned-for event was Sylvia. My daughter. She dashed all Marilyn's hopes of finishing dental school. And guess who took the blame? *Me!* For not taking precautions. I pointed out to her that she was responsible, not me, for taking the pill."

Connie began to laugh—she could not hold it back. She bent over laughing. "Sorry!" she said when she finally was able to stop herself, "Keep going."

"That's all there is," said Charles: "It was mostly downhill by then anyway. Nothing I ever did for her was quite good enough. She found fault in everything. To conclude, she could be a nasty bitch when it served her."

"Then why did you find her so attractive? What did you see in her to want to marry her?"

"What does anybody see in anybody else? That's why people go to psychiatrists and pay a lot of money—just to find that part out. We had some terrible rows, often over just trifles. If you knew me better, you'd know, I like my space. What she failed to learn was that she could back me into the corner only *that* far…What about your ex?"

He had been just a playboy and a womanizer Connie told him. At least Marilyn had kept her affair under wraps. Cliff had lacked even that scruple. Connie had described their relationship then and how it had unraveled. "How would you feel when you're carrying your husband's child and your husband is shagging your best friend? Joyce's little boy, Johnny, may be Cliff's too for all I know. I had absolutely no self esteem left."

"Sounds as if this Cliff tried to destroy your self-confidence," said Charles.

Why did you not see that yourself? You should have! she thought, thinking she ought to kiss him at that moment as a way of saying her thanks and what followed remained as unclear as her dreams that next morning when she had tried to explain before her mother and Alice why she had arrived home so late. What she did not want it reveal was that she had gotten flat out drunk, enough to have to be assisted into the car by Charles. Perhaps it was the blur of oncoming car lights and lights from the city at night flowing across her confused vision. She saw that other night from so many years before and Juan having to help her from the car. But it was Charles who was stopping before the aunt's house. Charles whose lips she had kissed and whose fingers she felt find their way under her skirt. The curious thing about it was they weren't even Charles' fingers doing it to her. She had known the hand was Charles' but in her numbed perceptions it might have been another's hand— *Juan's*—as she trapped it in her own hand while she decided. Finally—it could not have taken her more than a heartbeat to decide—she had allowed those fingers their freedom.

That New Years Charles asked her finally to marry him. Connie thought she would in the end, after months of vacillation and in the face of her mother's raised objections, "Mum, I know I should have listened to you about Cliff. But Cliff and Charles are completely different types. Charles isn't the unfaithful kind. His ex was not Charles! So tell me why you dislike Charles?"

"Dislike is too strong a word," her mother had said back. "I just find him odd is all. Inhibited."

"Mum, don't you think I already know that! Charles had a horrible childhood, raised as he was in that Catholic school for boys. Then that wife of his, Marilyn! Mum, Charles is a decent human being. All he needs is someone to show him a little respect." *Hardly words you would use to describe a lover* Connie thought, thinking *Then why did you marry him?*

But there wasn't a single answer. On the plus side was Charles' assured success with the Manchester School Authority and her fears for what the future held. She could picture herself a withered-up old woman like Isabel, only taller and with her long Scottish legs. But it was concerns over her daughter's behaviour that made her decide. Alice she could feel was slipping away from her spending for one thing far too much time with Elsie and *her* mother. "Whose house do you live at?" Connie had asked her daughter one evening, "Elsie's, or here with us? Because you're rarely at home anymore—?"

"Nor are you!" her daughter said defiantly back.

The words struck home. Alice had always been a self-willed child; Connie had no idea really of what went on in that precocious little mind and was almost afraid to ask. But she could sense her daughter was becoming too headstrong and impulsive, and needed reigning in *now* before she became any more difficult to manage. "Tell me, Alice, do you think I ought to remarry?" Connie asked her one afternoon trying to make it sound casual.

"I don't know, Mum. Why ask me?"

"Would you care?"

Alice fidgeted. "Dunno. It would depend on who."

"You don't like Charles much, do you?"

"Oh, Mum!"

Just the way she had said it, like an indictment! "Alice, I'm sorry you can't have your father back, but you can't, and *It Isn't My Fault.*"

"Then whose is it!"

How could she ever have explained what had happened between Cliff and herself to a twelve-year-old? Then came New Year's Day and with it the announcement that she had know would please her aunt alone. But just six weeks later Isabel was dead from cancer and Charles, now unofficially a part of the family, had attended the funeral also though he dreaded being forced to listen to the aunt's minister drone on through the rain. He would wander away for frequent smoke breaks during the service and later, as he poured himself a glass of wine from the bottle Connie now kept for him in her refrigerator, he said, "Well I knew he'd be a windbag, but at least he wasn't Catholic!"

So she would have had to vacate the aunt's house anyway, she told herself. Looked at that way, it had been a marriage of convenience—for Charles as well. Because, due to his new job title and status, he too needed more space than his smallish apartment provided. And since both were in education it made sense if the marriage were to take place at the end of the school year which would provide them with the time needed to readjust, Charles reasoned as the search for a house began.

Chapter 9

THE ONE THEY CHOSE WAS out in the Stockport area. It was a large, four-bedroom place with a spacious living and dining area, a full-sized kitchen, and a utility room that you entered through the garage, and which might do for the dog thought Charles. The bedrooms were all on one floor upstairs and the master bedroom came with its own shower and toilet, which pleased Charles: "I prefer not having to share a bathroom," he told Connie. Catching her questioning look, he hastily amended his statement, "— except of course with my wife."

But what really had sold the house for Charles was an unused bedroom that had already been converted into a study and would be perfect as the computer room: large enough to hold a table for his computers and printer, plus a desk for his writings and research. There would even be room enough for his leather settee! Originally it had been Marilyn's, Charles revealed. But he had formed an attachment to it, and they had fought bitterly for it during the divorce proceedings, until in the end his will had proven the stronger, he told Connie. Looking at it, she wondered how two people could fight over something of so little worth.

Also, those built-in shelves along the back wall, he pointed out to her, could hold manuals and his books all of a highly technical nature. These were exciting times in which to live, with the DOS system definitely in retreat before the new graphic interface (even though, he said, real programmers still preferred DOS). Then in an outpouring of almost boyish enthusiasm, he had announced before Connie and his soon-to-be daughter:

"But just think of the power you'll have in *this* one hand, *these* five fingers, as they grip that innocuous looking little mouse!" he pronounced as Alice simply stared. Yes, at two hundred thousand the house was not cheap. But with two salaries and bit of Charles' savings, it was within their reach. This house that would bring them together!

That had been in 1991. Nine years later she could see all her miscalculations, particularly with regard to her daughter. Alice and Charles had got off on the wrong foot from the beginning, she told her friend in the sunlit waters of that Turkish lagoon. Hardly were they settled into their spacious new house before Scraggles became the cause of angry dissention when Charles objected sharply to Alice putting an opened can of dogfood in the refrigerator. "Put it out in the garage where it belongs," he said.

"But it's just going to dry out there!!" complained Alice who hardly could believe her new stepfather.

"Well, it's not going to be allowed anywhere near human food that *I* eat."

There were two seemingly unrelated things that had turned Alice against him from the beginning: the refrigerator, and Scraggles. Charles had tried at the outset to prevent the little dog from being allowed inside the house proper either, to keep it outside completely (he had even suggested a doghouse for it), or in case of snow or unusually cold weather to allow it no further than the utility room. To that both she and Alice had said unequivocally *No!*

"Then where do you propose to keep the animal!" objected Charles.

"Scraggles can sleep with me," Alice said. "With *you?*"

Seeing Charles' look of disbelief Connie had explained how Scraggles fell into the habit of sleeping, if not with her, then Alice because of his greenstick fracture, and the poor animal's crying all night. Because, according to their vet, Scraggles had been so badly mistreated.

"Well, I'm not going to allow some animal that goes in the street and is full of fleas and *god-knows what-all* next to me," announced Charles. But in the end, he had given in to their pressure: the dog would be allowed into Alice's room. "Just keep it out of mine!" he said.

And there were other less tractable problems such as Charles' vegetarianism and how to allocate space in the refrigerator because, meat and meat by-products had to be kept separated from the beans and soy products he ate. Their first refrigerator, which had been Charles' from his prior marriage, failed to provide more than a storage shelf each with no way to separate their separate foods. One morning as she was preparing her face for school, Connie heard Charles' raised voice come from what must have been the kitchen. "What's this doing on my shelf!" Then her daughter's strident response as, dropping her eye-pencil, Connie rushed downstairs to hear.

"Have a cow!"

Charles stood before the opened refrigerator and held out two plates accusingly: the one containing Alice's cold lamb chop from last night and the second, his lasagna which he certainly wouldn't eat now! he said. Connie would have considered becoming a vegetarian if only to mollify Charles had it not been for Alice's refusal to even try Charles' food.

"Mum, if you want to eat rabbit food, you just go right ahead.

But don't expect me to!"

Nonetheless, Connie would sample Charles cooking on those occasions when Alice was not there to object and find it palatable. In some cases she might even be eating meat so clever was Charles at disguising the food he prepared. He always cooked enough for three people and at the start, when something he prepared really did taste good, she would urge her daughter to at least try it—but Alice remained defiant.

Other problems surfaced too. The dog had to be kept outside at mealtime. If she didn't put him out, Scraggles would whine at the door to be allowed at the table with them, which annoyed Charles, "Must that dog always cry whenever I sit down to eat!"

"Why don't we let him in?" Alice would say.

But Connie knew in advance what the scene that would provoke.

"No, Alice. Scraggles has his own food, we have ours."

Also, there was a certain way for the table to be set, with Charles' food at one end kept separate from theirs so that at mealtime they would face off from their respective ends of the table like two opposing sides. Nor were the sides, once set, ever to change. On one evening in particular that Connie had never forgotten—they had been married less than three months—Alice had set the two foods next to each other: Charles' dish of *quorn* right beside their grilled chicken perhaps by accident, but perhaps not—Connie was never sure.

"What is this!" said Charles, pointing to the plate of grilled chicken, his voice not raised but brittle, hard like broken glass, each word precise accusing. How different his delivery had been before a class, Connie reflected. Here there was no hesitation, no self-conscious grope for words. Nor did he reach for that ear.

"Ours—Mum's and mine," said Alice.

"And *this:*" Charles pointing to his own soybean imitation. "Rabbit food."

"I see," he said, his voice not even argumentative—only smug. "If you want to defile your own body by feeding it flesh, I can't stop you. But let me say it is not something I would knowingly do to myself. I have too much respect for my body."

"You're saying you can't eat *whatever that concoction is* because of Mum's and my food?"

"No. But I do insist, now that you've become my daughter, that you learn to set a table. So we'll begin by carrying everything back into the kitchen. Then we'll bring each dish back one at a time and place it as it should be placed."

Alice she could see was furious.

"God, so have a cow and you're not my father!"

Now it was she herself who rose up in anger: "Alice! Stop mouthing off to your father and just *do it,* stupid as it may be!" Still furious, she spun.

"And *you!* Stop being a child and start acting your age!"

In shocked surprise Charles' eyes had darted from mother to daughter. Then back as he rose flinging his serviette. He glanced at where it had fallen but made no effort to pick it up. Instead he stormed from the room and spent the rest of the night locked away with his computers.

"Help me clean this mess up," said Connie after a moment.

Because Charles refused to touch dishes with meat residue on them, or after they had even come in contact with other dishes that had, mother and daughter cleared the table as always, then loaded the dishwasher, after which Connie wandered into the living room finally and sat down facing the unlit television screen. After a time she felt Scraggles jump onto the couch beside her, felt the cold nose against her cheek as Scraggles began to lick. "Oh yes, Mummy loves 'ihm so much!" she said in as she pressed the dog to her.

Shortly after eleven when she got into bed finally, Charles' side was still unoccupied. After what seemed an interminable time, she heard him coming; heard water running in their shower and after more time, the electric buzz of his toothbrush. Then, seeing his dark form, she had switched on the bed lamp for him and looked up, waiting for him to say something. But he refused and instead she faced his hostile silence. She could feel his vindictiveness as he deliberately moved away, his back to her. *Let him be like that!* she thought.

But she could not fall asleep. She lay beside him in the dark thinking. *Was this what she had to look forward to? Was this her future life!* she thought, lying there sensing his hostile silence.

The next day the situation was no better. Charles went about the kitchen silently preparing his own breakfast and making himself tea, stepping wordlessly around both of them as if they were two inanimate objects, while Alice watched everything he did. "How is it, Charles," she said, seeing him reach for the bottle of milk in the fridge, "that you won't eat cheese but you'll drink milk in your tea?"

Connie saw his hand stop for an instant in the act of pouring; saw his angry look.

"And as for those cigarettes you continue to inhale, you do know they're loaded with chemicals. How do you know what is in those chemicals?"

"Alice, just *stop!*" she ordered.

"So what's got into him?" said Alice to her just as soon as Charles was out the front door.

"Maybe he really did have that cow!"

"I don't know where you picked up that expression but stop using it *now!* You're not helping things, you know."—adding miserably after a moment's reflection, "I guess I should have tried harder myself."

"Mother, don't you see, he's punishing you!"

"*Punishing me*? How do you know that!"

Mother, I'm not stupid. And I do have eyes. For making him look small. But it's not your place to give in!"

Had she? But she knew Alice was right. Knew also that she should not have said what she had in front of her daughter. Their daughter. "As I said earlier, you could try being more pleasant yourself. I know he may not be like your father—"

"May not? Mother, he is nothing like my father!"

"But you could try to like him, since you have to live with him."

Why did Alice continue to idolize a father she no longer saw, or but rarely; one who no longer tried to maintain any contact save the odd call at Christmas, or for her birthday? Should she tell Alice what Cliff was and had done to her mother? Alice, who was just twelve? A part of Connie wanted to, to put the matter behind them. But she was afraid of where the conversation might lead. Alice already saw far more than she should. More, Connie thought, than was either good or healthy for someone her age—and that was the worrying part: why Connie had to tread so carefully!

Dinner that evening got off on equally bad footing with Charles barely speaking. Even under normal circumstances, cooking was never without its problems. Only salt and pepper could be safely touched by all since their shakers protected them, while other things like tomatoes, lettuce, and seasonings such as parsley or chopped basil, were items Charles refused to touch after they had been handled by Connie or Alice if the hands of either had come in contact with meat first. And there were certain food enhancers or flavourings such as vegetable bouillon that Charles remained suspicious of. Whenever the three were together in the kitchen, before the stove or at the cutting board, Charles would watch the two of them constantly—each place their hands went. Aware of that, Connie had been especially careful in making the salad. Even so, tonight he refused it. Ate instead something he had made up from lentils the previous day, frozen, and reheated in the microwave. She especially opened a wine she knew he liked:

"Would you like me to pour you a glass of wine, Charles?"

"If I want wine, I'll pour it myself, thank you," he said. Finished, he pushed aside his plate, rose, and disappeared upstairs. There was nothing unusual in this; he spent most evenings locked away with his computers. As Supervisor of the school authority's newly named *Central Computing* and with his own business card, there was always work he would find to do. So she was used to seeing him disappear.

School nights she usually went to bed about ten. On her way she stopped before his door and tapped quietly. When she got no response she tried the handle and found to her surprise that it had been locked from inside. He never did that! "Charles," she called and waited. No response: "Are you all right in there?"

"…leave me alone."

"Just what did I do!"

"You know what you did."

"No I don't know. Can we at least talk about it?" Silence.

Miserable she continued along the landing to their bedroom where she undressed and slipped her nightgown over her head. In the bathroom she wiped her face with cleansing-cream then rubbed in her night cream before climbing into bed. Never, it seemed to her, had she been so consumed by doubt as she lay thinking over in her mind what she had committed herself to, seeing for the first time as she lay alone in the dark the magnitude of her mistake. How could she live a lifetime of *this!* And it was not just for herself, it was as much for Alice's sake that she had married Charles. But Alice had set herself against him!

They were two impulsive creatures that wanted only to clash, it seemed, like a pair of magnets when you try to force them wrongly together. Could she not have seen that from the start: that Charles could never be a substitute for Cliff. Charles was too introverted, too distant, not someone you easily felt drawn to, or comfortable with for that matter. And so for all he could give and was willing to provide—stability for one thing—there would always remain that one critical thing he didn't have to give—not to Alice who needed it!

So why had she married him? Not for love, she wasn't some giddy teenager, not anymore. She was a mature woman with her own teenage daughter (or practically teenage) and all the attendant responsibilities. Her mistake, if there had been one, lay in the belief that once those basic things, like a stable secure home where money was no longer the chief worry, had been found love or something like it would follow—or so she tried to believe as she lay in the dark wanting to go to sleep. She could see the luminescent numbers of the digital clock on her nightstand, they were like green teeth grinning at her.

She heard something click, like a lock, and rose to investigate. The landing was dark, and she crept along it, listening. It might have been her daughter she thought and stopped before Alice's door long enough to determine that her daughter was safe and well. She was. Connie could see Scraggles curled up beside her on the bed; see the two tiny eyes that glowed back at her look up.

Don't you dare bark! she said to herself as she eased the door shut.

Approaching Charles' computer room, she first listened. Hearing silence, she tried the door. This time it was unlocked. So she opened to find the room lit by a single desk lamp turned low. Behind it, lying on his settee, was Charles. She approached. He appeared asleep. "Charles," she said softly, "hadn't you better wake up?"

"I'm not sleeping."

"Then why don't you come to bed?"

"It's not a problem for me if I sleep here. I've done it in the past."

—*past?* "Charles, I don't know what game this is you're playing, but I am not amused. It's past midnight and we both have to get up. Now are you coming?"

"When I get ready."

The following evening, and though he joined them at the table, his mood remained testy. "Would you please hand me *that?*" he would say grudgingly, and point.

Nor would he have anything to do with her in bed. His desire for sex, always subject to erratic swings, had been replaced by a kind of accusatory resistance she already knew as she lay in bed waiting, listening to him shower. She had bought a pair of fancy *see-through* knickers and she had a sudden idea. She knew he liked looking at her in them and, slipping out of bed, she pulled them on and stood in the open bathroom door where he had to see her, she told Mandy the next day in Chester where they occasionally had lunch together: Mandy whom she had met on that children's playground eight years ago, and who remained the only friend she really felt comfortable talking openly with.

As she waited for him to finish showering, her vision fell upon the countertop. Always to the left of the sink stood his toiletries in an arranged column that she instinctively knew she was not meant to touch: the electric toothbrush, his toothpaste which he kept inside a glass which he would rewash at the end of each using, then his shaving tools and can of lather, and finally his bottle of Listerine mouthwash. Once—they had just married— she had bought a different brand and set it on the counter for him. "What's this doing here!" he had called to her from the bathroom. "The Scope? It's for you. I just bought it—the other bottle was empty."

"Well take it back and get Listerine."

"Why, Charles?"

"Because what you bought is a waste of money. Whether you know it or not, the mouth is one of the dirtiest parts of the body and Listerine is the strongest antiseptic."

She heard the water in the shower stop running; heard the shower door slide open.

Discovering her, he froze for an instant and she saw the surprise on his face as she turned and padded softly back to bed where she waited. In the past, she told Mandy, seeing her wear those knickers usually would arouse him. Tonight, however, he showed his indifference as he climbed into bed keeping to his side of it. At least he had not turned away. Instead he lay flat and faced the ceiling, waiting for her to make the initial contact she knew as she reached over.

At first he would not respond, except to allow her hand to remain there. But as she began to move her fingers down him slowly with feigned annoyance he pushed her hand back, "You needn't feel obligated to do any of this, you know," he said to her in a sulky manner. She had been in this situation enough times now to know what he was up to, she told Mandy. First he must make her feel guilt over something, some slight she had inflicted; and only then, after she had expressed remorse, would she be forgiven and allowed to make amends. Always it would be she that must come to him. Well, she was not going to this time!

Snatching her hand back, she rolled violently away, trying to hold back her sob and control her voice as she said, "Why are you doing this to me, Charles? Does hurting me incite *pleasure*?" A pause, then she felt his fingers reach for her.

"I didn't know—I mean, I *wasn't* hurting you."

Liar! "Just tell me what I've done to you to deserve this." Again a pause. She felt his hand slide onto her and this time she made no attempt to push him away. "Don't I have a right to know that much? We are married, Charles—or have you forgotten?"

"Well, I just, ah…well I don't appreciate it when females gang up on me is all. Marilyn used to do that: deliberately poison Sylvia against me. (Sylvia was my daughter.)"

"Are you're saying (or implying) that I'm poisoning Alice—?" she said, taken back.

"No, I'm not saying that, Connie. You always think the worst of me."

"But from what you tell me, Alice isn't exactly warm toward him," Mandy interjected. "And he must sense that."

"Alice admittedly is part of the problem. Something needs to be done," said Connie.

"Ever think about going to family counselling?"

"I don't think either would consent."

"No? Anyway, continue."

"We made up (as we always do). Had sex. The only time I think he really wants to spend anytime with me is after we fight and then make up. That's what turns him on. Last night for a good half hour until I went down on him finally. That's really what he's waiting for. Then he rolls over and before I know it, he's snoring.

He doesn't much like doing it to me though. He wouldn't admit that, of course, but he always finds some excuse. It's his back, or if not, then his neck that hurts…shall we have one more glass of wine?"

"We see each other so rarely, *why not!*" Mandy turned silent—thoughtful. "Then what about finding a marriage counsellor for you two (but more for Charles, I'm thinking)? Or psychologist if you intend to stick it out. Do you?"

"I have too much invested at this point not to," she told Mandy.

Chapter 10

SHE HAD TOLD HERSELF SHE didn't need the sex. No, they lived comfortable enough lives. Busy lives, and in her narrow world, beset by concerns for Alice's future and worries over her mother, dead to herself she saw herself in looking back as perhaps the one patient for which she could spare no time, not even to diagnose the malady let alone search for its cure. She could see her mother's normally robust health slowly weaken. Usually Connie's school day ended about four after which she would drive to the aunt's old house in which her mother still lived, to check up on her and spend a few hours, before going home to fix Alice and Charles their tea. At the back of Connie's mind was that dreaded word, *Alzheimer's!* Though not yet seventy, her mother could no longer be trusted to remember even a doctor's appointment. When the musical, *Les Misérables*, came to Manchester, thinking to treat her mother Connie had purchased a pair of tickets for the Sunday matinee. "Mum," she said, walking in, "would you like to see *this* with me?" Connie then handed her mother the tickets and waited, watching as her mother read one over. Then, slowly, she could see delight spread over her mother's face.

"It's been years since I went to the theatre. How sweet of you. Yes, I do want to go!" said Liz. But when Connie arrived that Sunday noon, her mother was still wearing slacks a worn house sweater. "Mum, you don't want to go to the theatre looking like that! Don't you still have that beige dress—the one I like?"

"Oh…Oh yes, I can't go like this—you're right."

While her mother was up changing, Connie noticed her purse setting at the end of the dining room table ready to take. She crossed then for whatever reason and opened the purse. Stuffed inside it, she discovered a plastic sack containing a sandwich and a half gnawed-at chicken leg. "Mum, what's *this*?" said Connie as her mother entered.

"That? Well I knew I was supposed to go somewhere today but I couldn't remember where. So I decided I had better take a sandwich." And on another afternoon when Connie stopped to check, her mother's first words had been, "Where is Isabel?"

Isabel? "Mum, Isabel's dead."

When Connie arrived home that evening, she had tried to share with Charles her concerns. She found him in the kitchen preparing his vegetarian lasagna and she could sense he was annoyed. "It's past seven," he peevishly said, "and I can no longer hold up my tea. Especially since I didn't know if you were coming home."

"Charles, I'm sorry if I'm late but it's my mother—again!" She started to tell him then some of what had been happening— describing the sack with its half-gnawed chicken leg but she could tell he was not interested.

"Maybe she should see a doctor," he suggested while she watched him slowly, painstakingly spread a layer of the quorn evenly over the pasta. "Oh, while I remember, I won't be here on Saturday. Paul Allen—*thee Paul Allen!*—is coming, and I just might be able to meet him *one-on-one*. You know how word gets out. Now *that* wouldn't hurt my image in the least!"

Charles was riding the crest of his successes in an expanding computer age, and the respect that had come with them. He had a staff under him now to meet the increased workload since all of the Education Authority's computers spread through its many schools had to be reprogrammed to accept the new Microsoft systems, including the Internet. Charles had just been offered a brand-new five-year contract with a salary increase. To the Manchester Education Authority, he was *Mister Computer* and the hefty raise in his pay was testimony to the high regard they held him in.

No longer was he required to teach night classes or pay visits to individual teachers who remained computer backward, his staff could do that. The MEA had even renamed the department.

Now it was called *Computer Operations Management* and his new business card listed his title as 'Systems Director'.

If Charles recent success had made him vainer, the transformation had not been entirely bad, Connie thought. Rarely now did he pull at his ear. But with his new self-esteem and worth came a certain overbearingness. If Charles had had close friends before his upgrade to Systems Director, he had fewer afterward. But that hadn't bothered Charles since what need her husband might have had for friends had been supplanted by sweet smells of success by his grand new title, which he loved to show off before the office staff and his close associates. If they chose to deride him for it—if he rubbed them the wrong way—they knew better than to risk doing so to his face. Only Alice could do that, "Mother, why do you think Scraggles growls at him? Because, Mother, face it, he's a *nerd!*"

Connie had tried to figure out from which side Alice had inherited her aggressive behaviour. Just where had that insolent tongue come from? Not her side!—of that Connie was certain. The genes could only come from Cliff, and were not Italians known for being emotional? Being easily excited? Then add to that her daughter's perceptiveness! That was the part that had always frightened Connie, that sometimes Alice saw *too much!*

Shorter, and with a tendency to gain weight, she was closer in appearance to her English grandmother than to her Scottish side, unlike Connie who had inherited her father's slender frame. But her eyes were Cliff's, Connie thought, hazel and—she also had her father's obstinacy— and would never concede defeat in an argument. But Alice's eyes lacked the same Latin warmth. To Connie they appeared judgmental somehow— piercing, and could turn instantly accusing like she remembered her dead Aunt Jean's doing back when she was a girl and did something stupid like the time she pulled her swim suit half down and rubbed up against her cousin's nakedness. Sometimes, on catching her daughter's probing look, she would find herself wondering afterward what veiled thoughts those unsettling eyes withheld.

While Alice still attended primary school, she would meet her mother each afternoon in the school parking lot and the two would drive home together. But when she began high school that changed. Rather than wait to be picked up by her mother, Alice sometimes announced she would walk home. Preoccupied with her mother as she now was, Connie did not question her daughter's decision. Alice usually arrived home before her mother. Connie always knew because, almost the instant she pressed the key to the lock and the door swung open, she would hear the ear-splitting blast of the rock-and-roll coming from inside the living room.

At first Connie was concerned. Did Alice not have homework to do? But as she entered the living room she would see her daughter's head, no more than feet from the record player, half buried in a school a schoolbook. Or Alice would be sprawled before the coffee table writing homework.

How could her daughter even think to concentrate with all that loud racket? she thought. "Alice, shouldn't you turn it down?"

"Oh, hi, Mum! Turn what down? *This,* you mean. No, it's fine."

Connie remained unconvinced. But when she looked at her daughter's grades at Christmas break and saw mostly A's, her doubts vanished. "Are you going to show Charles?" she no longer said *Your father.*

"Why would he be interested?"

But Connie had, that evening: "Charles, read this."

"What is it? Oh…but I wish you'd tell her to turn her music down. I can even hear it inside my study."

So long as Alice's grade average did not drop below an *A-,* Connie just assumed her daughter was living within the safe limits of what might be considered a normal adolescence. True, she did not know a great deal about Alice's friends except that there were a number—girls mostly, boys occasionally—that now phoned. At least she no longer spent her time with Elsie and Elsie's mother, and that of itself was a relief until one afternoon when she was called down to the Administration Office. There was a message for her to contact her daughter's school—it was urgent!

Something had happened, Connie could tell at once; it was a subdued Alice who waited for her inside the headmaster's office. Along with two other girls Alice had been caught smoking weed in the school lavatory, the headmaster informed Connie. Almost her first thought had been, "Does my husband know?" *Yes,* answered the headmaster, he had placed the call personally. Aside, he had assured Connie then, that given whom the parents were—Charles' rank within the School Authority—he would see to it the matter got pushed under the rug. Connie drove her daughter home then anticipating the worst: Charles hated being interrupted at work, especially over something like this! Connie fully expected a scene as she pulled up before the double garage doors. But the downstairs was empty. Charles had to be somewhere—his car was parked inside the garage: "Where do you suppose he went?" said Connie to her daughter.

"Probably where he always goes—hiding in his sanctuary," Alice responded.

"Sanctuary" was only one of the words Alice used to describe Charles' computer room, *"his cage"* was another. "And the first thing you're going to do is learn to control that mouth! From here on out you're going to speak respectfully to your stepfather. IS THAT UNDERSTOOD?" Connie waited, saw finally her daughter's reluctant nod.

Toward seven when Charles still had not shown himself, Connie went up to his computer room and knocked, "Charles, aren't you eating? I've taken the liberty of setting your food out also."

"I'll be down."

When finally he appeared, Charles avoided both their eyes as he approached his food, examining it instead. It passed inspection because he sat down then and reached immediately for the bread plate. Charles disliked direct conflict and would first tack away from it. So the meal began in silence. Finally, he laid his fork down and looked directly at her, his voice not even raised; the threat underlying it formal:

"You know who saved you this time *don't you?* But if I were you, I wouldn't press my luck."

After he had finished his meal and gone back upstairs leaving the clean-up to them, Alice had said to her, "Does that mean house arrest?"

But she had known it did and had already accepted its mandate, the results of which became apparent to Connie with her daughter's next school report. High already, her grades over the next six months improved more. Rather than walk home with her friends after school, she would stay with her English teacher until Connie arrived for her. The teacher, a Mrs Wilkes, rang Connie one noon to ask if they might meet—about Alice. Fearing the worst, Connie had approached the teacher's conference room with apprehension. But it was a smiling Mrs Wilkes who greeted her with a substantial folder of Alice's work, "You didn't know that I have Alice writing newspaper articles for me?"

"No!?"

"She comes in each afternoon, sits down and writes. I've got some of her work *here*," said Mrs. Wilkes as she opened the folder. "I think she may have the makings of a journalist. She hasn't told you then, I take it. Here, read this vignette."

"No, she's keeps things to herself, I'm afraid," said Connie as Mrs. Wilkes handed her one of Alice's articles to read.

"Also, she has a good, lively imagination even if her tendency is to overstate. But she'll learn. She's good with detail, her humour can be quite cutting. Here, for example, where she grotesquely describes her character pulling at his ear. I wonder, do you know where she gets her material?" said Mrs. Wilkes.

"I can't imagine," said Connie, shocked but secretly pleased.

"Her tendency is to over-attack; she can be perhaps too strident, but that will correct itself. I'm even thinking of turning the paper over to her next year if she continues. Hand her the job of editor."

Mrs. Wilkes had, and during her final year of high school Alice would bring home copies of the school's paper which Connie would open to the editorial page, to make a deliberate point of showing Charles Alice's name opposite *Editor in Chief*—perhaps to gloat a bit before him. Were her daughter's victories not hers also?

Alice finished third from the top in her class and with her acceptance at Leeds University for the following year assured, she was chosen to speak at the prize-giving ceremonies in the school hall that June. Liz was there; it would be one of the last times Alice was to see her grandmother. Also among those faces present was Cliff's.

Connie had not seen him in almost fifteen years and now there he stood, inside the auditorium where Alice had arranged to meet him looking after fifteen years a little down-at-the-heels and no longer the flashy handsome salesman Connie thought she remembered. Alice had agreed to go out with him after the ceremony while Connie and Charles drove Liz back to the aunt's old house where she still lived by herself. Returning home, Charles went immediately upstairs. But Connie waited at the window. Then, at eleven, her daughter returned looking disappointed, Connie instantly thought. "Where did you two go?"

"He took me to dinner at quite a good restaurant. Said he'd meant to do this before now. I didn't believe him of course."

"And? What'd you two talk about?"

"Everything and nothing. (Anyway, what do you say to someone who—though you still call him *'Dad'*—isn't, since he hasn't seen you for fifteen years. It's hard—it's like talking to a stranger you met on the street.) He questioned me on what I intended to do. I said I enjoyed writing articles and would probably study journalism after I got back."

"*Back*—?"

"From my gap year. I was going to tell you tomorrow, Mum. Karen and I have decided to buy European Rail Passes along with a couple others you haven't met, and that was when he handed me *this*." Connie watched her reach into her purse and pull out an envelope. "Six hundred pounds!" Alice showed her the notes.

"Ooh! So your father hasn't forgotten how to be generous."

"I wondered about that myself. *Why?* Unless it was to salve a guilty conscience, because how could he have known that I would need this money?"

"—And where are you going?" asked Connie after a moment. "Not sure yet. Spain. Italy. Some Greek islands maybe. The *usual*."

"And who are the other two you're going with besides Karen?"

"You don't know them, Mum."

"But I'm curious who they are. You must know their names." Was it reluctance she saw in her daughter's face? "Tell me."

"John Malcomb is one. Fred's the other. I don't know his last name even—they're Karen's friends. Mum, why are you looking at me like that?"

"You and Karen are going to run around Europe for a year with two strange men! Am I hearing right?"

"Mother, they're not strange men as you call them. I've known them for almost two years. We've even dated. So get off my case!"

"I'm not going to allow it, that's all."

"Why?"

"*Why?* It's not what a single young woman with any self respect would do. It would be making the biggest mistake of your life!"

"Mother, how can you stand there and talk to me about making mistakes after the ones you made! Anyway, how do you know that what I'm doing is a mistake?"

"But just to run off like that with two men—? It's not something girls do!"

"Mother, for your information, Queen Victoria has been dead for some time now. It's the start of the twenty-first century and I know exactly what I'm doing. I knew what your reaction would be and that's why I didn't want to tell you…You can't stop me!" she said and rose.

Still stunned, Connie's first thought was to pour a glass of wine and she turned into the kitchen. *You can't stop me, Mum!* She could only try—reason with her, Connie thought as she finished the wine and went up herself to bed. Charles would be asleep by now.

Unfortunately he wasn't. She felt him turn toward her: "Alice get home?"

"Yes."

She felt his hand grope for her then. "Don't do that, Charles. Go away! I've got a horrible headache and I need to sleep." But she couldn't, she lay awake in the darkness thinking back, seeing her life as a catalogue of mistakes. She needed first to discuss the risk Alice was about to put herself in with Mandy, Saturday. Fighting with Alice could make matters worse if Charles were to get dragged in!

"You'd be overjoyed with Alice for being able to do something like this were it not for the two boys, right?" said Mandy. "I think you just have to resign yourself and trust her— that's what I would do. If you don't, you're only going to alienate her more."

So Connie settled on a new tactic: *approval,* and one after- noon she brought home a large map of Europe which she spread out upon the dining room. She had already marked in felt pen places she had always wanted to see: Paris, Madrid, Rome, Venice. "Alice, come look at this map I found. Show you some of the places I'd like to go."

In return Alice pointed out cities she and Karen had already chosen, and others still to be decided upon and this led to more discussion. If you were going to Madrid anyway should you continue on to Sevilla? Or if forced to choose, which one should you see: Granada or Sevilla? With less than two weeks to go before the agreed upon departure date, Connie discovered a cheap flight to *Charles de Gaulle,* but the rail passes had yet to be purchased. Charles still had no notion of his stepdaughter's actual travel arrangements—only that she was going. Then Alice broached the question, "Does *your husband* have any idea who the others are that I'm going with?"

"No, and I think it best that way," replied Connie as if they were conspirators.

At last came the day of Alice's departure. "Shouldn't I come with you?" Charles unexpectedly offered.

"Why, Charles, when I am perfectly capable of driving her myself?" said Connie. It was not until they were all before the departure gate— Alice, Karen, the two boys, their parents—and she watched her daughter disappear into the tunnel without even a wave *goodbye* that Connie realized how alone she now was!

Alice had promised her to both write and email and at the beginning she did once a day sometimes, from endless internet cafes strewn like signposts along the meandering path of her adventures. Less frequent were the letters, but there were postcards, so many postcards! of places Connie had seen over and over in books and travel magazines: the Alhambra in Spain, the Coliseum in Rome. Each day Connie would await the postman. Then Alice e'd from an internet cafe:

> Hi, Mum! I just went swimming in the Mediterranean at
> a place called La Scala Spain.
>
> The water is warm here, I'm guessing degrees under a hot
> sun. It doesn't rain here.
>
> Love, Alice

The weather in Manchester that autumn had been wet and miserable, and the long-range forecast called for more of the same as Alice's letters began arriving less frequently. In early December Charles was invited to a conference on computer software in London. At the last moment Connie decided to leave Scraggles with Mandy and go just to escape the rain, she told herself, maybe take in a play if she could, or an opera while Charles attended his conference.

He had and returned ecstatic, "Connie, you'll never guess whom I met there!"

She didn't much care. "Who?"

"Paul Allen! And I still haven't told you, but I've reached a decision. I'm going to buy three hundred shares of Microsoft stock.

No, four hundred!"

"Buy them if you want." *Why tell me?* she thought, annoyed.

On her return she fully expected to find something, a postcard at least, as she quickly opened the letter box. It was empty. But inside she discovered a message on her answering machine: to call Manchester General Hospital and ask for a Ms. Wilson. With a terrible sense of dread she reached for the phone.

"What is it?" said Charles.

"Quiet!—Ms. Wilson? This is Connie Cullingsworth. You left a message for me call…Oh I see…Yes of course, I'm on my way." She must have gone absolutely white as she turned to Charles: "Don't even take off your coat. It's my mother—we have to go!"

It was a somber-faced doctor who had led them into the consultation room. The stroke had left her entire right side paralyzed and her speech gone, though her eyes could still follow movement which probably meant she had recognized Connie's face peering down at her.

"She still hears you," whispered a nurse beside her.

"Mum, I'm here. Get well soon, *please?*" *Please don't die!*

But she had already been told by the neurologist that the nervous system had suffered irreparable damage. "You do know what this means?" said Charles as they left the hospital.

"What?"

"You're going to have to start searching for a nursing home to put your mother in. They can't keep her here."

And that, she told her daughter by email afterward, had been the beginning of those three hellish months leading up to the second stroke. Finding a suitable nursing home meant days of searching by phone, then foot. Each nursing home had to be inspected and its staff carefully evaluated. Then there was the problem of what to do with her mother's furniture.

"I hope you're not planning on moving it in with us," Charles said.

"No, Charles, I'm not planning to unload any of it on *you.*"

Rarely did they have tea together now, Connie e'd; they were like two separate people—strangers—sharing a kitchen. Depending on how long Connie spent with her mother at the hospital each evening, she would walk in to find Charles in the kitchen preparing his vegetarian tea. Or, if it were later, he would have already eaten and there would be his dirty dishes stacked neatly in the sink waiting for her to load into the dishwasher. "And it does no good to complain. Your stepfather has little time for me these days. Or interest. Where are you now, by the way?"

"Innsbruck, Mum. Karen decided she wanted to ski."

But interestingly, there was no mention of the other two. Then in March her mother died suddenly of a brain hemorrhage. "Mum, I can't tell you how sorry I am or how much I will miss grandmother! I wish I could at least have gotten back for the funeral but there was no way."

No. A gap followed, during which time Connie heard nothing. Then for Easter a postcard arrived from a place called Nafplion in Greece:

> Cheers, and sorry for not sending this sooner, Mum. We are in the Peloponnese, in a pretty seaport with a castle atop a really high rock that I'd hate to climb after drinking ouzo (joke). Seriously, Karen and I are at present in a tiny two room apt waiting for the weather to improve. And for Karen to make up her mind on whether or not she wants to travel thru the Greek islands next summer. I'm thinking maybe I should try writing a book.
>
> Love, Alice

Book? Connie reread the card carefully. Next summer she would do the Greek islands with or without Karen, apparently *but what about Leeds?* She needed to be back home by August latest! Also, there had been no mention of the two male companions for some time—? If I understand you, Connie returned by email, all this including the island hopping is in preparation for studying journalism at Leeds? Don't forget, you should be back here by mid August! And what about those two boys you and Karen are with. Are they also going?

Connie waited. After two days the reply came back:

> Dear Mum:
>
> I totally forgot to mention: Fred and John decided to split some time ago. Things didn't work out.
>
> Karen now says she probably won't follow me as her parents want her to come home. I plan to take a ferry from here as soon as I can. Mum, these Greek ferries really are cool! They let the backpackers sleep on deck.

What had she meant by 'things didn't work out?' *What things?* If one of Connie's anxieties had been finally put to rest, another every bit as threatening had just replaced it as she hastily sent Alice another email: I want you to come home with Karen, now!

Mum, I can't, I leave tonight for Santorini. But you needn't worry—I'm okay.

Love, your daughter

And that was all for the next three months. Frantic, she had phoned Karen's mother. Karen, though back, could provide little new information. Alice was keeping a detailed diary, for future use she had said. As to whether she planned to return for college in the autumn, Karen didn't know. Then, early in August, Alice broke her silence and e'd:

Hi, Mum!

Sorry for not keeping you better informed. But I've been having really interesting experiences and gaining some good insights which I'll tell you about when I see you.

Right now I'm in Turkey, on the Mediterranean in a place called Fethiye. Mum, you would like it here. There is sun every day with no rain, and many here speak English. Most Turks here will bend over backwards to help you. If you ask a question and they think the answer will make you unhappy, they will lie to please you. And I got to know one quite nice bloke who's a diver and wants to teach me how to scuba dive if I stay, but I'm not.

Mum I know it's time for me to return if I want to go back to school (which I do). **The problem is my pocketbook was stolen and I will need some money to get home on!** Don't get upset. I'm in no danger or anything like that. But I need to buy an airplane ticket. Also to pay back my friends what I've had to borrow. So send £500. There's a Western Union here and the clerk knows I'm expecting it.

And <u>PS</u>: If you can avoid it don't tell Charles.

Paradise Visited

Chapter 1

WHEN AT LAST THE CLOUDS began to thin, then shred into tatters beneath the silvery wing of their 757 and Connie caught her first glimpse of blue sea below, she tried to hold onto that long- awaited emotion, store it in some special place in her mind where it would not become lost; and where she could always return to whenever the desire arose.

She tried to remember Juan's face but couldn't and the anticipated pleasure of seeing at last the Mediterranean, sea of her dreams, was tempered by her worries over Alice. Why had her daughter not come home with Karen in ample time to prepare for her freshman week at Leeds? Did Alice have no intention of pursuing her education? What had made her change her mind? And what in the world had made her decide to go to Turkey instead! All questions that had prayed upon her mind until she finally reached for the phone and rang Charles' travel agent. Then she had emailed her daughter the flight number and arrival time.

"Mum," Alice had sent back, "you needn't have gone to so much trouble and expense. (The money would have been enough.) But since you have, I've asked Ahmed to pick you up in his taxi. Look for a sign with your name when you leave the airport. Everything is fine so don't worry."

"Where will we meet?' Connie immediately sent an email. "At the hotel. Ahmed knows."

"*Ahmed?* thought Connie.

"What are you looking at out there?" said Charles from the seat beside her.

"The Mediterranean, Charles. Here, do you want to take a look?" She drew her head back from the window.

"I really don't care to. I'm bound to see it later anyway...I just hope this hotel your daughter booked us into is at least clean. If you remember, I warned you any number of times in the last three years that if you didn't step down on her, something like this would happen."

"Charles, you don't know that *something* has happened." He hadn't wanted to come and now she feared he would dampen any chance she might have of making a halfway pleasurable time of it. "Think of yourself as being on a week's holiday. Would you have rather stayed behind?"

"It's just a particularly bad time," said Charles, "with the entire system having to be up and running in just three weeks."

"But you have a staff you trained yourself you said."

"Yes, but they turn to me for help if things go wrong."

"Then be miserable."

"What?"

"Nothing. Just go back to whatever that is you're reading."

But as she sat with her face at the window and watched the last wispy tendrils of cloud float past, the glaze of bright sea far below, concerns for Alice's future sat like cloud-shadow over the joy of her holiday expectations. It was the end of gap year. Alice was a bright intelligent girl. Too bright to throw everything away, her education included, to live in some third world country and a Muslim one at that! Then she could feel the engines throttle back, and pressure build in her ears as the aircraft descended. Once inside the terminal and through Passport Control, she said to Charles, "Do you want to stop at Duty Free?"

"Oh, I rather think we'll need a stiff drink before this day is out!"

Then they were exiting into a canopied sunlight and heat, amid an encirclement of faces pressing forward. Connie saw there were many signs being held up and waved: placards bearing the names of hotels, and of tour groups, as well as individual names.

She spotted hers. "Charles, over *there!*"

Holding up a sign with her name was a swarthy, unshaven Turk. That had been one of the first things she had noticed about Turks: they often went about wearing several days stubble while Charles shaved sometimes twice a day, she noted as they approached the Turk holding up the sign and she introduced herself.

"I am Ahmed. I have taxi here for you," he said with a widening smile, extending his hand.

"Where is Alice?"

"In Fethiye. She say me to take you to the hotel. She will come later."

"So she's staying at the hotel—?"

"No she say me she will come to you there later," repeated Ahmed as he tried to take their suitcases. But Charles refused to relinquish his.

"I can carry mine!" Then they were stepping out into the direct sun and for an instant both stopped. It was like stepping through the door of a furnace. "How hot is it, Haymet?" said Charles.

"Ahmed! Today is maybe..thirty-eight. Very hot and it isn't just heat, it's thee..*ah..?*"

"Humidity?" she said.

"Yes." Ahmed smiled up at them through the rearview mirror as he started the taxi. "Next month better."

The taxi had a meter, but the driver did not turn it on Connie noticed as they went past the pay booth onto the road leading out. She still had little idea what Turkey should look like. Not a desert with camels, as she sometimes had pictured it. No, but what first surprised her was how green it was. Fertile, with fruit trees everywhere, and farms. But the country also had an impoverished look, she thought seeing the strewn garbage that littered both sides of the highway: an eyesore on what, if cared for, could be a pretty countryside. And there were those half finished structures everywhere: houses being lived in judging from the refuse strewn about, but which still lacked their upper part. Or, if the upper story was finished, an outside staircase of poured concrete would ascend, but without any hand railing.

Leaning forward to touch Ahmed's shoulder, Connie had asked why there were no safety railings?

"You are in Turkey, lady," Ahmed smiled back at them in the rearview mirror.

The highway seemed to narrow and become even windier; they were now climbing. The road surface was very rough and so patched that it resembled a washboard in places. Sometimes Ahmed would swerve to avoid a chuck hole, when the road wasn't too narrow. They had joined a column of slow-moving cars and vans and now, as they wound through a left hand curve, she glimpsed a slow moving truck at the head of the column; the honking cars impatient to pass. They were hugging the side of a mountain and she could look almost straight down: just how far down she could not see to know. She leaned forward and again touched Ahmed:

"Do cars ever go off?" She pointed down.

Again he glanced back at her smiling: "Oh yes, lady."

"I wish he'd just watch the road!" muttered Charles.

It was with a sense of relief that the taxi finally topped the last hill and started down and she saw in the distance Fethiye, spread out along the edges of a bowl-shaped bay. Closer, where the hillside slanted down, she could see blue water sparking in sunlight in the little bays and there were tiny islands, some little more than abrupt outcroppings of rock, against which waves broke whitely. Then they were on the flat driving through narrow villages of paint flaked buildings. A large white mosque atop an abrupt rise appeared then finally Fethiye itself: population forty-eight thousand, said the sign.

Ataturk Boulevard was the principal thoroughfare and was set back from the harbour where their hotel was located. But Connie could see it on her right, a multi-storied brown structure, and read its name—*Otel Kemal*—as Ahmed brought his taxi to a stop before the revolving glass doors and she could see the bellboy waiting *but there was no Alice*, she thought. She watched Ahmed opening the taxi's boot. "My daughter is *home* you say?"

"No home. Bea's," said Ahmed as he reached for his mobile phone and began selecting numbers. He listened. "Here Alice," he said and handed the phone to her.

"Alice?" she said into it.

"Hi, Mum. I see you made it safely."

"Where are you!"

"In Bea's Bar. Walk straight through the hotel, Mum, and out the front. Look right to where the quay does a ninety degree turn. You should see me in less than five minutes."

But first came paying their fare: Connie could see the meter still turned off as she handed the mobile phone back: "How much do we owe you, Ahmed?"

"For you, special. Thirty thousand."

Connie opened her purse and started to examine the new money. Ahmed quickly reached in and extracted three green bills: "These, lady."

"Why wasn't his meter on?" said Charles aside. "From what I hear you can't trust Turks."

"Keep your voice lowered!"

"You will follow me please, lady. Man."

They had, in single file through the revolving door and past the elevator and stairs to the lobby and reception desk, then out through the open bar and restaurant area which faced upon a busy promenade-like quay. She discovered bars and cafes along one side with ships tied stern first to the other. Some had two masts while others, mast-less, were double-decked and reminded her somehow of Manchester busses. A length of gangplank led from the mid-stern of each down onto the quay and there were tourists: sightseers, Connie saw: *but where was Alice?* It was unbearably hot.

"Here she comes, *there!*" said Charles, pointing to where the quay turned abruptly left.

Bordering it was a parking area and behind that were low squat trees and a path leading in. It was from there Alice appeared: Connie saw her daughter's radiant face, widening in a smile.

"So you two made it I see! But why do you stand out here when you could be inside with the air conditioning? How do you like your hotel?"

"I just hope the room is clean." said Charles.

"I told Suleyman who's the manager that you were picky about that, Charles. Let's go look," said Alice taking them first to the bar for cold bottles of *Effes* to carry upstairs with them. "And don't bother trying the lift—it never has worked," she said as she led them past it. Their room was on the second floor and, though plain, seemed at least clean Charles admitted. Mounted to the wall above the bed was the air conditioning unit which blew down a draft of cold air when Alice tried it. "Looks okay to me, Mum," she said and that *klima*—which is what the Turks had called it—alone made their next two weeks tolerable (or would have, Connie later thought, had it not been for those mosquitoes!). "Let's see what kind of view Suleyman gave you," said Alice then as she opened the sliding door, then screen, and the three stepped out onto the balcony to discover the busy quay below, and the harbour with boats at anchor beyond.

But the sea that rose and splashed against the concrete quay like water at the sides of a bathtub was filthy and they could see garbage bobbing on its surface: bottles and plastic of various descriptions, all floating in an oily scum. "It's just for boats, Charles—nobody swims in it," said Alice who could read her stepfather's thoughts.

"Mum, Charles, I have to go now. I promised I'd be at Sue's and I'm late."

"Who's Sue?" said Connie in surprise.

"The person I'm temporarily staying with. We met in Bea's Bar (which is where all the English ex-pat's go). Anyway, there's this English girl we both know (actually we're helping her hide). See she married this Turk who likes to beat the shit out of her. So she's going back to England, tonight and I promised her I'd say goodbye. So I've got to. Just be down in the bar by eight-thirty and we can have dinner at the Marina. Raquet, the owner's a Turkish woman but liberated (to the dislike of her husband). It's a nice place, right on the water—you'll like it, Mum. And yes, Charles, Raquet I'm sure can find something vegetarian for you. Until *eight-thirty* then?"

"Can we eat earlier? Like at five-thirty?" Charles objected.

"Mum—the both of you—just for your information, nobody eats here before the sun goes down and it turns a bit cooler. And, Mum, let me have your handy."

"My *what?*"

"Cell phone—the Turks call it a *handy*." She glanced hesitantly at Charles. "And a few thousand lira just to have—I was robbed, remember? I need to buy your sim card so we can text-message each other, and while I remember: How much did Ahmed charge you?"

"Thirty thousand!" said Charles. "He didn't even turn his meter on. I figured we were getting taken."

"No, Charles, you were not being taken—that was probably the actual cost of the petrol. He did it as a favour to me…Now I have to leave you, until dinner."

They had walked with Alice through the lobby. Connie watched her daughter disappear into the crowd of Turks and sightseers on the quay—a person with a place to go and people to see and while Alice's apparently easy successes—the fact alone that she could claim friends in so short a time, had only to ask cab drivers to do her favours—pleased Connie even though she knew nothing about her daughter's actual involvements themselves. That caused her a stir of uneasiness. Nonetheless, she couldn't resist the opportunity to say before her husband, "It appears that Alice isn't so moribund as you thought, Charles!"

Alice came for them in the Kemal's bar at a quarter past eight; dusk, with the air still uncomfortably warm as they set out along the quay and Connie saw before her an unbroken line of boats of varying sizes moored stern to stern. There would be a small craft capable of carrying perhaps only a dozen passengers sandwiched in between larger ships with two decks capable of carrying perhaps a hundred, Connie thought. "Why in the world would anyone want so many boats?" said Charles. "What do they do with them all?"

"Charles, not you I know, but many just like to swim," said Alice. "Out there are what is called 'the Twelve Islands' and at the height of the tourist season most of these boats leave filled each day with people who want to see the islands, swim, drink beer, and to have fun."

"In a Muslim country?" said Charles.

"Yes. There's no law against it yet. Mum, it's such a pity you don't swim!—Oh, now look ahead. See where the quay turns? Well that's where we're going."

The quay bent left, and just beyond the bend was the Marina Bar and Grill. Connie could see its tables facing the water and standing sentinel before them was the proprietor and her friend, Raquet, said Alice. Connie watched the two exchange hugs and kisses. "Raquet, this is my mother, Connie. And this is Charles." Raquet was darkly attractive, and very made up, Connie noticed as she bent close to kiss her cheek. Then Raquet showed them to a table and no sooner were they seated than a waiter appeared with a chilled bottle of white wine and an ice bucket. Charles took the first swallow to sample, then nodded. But the waiter was barely gone before Charles turned to her and said,

"Crappy wine!"

Tied to the quay directly before their table were ships of a different kind. They had tall masts Connie saw, and she could see furled sail between the bowsprit and foremast of each. They were long and graceful, and their polished wooden hulls gleamed in the darkening light just like someone's favourite polished table. Never had she seen boats so pretty! One, she further observed, had a squared stern with two rear windows that were quite large and made her think of a pirate ship, or even a Spanish galleon! "What lovely boats! What are they?"

"Gulets, Mum."

"And can you go out on them?"

"You go for a week on those. Take what the Turks call 'a blue voyage.' They're like hotels and sail up and down the coast. Wine and dine you.

Spend your night in some little cove, or cool bay. The only thing against them is, they're expensive."

Charles considered it a moment: "But if you were out there that long with nothing to do, wouldn't you get bored?"

Their dinner was quite good. She and Alice had grilled fish; Charles, lentil soup and a vegetarian pizza; and though it was quite dark— too dark in fact to see to examine the food in the pale light of the table candle—he ate greedily. "So what are Turks like?" lowering his glass he asked Alice— they were now on their second bottle of wine.

"Pleasant, Charles. Accommodating," she said as she swatted at something on her wrist: "Got you, you little shit! Oh and one thing I forgot to mention," she said, holding something tiny for them to see under the light of the candle: "Mosquitoes! This time of night they can be especially bad. I hope you brought repellent. If not, we have to stop."

They had on their way back to the hotel. Leaving Charles to wander, the two set off in search of the *Off.* "So would you stay here?" asked Connie—it was their first real moment alone.

"*Here?* What gave you that idea, Mum?" said her daughter. "From some of your emails. And what Karen said." Connie

could read in her daughter's smile nothing—free as it was of any resentment or ill-feeling that she could find.

"Well Karen misunderstood me is all...I will admit the thought crossed my mind. But without money how could you exist here? Marry a poor Turk?"

"They think the English are all loaded by the way, so be careful!" Alice warned as she left them before their hotel with a promise to show up in the morning. "See you both about ten and I hope you find the hotel comfortable, Charles."

But her first night in Turkey had been anything but comfortable! First Charles had fiddled with the '*klima*' which was mounted to the wall above their bed, trying to moderate the flow of air that blasted directly down on them and made them cold. Yet turn the klima off and within minutes the room was uncomfortably hot again. They had only a double mattress while they were used to their king-sized at home, so the bed seemed narrow. Charles always sweated anyway; she could smell him and feel his heat as he lay beside her. Each time she tried to move away he would follow in his sleep. She was at the edge of the mattress already and had to keep pushing him back, "Stay on your own side!" she would tell him. Then add to that a pair of mosquitoes that kept waking her up as they whined past her ear. Charles managed to kill the first as it landed on him but the second was more clever. When she turned on the light they could see it above them at the wall, or over their heads on the ceiling. But Turkish ceilings are high and they had nothing to swat with anyway. What was worse, she had been bitten earlier at the restaurant and during the night the bites began to itch.

But she must have slept somewhat, because it was fully light when the buzzing of her handy woke her. It was a text message from Alice:

> Sorry Mum, forgot I can't make it. Have appointment I must keep. Suggest U shop before it gets 2 hot. Charles will need shorts, sandals. Buy yourself a swimsuit for when we go to the beach.

Connie had tried then to call, but Alice had her phone shut off.

By eleven the streets were already oven-hot and Connie's mosquito bites were red welts that itched fiercely. At a pharmacy she stopped for antihistamine cream and more repellent before continuing her search for beach wear. Connie found the swimsuit shop Alice had told her of. It was air conditioned, and Charles did not mind standing there while she went through the racks trying to decide whether she should buy a single or two-piece costume. She selected a two-piece that didn't appear too risky and went to try it on.

"Charles, how does it fit me?" she asked as she presented herself.

"It seems okay to me."

"How do I look in it?"

"You must know."

"Hadn't you better try on a swimsuit yourself?"

"Oh I doubt that I'll want to go in the water."

She remembered the old saying then about dragging the horse to water. But Charles was a shy horse and shyness often took the form of stubborn resistance. So she had simply told the salesgirl to include a pair of trunks for him, before returning back along the quay to have lunch at the hotel.

Afterwards they tried sitting out on their balcony which was shaded, looking down at the water, drinking scotch which only made them sweat. "I know," said Connie finally, "why don't we try and find Bea's?"

Chapter 2

IT WAS NOT DIFFICULT. FROM mid point in the park she could see it, set in with small cafes and other bars facing onto a street that bordered the park, and that was really more a pedestrian lane. As they drew closer Connie knew it must be Bea's not by the sign, but by the clientele. Not a few were *getting on* in age, she saw, and they sat before a confused array of tables, some round while others were rectangular, and drank from fat brown bottles of *Efes* though she could pick out the odd glass of wine. All looked and sounded British and except for the fact that they drank Turkish beer, and the sun was hotter and brighter than it ever could get in Manchester, she might be at a gathering for English retirees.

"Are you perhaps looking for someone?"

Connie saw a tallish, white-haired lady with friendly blue eyes and the welcoming hint of a smile approaching. "You must be Bea?"

"I am. And who have I the pleasure of?"

"Connie. I think you know my daughter."

"Alice's mother!" Connie saw the smile widen. "Then you must be Charles? Normally Alice is here by now. Let's see where I can find to put you... so when did you arrive? Where are you staying?"

Connie explained events of the last forty-eight hours to her hostess as she led them to a table. There were three others already seated and as they approached, one—a small, wiry man with splotchy-red cheeks etched by a mosaic of tiny blue veins, narrow nose, and a pencil line moustache above equally thin lips—held up his glass of Coca Cola Connie first thought:

"Bea, *old girl*, did you short my brandy?"

He spoke with the urbane manner and exact pronunciation of an English public school boy, observed Connie. "*No,* Eric! And if it had any less coke, you'd be drinking straight brandy (which you almost are)," said Bea, angered. Connie and Charles both ordered bottles of *Efes* and as they waited Connie could feel Eric's eyes focus upon her.

"I'm Eric and I already know of you, dear lady, from your daughter."

"Alice! Yes, I'm Connie and this is my husband, Charles."

"Indeed, pleased to make your acquaintance, both. This is my *paramour*, Maureen."

Once a pretty face, it looked unattended and badly eroded by myriad wrinkles. The eyes, Connie noted, shone but weakly, and the hand as it was being extended, shook badly.

"Maureen keeps urging me to tie the fatal knot. Are you two here to stay and join our tight knit little community, or are you going back, Charlie?"

"Charles."

"Oh, sorry old chap! and this is Martin. Your daughter said you teach school. Martin is, take note, also a schoolteacher. I'm afraid you'll have to excuse his state of inebriation however."

Martin was a large man, fleshy with a round face, maybe forty-five, thought Connie and as he stared with a sort of silly expression across the table at them, Connie was unsure he saw much of anything at all.

"You taught art, didn't you say, Martin? Martin, meet Charlie and his, I believe, wife."

Connie noticed two people leaving. "Come on, Charles!" She rose to claim the table. Bea followed with two cold bottles of E*fes* which she set she set before them: "Eric gets like that after he has too much to drink. I'm afraid you have to put up with him."

The beer was very cold. Connie even held the bottle up to her face to feel the cold before she poured and drank thirstily. Charles had already finished his first glass and was pouring the second when Bea appeared with two more bottles. "We didn't order those," said Connie.

"No, dearie, they come from the young man at that table *there*. He knows Alice. He was the one who helped her out after I introduced them."

Following Bea's finger Connie discovered a young nice- looking face tanned from the sun, and with intense dark eyes looking directly at her. "Cheers!" she saw his lips say to her and responded in voiceless speech *Thank you very much!* as her eyes continued to meet his. A quality in them held her, until she forcibly drew hers away. Curious, she glanced over at his table twice to see if he would return her look. But he was occupied with someone she saw, and when she looked a third time he was gone.

Alice had promised to pick them at the hotel at ten that morning. It was not until two that afternoon that Connie finally saw her daughter's face appear looking apologetically for her in Bea's. It had been an eventful morning. First, another of her girlfriends had had to return unexpectedly to England after her father had suffered a stroke Alice said, and she had been busy helping her friend find a cheap flight back. Ordering first a cold bottle of *Efes,* Alice sat down across the table, "Well, Mum, which do you want first, the good news or the bad?"

The good had been that she was definitely going to attend Leeds and be there in time for her freshman week. The bad was that, while helping her friend, as he had found a super cheap flight for herself and would return to Manchester Thursday morning. "That leaves us just tomorrow, Mum. How's that for irony though?"

Alice said with a laugh, "It was me that was stranded, you thought. Now it turns out to be you. But only for two weeks and, who knows, you might like it, Charles."

That next day, their last, Alice had taken them by water taxi across the bay to Chalis Beach. Carrying about twenty-five each, the taxis left every half hour from beside the quay not far from their hotel. At least this way they would get out on the water where it was cooler, said Alice. This time, true to her word, she did arrive for them at ten. Fethiye Harbour this time of morning was crowded with craft of all descriptions from the bigger gulets, outbound for pretty places along the coast, to the many swimming boats off on their day's adventures through the twelve islands.

The water taxi delivered its passengers to Chalis, and while the beach was itself rocky the view—the sparkle of the water, the hazy-blue shapes of islands in the distance—was new and so pretty, she immediately thought. There were sunbeds and umbrellas for rent on the beach. She watched her daughter strip out of her tank top and shorts to the swimsuit beneath. "Come on, Mum, try the water: you can paddle anyway. It's a pity somebody doesn't teach you to swim. Coming with us, Charles?"

"No, I don't think I care to, today."

"Charles, you really are a fish out of water. Then you ready, Mum?"

It had been a lovely, fun day Connie reflected: bittersweet in the knowledge that it was also to be their last.

Chapter 3

THE NEXT DAY HER DAUGHTER had had little time for her before Ahmed took her away in his taxi. "And don't forget to kiss Scraggles for me!" Connie had called after Alice as she watched her daughter climb into the front seat.

"I'm getting him first thing, Mum!"

Then she watched as Ahmed set the taxi in gear. Afterwards she and Charles returned to their room, Charles with a bucket of ice from the bar. But the scotch-and-sodas had done little to lift their spirits, and only made them sweat more. Charles seemed moody and irritable, and Connie thought she knew why. She felt herself as if she had been suddenly abandoned. The next morning after breakfast and with little better to do, Charles announced he was going to look for an internet café; find out, if he could, what had happened during his absence at *Computer Operations* by contacting a friend or two. "Do you want to come?" he asked. "There's nothing to do here."

"But what's there at an internet café and anyway, I don't care to know what's happening. So *no*, Charles, and if I shouldn't be here when you return, I'll be—I don't know—walking."

"In the heat! What if I come back and you're not here? Where should I start looking?"

"Charles, I'm hardly going to get lost. I'll be back when I'm back!"

As lunch time approached, she tried to decide what she would eat: lamb kebab at the restaurant opposite the post office? She wondered if Bea served any lunch. She was sure *not* as she wandered along the edge of the quay and gazed down at the filthy water. *What would she do were she to fall in!* she thought as she followed the quay to where it turned. But she did not turn with it—instead she cut directly across and entered the park.

Bea's was crowded with many of the faces she remembered from yesterday: one or two even by name already as she passed by their tables hoping Eric's face would not be among them.

"Connie! I was hoping you'd come back! Your daughter made it off safely? We haven't formally met, I'm Omer. Come sit down beside me and what can I get you to drink?"

But she already knew his name and she liked the face before her, its high forehead, receding hair and bushy brows, and those warm black eyes inviting her. "Omer! I know. Alice mentioned you in her email," she said, returning his look: "How pleasant! Yes, thank you, I believe I will," seeing him at once rise and draw back the chair for her. That had been Connie's first and her lasting impression of him: the attentive concern he had from that first moment lavished on her. She had not wanted *Efes* but a white wine if Bea had it.

"Bea, look who came! Do you still have that white *Antique?*

If so, and it's cold, could you bring it?"

While she waited, Connie looked more closely at the face before her. He had a nice smile: clean, pleasant teeth, she observed; but it was his eyes that struck her most. They were darkly alive and within their depths she could, upon closer inspection, make out instant flecks of light, like the flashes of fireflies back in Scotland when she was a girl. The only thing she disliked was the perhaps three days of stubble and she wondered why Turks all looked so unkempt, until she remembered that Juan would sometimes come to class unshaven. Then Bea was there, holding the wine before Omer.

"Oh that's cold! Yes, we'll have that bottle, Bea," said Omer. "Do you have an ice bucket?"

The wine had had just enough fruitiness to taste cold and very good, perhaps *too good! "Prost!"* Omer had said and held up his glass to hers.

"Cheers!" she said as she clicked the two. "Prost—that's German. You're not German?"

"Jawohl, Madam! I was raised in Berlin and almost carried a German passport, not the Turkish—but that's a story with twists and turns, and not always happy. So let's talk about what is: you! You're here for a fortnight and want to learn to swim, and you want me to teach you."

She had had the uneasy sense that she was being lied to—lied or *charmed to*—and that she ought to stay wary. Equally obvious too was "You and Alice have been talking about me!"

"We have and I wouldn't deny it," said Omer, raising his wine in salute. "Nothing bad, I promise. And we came to the same conclusion—that I should be the one to teach you."

"That's what you do professionally—teach people to swim?"

"No, Connie. I'm a diver."

"So it was you who offered to teach Alice scuba diving! *How*—when did all of this come about?"

"After your daughter had her money taken. Bea came to me asking if I couldn't let her work with me on the diving boat for a few days until she could get money sent. There wasn't much she could do not speaking Turkish: collect the air tanks...carry drinks to customers. But in the end I couldn't say no and let her stay on board for a few days, until she could find herself a place to live— though it was risky."

"Risky *how?*"

"All it would take, Connie, is for anyone to tell the police that *Diving Delight* has an English girl working on one of their boats and we'd get a big fine, plus your daughter would be deported. It happens."

"*Ooh,.* So you're her Good Samaritan!"

"What's that?"

"Her friend in need. She said you're a diver!"

"I used to be. Do you know what the bends are?"

"I—no. Not exactly."

"That's when you surface really fast. I was down too deep and ran out of air—I had only fifty bars left and had to come up before I could get all the nitrogen out of my blood. That's how you get bends. I mean, it could have been worse, Connie—if my lungs had exploded, I wouldn't be here."

"But you can no longer dive?" She could read the answer in his face.

"The one thing in the world I loved more than life itself was to strap on those tanks! The property, my family inheritance, mean nothing! I would give them all up, Connie, my claim to that property, wealth, everything if it would just undo those fifteen minutes. Do you want to see my boat, Connie—the one I was diver on? And your daughter went out on? Finish up your wine and we'll take a short walk. Do you want to?"

She did, and they had, beside the quay. Charles would be back at the hotel, worried by now.

Perhaps he would come looking! But she had had enough wine and didn't care.

They walked past the hotel and continued, Omer leading her. It was afternoon and with the swimming boats all out, the quay ahead looked boat-less, though out in the bay beyond she could see an occasional ship at anchor. One caught her fancy. It had a very graceful look she thought. Its hull a light ash trimmed in pretty blue. White masts with blue sail covers. The sun awnings above the large, polished table at the stern, and over the sun beds further front were the same matching blue.

"Omer," she pointed: "Do you know anybody with a boat like that?"

"The gulet? Do you like it?"

"Yes *very!*"

"It shows me you have good taste, Connie, but *no.* At least not here. I did, but he moved the boat to Kas."

She had had no idea where Kas was. "Hundred kilometres *that* way," Omer told her. "My friend sails to Kekova Sound, where you would like it, Connie. The water is very clean there plus there are so many things to see."

"Like *what?*" she asked.

"Like the Sunken City thousands of years old, Connie, that you can only go to by boat. Maybe I can take you there—who knows? And now I must stop, but only for a minute."

They faced a quayside café. "Here?"

"Down *there* is where I keep my silver."

Next to the café was the entrance to a sort of alley. Down it she could see stalls side-by-side. They were set facing each other in a row and before each stood a Turk. They sold trinkets, jewellery—things of that sort she thought. "Can you wait for me here, Connie? It won't take me long," said Omer.

She watched as he approached one of the stands. Its attendant looked to be a teenager and she saw Omer talking with him—the teenager repeatedly glancing her direction. Then she saw him open a door beneath the display case and both knelt before whatever was inside—a cash drawer or money box, she imagined, because the youth held a key, and then she could see Omer stuff money into his pocket. Then he was coming toward her, again with that smile and those eyes she liked.

"I told you it wouldn't take me a minute," said Omer, returning, taking her arm. His boat was moored but a short distance away and she could read the name *Dolphin* as he led her up the narrow gangplank onto the stern and called out loudly to see if anyone might be aboard. The boat appeared deserted.

She had never been on one this size before and she looked curiously about at all it held. Tall silver cylinders: oxygen tanks, he said—and hanging before her were heavy-looking black overalls: they were "wet suits." And she saw smaller tanks that you strapped on, and hoses with attached gauges hanging. Those, he told her, kept track of the amount of air you had left—and that was where he had gone so wrong! he said as he led her to a descending stair.

"What's down here?" she said.

"The galley. A head. Plus there's a cabin with two beds. Nobody ever sleeps down here, Connie, since the boat returns each night. Here, look inside."

But one of the beds had been hastily made. She saw the crumpled sheet as Omer opened the door, and there was someone's underwear, bra and panties, and a handbag shoved she saw into a corner. "Oops! It looks like somebody is using this place!" said Omer as he drew the door shut: "Best leave them."

"So now that you've seen a diving boat, Connie," he said when they were back on the quay, "there's a special ice cream shop that I want to take you to."

"I can't, Omer. Charles must be wondering what happened to me."

"Fresh peach ice cream? You can't disappoint me now, Connie!"

She gave in to him again. Taking her by the arm, Omer led her along the quay, for peach ice cream. "Delicious!" she pronounced, and Omer ordered her a second. Then, facing the water, under the shade of their parasol he again raised the question of swimming lessons—why not tomorrow! "Do it, please, *for Omer?* You'll thank me in the end, Connie."

Back at the hotel, Charles at first refused to take any part in the swimming lessons. He had been worried about her all afternoon and now he was angry: "So where did you meet this— *Omer!*"

"Accidentally, Charles—we just happened to meet, is all. We had lunch together and he told me about being a diver but getting the bends. He's offered to take us swimming. So why don't you want to?"

"I just don't. It's not something that interests me."

"Charles, why is it always *you!* You know how much I've always wanted to be able to swim. And he's picking us up by car. So what do you intend to do over the next two weeks—sit here, sweat, and get eaten by mosquitoes? At least a beach will be cool, and I'm sure you can buy cold beer there, Charles."

Chapter 4

"SORRY ABOUT THE CAR," SAID Omer as he ushered them into the rear seat. "Mine had to go into a shop with clutch problems this morning."

It wasn't a very new car and the seats which had cigarette burns were badly stained. But she hadn't cared as they wound slowly up a steep saddle between mountainsides of dry pine. Then the road levelled and they were passing restaurants, a cemetery, before they descended without warning and she saw blue sea spread suddenly below, turning hazy further out where it seemed joined to the sky in a seamless weld, and where there were faint, two-dimensional shapes of what must be islands, she thought. In the foreground below were the red tile roofs of some very good hotels, said Omer.

Then they were beside a beach, the famed *Oludeniz,* and she saw the sea's incredible colours: greens and turquoise blue— iridescent as it crashed with muted thunder against the beach, then ran whitely back. But it was not a place for her—not yet, said Omer as he drove past to turn instead into the *Seahorse Beach Bar and Restaurant* that faced onto the Blue Lagoon, sea- fed by a narrow channel before which the gulets would often moor like elegant sea creatures at rest.

The beach was of sand and already crowded, with English for the most part though she heard other languages—German, she could pick out. After a search they found three sunbeds and umbrellas together, and prepared to go in—even Charles, to her surprise. She watched him remove his sandals.

"It's not the cleanest place," he muttered, more to himself as he stripped off his socks. "Are we set?" said Omer.

But the sea to her shock was like tepid bath water and standing about in it sometimes up to their necks were other bathers, often in groups, talking. The water inshore was almost a split-pea colour and looked unclean. Spread over its surface was a thin greasy film, and in it she saw bits of plastic and a discarded ice cream bar wrapper, all floating. The greasy film, said Omer, was sun lotion and it was attacking plant life on the sea's floor, slowly killing it off. Because of people the Mediterranean was dying, he told her as, leaving Charles behind, he led her around and between bodies. Out some distance the water changed its colour, became blue. That was where they wanted to go, said Omer, out *there* where the water was cool and clean.

It would be over her head! She froze in a panic and would have turned back, but he held her. "You can't learn to swim with people around. It has to be just the two of us. I'm not going to let anything happen, Connie, you're my *Gnadige Frau.*"

"What is *that?*"

"*Pretty girl*," he said, meeting her eyes.

Later she thought, *that was why she'd trusted him.* Because of those eyes; they had coaxed her out far beyond her depth.

At first he had walked her through the water, holding her like you would if you were calming a terrified child, taking her still farther out.

"Don't let go of me!" she would implore. "No, Connie," he would say:

"Everything we do I explain first."–tricking her in that manner, taking her farther and farther out.

"Can I still stand?" she would suddenly think to ask. "No, Connie, not here."

At first she was frightened and would demand to be taken back. But after the third time, and then the fourth, she stopped asking and simply surrendered to his will. "Do you believe in fate?" he asked while he treaded water beside her nakedly floating form. Fate *how?* she responded.

"That it was because of fate we come together?" he said as his eyes moved appraisingly over her whitish body spread all but nude before him. "You have such a pretty body, Connie— streamlined. The whole girl is perfect!"

She loved him calling her that! No one had called her a girl, since— she could no longer remember exactly. Charles never had! Then another thought intruded, "My husband isn't watching?"

"He can't see us out here, Connie. Does it matter—we're not doing anything we shouldn't."

"Of course it doesn't!" she would say.

What mattered was that he stayed close to her! With him holding her this way and running his hands along her, she felt secure, almost like when she had been with her father, curled up beside him and they had listened to music together. When toward the middle of their beginning lesson he had ordered her to swim to him using her backstroke, her first thought was that he would leave her alone there! She was gripped by panic.

"I'm not going to leave you, Connie. I'll only be two meters away at the most, and I want you to swim to me when I say so."

"You'll catch me, won't you?"

Being left alone in the water for even those few minutes at first made her uneasy. But when she swam on her back she could move fast through the water, and it was such fun to have him catch her that way, sometimes by the ankle, or sometimes by an arm around her thigh. He would pull her in to him then and hold her so tightly that she could not get free—but pleasantly as his hands slowly explored her.

"Oh, what is this? You have a nice little tail bone!"

"Do I? Is it not the same as yours?"

And that was when she first learned to tread water because she'd had to, to free herself so that she could feel down and find the bone.

But she had felt far from secure in the water, afraid her face would go under, and so she had clung to him for life feeling his upper leg coax her thighs apart: *If you keep doing that, you'll force me to kiss you!*

Her first day in the lagoon had been as productive as it had been, to her, an adventure and it was mid afternoon before either thought of going back in for lunch. At first she was afraid that Charles would be angry for having been left alone on the beach for so long. But, in fact, it worked out just the reverse. He had, over beers, Charles said, met an Englishman who was living here—for two years already! They'd spend most of the morning drinking beer, the Englishman describing to him in detail just how stupid Turks were.

To Charles' pleasant discovery, the Seahorse menu listed a number of vegetarian delights and he settled finally on grape leaves stuffed with rice. Lunch over, Omer had asked her did she wish to return to the water. *Oh yes!* but then she remembered Charles, "Do you mind terribly, Charles, if I leave you alone again?"

"No, actually I've gotten to like it here. You were right—it is cooler than at the hotel. Besides I've got those journals on the latest computer analysis and application that I brought—all stuff that needs to be read—and I still have yet to crack even one!" As she let Omer float her out, looking back she saw Charles on his sunbed with his head inside a book. She knew it had to be him by the socks.

It was past seven in the evening when Omer returned his passengers to Fethiye. As he drove down Ataturk toward their hotel, from the rear seat Connie could hear Omer's *handy* ring. She saw him reach for the phone, read it, then drop it back in his pocket as he turned in before the hotel:

"Tomorrow I come for you two, Connie, like today. Same time, *tamam?*"

"At eleven then, Omer!" said Connie, directing at him her best smile as she followed Charles out.

Omer watched her as she entered the hotel but did not leave at once. Instead he reached for his *handy* and, carefully selecting buttons, dialed waiting to see it ring.

"Ali? Omer! I just dropped them off…no, everything went as planned… of course. I think she wants to go on a gulet..Evet.. evet.. Gorusuruz," he then said and, dropping the phone back in his pocket, put the car in gear.

"Would you like to go out on a gulet with me, Charles?" Connie had asked on the evening of her third day of swimming lessons. They were having supper at the Marina and tied to the quay before her were three. She picked out the prettiest and pointed: "If it were one like *that?*"

"Not especially."

"It would be much cooler on the water."

"But didn't Alice say they were expensive?"

"But if it didn't cost us anything, would you?"

Earlier that day while she floated beside him, Omer had said to her,

"When do you go back, Connie?"

"To England?" She counted: "In five days."

"Tuesday! I don't want you to go, Connie."

She could see his disappointed face above hers in the water. "Afraid I have no choice, Omer, I'm a teacher. Plus Charles is responsible for all the schools' computers. He has to be there!"

"Will you come back?"

"Charles would never agree to it."

"Come without him!"

She could feel his eyes plead. "I just can't, Omer."

"Not even if I said I'm falling in love with you! Because I can't help it, *I am.*"

She could feel his eyes, so honest, and she was forced to laugh. "I don't believe you, of course."

"I wouldn't lie to you, Connie."

"And if I said, 'Come to England with me,' *would you?*"

"Just to see you, you mean? I might."

"But you wouldn't stay?" she said lightly.

"No, Connie, I would miss Fethiye.

"And you don't think I'd miss England—?"

"You like it here better, Connie. Look at all the English women living here that prefer Turkey to England."

"Yes, and I know what happens to some of them," she said, seeing his silence.

"Then you won't miss me?" he said after some moments. She reached for his hand to just hold it, "Omer, *I can't!*"

"And I suppose then you wouldn't consider going on a *blue voyage* with me, not even if I found us a nice gulet, like that one you liked?"

Her heart quickened. "Before I leave?"

"Just as soon as I can find one, God willing. See, Omer knows how to make his Connie happy. Tomorrow even!"

But the next morning when Omer picked them up, Connie sensed disappointment and as he swam beside her that day his mood was changed. It lacked the playfulness that she had so looked forward to. Finally, she could hold back no longer, "You weren't able to find a gulet?"

"No, Connie. Don't look sad. I phoned everyone in Fethiye I know. For you I would do anything, you know that."

"It's all right, Omer," she said, and for a moment considered kissing him. "What about your friend in—*Kas* didn't you say?"

"I called him too, Connie. But he's got a problem with the propeller and he doesn't know when they can fix it (And it's almost a new boat!)."

Then that evening as she and Charles were preparing for bed, the house phone rang. *Alice,* she thought as she walked to the nightstand to answer, or Omer, unable to take her swimming in the morning?

"Omer!...Yes!...yes I do and can!"

"What is it?" said Charles.

"Omer may have found a gulet for us. But he needs to talk to you first."

"Omer. We were just about ready to go to be'—you do!

"Oh..oh. Well does it have a satellite, because if it does..I see… Well tell him I can at least look at it…Yes. Cheers!"

"I guess this captain friend of his bought a computer but can't get it to work. I asked Omer if the boat has any satellite signal, but he doesn't seem to know what I'm talking about (I mean, you'd think even a Turk would know that much.). I don't dislike Omer as Turks go. I even like him. So I said I'd come down for a day or two, see what I could figure out. Humour them, I thought. You know, *when in Rome*!"

Chapter 5

"CONNIE, CHARLES, OVER *HERE!* I want to show you this Roman swimming pool. See *look*, it's even got a small wading part for kids."

"From *five-hundred BC* did you say?" said Charles.

"The Lycian agora is. I already walked you through that. This is Roman. What you see here is from when Julius Caesar was killed by—*who?*"

"Brutus!" said Connie.

"Yes, and then he attacked Zanthos and the Lycians committed mass suicide by throwing themselves over the cliff I'm going to show you next."

"You wonder where he picked up all this history?" breathed Charles into her ear as they followed Omer up the rough dirt path between weed-choked bits of walls that were two-thousand five- hundred years old, he had told them.

"Here! But don't get too close to the edge," Omer cautioned. "This is where it happened. They all jumped from this corner rock we stand on. Brutus's army scaled these walls. Then Anthony and Cleopatra arrived and attacked Brutus, and the rest you know, how they delivered Brutus's head to Anthony on a platter."

"Omer, this is incredible!" said Connie, voicing her emotion, to think she was standing at the spot where famous personages of history had themselves once stood, and where events older than the Bible, storied in Shakespeare, had played themselves out!

She felt a glow of happiness as she followed Omer back through the ruins to the parking area and while they waited for Charles who had gone to use the public toilets, she couldn't stop herself. She ran her fingers up his arm lightly, then squeezed.

"So you're glad I stopped and showed you?" said Omar with that smile she so liked. They were at Zanthos, Lycia's ancient capital, halfway between Fethiye and Kas. "This is nothing, I promise you, compared to the *Sunken City*. You'll see it all, tomorrow, Connie!"

Kas was much smaller than Fethiye, but prettier! Connie saw as they wound down a crowded narrow street and the harbour was suddenly there before her vision. It was U-shaped, pleasantly small, and busy with boats of all kinds. To her left was the large town square lined by outdoor cafes and restaurants, all set finally before steep hillsides that, higher up, merged into a vertical cliff face of reddish rock in which she could see cave entrances. Tombs! Omar said, carved out by the Lycians between two and three thousand years ago.

A jetty of huge boulders formed the outer part of the harbour's right side. There was a high concrete sea wall that, in bad weather, protected the little harbour, behind was open sea. It was along this side that the larger gulets were moored, theirs among them. Omer had phoned on his *handy* to announce their arrival and its captain was already waiting for them to help carry extra food for Charles, plus the clothes they would need and her vanity case, to the *Gul II* as she was called. The captain's name was Ali, a short, barrel-chested man, middle-aged and swarthy, with a rounded flat face that, as it smiled, showed three days perhaps of black stubble to Connie. But he seemed jolly—even a bit clownish, she thought, as he pointed ahead at the gulet that was to be their home for the next two days.

It had pleasing lines, she saw. Its hull and superstructure were a polished chestnut; awnings, and the sun mattresses that lay spaced in rows across the roof before the large front windows of the wheelhouse and salon, a maroon. There were others already aboard, Connie discovered. Occupying two of the mattresses were women in bikinis watching their approach. "So are there others going?" asked Connie: Omer had not mentioned anyone.

"Just two more couples," said Ali. "But next week boat will be full."

"How many does it carry?" asked Connie.

"Eighteen," said Ali as he led them to the gangplank. "I have seven cabins forward and two *here* —you are seeing at their windows." They were like the pictures of Spanish galleons that Connie remembered. "And now take off shoes," said Ali.

"Take off my shoes!" said Charles.

"Tamam, I have teak deck. We must keep it clean," said the captain as he removed his own and dropped them inside a wicker box fastened to the outside of the hull beside the gangplank.

Across the gulet's squared stern and extending partly up the sides were cushions like sofa cushions but specially made, Connie saw, of the same matching colour as the sun mattresses and sail covers. Thick and soft, they felt pleasant underfoot as she stepped from the gangplank down into them. Then down again, the captain offering his hand, to the deck before a large table of brightly polished wood. The captain's table and it was like stepping into a perfect dream! she thought as she gazed about her at the pretty ship.

The women in bikinis emerged one at a time from where the deck narrowed beside the salon so that only one person at a time could squeeze past. In single file behind came their husbands, to meet the new arrivals. Captain Ali made introductions and when Connie discovered that both couples were German and spoke almost no English, she felt immense relief. "Come," said the captain, taking their suitcase, "I show you two below."

He led her then past the large ship's wheel with its radiating spokes and down several steps, to the salon where she discovered another dining table, overstuffed furniture, and a second steering wheel before the ship's slanting front windows that were left raised to allow in whatever breeze came.

Beside the wheel were the ship's controls. Charles paused to examine the electronic equipment. "But you can't get a satellite signal?" he asked.

"Afraid not, said Captain Ali almost apologetically.

"Then there's no way of getting the Internet in on your *laptop*…But I can look at it."

"Afraid it's not possible," said the captain. "But Omer led me to believe—"

"Afraid I drop it," said the captain apologetically.

"It might not be all that damaged," said Charles. "I'll look at it."

"Afraid I don't have it anymore."

"Where is it?"

With a grin that was more grimace, Captain Ali pointed.

"You dropped it overboard!" said Omer incredulously. "How? Why?"

"Last night. When I was trying to see at it."

"What a terrible thing to happen!" said Omer. "So, Charles, it appears I've dragged you all this way for nothing. I'm so sorry. It looks like you're going to just have to enjoy the *blue voyage,*" Omer concluded with a friendly smile. "Now I show you your cabin which I hope you do like. We want to leave, and Ali needs my help with the anchor."

The passageway between the forward cabins was unlit, narrow, and hot! Connie had wanted one of the other cabins with the large pirate ship windows where she could lay and look out. But they had both been taken by the Germans. However, the cabin Omer showed them was spacey and light, with a queen- sized bed and built-in wardrobe, all done in what she thought was a mahogany. The cabin had its own toilet and shower, and a sink with mirror and space for her combs and make up. *Yes, Omer, I could learn to like this!* she thought. The only problem, she realized, was the heat! As she changed into her tiny new bikini bought just that morning, Connie heard the rattle of chain above her head. The ship was moving! She left Charles to fuss about the cabin and hurried on deck to find Omer.

There he was! At the bow peering into a hole in the deck into which wet anchor chain noisily streamed. She made her way forward along the side of the wheelhouse, carefully since the deck was narrow here, gripping the wooden handrail at the edge of the roof. The outer railing was twisted steel cable strung through the eyes of stanchions not even waist high. If the boat rocked even a little you could easily lose your balance and fall overboard! she thought as she tripped lightly forward barefoot, showing herself. Omer was standing in front of the jib sail smiling, waiting to catch her. The boat was beginning to rock, gently and evenly, from side to side. "So how do you like your cabin?" he asked as she fell a little into him.

"It's all still a dream!"

Their ship was gliding effortlessly past the bowsprits of other gulets, masts and hulls mirrored in the wavy-smooth water and there were ships she'd never seen before. One had a high, rounded front a little like a tugboat—only it was much larger, white, and she read painted on its side in blue: **Glass Bottom Boat**. "Where does that one go, Omer?"

"Same place as you. To the *Sunken City.* Would you like something cold to drink, Connie?"

"What do you have?"

"Whatever this girl might want," he said back, his hand lightly upon her waist, guiding her past the German couples lying on their mattresses and protected from the sun by the maroon awning held taunt above their heads by ropes fastened to the ship's rigging. Omer greeted them as he and Connie passed:

"Guten Tag!"

"'Tag."—Omer protecting her from the roll of the ship. They continued back toward the wheelhouse where she found her husband, on deck dressed in shorts. How unhealthy, *pale!* his body looked when she compared it to Omer's. Standing at Captain Ali's side, Charles was examining the ship's radio gear and other components.

"You've got some pretty high-tech stuff here, Ali. You know you could get satellite." But Ali had no time to listen. Entering the harbour directly ahead was a large sailboat and the two craft must pass within feet of each other.

Then they were past the harbour mouth and jetty, being struck by swells. Ali spun the ship's wheel right and the deck dipped left as Charles' expression changed—became suddenly concerned. Connie would have lost her balance had Omer not caught her and guided her to the cushions at the stern. "Charles, it's going to get a bit rough," he said, "Better sit down!"

The ship leaned sharply, then came back as the sea fell, then rose again almost to the deck, she saw. In front of her was the long captain's table, and in front of it, to the right of the companionway opening down to the ship's saloon, galley, and cabins, was an oblong white refrigerator fastened to the deck. The salon was rarely used, except in bad weather. It was up here on deck that crew and passengers *really* hung out! said Omer— where they ate and drank and socialized, he said.

"We Turks like to live outdoors. That's because we're nomads. Charles, you don't look like you're feeling so well."

"You do look white, dear," said Connie.

"It's my stomach," admitted Charles. "It's queasy."

"You could be having seasickness. Think an *Efes* might help it, Charles?" said Omer, and without awaiting a reply he rose and worked his way forward by gripping the edge of the table, to the refrigerator. "Connie, would you like a beer too?"

"Mmm..I might have a sip of yours if you have one."

Omer waited until the deck was level, then crossed with the uncapped beers.

Charles eyed his with some doubt before finally swallowing. "I don't suppose you remembered to bring any seasick pills, did you?" he said to Connie.

"Why was it up to me to remember!" she said back and, seeing that Omer was watching, regretted at once the tone of voice she had taken. The *Gul II* was turning direction, staying close-in to the shore and she could see large rocks; watch the seas rise and break over them, only to fall back. Then Charles was up rushing to the side and she could see him spewing beer and whatever else over the rail as Omer rose to help.

"Think I want to lie down," Charles said.

Omer had helped him to his cabin. Connie followed. They had assisted him onto the bed where he just laid, as if dead, and then both retreated back along the hot passage. "Do you want to lay on one of the mattresses, Connie?"

"If you do," she said and followed him, forward to the sun mattresses atop the cabin roof, before the opened windows of the wheelhouse.

But as she crawled a mattress over to make room for him, he said, "I'd better go check on the Germans," and continued past. She watched him visit with them further up the deck, talking in another language. *Why did he suddenly want to talk with them?* "You don't have to come back if you don't want," she said to him with suppressed anger when at last he lay down beside her. She saw his surprise, then those eyes she liked turn critical:

"Connie, you're here under special circumstances which I won't explain, and so am I. Those Germans paid out a lot of euros to be on this boat." He paused, his unfathomable dark eyes holding her fixed and when he resumed his voice appealed to her softly, "There's only one reason for my being on this boat and you already know it. The *same* reason as you, Connie."

Had she—known? She must have, but simply hadn't spelled it out yet in words. She felt his hand feeling for hers, to squeeze. She squeezed back. *What circumstances?*

Chapter 6

IT WAS EARLY EVENING WHEN they reached their moorage for the night in a tiny bay surrounded by ruins of what Omer said had been a boat repair yard in Roman times. On her right rose the island itself, Kekova, with its famous ruin half of which, though still visible from the surface, now lay beneath the sea due to a massive earthquake that had split the island causing a portion of it to sink. It was the upper part Omer intended to show her, tomorrow!

But seeing how far from the beach the ship was, Connie wondered how he could expect her to ever swim such a distance. Earlier they had dropped anchor out near the middle then Ali had backed the *Gul II* in toward the rocks as Omar stood perched precariously on the ship's stern with a coiled rope, waiting until they were sufficiently close to the shore for him to dive. Then he had, with but little splash, the rope uncoiling behind him. How cleanly and powerfully he went through the water, how gracefully! she thought as she watched him climb onto the shore trailing the rope, looking for a suitable rock to secure the ship to. Captain Ali was standing beside her, in his hand another coil of rope, watching Omer's return to the *Gull II.*

When he was sufficiently close, Ali threw Omer the second rope which he swam to shore with, then tied, this time to the trunk of a dead tree he found; and that was how the gulet was secured for the night from the bow by her anchor chain, and by ropes from the port and starboard sides of her stern. Connie watched Omer swim back to the gulet. How he loved water! *Why?* since he said he had been raised in Berlin? She was curious to find out more, but the chance to ask was not to come until well after dark. Now, in the remaining light, fixing supper was the first priority. "Who does the cooking?" asked Connie as she watched Omer stuff kindling and charcoal into a metal box and grate used for barbequing, and that was attached to the outside of the ship's rail above the anchor.

"Ali likes to—it's his boat," said Omer, glancing up from his work, smiling. "But I also cook. That's something we Turks as males do."

"Why is that?"

"Just is. Like we bake the world's best bread. I'm a good cook, Connie. I promise I'll show you sometime."

With the coals started, Omer went below to help Ali in the galley. The Germans had all assembled around the big table and were drinking wine. For a time Connie tried to join them. She would have expected that being German, they would speak English—but they didn't. So she had gone below to check on Charles.

The cabin was stifling! She knelt on the bed and reached up to slide open the long narrow windows that looked out at deck level, seeing Charles' colourless face peering up at her with dulled interest. She could smell the faint sour reek of vomit. "Are you coming up to eat with us?"

"I better not."

It was dark long before they had finished eating and Ali tossed overboard the food that had been left, chicken bones, bread, Charles' bulgur. "I feed fish good meal too!" said Ali.

As she watched the Germans return to their deck mattresses, some carrying a light blanket or sheet up from below, the thought of staying in that cabin next to Charles filled her with distaste. Omer expected her to sleep on deck, under the stars, and why shouldn't she? It wasn't as if she were planning anything! Filling her wine glass full, she carried it forward. Selecting a mattress, she lifted her knee and climbed onto it, careful not to spill the wine. Then she moved in, as far from the deck as she could and still view with the canopy just over her head the glittering mosaic of stars. Looking about to see first where the Germans were located, she waited. Connie had sensed his shadow coming then, before she saw his actual form or heard him beside her: "See what I bring you, Connie."

Wine! In the pale light from the stars she watched him fill her glass, then his and click them. Cheers! How good the wine tasted!

"How is Charles doing?" had been Omer's first question.

"Still seasick—but I haven't checked," she said. "Maybe I should."

"No!"

She felt his hand: "Why did you marry him, Connie?" Adding when she struggled for an answer, "I'll know if you lie to me."

On the rebound, she had told him, slowly, in a quiet way, picking carefully over her words as she described first Cliff. Then meeting Charles whom she had felt sorry for.

"And that was why you married him? I knew you couldn't love him, Connie."

Was it so obvious? "No," she admitted. "Though I thought I would, eventually," she told him in answer to a question that had no single or simple answer she said and *that* at the time had seemed the best thing for her to do, is all. For one thing, Charles wasn't in the least like Cliff—they were complete opposites. With Charles she knew she could feel secure. "Now tell me why you're not German if you were born there?" she asked in turn. "Berlin is a city I always wanted to see," she said and wondered immediately why she had said it.

"You'd be disappointed, Connie. Berlin is only a city. It's so much prettier here."

"But that isn't why you're Turkish, not German—?"

"I could have been either one, Connie. But if I stayed, I would have had to go to jail."

"You mean *prison?* Why!"

"For doing stupid things. I got running with street gangs after my father showed me to the door with the toe of his shoe."

"Kicked you out, you mean—?"

"I was nine the first time and don't forget my father was a strict Muslim. See, Connie, there's a lot you don't know about Turkish fathers. They spoil their kids rotten for the first seven years. Then after that they beat the shit out of them!"

"So how did you survive?" But she saw him look up and felt him suddenly disengage:

"Charles! We're over here."

She rose to her knees and would have scooted across to the outside mattress had Omer's hand not checked her.

"I'm in here, Charles, sharing a bottle of wine with your wife.

Get yourself a glass and come join us."

"Omer. No, thanks, I don't want to chance it."

Then she saw his face peering at her beneath the sun canopy: "Connie, aren't you coming to bed? I can't sleep. Does this boat never stop rocking!"

"I'll come, Charles, soon as I finish my wine."

Connie watched his form disappear. She finished the rest of her glass, thought, then poured herself another which she swallowed down. "I have to, Omer."

"*Tomorrow!*" he whispered behind her as she slipped off the mattress, down, and retraced her way back along the deck toward the salon companionway that led below.

She must have slept poorly, because she heard Charles snoring, and once she had even seen him reaching for his distended ear. She had given up trying to break him of that habit. "Where are you going?" he said, opening his eyes as she rose.

"For a cup of tea, Charles—it's morning."

"I know it's morning, I've been awake for hours. This boat stopped rocking for a while last night—did you notice?"

"No, Charles, I was asleep."

Before the bathroom sink, she examined her wrinkles in the mirror. The crow's-feet had gotten, if anything, worse overnight. *Little wonder,* she thought as she carefully worked the cream in, first around her eyes. Finished, she emerged onto the bright deck as Ali was lifting a length of wooden ladder down from the roof of the salon. He hooked it over the ship's side. "Want to go for a swim before breakfast, Connie?" he said as she watched.

The German's were already at the table waiting as Omer carried up platters of tomatoes and cucumbers. Sheep's cheese, marmalade for the bread, and finally the eggs, scrambled. Charles appeared for just tea and a little bread, to test his stomach and afterwards, their coffee drunk, the Germans disappeared as Omer helped clean away breakfast before heading below himself.

When he reappeared he was wearing swimming trunks. "Think I'll go and explore those ruins." He glanced about at the faces: "Anybody want to come?"

"I will," said Connie. "You don't mind, do you, Charles?"

"No, enjoy yourself if you like, Connie. This is something you only do once."

Standing before the ladder Omar dove and, after moments, resurfaced. Connie backed herself down the side of the ship feeling from rung to rung while Omer waited below her. "Now just fall backwards and let yourself go," he said. She had, pushing herself out from the ladder, and then his arms were holding her beside him in the water. "Do you want to try swimming on your own to the beach?" he asked, and she could feel his eyes—playful. "You should."

"Yes, on my back." That way she felt safest. On her stomach meant sometimes having to get her face too close to the water and if her mouth accidentally opened she would taste salt. But on her back she flew!

"Omer, where are you—I can't see where I'm going!"

"I'm here beside you—you're going fine."

After a short time she decided to give up, just float and let him take her the rest of the distance. She could feel his hands. "Omer—"

"Yes, Connie? You have a lovely body, did you know that?"

"Do I? Finish telling me what you started to. Last night."

"My father kicking me out, you mean?"

"How did you eat and where did you sleep?"

"Park benches. When it rained, in the subway. Or the train station when it got really cold."

"How did you eat?"

"I was like the organ grinder's monkey and danced for my supper. Don't look at me like that; I got very good at begging. Old ladies especially would feel sorry for me. And when that didn't work, I'd steal."

"How long did you have to live like that?"

"Never long at any one time. See I'd get reported truant by the school. I'd get picked up and returned home."

"What about your mother—she's also Turkish?"

She saw his eyes change—become perhaps guarded, if only for an instant. "German. I have two half-brothers and a half sister in Berlin. At least I think they are still there."

"But you don't stay in contact…Do you miss Germany at all?"

"Now I'm touching bottom. You can stand up, Connie."

She could see on the hillside to her left joining walls of rectangularly cut, perfectly fitted stone, and judging from the size of each block it must have been impressive building once.

Below it seen through the trees and brush was an empty doorway—just the doorway, alone, still standing and back of the beach that was part sand, part pebble, were more fallen buildings. Chunks of roman brick, arches and cornices, lay in the sand half buried. But what surprised her was all the litter: garbage of every kind and description from old Coca Cola cans to discarded *Efes* beer bottles. There was broken glass, paper cups and juice cartons, and plastic sacks—everywhere!

"It's disgusting!" pronounced Connie.

You can always know where a Turk has been by the trail of garbage he leaves, Omer had told her. "This way," he said, taking her hand. "Careful where you step *here*."

"Where are we going, Omer?"

"There," he pointed. "We'll be alone just the two of us, Connie."

The hillside rose impossibly, a mass of trees and brush with, here and there, parts of walls: a window left; steps leading to a doorway that wasn't there. "I can't make it up there," she said and started to hang back.

"*Connie*—" But he held her so close, his arm about her waist: "*please* trust me. You're my *fantastische Frau*. Do you know what that is? What I'm saying to you, Connie?"

She thought she half did: "That you love me?"

"Oh yes, *meine Liebe!* And that you've become my life. My reason for living.

Connie..."

It was his eyes she knew she couldn't refuse that made her legs go weak.

"Connie, we need each other. You need me as I need you. *Du! Mein schones Fraulein.*"

She let him lead her, through rocks and brush, half stumbling over the unpredictable ground, up: feeling his words caress her in a tongue she did not know. She could feel her heart pound inside her rib cage.

They must be near the top now, she thought. How much farther must she go! He stopped to look around. The sun was becoming hotter. "We need to stop, Connie."

But where? He spotted a clump of olive trees and beneath them, shade. She rested on a flat piece of rock. "You wait here," he said to her.

"Why, where are you going!"

"Just over *there*. Make sure I know where we're at."

She watched him walk back into the sunlight, look about, then choose a direction. He continued in it a short distance, then stopped and again looked about, slowly. "Connie, come look at this."

She rose. "Why—what's there?"

"An incredible view. Our boat directly below us, for one thing."

"I want to see it!"

But as she approached, he warned her, "It's a solid drop-off. Don't get any closer. Look across the water to the other side, Sibena, with the ancient castle on its top. Below us is the submerged city."

She looked across the glistening expanse of sea. It was like a scene from *Gulliver's Travels:* the diminutive world spread below her and, for an instant, that made her think of her girlhood in Scotland. Almost straight down and to her left she saw their gulet. "And there are people swimming around it," she said to Omer.

"Do you know what standing here looking out at the sea like we are reminds me of, Connie? A movie I saw about two years ago."

"Which one?"

"I can't remember. It's about someone who's shipwrecked. He's swept from the sea and survives somehow, in a foreign land where they speak a different tongue. Because of that he's like a cast out nobody wants. The only person to befriend him is this girl who finally marries him. But because he comes from a different place she can't understand him either and is cruel. In the end he dies. I remember his name—Yanko—because in a way I see myself like him."

"Conrad's story! I read it in college. I didn't know they made a movie." She could see below them the *Gul II*, and people swimming beside it. "Those must be the Germans—it couldn't be my husband swimming." she thought. What was Charles doing—starting to wonder when they were coming back? He might be seasick again. Or reaching for his ear to pull. All those lost years, how barren her life had been! "Omar, let's go. Take me somewhere else."

"But *where?*" He took her waist. "I'll find somewhere."

She submitted—will-less. She could feel her heart race.

"There!" He pointed to trees: eucalyptuses, and as they approached, she saw shade beneath, and what were once rooms. Where there had been a floor was now bits of rock and dirt, and debris from the eucalyptus trees. He knelt and began throwing the rocks aside.

"Help me, Connie—collect eucalyptus leaves," his eyes radiant with anticipation.

Frantically they stripped branches to make the bed of leaves. "Now put our swimsuits on top," he said. His back half to her, she saw him strip. Turn, and she could see his excitement, his eyes exploring her. "The whole girl is lovely. I just want to look at you, Connie!"

She had never seen a circumcised male. She'd seen photos of them of course limp. But his was the first one she'd seen standing up for her like this! "You're a handsome man, Omer!"

Then she was lying herself down as he arranged her bed under her, his eyes so caring. But laughing too, with a devilishness she liked. "Connie, I need you and want you. *Mein Schatz*," he whispered to her ear. It was all like a dream and she did not want the dream to end, his hands ever to leave her.

"Afraid it's not the most comfortable bed," he half apologized.

But she had not cared. *Just do what you're doing, my organ grinder.*

It had been morning when they left and now as they returned it was late afternoon and the sun was at its hottest. Going downhill was, in one respect, harder than the trip up had been since in holding her legs back she was forced to use muscles that hadn't been tried in years, so that she was soon exhausted and *very* thirsty, glad just to set foot again on the deck of the gulet. Now all she wanted was to sit in the shade of the deck awning and drink something cold.

Charles waited beside the ladder as she climbed it to the deck. "You were gone a long time. I was beginning to wonder," he said.

"We lost our way up there, Charles," she replied.

"The trail isn't always easy to see and we strayed off it in a couple of places," said Omer as he stepped onto the deck behind her.

"So was the climb worth it, Connie?"

"Oh *yes*, Charles!"

"Well, you look like it was. I must say in fact, you look radiant, Connie."

"Right now I feel exhausted and just need something cold and wet to drink," she said.

But first she had gone below to change into a fresh bikini. Returning, she found Charles waiting for her at one end of the captain's table—the other being occupied by some of the Germans.

Omer brought her a cold *Efes* but could not join them since Ali required help getting the dinner going. "So was it hard getting up there?" asked Charles.

"Almost impossible. There were places I could never have made it except for Omer. But the views from up there made it all worthwhile!"

"As I say, Connie, you look like you enjoyed yourself."

"What did you do while I was gone, Charles? How's your seasickness?"

"Better. Captain Ali remembered some pills he had. They seemed to have helped. Not a bad bloke, Ali! We talked about computers. Would you believe it, Connie, he's not sure what brand that computer of his was he dropped overboard!"

"Then you weren't bored?" she said.

"Not really. We drank a few beers, and played backgammon (which Turks call 'tavla'). Then I tried to teach Ali a little chess and was surprised that he could pick it up. But you know, I still can't get over him not knowing what kind of computer it was. He says, now that I've gotten over my seasickness, he's going to cook something special."

Ali had aubergines prepared in yogurt and olive oil with peppers, garlic, and bits of tomato. Omer carried a large platter of them up from the galley and you didn't have to be vegetarian to enjoy it, Connie discovered. The platter was emptied and she watched as one of the Germans wiped it dry with his bread.

"Compliments to Chef Ali!" said Charles as he raised his wine in a toast that was taken up all around the table. She had not seen Charles in such an outgoing mood in quite some while. After dinner the four Germans returned happily chatting to their sun mattresses up in the bow while the remaining three plus Ali stayed seated at the table on this, her last night. Early in the morning the ship must return to Kas, said her captain, to be cleaned and provisioned for a full seven-day blue voyage with a new compliment of guests. *Lucky them!* thought Connie as she watched the last pink fade from the water, and night encroach turning the rugged hillside she had climbed just that morning with Omer into a flat imposing shape above the motionless ship. Velvety at first as the last light drained, the hill with its ruin rose two-dimensionally and black above: a craggy broken outline against the glitter of myriad stars. She felt someone's foot touch hers under the table and drew her own back. But when the foot followed her, she realized it was Omer, and discovered his warm eyes trying to catch hers.

"Something that struck me, Omer," said Charles, his face lit by the electric glow of a lantern suspended beneath the protective awning that shielded the quarterdeck. "England is a seafaring nation. Yet we don't many of us even know how to swim, not like you Turks!"

"Yes, Omer, if you were born and raised in Berlin, where did you learn to swim—not there?" it occurred to her to say.

"Izmir, after we were forced to move there from Istanbul."

"Who is *we*?" she asked.

"What I haven't told you yet is, I was married," said Omer and reached for his glass.

It was empty. And so was the bottle. "Wait, I'll get another." Omer rose along with the captain, who disappeared on deck while Omer searched about the refrigerator. She heard the pop of a cork. "Who needs wine? You do, Connie."

She watched him fill her glass. "To a German or Turkish girl, Omer?"

"Turkish. Her name was Seda. I told about having to leave Germany, move to Istanbul. Well I met her there, and to make a story short, she became pregnant. Had a baby girl, so I married her. But—and this is important—you remember asking me if I was Turkish or German. You can't be born, raised, and go to school in one culture and not be part of it. That street gang I told you about—they were German kids I ran with and that's really what turned my father against me. Because, though he lived in Germany, he remained a Turk, and though he may have driven a taxi in Berlin he didn't socialize with the Germans."

"—while you did?" said Connie.

"*Ja,* while I did. And that's the real reason for him throwing me out. Also, the reason why for years after I came here, I still thought of Turkish as my second language, *ja?*

"But if you think about it, it's not the language, it's the customs that make you different, like with Yanko," he said, his eyes seeking hers. "Here's one example I know well. German fathers change their baby's nappies all the time. But Turkish fathers won't—it's something they just don't do, period!

"Well, my wife was out with her girlfriend one day, doing I- don't-know-what. Something, anyway, I was home with the baby. She started crying and I thought she might need changing, so I put my nose down there, did the sniff test, and determined she definitely did. So I takes off the dirty nappy and am in the middle of cleaning her little bum when the in-laws walked in on me: my *Schwiegermutter* and one of the aunties. They see me and think I'm doing something I shouldn't! *To my own daughter!* I don't know if you're aware of just how much Turks like to talk about each other.

And if they don't have anything juicy, they make it up! I never could clear my good name and that, finally, was what led to our break-up. More wine?"

"I'll have a glass," said Connie. "So do you still see your daughter?"

"She's dead."

"*Dead!*" said Connie.

"How did it happen?" asked Charles.

"Bus accident. We were going from Antalya to Marmaris.

Three-thirty in the morning. She died in my arms." They had all stared back in curious disbelief.

"I'm not making it up. I can prove it to you!" He rose. "Where are you going, Omer?" said Charles.

"Below. To get my wallet."

"Poor bloke!" said Charles as they waited for his return.

He had, and they watched him search through the wallet for something. A piece of paper, folded and refolded so many times that the paper was beginning to disintegrate. He carefully unfolded it: a newspaper article. "It's at night so you can't tell much from the photo, but it was head-on. The impact pitched my little daughter out of my arms against the windscreen. Ali, did I show you this?"

The captain's face appeared suddenly from out of the darkness of the deck. "That terrible accident where your daughter got killed? I already saw it."

"Sit down and have a glass of wine with us, Captain," said Charles.

"No, I go now to my bed. I must leave early morning," he said and disappeared.

On such a warm night, all those aboard had slept topside under the fierce light of the stars, even Charles. All that wine had made Connie tipsy, and he had had to help her a bit as she led him along the deck beside the cabin roof upon which were spaced even rows of mattresses.

She picked for herself and Charles mattresses at the edge of the roof beside the deck so that she could gaze up at the sea of glittering stars. But toward morning a breeze came up. She woke, chilled, to discover Charles gone. He had, at some point, returned to their cabin. Connie rose and, unable to locate Omer in the dark, went below.

"Charles, you're taking up all the bed. Move!" she had said, poking him and that was the last she remembered until the sound of the ship's engines woke her. Then, as she listened, there was the rattle of anchor chain above her head, and she could feel the ship moving.

By eleven they were back in Kas; she had given Captain Ali a goodbye hug. Even Charles had hugged the captain and by one that afternoon they were before their hotel with plenty of time to pack for the flight to Manchester. Omer would take them to the airport he said, "If I'm back here at five, can you be ready?"

"Sure you want to drive us, Omer?" asked Charles. "Nothing makes me happier, I promise."

They had already exchanged phone numbers and email addresses before leaving the *Gul*, so there was no further reason for Omer to stay there with them. "Five then," Connie said and bent forward for the *goodbye* kiss. But instead he took her hand which disappointed her, until she discovered he was trying to slip something into her palm. A folded scrap of paper. In their bathroom upstairs she unfolded it and read:

I wait for you at my silver stand at 2:30 meine Liebe!!

"Bloody hot out there!" said Charles as he played with the remote control for the air conditioning.

"Hadn't you better go check with the Internet, see if our flight's on time and reserve us some seats, Charles?"

"We can get them at the airport."

"But I thought you were supposed to check in with the airline twenty-four hours in advance?"

"They're not going to sell our seats," said Charles. "But what if they don't give us seats together?"

"Then when are we going to do the packing?"

"I'll take care of the packing. Just go!" said Connie.

She saw him to the elevator then, after examining her face and mini dress in the mirror beside it, she chose to go down the stairs instead, past reception, and through the restaurant to the quay, *What if they shouldn't find each other!* Then she had another thought, *Did it matter?* This time tomorrow she would be back in Manchester and would be forgetting all this—putting it behind her. But she was lying to herself and knew it.

What time was it? She could see by the clock inside a café she passed that she was even a bit early. So she made herself slow down. What if Charles returned? What she was doing made her uncomfortable. Then she discovered Omer walking toward her were those eyes and that smile she loved.

"Connie! I was afraid something would happen to prevent you from coming. Oh, I don't want you to leave me, *Schatz!*"

"And I don't want to leave you, Omer," she said as he pulled her to him. She kissed him hard, using her tongue and, releasing him, let herself be taken—she scarcely cared where, to his old boat, the one he had shown her the first day, she thought. But to her surprise he stopped before a different boat. "This isn't yours!"

"No, mine's not here today," he said as he led her up the gangplank.

She knew where she was being taken—the boat's design was much the same: below deck to the cabin at the bow. Only it was smaller and more cramped than the one she remembered, and not very clean. In the bunk was a single mattress, old and stained—she did not want to think *with what* the uses this mattress had been put to. The entire cabin was badly in need of a coat of paint. "Sorry, *Schatz,* it was all I could find on short notice."

Short notice: the words jarred at her being as he began to undress her.

She let him, much like a quiescent child might, knowing as she saw him quickly strip, and watched his penis spring up at her, that she was prepared to lie down beside him and do anything he might want of her because she would never see him again, not once until, after a time, the memory itself would fade and finally disappear.

"Meine Liebe!" he whispered. She felt him enter and did not know if she would cry or not.

"Connie, what is the matter, my love?" he said afterward.

But she couldn't decide. "I have to get dressed!" She felt him begin kissing her.

"You know how much I love you, Connie! So tell Omer. You don't love me—*is that it?*"

"It's not it," she said.

"Then what, *liebe Connie?*"

"Maybe I'm just not good at this."

"At what?"

But she didn't know. "I have to leave. Charles will be looking for me."

"Then I won't keep you," he answered, coolly she thought.

Was it sarcasm she heard? She knew how unhappy he must be with her as they walked along the quay not speaking. "What will you do when you get back?" he asked her finally.

"Be very busy teaching. I won't have time to think of much else—which is probably a good thing."

They continued along the quay again in silence until he drew up. It was as far as they dared go together. "I'll pick you and your husband up at five," he said, almost formally she thought, and turned, not even leaving her with a kiss.

She had not wanted to part this way! Despite the heat, she hurried the remaining distance back, angry at herself, at Omer. Only when she got close to the hotel did she slow—try to make herself breathe normally.

Upstairs Charles waited—he was visibly worried. "Where were you!" he said angrily.

"Just over saying goodbye to Bea."

Chapter 7

HOW EASY IT HAD BEEN to do what she had, and not care a twit about the consequences! she thought on the flight back. If stepping from the terminal building at Dalaman had been like walking into a furnace, Manchester had felt like a frigid steam bath, she told her friend Mandy.

"Thank god we're back!" said Charles.

Alice was waiting to meet them with her umbrella. "So did you enjoy yourself?" she asked on the drive home, "What did you do for all that time?"

"Learned to swim—or at least stay afloat. Plus spent two days on a gulet."

His stub of a tail wildly beating, Scraggles was behind the front door waiting to jump up on the first one to enter, which was Charles. He pushed the dog away from him with his shoe and turned to go upstairs to his computers first. "That animal smells!"

"You stay away from that horrid man!" Connie bent and scooped the little dog up in her arms. "Connie missed 'ihm so much! Oh ye-es! You just smell doggy, is all," she said as she released the dog and they turned into the kitchen where Alice made them tea. "So how did you happen to wind up on a gulet, Mum?"

"Omer arranged the trip." She saw her daughter's smile momentarily disappear. "He has a friend who owns quite a nice one and we went to Kekova Sound."

"Charles too! How did he take it?"

Connie described the *Gul II* and the part about Charles' sea- sickness.

Nonetheless, they all had had what really turned out a marvellous little adventure—even Charles despite him getting sick! Connie told her daughter who was pleased. "I'm glad, Mum! So now I suppose you're all set to go back into the classroom?"

For the first few days Connie had been simply too busy to find that part out. Her mistake, she told Mandy when finally she had, was in having assumed that life would continue the same once she was back. "Think of a river that for untold time has flowed inside its banks. They're neatly trimmed and cared-for banks and all it's ever known. Then something happens and it bursts them and runs wild, just for a very short time. But long enough for her to discover paradise and, really, discover she doesn't want to return."

"*The river* you mean," said Mandy. It was the first chance they had found to have lunch together. "And Charles, I take it, is quite happy to return to within his banks."

"Not to confuse metaphors," said Connie, "but like my daughter said, he was a fish out of water."

"And now that you're both back—things are peaceful?"

"I wish they were. We already had one nasty go-round. While we were in Turkey Alice threw what must have been a wild party. She cleaned up afterwards, got the refrigerator back to where it would pass inspection. But somebody must have been in playing with Charles' computers because he found a roach up there."

"Oooh! Charles' computers become a serious matter," observed Mandy.

"*Very!* But so was the roach. And of course he comes back at me for my failure to control her. It winds up with him calling me some of his choicest words."

"Fortunately, Alice will be gone in another two weeks and you'll both have settled back into your separate grinds by then," Mandy reflected.

But she no longer found the classroom provided her any escape. Not since those Valium-filled years following her break- up with Cliff had she felt so depressed. Life was an unending series of meaningless acts; daily repetitive routines performed— she scarcely knew or cared how. She saw herself as though operating in a part trance, her very motions the motions of someone who had died but was denied even the time to decently lie down. Because paradoxically there were always things to do and tasks to perform to fill those meaningless hours. School and schoolwork took up most of her day. The remainder she divided between Alice, and Scraggles' increasingly frequent trips to the vet.

Alice had been the first to notice that Scraggles could be losing weight, after her return when she went to pick him up from the kennel. "When they brought Scraggles out my first thought was, they hadn't been feeding him! We've spoiled him anyway and he probably didn't like just dry dog food. But, Mum, I don't think it was that now."

"Has my *lovey* lost weight?" said Connie, looking down at Scraggles who met her gaze with sad brown eyes. It was decided then that they make a special trip to Tesco to buy things Connie knew Scraggles would not turn down: steak, some marrow bones. "And why don't we get him these oxtails?" said Alice, pointing.

"What are those disgusting things for!" Charles said as he opened the refrigerator and discovered the oxtails.

"For Scraggles. We're trying to put a little weight back on him, Alice and I." She could sense the sight of those tails upset him.

"Well you'd better keep them well away from *my* food!"

Connie could sense the sight of ox tails and marrow bones upset Charles but from them she made Scraggles a tasty nutritious broth while the oxtails, she thought, would provide Scraggles with vital calcium. But to their surprise, Scraggles refused the rich treat and turned to his water bowl instead. Why or what could make the little dog turn down even good steak? "Have you notice how much water Scraggles has started to drink? Mum, something's not right," said Alice. They had to find out, so late one afternoon after returning from her day of teaching Connie clipped the leash onto Scraggles collar and was leading him to her car when she saw Charles arrive.

"Where are you taking that dog?" he asked. "To the vet, Charles."

"Why, is there something wrong with it?"

As he checked Scraggles over the vet had asked Connie a second time on just how much water the dog actually drank. "So what did the vet say when you told him?" Alice asked over supper.

"He doesn't know anything for sure yet. But he took blood and is waiting for the results. The blood work should be back in a couple of days"

"So we wait and hope it's nothing…oh, and I nearly forgot," said Alice, "You'll never guess who sent me an email today. But really, Mum, it was addressed to you. Omer."

"*Omer!*"

"Oh and I'm to tell you, Charles, that Captain Ali also sends his greetings, and thanks."

"He did!" Charles looked pleased. "You might, if you send Omer a greeting back, ask him to ask Ali if he ever bought that *Toshiba* I suggested," said Charles, and resumed eating his *quorn*.

"I wonder why he emailed you?" said Connie to her daughter as they cleaned the supper plates.

"He said he sent one to you too, Mum."

When? She made a point of checking her email at least once a day, usually when she walked in the door from school. She had expected something from him and when nothing arrived, she considered initiating the contact. But each time she was about to, numerous reasons why she should not, would stop her. After the dishes had all been cleared away and Charles was back with his computers, Connie went quietly up to her own *pc* which she kept at her vanity. She turned it on and with her mouse clicked to *Hotmail*. The email had arrived yesterday late:

Liebe Connie I miss the girl!

Do you never think of your Omer? The weather here is always wonderful, like my memory is of you and I can't believe that you will never come back to me, Connie. I think of you all the time and am here waiting for you when you do.

With all my love, Omer

As she reread the lines she trembled with a mix of feelings. She quickly e'd back: Everything including the weather is bad here. Horrid!

But she stopped. How really should she respond? Not *I love you too, Omer!* Why, since it would only intensify their feelings of loss—and what was there to be gained in that?

Nothing, since she could never talk Charles into spending another fortnight there. So instead she devoted the rest of her email to her worries over Scraggles, describing her trip to the vet. Charles' lack of caring, and how she anxiously waited for the results of the blood work, signing it: I love you too, Connie.

No *erase it* she rethought and wrote instead:

Take care, Omer. Stay in touch. Never will I forget the
Sunken City for reasons you know.

You live in such a beautiful place while all I do here is lead
a slave existence. Connie

Alice's concerns had been well founded as results from the blood
work showed the next day. There was a message on Connie's answering
machine for her to phone the vet. The receptionist answered. She must
bring Scraggles in as soon as possible and it might be best if her daughter
were also along.

"What's wrong with him?" asked Alice.

"It's what I was afraid of," said the vet to both, "but I didn't want to
alarm you needlessly until I was certain that it was diabetes."

"Diabetes? I didn't know dogs got that!" said Connie.

"They get most of the things we get and that's why I wanted you here
too, Alice. You need to both know how to give Scraggles his insulin." The
vet then showed them how to prepare the needle by forcing the air out
first; then where to best insert it: basically wherever you found loose skin
enough to grip between your fingers, he said as he prepared the syringe.

"Doesn't it hurt him?" said Alice.

"Not if you do it like...*this,*" said the vet, inserting the syringe. "And
life continues the same except we have to give him his injections?" said
Connie skeptically.

"If you watch his diet. No more steaks. And nothing with sugar, which
rules out normal dog food. You need to buy one made for diabetic dogs.
Pet stores sell it."

"The part about not letting Scraggles have any more meat should please
Charles," said Alice, holding the little dog in her lap as they returned home.

"You're going to have to eat like Charles now!" she said to it. But when
they discovered the cost of Scraggles' new food, Alice had another thought,
"Think if I were you, Mum, I'd hide the price from Charles."

As the vet had predicted, giving Scraggles his injections became almost
routine once they had overcome their fears of hurting the little animal
with the needle or, worse, accidentally injecting a trapped air bubble which
could kill him. "Come, Scraggles my baby, come with Mummy and get

'ihm's shot." As though the dog understood his mistress's words he would obediently follow the two to the kitchen and patiently allow one to hole him while the other administered the insulin and as Scraggles lost more and more weight, loose hanging skin provided easy places to insert the needle. One morning while she and Alice were giving him his shot, Charles entered and would have walked into the three of them.

"Charles, watch out where you step!" Alice said sharply.

He stopped. Looked down to observe Connie carefully fill the syringe to its correct dose level: "How long are you going to have to keep giving him those?"

"For as long as Scraggles is with us," Connie answered. "Could be years—so maybe you'd better learn how to do this, Charles. In case you should have to once Alice is away at college."

"I'm not about to do anything like that!"

"It's not hard, Charles," she said.

"I don't want to know."

Then have it that way! said Connie to herself.

While she remained home, Scraggles' increasing needs were administered largely by Alice since he slept practically beside her. For years Scraggles would go all night without having to be let out but with his diabetes that changed. Now, once, or sometimes twice a night, he would scratch to be let outside, which meant Alice having to take him downstairs, then wait by the back door until he could relieve himself. Connie emailed to Omer: Awakened, it was difficult going back to sleep because she would hear her little dog scratching from inside Alice's room to be let out and wonder how she was ever going to manage once Alice had left for Leeds? All she knew and very much feared was that, whatever happened, it wouldn't be easy, or pleasant!

My poor *Schatz!* Omer e'd. When does Alice leave to go to college?

Saturday, Connie e'd back. Alice had managed to find a house for students within walking distance of the campus. She and her mother loaded all her clothes plus the CD player and her laptop into the boot of Charles' car. The two gave Scraggles his insulin and while Alice carried his food dish into the garage to refill, Connie made sure Scraggles would have enough water. The two placed Scraggles food dish and water bowl in the most secure spot in the kitchen Connie could think of. "I hope Charles won't walk into them here."

"You'd better warn him about that, Mum!"

At last, with the car packed, it was time for them to leave. "And Charles," Connie had said, "In case Scraggles needs more water, his bowl is here."

"Oh…I'll take care of it."

Alice bent down and hugged the dog goodbye. Rose and faced Charles hesitantly. "Well, Charles, see you at Christmas then…Thanks again for everything."

Odd thing to say—? Connie thought, watching the two. "Well aren't you going to at least hug your daughter, Charles?" she said and both had then—though not very convincingly. Then mother and daughter were in the car headed for Leeds where they found the house Alice would be living in and unloaded the car.

But Connie hadn't stayed to help Alice settle in. Concerns over Scraggles forced her to return instead. Connie approached her front door and opened expecting to find her little dog waiting for her. But he wasn't!

She hurried on through the house to discover that Scraggles' food dish and water bowl were no longer in the kitchen. "Charles!" she yelled up: where was he? *Upstairs* she thought and turned out into the garage where she heard Scraggles scratching at the utility room door.

"Connie, we're going to have to come to some understanding over that dog," said Charles.

She had been helping herself to wine from the fridge when he entered and discovered Scraggles' food and water back in the kitchen where she and Alice had placed them that morning. "Why, is there something wrong with it here?" she said bolstered by the wine but fearing him.

"I want it outside! And two, where is Scraggles going to sleep now that Alice is gone?"

"In here, Charles."

"Around food? An animal free to go in the street and do *you know what he does?* I've watched him, he smells where other dogs have been and then he smells their droppings! God knows how many flees and whatever else he brings in with them. And if you don't think he doesn't smell, think again!"

"He gets a bath every weekend, Charles. Don't you, Scraggles?" she said, addressing the dog who looked up at them through interested eyes as though following the exchange that was to determine his fate.

"He still smells and if you don't believe me, just walk into Alice's room."

She had and knew. She faced him silently defiant.

"By rights," continued Charles, "it shouldn't even be allowed inside the house. And how old is that dog by the way?"

"We think maybe thirteen or fourteen," she was forced to admit.

"So he can't live much longer. And now with diabetes? How can there be any quality of life for the animal? The kindest thing would be to have him put to sleep? I would, if it were my dog."

"It isn't your dog, Charles!" she bristled back at him. But in the end, Connie emailed Omer; she had bent to Charles' pressure and agreed to make Scraggles sleep in the utility room:

And how did it work out, *Schatzi?*

It didn't, Omer, she emailed back. And I haven't had what you would call a real night's sleep since Alice left.

She had constructed a good bed for Scraggles right beside the boiler where it stayed warm. She'd put an extra bowl of water beside him so that he couldn't run out and spread papers down. Kissing her dog goodnight, Connie hurried out and drew the door shut trying not to hear the frantic scratching his nails made against the door, or that pleading whine. As she climbed into bed beside him Charles asked, "Did you put paper down?"

"Yes, Charles, I laid plenty of paper down."

"Well that's one problem solved...How does it feel not having Alice here?"

"Being alone, you mean?"

When Connie returned home that next afternoon there was a message from Alice to call her. After letting Scraggles out of the utility room, Connie had. "I want to give you the number of the house phone here, Mum. And find out how things went last night."

Connie told her, knowing beforehand that it could only upset Alice.

"What will you do, Mum—I can't come back!"

"Don't be silly—I don't want you back."

It was as though her days were now metered. She must wake before Charles, get up and hurry downstairs to let Scraggles out, crumple up the messed-on newspapers, and wash the floor if need be, before Charles could see it. Then, while she made herself breakfast, she would fill Scraggles' syringe with insulin and administer the shot and after her day spent in the classroom, she would rush back to free Scraggles and again clean up his mess before Charles found it. Dinner over and the last of the dishes stacked into the washer, she would go directly to Alice's room since only in there was the dog permitted. Such routine became her day; it was to get worse.

When she took Scraggles in for his follow-up visit the vet first weighed him and found he had lost more weight. It was not a good sign the vet told her and the new blood work indicated that Scraggles' condition had indeed worsened. "So what will happen said Connie, afraid.

"I'm going to change his dog food again," said the vet, writing its name on a prescription form. "Unless you feel you can't afford to pay that much. I warn you, it's not cheap."

"The money I don't care about!" said Connie. "Tell me what will happen."

"If we don't get his diabetes controlled you mean? Quite a few things. He could go blind. He can lose partial control of his bladder."

She thought she already was seeing the start of a bladder problem, but it was the blindness that scared her. "How will I know if he goes blind?"

"You'll see him walk into things."

None of that must Charles be allowed to find out! she thought as, returning home, she immediately retreated upstairs to Alice's room with her sick Scraggles tucked under her arm. After setting Scraggles' special food down, and plenty of water, Connie corrected papers and did her lesson plan, coming down only briefly to make Charles his tea. Then at ten it was back to the utility room with Scraggles and another night of incessant scratching that she would listen for trying not to hear.

After a week Charles gave in—not to the scratching but because the dog's nails were destroying the utility room door. So Scraggles would be allowed to sleep in Alice's room, as a trial and just to see if the scratching would stop. Connie carried the dog food and water bowl upstairs and placed them where they had been in the past, seeing Scraggles' stumpy tail beat in approval. Because of his weakened state which prevented him from jumping onto Alice's old bed, Connie made him a comfortable new one on the carpet beside it and spread protective newspapers over the rest of the room. Then she would lie on the carpet next to the dog for a time, petting him, before escaping, creeping out and down to her own room hoping to find Charles asleep.

Some nights he was; she could tell from his breathing even when he didn't snore and she would creep quietly into bed. But one night she had been fooled. Thinking him asleep she had slipped in beside him and started to turn onto her side when she felt his hand grope for her beneath the covers. "Charles, don't!" she said batting his hand away.

But it came back, this time finding her hand which he dragged onto his penis before she could pull it free. "Don't! I said. I am not in the mood."

"You never are," he mumbled at her, "except for that mutt of yours you dragged in off the street. –Where you going now!"

She had risen without telling him and fled, along the landing to Alice's room where Scraggles met her in the dark. She scooped the little dog up, felt it start to lick. Only his nose was dry, hot: not cold and wet like she knew it should be. "Oh yes, Mummy sleep with her baby."

"He's jealous of it!" said Mandy that Saturday when they met at the usual place for lunch—their last, since Mandy announced she was moving to London.

"Of *a dog?* What am I to do, Mandy?"

"At this point? It's slightly late for marriage councillors I think, don't you? I can only tell you what I would do—leave him. If you recall, Connie, I warned you at the time you met him to think before you jumped."

Both reached for their glasses. They had met so long ago now, on that playground where Alice and Mandy's boy liked to play. Where Alice had had her fall. Mandy was divorced even then and had never remarried: content to live her life without a man it seemed though she, Connie, couldn't!

"So did my mother—try to warn me…If I did leave him *then what?* Besides, divorces are horrible things as you well know. And where would I go *afterwards?*" She did not want another English male—of that she was now certain. Omer was thousands of miles away and *really* what did she know of him? That he had a German past. That he'd had the bends and couldn't dive. But she didn't even know how he lived, not really, or on what?

Apparently, he owned a silver stand and sold trinkets. But even if he still had the diving boat and she could go back, she still could not because there was Scraggles. Poor sick little Scraggles who was as helpless as a stricken child and whom she would never abandon!

Chapter 8

THOUGH CONNIE HAD NOT RECOGNIZED it at first, with Alice off to college and with the departure of Mandy for London, a new phase in her life began: not a turning point exactly, yet. At first she only knew she faced struggle alone. More than her daughter even, it was Mandy she really missed: Mandy whom she could open up before, explore her past mistakes, see her many faults which she had gone to some great length to hide.

With Charles the anger of that night had been muted and again they were amicable. If anything, there was less fiction now than when Alice was home—perhaps because of it. But they lived separate lives, he immersed in his *Computer Operations Management,* while she made the daily trek to school then back to tend to Scraggles. But it was not even an armistice between them, so much as it was an uneasy truce. On the surface Charles even tried to tolerate the little dog since he knew that to do anything else would be to violate the terms of the truce. He had given up telling her that it would be best for the dog—the kindest thing in the long run, given up complaining about the vet bills, saying to her, "I could see it, Connie, if it were a valuable dog even."

The truce seemed on the surface congenial. In the kitchen at night they would prepare their suppers together, he his food and she hers, but they were careful to avoid touching, a little like two shoppers do when rummaging at the same time through the same supermarket shelf for items they need. The meal finished he would run upstairs to his computers. She would put the supper dishes away, then go see if there was another email from Omer. She liked it when he described for her Fethiye with all the tourists gone and where the harbour lay empty of craft.

Where berths along the quay and over in the yacht harbour were completely filled with ships of all kinds, from swimming boats and small pleasure craft to big gulets, and fresh white sails for a new season were already being fitted to many. It had cooled. Any day now expect snow on the higher peaks that you could look up at from the quay. And for the adventurous and the lucky who just happened to have a hundred thousand or more in their pocket, it was that time of year to shop for your gulet! She would love to own a gulet and emailed back: Dream on for both of us, Omer! He e'd back immediately:

> I am serious, Connie. Some day soon, God willing, I will buy us that gulet. Am to meet with my advocate Friday. He seems to think the court date is finally going to be set. He thinks I have a very good chance of getting that land which I told you about put into my name. I told you I think how it should already be mine. And would have, had my father just signed those papers from my grandfather like he was supposed to.

> Love, Omer

She thrilled at the prospects as she emailed back 'Good luck, Omer!' Let me know when the date for the litigation is. I'll burn candles for the both of us. Love you!

Never very strong, the truce between Connie and Charles ended abruptly one evening when they returned from seeing Alice. Connie was driving. She pulled up in the driveway before their garage door and was still locking the car when she heard Charles shout from somewhere inside the house: "You fucking cur!—heard Scraggles' yelp of pain and she dropped the keys and ran into the garage where she discovered Charles standing just inside the utility room door and stopped dead! In their absence Scraggles had messed all over the utility room and Charles had stepped into it. She rushed past him to find her dog lying back down on the floor, shivering. Connie was shaking almost as much as she scooped the little dog into her arms, then turned to encounter her husband's rage as he stared furiously down at his shoe.

"I'll clean it up."

"Well, somebody had better!"

"And take off the shoe, Charles."

For the next two nights she slept instead with her dog. In the morning they would face each other over the breakfast table then go their separate ways. The second day when she returned there was an email from Omer:

> Schatz, if I can come up with half the money for the gulet, would Charles put up the rest? Tell him he will get all of it back from what the boat earns in just the first season!

> Even if true, Charles invest in a gulet? she typed into her laptop, You have to be dreaming, Omer!

> Then can you? he sent back.

Where would she find that kind of money! She had about ten thousand pounds in savings from before Charles, and there was perhaps two thousand more in their joint checking account. Her wedding ring from Charles and the string of pearls he had given her one Christmas might fetch a thousand, but she didn't know. "I just don't have any way of coming up with even half the amount. I only wish I could!" she typed.

The third Thursday of each month was union meeting night, and the upcoming one was of particular importance since their new contract had to be discussed before ratification. With no way around it for her Connie decided to attend so she closed Scraggles in the utility room with food and water. Then she went upstairs to tell Charles that she was leaving and he needn't bother checking on Scraggles, he would be fine.

It was a long union meeting, tedious. She tried to follow the arguments for and against but had difficulty in paying attention.

She kept glancing down at her watch: 9…9:15. Finally, a little be- fore ten the meeting broke up and by ten-thirty she was parking her car in the driveway.

She slid her key into the front door and opened. The house struck her at once as deserted—quiet as a tomb. Was Charles in bed asleep? He could be in his computer room working. He was spending more and more time up there by himself, if not at one of his computers, then sitting tilted back in his chair before the desk. Or sometimes she would walk in to find him on that discoloured old couch that had been his first wife Marilyn's, just laying there staring up at blank space—thinking she couldn't begin to guess what, or what thoughts, feelings went through his mind. Why he still kept that unsightly old thing was another mystery.

But she really didn't care as she passed though the kitchen into the garage where she saw Charles' car. Then she discovered the door to the back yard stood open, and so did the utility room door! Seized by panic, she rushed into the utility room. *Empty!* She looked down at Scraggles' untouched food and water, then at the newspapers she had laid out: they hadn't been walked on even! She rushed into the back yard searching it for two glowing little eyes she knew so well. But encountered only empty darkness as she repeatedly called, "Scraggles! Mummy's back!"

Almost hysterical, she turned again through the house: Charles could still be at his computers…no, the room was dark. She hurried along the landing to their bedroom where she discovered his shape in the bedcovers. He appeared asleep. But as she snapped on the light he bolted straight up.

"Where's Scraggles!"

"Scraggles? Didn't he come back?"

"What did you do with him, Charles? I expressly told you to leave him where he was!"

"He was scratching, Connie. I thought he had to go out. You mean he's still not back," Charles said and reached for his ear. "Where you going?"

She turned. "Look for him—what else would I do, Charles?"

She found a torch with good batteries from the garage and started through the neighbourhood shining her light all directions, under bushes, behind hedges, calling! As she started she felt the first cold drops on her face—it was beginning to rain. She cast her light onto the pavement in front and behind, under parked cars, and into the street afraid of what she might see. It was raining harder. The water ran in cold droplets down her face. She could feel it run down her neck and inside her blouse, feel its coldness in her cleavage. Not since she was a girl making her way home to the aunt's house had she walked through rain like this and with a cold sinking fear that she could feel down her spine, she seemed to know that she would never hold her dog again.

Charles was waiting for her in his bathrobe when she returned. "Did you find him?"

"Does it look like I did, Charles?"

He appeared to search for words. "You're wet," he said.

And when she said nothing, only stared back, holding him in her icy silence: "Connie, I know how much that dog meant to you…Look, if he's not here by tomorrow night when I get home, we can tape signs up to utility poles and offer a small reward. But you've got to get out of those wet clothes before you come down with something. Here, I'll help you. Connie. I still love you."

"Just stay away!" She kept the table between them. *You never loved anybody in your life but yourself!*

He groped for something more to say—unable to meet her stare.

"Well I'm going to bed, and I suggest, dog or no dog, you do the same. I have to get up at six-thirty. No dog is worth losing your job over… He'll be back in the morning…"She watched him disappear upstairs. She stripped out of her wet clothing, found something she could wear in the dryer, and laid down on the couch. But she couldn't sleep, pursued by horrible dream images in which her dog was abandoned and lost in some terrifying place: dumped to wander about half blind and in need of his insulin. Or perhaps somebody had picked him up, and in kindness taken him home not knowing—how could they!—that Scraggles' life depended on getting insulin. Or perhaps he had already been hit by a car in the street somewhere and lay unable to move! She felt ill—physically sick.

Charles came down in the morning and found her. "You're not going to work then?"

"No, Charles." She was glad that he kept his distance.

Exactly at seven Connie phoned the school to report herself sick—and to call in a substitute. After tea with a bit of toast, she set out in her car slowly, searching street after street. Finally she stopping before the vet's. No, no one had brought Scraggles there. So her little dog might still be alive. *But where?* Worse even than knowing was the *not knowing.* He could be lying in some street even as she was thinking it—injured and crying for help! The thought made her ill and she thought of her Valium— but she had thrown the remaining pills out years ago. Returning home, she went up to her laptop to check if Omer had emailed. He hadn't, so she began typing a message: Dearest Omer, how are you, my love? Yesterday night something horrible happened! She sent off the account of what had in some detail and waited. That afternoon a response came back. My poor poor Connie!

I just wish there was something I could do, if it was only to hold you in my arms again and comfort you. You know how much I love you, Connie!! And just want to kiss you like I kissed you in the Sunken City—remember?

How could she not! There was a *PS:* I was going to email you anyway, Connie. And while this may be a bad time, I have to tell you because its important. Captain Ali owes money to various people and may be forced to put the *Gul* up for sale. It could be yours (ours) if you are interested.

Love to the girl of my dreams! Omer.

She emailed back. How much is he asking? And what does the word 'Gul' mean, if anything, Omer?

Gul is Turkish for 'Rose', Schatzi, Omer e'd back.

Connie liked the name *Rose* for a boat! She waited, checking her Hotmail every two to three hours. Finally the response came:

Ali says the boat will be appraised for at least a hundred and seventy-five thousand. But for you he will come down.

Ask him, Omer, how much is 'down'?

Connie waited and waited. Charles came home early that evening. His first question was of Scraggles—had he come back?

"What do you think?" she answered in a quiet, almost disinterested way,

"Do you want me to put up notices in the neighbourhood offering a reward?"

"Go ahead if you want, Charles."

"How much reward?"

"A thousand pounds."

He looked startled but didn't object. Returning, he sat down to with her and announced that he would be travelling to London next week for a computer conference.

How long will you be gone, Charles? she had asked then and heard him say, three days. *Only three?* She stayed home sick from her job a second day, waiting for Omer's response.

Ali said a hundred and fifty is the lowest he can go, even for *you,* my love.

There was no way she could come up with anywhere near that she emailed and waited half in despair for the response. It came the next day:

Schatz, didn't you say your house is worth a half million? Couldn't you borrow some of it? By selling my silver stand I can come up with something. What should I tell Ali? He needs an answer as soon as possible.

Try and stall him, Connie emailed back even though she knew the situation hopeless. She waited. This time the response was longer in coming:

> Schatz, I told him that you would raise the money but that it might take some time. He said that he needed the money bad and could only wait so long before he'd be forced to sell it to someone else. Connie, we will find a way yet! If ever two people were meant for each other's arms, they are us! Think of the life we will live, just the two of us together.

> Think of paradise!

Connie returned to her teaching the next day, and that afternoon on her way home she stopped along a busy avenue of stores where there was a jewellery shop she knew. She entered and approached the owner with her rings. "If I were to sell these, how much could I hope to get?" She watched him weigh the wedding band then inspect the diamond ring with one of those small eye pieces jewellers use. Finished, he gazed up into the neon-lit ceiling, deciding.

"Eight hundred pounds…Nine, maybe."

That was all! She thanked him and left. On her return to her car Connie passed an estate office where she stopped look at photos of houses for sale in the window. She knew theirs had increased considerably in value—perhaps it had even quadrupled, it might have. One of the teachers she worked with and often encountered in her free period had just sold his house, so Connie decided to ask him that next day what sort of a market it was? Seller's! because interest rates were so low. He had listed his with the agent on a Friday and by Monday it was sold!

Charles would never sell, she knew that, but what about a second mortgage? Connie decided to wait until the following week when Charles would be away at his conference before phoning the bank. She rang and was rerouted to someone in the house loans department. With the interest rate at a low four percent, the time to refinance was *Now* said the voice in the phone. If she wished, the bank could mail her the papers. Yes please! she responded. "And could you rush them?" Glad to! said the voice. Most of the required information could be filled out at home which would expedite the process. Then she and her husband need only make an appointment to see one of the loan officers.

"My husband is in charge of the local school authority's computers and may not be able to come in—he's that busy!"

"Unfortunately, Madam, you both have to sign plus, we need to discuss the loan with you."

She dropped the receiver back onto its cradle and spent the rest of that day wandering about in a depressed state. Not even in the days following her break-up with Cliff had she felt more down and as she pictured the life before her having to live with Charles after what he had done, the thought of suicide crept back. She was on the verge of going upstairs to tell Omer just how hopeless the situation was, when she remembered something. The last time she had gone to London with him, Charles had met Bill Gates and had returned to their hotel room wanting to buy Microsoft shares. She had no idea if he actually had but, if so, they might be locked in the safe inside his computer room closet. She knew where he kept the combination to it hidden, but she had never been interested enough in his world to bother opening the safe since she believed she knew what it contained: insurance policies and documents such as their house mortgage. So she was surprised to discover letters, some from before their marriage. A few old coins of little worth as far as she could tell, and other items: a locket that wasn't of real gold because it had turned partially green. A yellowing photograph of some woman's face. *Marilyn's?* It was possible, but how could she know? No—at least she did not think so. They were windows into his past: uninterested, Connie pushed them aside.

She did not know what she was looking for, really, as she continued pulling items from the safe. Then she discovered a bundle of papers that looked more interesting. They were held together by a large paper clip and when she saw the word **Apple,** she sensed she had found something of interest.

It was a stock certificate she slowly figured out: for three hundred common shares issued by J.D. Powers, Stockbrokers, and what must have been the original purchase price and date-of- purchase, signed by someone. She could see the stamp of the brokerage house, and that it was initialled. *Yes, this might be what she had been looking for only didn't know it!* Her heart raced as she carried the stack of documents to her dressing table, removed the paper clip, and started thumbing through them. They were all certificates of stock purchases Charles had made over years from two different brokerages, one in London, one located here in Manchester. The earliest she discovered was from before their marriage, for a stock called *Sage*.

She was amazed! She'd had no idea he was into stocks! But how much were they worth? Newspapers carried daily stock price quotes and she still had a stack in the garage that she'd kept for Scraggles. Connie ran down to the garage where she found what she was looking for and rushed back upstairs. Thumbing through the stack of certificates, she discovered that Charles had purchased *Sage* shares on six separate occasions. She added up the number he now owned and the total amount paid. Then she located the share price listed in her three-day old newspaper, multiplied it by the number of shares Charles owned, and could have danced as he watched those little green numbers appear on the calculator screen.

She was holding in her hand the equivalent of eighteen thousand pounds! And there were more shares of *Hewlett Packard, IBM,* and other high-tech companies. There were eight hundred shares of just *Microsoft*!

Her first impulse had been to email Omer the good news but she stopped herself. She was not at all certain she could sell the stock without Charles or even whom to approach with the question. She forced herself to stay calm, and in command just as if she were standing in front of a class as she walked down to the kitchen to put on some water for her tea thinking *Your whole future depends on what you do next. You can't afford even a single mistake.* Returning upstairs with her tea, she sat before the dressing table and examined the certificates closely. Most were from a London brokerage house.

She had an idea and found in an old Manchester phone book a listing of local stockbrokers, selected one at random, and dialled. Her hands were trembling despite her best efforts to control them and as she listened to the repeated ringing, she practiced over in her mind what she would tell them. Then she was saying that she and her husband had purchased some stocks in London years ago and now they wanted to sell them. Could that be done here in Manchester, or must the stocks be sold where they were purchased—she and her husband had just no idea of what to do or how to proceed. Then she was told *wait* while the call was being transferred and she heard herself repeat the question to yet another voice. She could have kissed the phone when the reply came back:

No, any brokerage firm could sell the shares: she had only to turn in the certificates. But how would they receive their money, and when? she then asked. Within two weeks—by check in the mail. Connie always arrived home before Charles, so that part would work out. "Can I initiate the process by phone?" she asked next and was asked in turn the name of the stock and the certificate number. "It's that ten digit one there to the right," said the voice.

Connie found it and was told to wait. She had. It was some minutes before the voice returned and read back to her the number of shares and the price at the time of purchase, by Charles Cullingsworth.

"That is my husband!" said Connie. "And whom am I talking with?"

"Constance (also with a *C*). Cullingsworth." She tried not to be nervous.

"..Oh yes. And do you want me to put in the sell order now, Madam?"

"Oh yes please!" She couldn't believe how easy this was!

"Alright. That's four hundred shares sold at thirty-eight and three quarters. And, Madam, you'll need to deliver the certificates here within three business days, by courier is safest— or you can bring them in."

"Yes, I'll bring them in," said Connie.

But scarcely had she placed the receiver back down when she realized her mistake. She would need his identification too! Plus they would ask her personal questions just to trip her up, or perhaps they would phone Charles! She was not sure if what she had just done was actually against the law, or what the offence was? Part of her did not want to know. In England property was divided evenly between the man and wife, she thought—but wasn't sure. What if what she had just done was criminal. Knowing that, would she do it still? She was only giving Charles a little of what he deserved.

Another thought! What if Charles should discover the missing certificates? But that was a risk she would have to accept—until she had a second idea. She knew of a good copy place in town, and as soon as she had emailed Omer the good news she drove there and spread the certificates out on the counter before an employee telling him she wanted the copy as near perfect as possible.

It was. She could not distinguish between the original and fake. She would reassemble the stack of certificates to just as she had found them, leaving the top one authentic even though Charles would likely do no more than glance at the bundle (if he did even that). And something else occurred. She would need to deposit the arriving checks—*but where?* Her own bank knew too much about her. So that afternoon she drew five thousand pounds from her savings and with it opened a new account just down the street. When she returned home, she found an email waiting:

Dear, Connie:

How much money did you say? When will you get it? I was talking to Ali again and someone else he thinks is interested in buying the Gul.

Connie's spirits sank. She e'd back at once that she didn't know exactly how much the amount would be in the end, or how long it would take until she got it. She understood that it was their future that now was in her hands and for that reason alone she had to proceed in such a way as to not make Charles suspicious. Schatzi! Omer answered, the Gul will be ours yet, God willing. You don't buy a gulet like you would a car. Before the boat can be sold it has to be appraised. And for that to happen it first must be inspected out of the water. So there still is time.

Charles was due back by train that next afternoon. She was there to meet him when he stepped from it. "So what's been happening in my absence?" he said as she pulled into their driveway.

"Nothing, Charles. It's been the same boring existence."

It was amazing how skillful she had become at lying she later thought to herself, so skillful, in fact, that it was accidentally telling the truth she now feared as she continued to plan. She would rush home each day to check the mailbox and should another check be there, she would rush it down to the bank and be back in time for Charles to find her in the kitchen preparing tea for the two, adding in her mind the amount of each new check to the existing account until her mind signalled her to stop, there was now enough! Her mind was telling her she must now leave, that it was time—all the while trying to appear normal, pleasant even as she avoided contact with him, since everything about him was repulsive to her.

She emailed Omer the date she would leave and the flight, and in the morning just as soon as he had left, she packed. Originally, she had considered resigning, walking in and telling them she was cancelling her contract. But they would try to track her. No, better to just disappear, leave no trail—nothing. Vanish. There was just one thing yet to do, close out her old bank account. There was only seven thousand pounds left in it that she would take hidden on her person.

Returning home, she poured herself a stiff brandy and waited until it was time to ring the taxi. She poured herself a second drink then she was in the cab, being dropped off. She thought, if she could just make it through airport security, make it down the ramp, she would be alright. She knew that once she was on the airplane it would be too late to turn back. She stowed her carry- on in the overhead bin, took her seat, and sat gazing trancelike out at the wing, thinking of Omer's face waiting for her, and Alice's. And her dog as she felt the airplane being pushed away from the terminal.

Then begin to roll. *Please don't hate me, Alice.* She felt tears slide down her face as she thought of never seeing her daughter again. Perhaps she would email her, let her know she was with Omer and quite happy. Charles would think her dead. He would have the police look for her at the beginning. But in the end, he would forget even her existence—as she had his.

She felt the airplane turn sharply and again start to roll, faster. She heard the sudden crackly roar of the engines and gripped her seat rest. Never before in her life had she been this afraid.

PARADISE

Chapter 1

SHE DREAMED SHE WAS IN a taxi. It was night and she is being taken somewhere. The driver's face is veiled yet, somehow, she seems to know his identity. She is being driven to where she has never before been and feels concern over her safety. As the road climbs it becomes very rough and she can sense through the windscreen how dangerous it has become. The taxi driver is telling her that it is impossible not to go over the edge. Then she is falling, falling and falling past strange curious shapes that, as she watches, come threateningly close. She sees the bottom. Frozen, terrified, she is rushing helplessly toward it and will hit! But the landing is surprisingly soft.

When she woke it was to bright sunlight pouring into the room where she lay. She sat up in bed and saw red rose petals mixed in with the crumpled bedding. She had been met with red roses, she remembered; and more had been waiting for her inside the apartment. The sun's brightness streaming through the window made her divert her eyes and she saw last night's bottles lined up near the doorway, *but where was Omer!*

"Omer?" she called out. She rose and started toward the bedroom door as her lover appeared in it to catch her as she fell against him.

"How's my *Schatzi's* head feel this morning?" he asked, his dark eyes laughing at her.

"I've got a headache that will not stop. What all did we drink last night?"

"After the champagne, you mean? We finished drinking up the rest of my raki."

"Ooh, that's why. You must feel pretty rotten yourself."

"Not so bad, Connie. I think I'm more used to it than you are. How about breakfast? Remember when we were on the boat and I said I was a good cook—which reminds me, Special greetings from Captain Ali."

"And he hasn't sold the *Gul*? My fear—why I came as quick as I possibly could—was that he might. (I thought there was somebody else who wanted it.)"

"Oh no, Connie."

"Or change his mind?"

"About selling it, you mean? No, he has to, Connie."

"Why does he?"

"The court will make him. He owes some English a lot of money."

"For what?"

"Selling houses he shouldn't have, because now the people can't get their *tapus*. I mean, that's rumour—I don't know it personally. It's not my business, Connie."

"What's a '*tapu*'?"

"It's a paper that says you own the property."

"A deed?"

"Maybe, and now the English want their money back."

"I see." She had another thought, "But Ali's free and clear to sell the *Gul* to us?"

"I'm sure, Connie. I've known Ali since I first came here and he wouldn't lie—not to me. But we'll find out. It's part of what we're paying a lawyer for. Are you ready for breakfast, Connie?"

"When can we go to Kas and see the *Gul*?" she said.

"It's probably not there, Connie. Ali said he wanted to move it to Finike for the winter."

"To *where*?"

"A place about two hours from Kas. Where captains like to take their boats because repairs are cheaper. Or to just store them. I text messaged him that you were coming but he hasn't texted back yet. Now breakfast, *Schatzi*. Remember what I told you on the *Gul*. Now I can prove it to you. Ready?"

They dressed then she followed him into the kitchen which was also in sunlight early, before the sun could cross to the west. Beside the kitchen window was a door that led onto a balcony and she said, "Can we go look?"

"Of course you can, my love!" said Omer, and opened for her. Though the sun looked warm, the day was actually on the chilly side, she discovered as they stood side by side and she looked around. Of course, for Manchester this would be almost summer weather. Still, she felt the goose pimples on her arms and huddled into him for warmth. The apartment was four floors up and she could look directly across to the opposite balcony, see a table and chairs, a tot's toy scooter with training wheels, some cardboard boxes and other items: a burned pot. Directly below them she discovered a cement walk and lining it, rose bushes still in late bloom. *Was it from there the roses he had met her with and had laid out so artfully atop their bed had come?* she wondered. She could remember climbing those four flights of cement stairs smelling of dampness, of shoes left before doors, and perhaps of things mildewing, in the dark with only a single naked light bulb at each landing to see by.

"Don't any of these buildings have lifts, Omer?"

"No-o, *Schatz,*" Omer answered with his saddened dark eyes, "You're living in Turkey now."

Huddling beside him, she turned to go back in, but was still cold as she cast her eyes about the kitchen, looking for a radiator. "Where do I turn on the heat, Omer?"

"You get used to sweaters, Connie. Turks say that it never gets cold enough here for heat. When we go into town later, or sometime tomorrow, we can buy a space heater. Do you have a sweater?"

"I was under a lot of pressure to leave and didn't think to bring any, Omer."

"Here, I'll get you one of mine till we can buy you some."

Thoughts of the *Gul II* aside, it would be a busy week just getting settled in, since she had come with just what could be stuffed inside one suitcase. A busy future: one she looked forward to! The first thing after breakfast would be to find a bank,

she thought as she watched him assemble breakfast for them: fresh bread, marmalades, and eggs with diced bits of green pepper. Sausage, and even bacon from *Tansas!* Their supermarket—she remembered it as she watched him carry the pan over. In it were six slices. She watched as he lifted four onto her plate and the remaining two to his. "So you do eat bacon, Omer."

"Of course. Why wouldn't I, Schatzie—is pork unsafe?"

"I thought being a Muslim country— But you must have eaten it when you were a boy in Germany."

"Are you kidding, *Schatz!* If my father ever thought for a minute I ate pork, he'd beat the shit out of me. That and alcohol. As I say, he could be a real asshole when he wanted."

"Did you resent him?" Connie watched Omer stop in the middle of eating.

"When he used to throw me out?" She saw him shrug, "I came to expect it. After the first two times it was like a game we played. I used to enjoy it when I could get his dandruff up. In German we say—what are you laughing at?"

She couldn't help it; she was still wearing her thin nightie and could see his eyes even as he spoke looking through it at her flesh and see their flirtatious sparkle. "You're too much for any woman, you know. You should attach a sign to yourself: '*Dangerous!*'"

"*Me?* Is that why you're asking me all these questions?"

"I'm curious about you—shouldn't I be?"

"Maybe you'll find things you don't like about your Omer. Maybe you'll decide to leave."

"If I ever decide to do that, first I'm going to cut off three parts of you and take them with me. Do you want to know which parts?" She could see his eyes, how they shone back at her in merry anticipation as she rose and walked around the table to him: "Empty your mouth out. I'll show you the first. I can bite it out," she said as she pressed her lips to his.

"How much money did you bring, Connie?" asked Omer after breakfast was over and as, together, they finished unpacking her suitcase. "And what do you want me to do with *this?*"

Connie turned and saw him with her computer. "Just drop it there on the bed." Her laptop was another problem she feared she must face sooner or later.

Later. Connie went back to placing and arranging her under garments inside her dresser drawer. She would need more of everything, from half slips to fancy little bras and panties that matched. The list her mind quickly assembled was practically endless.

"How much did you say, *Schatz?*"

She hadn't. "Seven thousand pounds," she said as, turning, she watched him search for it, "But don't think it's in there— I'm not that stupid. I stuffed it in the bottom of my purse. Customs didn't even look. Plus add that to the five I sent you. Then ten, which I presume the bank received."

"They did and it went straight into my savings where it still is, waiting for your arrival. Want to see the bankbook, *Schatz?*"

"I believe your word, Omer."

But he had dug into one of the dresser drawers for it anyway. "See here. And, *here* below it, Connie."

She had never seen a Turkish savings account book before and didn't know what the rows of figures meant, or the symbols atop them. "That's all Greek to me, Omer."

"I know, they're confusing," he said and slipped the bank book into a pocket: "I was thinking, *Schatz,* if you don't want to go to the trouble of opening another account, you don't have to. Do we need more than the one between us? It's up to you, of course."

She had considered doing something like that on the flight out. She still had ninety thousand pounds hidden in her secret account in England and had mulled it over in her mind. Should she send for the entire amount at once, or have it brought over so much at a time? Choosing the last for no clear reason, she then decided to open an account and have money forwarded. "I think I should open my own account, Omer."

"Probably a good idea, my love."

It was afternoon before they were ready to go into Fethiye. Her trip from the airport to Chalis Beach had been at night. Now, in daylight, as she looked at the car in which Omer had picked her up, she realized it was not the same one she remembered. "You didn't have this car when we went to the lagoon—?" she said.

"No, Connie. I had to borrow this one."

"What about the other?"

"It wasn't a very good car, remember? So I traded it."

"Traded it? I don't understand, Omer."

"For the apartment."

"*Our apartment?*"

"Connie, you couldn't have lived where I was before, believe me. And I wanted to pick a nice place for my *Schatzi!*—where most of the English live. I want our relationship to be perfect! You still haven't seen the Chalis sunsets, have you? Maybe I can show you this evening if we get back in time. You wait. When people see us walking arm in arm along the beach they'll point to us and say, 'See those two walking by the water that are so much in love? They're that new couple!' And pretty soon all the people living in Calis will be talking, Connie—that's what will happen."

"I don't want to be talked about, Omer, even nicely. But instead of trading the car, why didn't you use the money I sent?"

"Connie, I didn't want to touch that money without your approval. I wanted this relationship to be not just perfect—but better than perfect, *Schatz!*"

She could see the sincerity in his eyes.

"Thing of it is, Connie, I owed him money anyway. He's been asking for it back and that's another thing you don't understand.

There are people who owe me money—okay? But it's very hard to get money out of Turks, particularly in the wintertime. If I could get even some of that back, then I probably wouldn't have traded the car. But this way we get three months rent free. Now do you see?"

She didn't, but no matter! "So where are you taking us? And do I assume you'll need to return the car to someone?"

"Mehmet—he's a good friend. I can return it tonight or tomorrow, Connie. Now first we go to the bank. Then you do shopping. But I need to go with you, *Schatz.*"

Driving in, she saw the harbour in winter as an endless panorama of fresh white sails greeted her eyes, the sea like a mirror reflecting them. Because of all the stores and tiny boutiques Omer insisted she see to begin their new life together, he said, he parked in the lot behind the post office where she could look up at the first snow and see closer down the crumbling walls of what had been a Crusader Castle, like an inverted row of broken and sometimes missing teeth. It really was a beautiful place! she had remarked. A place ideal for honeymoon couples! Omer responded as he slipped his arm about her waist. "You have such a nice little waist, *Schatz!*"

Perhaps they had been the best few days of her entire life! she thought, thinking back on it. After opening her a savings account at *Finance Bank* and applying for their Visa Card, Omer had taken her on her first shopping spree through a part of Fethiye that backed against the steep, sometimes near vertical, bluff beneath the ruins of the castle, and where the oldest portion of the town lay spread, sandwiched between mountains and the sea. Here the streets all were of stone and too narrow for cars to be allowed in. Here she could find the smaller, more exclusive shops: a good place to window-shop and take the town in, said Omer holding her hand.

She needed virtually everything. Earlier she'd made herself a list: long under slips, waists for when she wore a skirt and blouse. Nylons, socks, tank tops. They were opposite the old *hamam*. Omer pointed it out to her—it was one of the few buildings to withstand that horrific 1957 earthquake. Had she ever had a real Turkish bath before? he asked. *No* she responded.

"Then I must bring you," he said, "You'll like it—a Turkish bath will be good for the girl, especially her complexion—not that there's a thing wrong with it now, *Schatz.*"

She noticed the building directly across from the *hamam*. It was black, totally black—even the doors which were closed tight—and windowless. It's sign above her head read *Bananas*.

"What's that, Omer?"

"A place to go dancing. It only opens at night. Do you want me to take you dancing, Connie?"

She could have kissed him there in that cobblestone street! Not since her marriage to Cliff had she gone dancing. Charles refused! "I'll love you forever! I'll be your slave even—but I need to buy heels! I left all my shoes behind!"

Arms entwined, they strolled past more store fronts until she came upon a window displaying women's clothes she liked: scant see-through things. "See anything you like, Omer?"

"That sweater would look good on you, and you'll need sweaters!"

"Will it get colder than this?"

"Oh *yes!* January and February get quite cold—so you need them. And see those red knickers *there*. They'd look good on you, *Schatz.*"

Giving him a quick squeeze, she led the way inside. It was quite a large store with two upper floors, one of which was just for women. Yes, this was the place she had been searching for. This was like a *Marks and Spenser's* almost, and shop they did methodically searching through the racks of clothing for items Omer thought would look best on her until, with four or five selected pieces, she would walk to the changing cabin while Omer waited outside the curtain for her to emerge wearing a new tank top, or skirt and blouse. "How does it look on me?" she would say, already knowing the answer just from the way his eyes in that moment would take her in.

Skirts and tank tops were one thing—with those she could walk through the store—but when trying on the underwear he picked out for her, they had to be less obvious. He waited just outside the changing cabin as she undressed. Before the mirror she would step into the thin, see-through nylon knickers, slip the pretty lace bra around her waist to fasten the hooks before giving it a half turn. Then adjust it into position in front of the mirror conscious of her flatchestedness, though the padding inside the bra helped. Ready at last, she would call out to Omer to open the curtain and stick his head in knowing how eagerly he waited. Charles too had made a fuss out of how she must dress for him before they had sex. Net stockings and garters excited him the most—though *why* he never said. Quite likely he didn't himself know she thought, but after their fights and when they made up, to appease him she would appear sometimes dressed like a tart. Like some streetwalker from Whalley Range showing off her wares, seeing his excitement. She had done it because she knew she must, it was part of *making up*; but she had never felt right about it in herself. "Omer," she called to him in a bare whisper, "slide the curtain back and tell me if you like what you see."

It was getting to late afternoon and she was tired, also a bit hungry. "I've shopped enough for today," she announced.

"Do you want to go home now, *Schatz,* or see the sunset?"

Was there still time? she had asked and moved toward the sales counter at the rear of the store thinking it was lucky she had foreseen something like this and was carrying a thousand Turkish lira from Finance Bank in her purse! But Omer's hand stopped her, "Connie, let me handle this. Don't say anything and don't show your money! In fact, just wait here."

Connie hadn't the faintest idea why she had been told to stay back but she did and watched Omer approach the counter.

The salesclerk was only a young girl. Connie watched the two talking and there seemed to be some disagreement, over something; the girl kept glancing in her direction and looked very uncomfortable, thought Connie who wished she could hear what was being said. But it would be in Turkish anyway! she realized, watching the two apparently argue. Then a middle-aged man appeared from somewhere: *the store manager* she thought as she saw Omer turn to him, gesticulating with his hands, pointing. Their conversation must be about *me* thought Connie, because the manager too kept looking over at her.

She started to become uneasy. Then she saw Omer remove a card from his wallet and hand it to the manager. *A business card?* More conversation followed punctuated by the manager's frequent glances over to her. At one point it appeared that Omer would walk away. But the manager must have said something because Omer returned to the counter and Connie saw the manager draw a notebook from under it which he then spread open beside the stack of her clothes still to be purchased. They would discuss the price tag of each item, sometimes heatedly she thought, then the manager would make an entry in the book. Finally Omer drew money from his wallet and handed it across the counter. Connie watched the manager count it. Omer reached for the bagged merchandise and motioned for her to follow. The store manager was holding the door open for Connie, and as she approached he smiled and said to her in English, "Welcome to Turkey, Madam. I hope you like our country and we will see you in here many times. If you can't find something, just say me and I am sure to find it."

"I shall. And thank you," she managed. Once in the street, she turned to Omer, "What was that all about! Were you two arguing?"

"I was opening an account for you, *Schatz.* The argument was over prices. Those they have marked are for tourists and foreigners. Turns would pay half that maybe. So when I told him I wasn't going to pay English prices, that I was going to walk out, he agreed to forty percent off."

"Forty percent!"

"I said *fifty* but he wouldn't go that much. I knew you needed the clothes, Connie, and so I settled for the forty."

"So how much did you have to give him in the end?" she asked.

"A hundred lira down. The rest I said I pay off weekly and he agreed. It was that or I take my business elsewhere. You couldn't have done that, Connie. It takes a Turk!"

You said you weren't Turkish—remember? she nearly said back.

Omer stopped briefly at a hardware store to purchase two space heaters on their return to Chalis. They quickly dropped the day's purchases at the apartment before continuing on to the Ana Bar for dinner and to watch the sunset as he had promised. Parking on the back side, they had entered at the rear of the restaurant. There was a bar along one entire side, she saw. In the middle stood a row of billiard tables, then a small dance floor and tables, all facing out upon the promenade, and the sea beyond.

Omer ordered large glasses of *Efes* draft and they walked out through the folded glass doors onto the promenade to choose a table facing the surf as the waiter emerged carrying their beer and menus. After some indecision, Connie picked the pepper steak while Omer chose *kofte*. The waiter drew Connie's attention to a faint shape on the horizon that seemed to hover mirage-like. That was the Greek island of Rhodes! he told her, but Omer disagreed. He and Connie clicked glasses then—*Cheers!*—and drew close to each other to watch the slanting sun, now only a liquid ball of pulsating light low in the sky; its last effulgence in scattered retreat over the sea's slow roll, as the headlands darkened and became flat two-dimensional shapes against a crimson sky. It was perhaps the loveliest sunset she had ever seen and she was glad she was here, glad to be held like this by Omer whom she loved and always would! Thinking *if she were a kitten and could purr, she would, now.*

Chapter 2

IT HAD NEVER OCCURRED TO her that she would ever be cold in Turkey. Until now summer heat had been the problem. But hardly had the sun dropped below the headland before darkness came on bringing with it a chilling cold. And it wasn't the cold as such, said Omer, it was the dampness both felt as they returned to the restaurant and picked a table close to the wood stove which the waiters had since lit. Omer watched her move closer to it. "Just have to get used to sweaters, Connie."

That meant inside their apartment too, she was to discover. Stone buildings were plain cold! By burning the space heaters you could make the living room bearable, but the bedroom remained like a refrigerator. Don't they put central heat in anywhere? Connie had asked. "In a few houses, but never apartments—it would be too expensive," Omer told her. "Now if you bought the apartment while it was being built and before the floor tiles were put down, you could have the pipes specially laid. Here you would have to run them out in the open and they're hot don't forget. Installing the radiators wouldn't be a problem, but where would you put the boiler? Or the tank for the diesel? It just doesn't stay cold here long enough to justify the expense, even for Turks who can afford it."

She couldn't imagine living in a house in the UK and being unable to heat it. "So how long will it stay cold like this, Omer?"

"Till the end of March. Or April."

She counted. "Four months of having to live in a cold unheated apartment!" She hadn't foreseen this, "I thought you said it didn't get cold here, Omer!"

"I know. But I didn't want to make you unhappy, *Schatz*."

"So you lied instead." Hadn't Alice emailed her that if a Turk thought saying the truth would hurt, he will make up a lie to please you!—sensing affirmation in the innocence of those beguiling black eyes that Connie knew wanted her unequivocally without pretext, without the need for a right or wrong—and that she also sensed she could not refuse. "It's a small matter," she said to dismiss it. "When I get cold I'll just have to huddle up next to you."

But as she began turning it over in her mind, she was assailed by her first doubt: no matter the motive behind it, it was still deception and for that she had abandoned, simply thrown aside, all she had ever known—her life as a teacher and what friends she still had. She had committed serious theft (though Charles deserved it!) and so could not return to Manchester. Forced to hide, she might never see Alice again!

Where was her daughter at this moment? What would she be thinking? That her mother had mysteriously vanished and taken the money from Charles' stock certificates with her? Or perhaps Charles hadn't yet discovered the certificates were missing: that he had only glanced at the bundle of copies Connie had left in their place and so was not yet suspicious. But he would be—it was only a question of time before he discovered what she had done to him *and call the police?* But they already had her down as missing probably. Charles would have contacted Alice who would immediately notify the police. Of course, they could not possibly know where the money was—where she kept it hidden. *Even so* she thought, she should have the remainder of the money transferred as soon as possible and the account in England closed (unless she decided to keep some back?). Finance said it could take up to five days to transfer money. Then she would just have to go to the bank each day and ask: Is it here yet? She really wanted to phone Alice to tell her she was quite safe and happy here with Omer and not to worry about her. She wanted to, she felt terrible over what she had done to Alice but as she lay in bed beside her sleeping Omer and huddled against him not just for his physical warmth, but to draw reassurance from his incorrigible optimism (which too was a defining Turkish trait, she thought), she knew she couldn't do that either.

As the sun of early morning slanted onto her bed and brought its healing warmth, last night's fears retreated. How different it was waking to sunlight! she thought as she rose, slipped inside her bathrobe, and went to find Omer. He was already preparing breakfast. "I'm just frying you your bacon, Connie," he said as he greeted her with the *Omer smile.*

"You know I like to be spoiled!" she confessed.

"And I like nothing better than to spoil the girl!" he returned as he began carrying over dishes and plates: sliced tomatoes and cucumbers; olives and cold meats decoratively arrayed. Her bacon he brought last and separate. "Oh, and Captain Ali called me on his *handy*. I was right—he sailed the *Gul* to Finike for the winter as I thought."

"And he still wants us to buy it?"

"If not us then somebody else. He's got no choice."

"Did he say for how much?"

"No, I don't know, Connie. We have to make him an offer. But only one problem: to do that we have to go to Finike somehow and negotiate."

"When?"

"That we have to figure out. Right now Mehmet wants his car back."

"Then we'll be carless—?"

"That's the problem; you just touched it. We can take the bus there. But then what do we do, *Schatz?*"

"Can't we rent a car? Or better yet, lease one like you can in England."

"No, Connie, Turkey isn't England (I wish it was.). Either we buy one, or each time we need a car we have to borrow it or find some Turk to rent it off."

"And I suppose we'll be needing one—?"

"Unfortunately, *Schatz*. I just didn't want to burden you."

"For two people who love each other it's no burden," said Connie who had another thought, "Do you still have your silver stand?"

"I do. I could always sell it. Trouble is, nobody has much money. It's the wrong time of year. How's your breakfast, *Schatzi?*"

"Delicious! Tell the cook as always, he knows exactly what Connie likes!"

Following breakfast they drove Mehmet's car back into Fethiye for a final shopping tour before Omer surrendered it. She still needed to buy a coat badly and she had practically no shoes; certainly nothing she could go out dancing in! Her purchases made, they had shopped for a week's groceries before returning to the apartment. Hardly were they upstairs, the car unloaded, before Omer's handy rang and she watched him answer, "*Efendim..Evet, evet. Tamam!*" He dropped the phone back into his pocket: "Connie, that was Mehmet."

—wanting his car, she knew. "But how will you get back?"

"Walk. I'm used to it."

She followed him out onto the landing to give him a kiss before the stairs. There were three more doors on the landing and before each stood a neat row of shoes. The landing looked cold and felt dank; a place more for mildew, and whatever else that sought cold damp places. Why did the Turks always leave their shoes outside in the wet and cold, she wondered. It was alright to do that in summer, but *winter?*

She returned to the apartment—alone, and by herself for the first time she realized as she allowed her mind to wander about the room aimlessly. It was even a pleasant apartment (or would have been had it not been quite so cold); light and airy, and she realized what a difference it made to her whole outlook to wake and find, in place of cold grey skies and rain, sunshine and brightness! He had picked this apartment for her, he said because of its location, so close to the sea; and because, by his own admission, she would have found the place he'd lived prior to this intolerable. What had he meant by *intolerable?* She still knew nothing about him or his life, how he lived or on what? She only knew that he was the most seductive male she had ever met including her first ex; including even Juan upon whom she had lavished (and wasted) her love. And now because of it and because of wanting to swim, she had cast aside all she had so painstakingly constructed since to keep her safe from further harm: her teaching career. Alice. But what really did she know of him?

That as a child he had been given the boot by his Fundamentalist father and had learned to survive somehow. She could almost picture him, a sort of present day Oliver Twist forced to exist by which ever means, wit or cunning, in the streets and back alleys of Berlin. Then, still a teenager, being caught by the police for something and deported, to arrive finally (cast up, he said, like a *Yanko*) on Turkey's shores. And, like Yanko, he had married a young girl after making her pregnant—only the family had misunderstood him (or something) so the three had fled somewhere. Antalya, she thought, where the baby daughter had died in his arms, in a bus crash while he was on his way to somewhere else. And some place in there was his stint in the military and coming here to Fethiye for an undisclosed (and apparently unrelated) reason and somehow discovering that he ought to have inherited property from a dead grandfather that would (and still could) make him wealthy. Evocative images in themselves, she thought, but how did they relate? Where did they lead? They were like incomplete episodes. Like random parts of a puzzle in which many of its pieces still were missing. Yet she had trusted him with her life, quite literally when they had entered the lagoon together and she had allowed him to take her out beyond her depth.

What else did she know of him? That he owed money to one or more Turks but attached to it apparently little importance (and certainly no urgency). That they still owed the store for most of the clothes she had just purchased. He had insisted they pay the bill off a little per week. *Why?* when she could have paid it in full—the money was still in her purse! Lastly, he had traded his car for this apartment which, as she cast her eyes about, also told her little.

Upon closer look, the furniture, what there was, looked well used—perhaps it had always been in the apartment. There was a small unused fireplace tucked into one corner, its opening, which was tunnel-shaped, plugged with a piece of cardboard cut to shape and not far from that was the television, set inside a finished wood cabinet that was large enough to hold a *CD* and a *VCR* player, but which now held odd books, some magazines and temporarily, her laptop.

For now the laptop was just there—useless since to plug it in would require an adapter to fit the Turkish wall socket and anyway, without a phone line she couldn't read her Hotmail (Omer had said, many places here didn't have phone lines because they were expensive to install, and now with *handies* you really didn't need them.). Not that she would risk reading her Hotmail even if she could. Being a computer whiz, Charles would have looked there first to see if she had left a trail. Alice would have emailed her. And/or Omer! But Omer wouldn't have given them away— and would have said something: *unless he had not yet been to the internet café.* She must ask. Warn him not to, she thought as she stared transfixed at the thin snapped-shut black case that she half suspected might yet lead her to undisclosed grief and anguish. Underneath she still felt guilty and were it not for Charles, she would rush to the nearest internet café. Say to Alice *Please don't worry about me. Your Mum's never been happier! She's with Omer in Fethiye and things are just fine. PS: What was Charles' reaction?* No, she wouldn't add the PS even though the question worked upon her fears. Except for Charles, Connie would already have emailed Alice telling her everything.

She turned then to the few books, and magazines which she thumbed through: *Vogue* and *Vanity*—except they were in Turkish. There were even a few English magazines mixed in, old and badly dog-eared, and she doubted they could be Omer's as she set them aside to examine the books. One because of its gold edge and quality binding caught her attention, and she reached for it: the Koran. She had never held a Koran before—it vaguely interested her because of its foreignness. She sat down with it but discovered as she began thumbing its pages that it too was in Turkish. What did she expect? she thought as she turned still carrying it to the bedroom.

With the sun now gone from that side of the building, it felt cold! Laying the Koran down at the edge of the dresser, she crossed to the window, and reached for the space heater below to turn it to high, that would take the chill off in minutes, she thought as she glanced about the room trying to decide. She would look at his clothes hanging in the closet first. But there wasn't much there really that was his: two quite dressy suits— one might even have been new. Slacks, but mostly jeans.

She turned away, turning to the dresser now. In one of the drawers she found swimming suits and his underwear and, hidden perhaps at the bottom, some photographs. One was of an older woman—his mother? Possibly. There was a group photo taken on a boat, all wearing swimming gear—his diving days? Another was of him and a woman, maybe thirty, Connie thought. His arm was around her and both smiled: was she English or Turkish, Connie wondered as she laid the photo aside and reached for a silver locket and chain she saw next to it. *Whose?* She didn't think it was from his silver stand judging from its age and condition. He hadn't mentioned the stand any more except to say he still hadn't sold it. But it was on that business card he had showed the clothing store manager that first afternoon and he was listed as owner, she was nearly sure. *Omer, I want you here!* Where are you? she thought as she walked to the kitchen to pour herself a glass of wine and wait.

If he didn't have his key he would push the buzzer telling her to trip the lock downstairs before he could enter. *Do you know what I'm going to do with you, Omer, do you!*

The Meri Bar was a long block in from the beach and one of the more popular places of Chalis, both to the English and the Turks. As Omer pulled the car up before the curb, he could see Mehmet at one of the outside tables, enjoying an *Efes.* Plunking the car keys down before his friend of long standing, Omer ordered himself a beer and sat down. "So how did it go?" asked Mehmet.

"It couldn't have gone better!"

He had met Mehmet seven years earlier in Marmaris when his friend had occasionally spelled for him as bartender during that brief time he had lived with another English woman, Angela, his first, and they had taken over the lease of a bar. When the venture failed and the pair split, and Omer had decided to try Fethiye, and diving, Mehmet found a job waiting tables in a restaurant there and so followed him.

"What did you say her name was again?"

"Connie."

"And she's really going to buy you a gulet?"

"It's what she wants." Omer reached for his beer feeling Mehmet's eyes interrogate him. He knew the direction of his friend's thought. "If God's willing," he added and turned silent. He enjoyed his friend's envy.

"What's she like?"

"Nice. She was a schoolteacher. I don't know what she's like in school, but I know where she likes to be! Plus she's not that old. She's still got a good figure—tits might be small."

"Bet she's not as good as Doreen. Doreen can fuck!"

"But Doreen is a fat cow and those aren't tits she has—they're udders!"

"I saw Doreen in Fethiye two nights ago," said Mehmet, staggering out of Bea's. I wonder what she does for money?"

"She gets a pension in England is about all I know." Omer reached for his beer glass, "I've got to get back."

"Now May was the one with the nicest tits I've ever seen on any fifty-year-old. Wonder what happened to May?"

"She went back to England I guess because she had no choice. She ran out of money and from what I heard, her husband agreed to take her back again." Omer swallowed the last of his beer and rose.

"Then you think you'll stay with this new one, Omer?

"Yes!" *So don't get any hopes up—this isn't like Doreen.* "This time it's different, and I *do* like her. She's not been spoiled. Now I really have to!"

He turned out onto the street in the closing darkness of early night and walked fast, hurrying it would take him less than ten minutes. *Yes Mehmet!*

he intended to keep her, he thought because for him her love seemed new and refreshingly different. She remained unsoiled—if only because she had not yet been passed from hand to hand. *Yes,* that was why he found her love so pleasing, because he was its recipient. Because never had he met a woman who could love with such intense abandon. In a sense she was like a precious but fragile cargo that had been entrusted just to him for its care and now, in return, he would watch and protect her—keep her away from Turks! he vowed as he turned into the dirt street before their apartment complex.

The way was unlit and he had to choose his path carefully in the dark. Fethiye had had two days of heavy thunder showers the day before Connie arrived and there were still a few standing puddles, and places where car tires had churned the earth into mud. Omer knew where the puddles were and avoided them. The muddy patches he traversed as though he were walking over egg shells and trying his best not to break them, until he stood once more on clean concrete before the apartment building's outer door which remained securely locked night or day to discourage any would=be robbers. Burglaries were always a problem in winter particularly because so few had money. Omer pushed the button for their apartment, waited.

Heard almost immediately the lock click free and pushed his way inside—she had been listening for him.

"Omer, I've been waiting!" she said down to his head, the swarm of black hair as it appeared in the mid-landing below, "Is it cold?"

"Brr!" he said and smiled up at her as he climbed the last few stairs to their floor. They kissed, then he bent and removed his shoes at the door just as he had always done, dirty or clean, since he was a small child. In the kitchen he found the salad made, the food out and the lamb chops waiting for him to grill them. "Don't you know how to cook, Connie?" he asked, his impression being that she didn't.

"Not like you do, Omer. I did only because I had to for myself and Alice (Charles being a vegetarian). You haven't stopped by an Internet café—?"

"For what?" But he knew from her face: "Alice."

"I wonder if she knows I'm here?"

"Connie, it's been done, and you can't go back. You know we were made for each other's arms, just as sure as there is paradise. We'll be happy together, *Schatz*. I'll make you happy! Starting tonight." He knew how to bring women around if they were sad or having other thoughts, and she was no exception. "Come here to Omer." He opened his arms to her, beckoning. They held each other and kissed, he slowly rubbing her back up and down, caressingly as he whispered close, "We only have each other, it's all we have in this world and all we need—each other, Connie. Tell yourself we'll be happy together and we will! Tell yourself like I tell myself, every day, every hour. *Do it* and wait for tonight. I'm going to make love to you like you've never had love made to you I promise. *Tonight!*"—seeing her eyes shine in the radiance of her anticipation as he released her finally and turned back to their dinner. "What kind of wine should we open, Connie, for this special occasion?"

"Is it special, Omer?"

"*Very* special, as I intend to show you, *Schatz*."

"Do you?" She liked Omer when he was in this mood. "Then why not champagne?"

"Sorry, we drank it all, *Schatz*," he said looking up at her. When he chose to, he could look so apologetic, she thought and remembered there was a bottle of white wine still.

They sat down across from each other then, his eyes repeatedly seeking hers, holding them with their signalled intent which her own eyes could read from his secretive depth, alive with the desire she too felt. Supper soon over and the last swallow of wine drunk, Connie rose and started to collect the dishes.

"Leave them!" he said had drew her by the hand from the kitchen.

"Where we going?" She had thought to the bedroom. "Shower first. Did you put the heat on in our room?"

"I had it on earlier."

"I'll turn it back on. You just get undressed."

She obediently did as told. Showers with Omer were events in themselves and how she looked forward to the way he so methodically soaped then washed and rinsed every inch of her. How she loved to be touched—loved it just to feel his body rub against hers amid the cascading warmth of water plashing over them and seeing his dark eyes—their boyish excitement as he reached to turn the water off:

"Come, *Schatz!*" Then he was towelling her dry, and in the cold, both ran back along the hall to their warm bedroom. Before the bed, both stopped. She waited watching him climb in first. How she loved just seeing him. The amazing thing to her was when he tried, how long he could hold it. Hold it and hold it. Just the opposite of Charles. With Charles, it was over in minutes. Or less. She didn't want to have to think about Charles any longer.

It's you I love! she thought watching him spread himself out on the bed and wait for her. She tried to think of something completely unexpected that she could do—that would amuse both. She wished she just had some whipping cream—why did she not think ahead and buy a can! *Never mind* she crawled slowly over the bed toward him as though she were stalking: she knew to a science what she must do to make him first moan, then cry "Do that, keep doing *that!*"

"*This* you mean?" But he suddenly pulled away from her: "What is that?"

"What is *what ?*" Looking up, she followed his finger to where it pointed. "The book, you mean?"

"That is my Koran—!"

"Yes. I was glancing through it earlier."

"Well, it shouldn't be in here!"

"No? Why?"

"It just shouldn't, Connie."

She felt him disentangle himself. "Where are you going?" she said, watching as he rose.

"To put it back. It needs to be set in a high place alright. But it can't be in here while we're having sex, Connie."

Chapter 3

BUT WHY? CONNIE PUZZLED OVER afterward unless in their religion sex and guilt were in some way entwined, and that could only lead to Freud!—though *how* exactly she would probably never find out. The answer, when she finally did stumble onto it, astounded her.

December was to be a near perfect month: the temperatures like Manchester at the end of April, or May even, as they would stroll the Promenade afternoons dressed just in shirtsleeves, Omer holding her, and gaze down at the water lapping against the beach. Even so, at unconscious times a certain longing for things of her English past—moments, faces she'd loved and that were now gone, forever banished—left her not depressed exactly, not regretting what she had done, but moody somehow—taciturn. Christmas was one such day; her first without a lit tree and presents, without seeing Christmas decorations in all the stores, or feeling any Santa Claus cheer. In Turkey it was just another working day and they spent it along the beach drinking beers at Anna Bar, planning their future. "Today's Boxing Day," she remembered aloud.

"What's Boxing Day? That's something they don't have in Germany. Is that when you give presents, *Schatz?*"

"No it's the day after Christmas. In England we give the presents on Christmas Day."

"Do you miss Christmas, Connie?"

"Not exactly." She wondered where her daughter was at this moment and what she would be doing. Would she think of her mother on Christmas? Connie wished she could email. "There were good things about it. Christmas parties we would go to when I was younger (with my first husband). Opening the presents…You didn't do that in Germany either?"

"No, Connie, only the Germans. Turks just celebrate Ramadan." He paused…"I know!"

"What, Omer?" Something would come—she knew from his eyes.

"Don't you want something for Christmas, Connie?" he asked her, and that evening he was constantly on his handy making or receiving calls in Turkish, calls she sensed had to do with her. The next morning she watched him mysteriously prepare to leave and asked *to where?*

"I can't tell you, Connie, except it involves your Christmas surprise—remember? Oh, and I'll need your credit card."

Suspicious, she went nevertheless for her purse. "Shouldn't I come? I'll need to sign it won't I?"

"No-o, Connie, all of Fethiye knows by now that you're with me. Word travels. But I do need your pin number."

She wrote it onto a scrap of paper and followed him out as far as the stairs. "When will you be back?"

"I don't know. If you go somewhere don't forget to take your *handy*. —Are you?"

"I may go to the beach," she called after him and watched his thick mane of lustrous dark hair disappear on the mid landing. To have questioned him on how he was going to use the Visa Card would have led to the notion that somehow she mistrusted him, and that was the very last thing she wanted! But there was that other simultaneous thought in the back of her mind: that he was good at manipulating people. She couldn't help it. Turning the card over to him still made her uneasy as she set out for the beach. She wasn't worried about money *as such*, not with all but the few thousand having safely arrived, she had decided to leave in England for the present and her bankbook now showing almost eighty thousand pounds. Plus add to that the fifteen thousand she had sent to Omer. Possibly it was the idea that she would soon be forced to hand most of it over to Captain Ali (she assumed she would have to pay cash for the boat). That must be why, she decided, because, though the *Gul* would be hers (*theirs!*) it would not earn them even one Turkish lira before May at the earliest and now Omer was out apparently buying her a Christmas present. She feared it would be nothing simple and inexpensive like a dress (which reminded her of that clothing store bill still to be paid). Or a necklace and matching earrings from his silver stand which would cost nothing—unless of course he kept it empty over the winter and that she didn't know—he never once talked about it. But he would have to store the silver somewhere—*where* she would be curious to know. Why did he not he not show her the stand? She was eager to find out everything she could about her lover, even the secrets he kept—and know him like she knew herself.

The beach appeared deserted except for two Turkish peasant women she observed down at water's edge. Both were very old and needed canes fashioned from lengths of a tree branch in order to walk: the one, she noticed, walked almost doubled over with osteoporosis. They were searching the beach for anything of value the tide might have brought in and it was amazing to see just how much weight they could carry on their backs even bent over: loads of twigs and firewood. Trash found in garbage cans. On two occasions since her arrival, Connie had watched them carefully pick through garbage inside those large metal bins placed at the edge of the road near street corners usually, and had wondered what they thought—what went through their heads, seeing her in turn? Only the simplest, most rudimentary thoughts: what passed through the minds of small children raised from the time they were toddlers in the fields to be little more than work animals in their headscarves and their loose shapeless brown or grey pyjamalike tops and bloomer bottoms (she doubted any of them had ever worn a bra or even knew what one was.). And what did they see when they saw her, Connie. Did they see a Western woman who dressed to make herself look attractive, and who kept her face cared for and clean? Nothing, not even the curiosity that she herself had for them, and so there could be no communication. Connie drew her attention elsewhere.

At the opposite end of the beach from Anna Bar she had discovered a small café that opened each afternoon, and she turned toward it seeing a new couple sitting at one of the tables before the water, the man drinking an *Efes*. Curious, Connie approached and introduced herself. They were Americans, from Seattle said the woman, and had come here to Turkey to explore the ancient sites. Connie decided to join them and had just sat down, hadn't had time even to order, when her handy began to play *Eine Kleine Nacht Musik*. She dug for it in her purse and opened, "Hello, love!"

"*Schatz*, where are you? Come to the Anna Bar then walk through to the back *now!*"

It took her only minutes to find the Anna Bar which she quickly passed through to the rear, then out the back door to the parking lot behind. She heard a car horn and, turning, saw a new- looking sedan with its driver's-side door standing open and someone motioning at her. Omer! She rushed over.

"So how do you like your Christmas present, Connie?"

A gleaming white Toyota *Corona* less than two years old! More by luck than anything he had chanced upon its owner, Omer said, a Turk about to lose his business and in need of cash, desperate to sell! "I hope you're not disappointed, Schatz? But get in! And do you have your bankbook?"

She wasn't angry. They would need a car and, if anything, she was pleased as she walked around to the passenger's side. "How much does he want for this?" asked Connie as she got in opposite her lover.

"He started out asking twenty-five thousand, but by promising him cash I got him down to nineteen finally," Omer told her. "It's a good price for here, Connie—about what you'd pay for a car of this kind in Istanbul. And that's why we have to get to the bank!"

"So you didn't need my credit card after all—?"

"Oh yes I did, Connie, it was that credit card that swung the deal! When I showed it to him and he read your name and saw you were English, that was when he believed me—when he decided to hand me the car keys. Look and see if you've got that bankbook, Connie!"

She didn't. So the first stop then would be their apartment. "I'll just double park in front of the bank while you go in, *Schatz*. And once we've got the money, I'll just drop you back at the apartment and then go on."

"You don't need me to come?"

"Just to hand him the money? No, why?"

"But there has to be more to it than that, Omer!"

"Oh there is, *Schatz*, it gets complicated. First we go to the police for the *klegi* which is a paper saying the owner can sell the car—that there are no fines against it. Then we find a notary who makes up the papers for the sale. Then after we both sign and I pay the car taxes, it's back to the police."

"But you'll need me to sign the papers if the car is in my name."

"No, Connie. Because it has to be in my name."

"Why your name?"

"Because you need to be here six months. Then you apply for residency, and we can put the papers in your name then if you still want. We're together now, *Schatz*, we're like one don't forget!" *I love you, Omer* she thought, and gave his hand a squeeze.

It was already late in the afternoon as Omer double-parked and Connie rushed inside. The money drawn, he dropped her back at the apartment to wait. She had waited and waited pouring herself first one glass of wine, then another as she watched the sun slowly drop behind the adjacent apartments and the last afterglow fade and become dusk. Then dark. With night came the cold. She turned on the space heater in the living room and sat close to it, looking repeatedly at her watch: *Where was he and what was he doing all this time? The notary must be closed,* she thought and refilled her glass. She was not worried exactly. But as night progressed she began to. This wasn't like Omer!

She remembered his *handy* and decided to try phoning him. But he didn't answer—instead a woman's voice came on. It sounded like a message, but the words were in Turkish. She could only wait. Then at a little past eleven, to her relief she finally heard the bell that told her to release the lock downstairs. She had and waited at the top of the stair; and when she saw him in the mid landing below, she could sense at once from his loose walk, and by his grin, that he had been drinking. As he kissed her she knew from the liquorish taste on his lips, "You've had raki!"

"I have, I wouldn't hide it from you, Connie. But only because I was forced to. Ahmed forced me!"

"Who's Ahmed?"

"Another Turk I know," he said grinning.

"Obviously. So what were you doing with Ahmed?"

"He wanted to see the new car we bought. You bought."

"So let me understand: You phoned this Ahmed."

"No, Connie. I phoned Ishmael and Ishmael phoned Ahmed." She was beginning to see. "So you were out all this time showing off the new car to your friends!" She knew by his eyes, by the devilish, carefree way they looked back at her. She ought to be angry with him, "I was beginning to worry. I tried phoning you."

"Guess I must have my phone shut off, *Schatz*. Sorry," he said as he pulled her to him and kissed his apology.

"Next time just phone me, Omer, so I won't worry. You do know, if something ever happened to you, I'd be completely helpless."

"Really sorry, *Schatz.*" But it irritated him that she had wanted him to account for his time—having lived all his life free of such constraints. Angela too had demanded to know where he was at practically every minute—always afraid, he supposed, that he might be with another woman.

Chapter 4

IT WAS THREE DAYS BEFORE their new car registration showing Omer as the owner was ready, three days before they could leave for Finike. In the meanwhile, curious about his silver stand, Connie had asked several times to see it. They were in Fethiye anyway. "Is there a reason you don't want me to now?" she said and saw his surprise.

"No, Connie, it's just a stand—you've been there. I would show it to you now except it's locked up and the key is at home. Tomorrow I'll show you when we come again to see about our car papers. *Schatzi* don't forget, nothing happens fast in Turkey. Tomorrow *ja?*"

To reach the silver stand, they had to practically pass Bea's. Connie was still afraid to go in.

Afraid someone really was looking for her: Alice (who should be attending class at Leeds, perhaps even as she and Omer strolled arm-in-arm), or Charles? Or *Interpol!* "Don't be silly, Connie!" Omer told her. "Bea knows you're here and is probably wondering why you haven't shown your face. You can't keep anything a secret—not in Fethiye!—and if somebody is looking for you, don't you think I would have heard?" So she agreed to at least stop and show herself to Bea.

"I say, that is you, Constance! You did come back just as I predicted you would!"

She knew Eric's voice before she discovered the face or saw the hand wave. Beside him sat Maureen, smiling, nearly upsetting her drink as she raised her hand in shaky greeting. "Ignore them," whispered Omer. Then Bea's aged pleasant face and welcoming blue eyes were before her:

"I've been expecting you!"

"I wanted to come before this," Connie lied, "but just haven't found time." The part of Bea that never changed was the candour Connie found in those mild blue eyes, warm, they never left yours. Bea's was a face you could confide in and trust.

"So you're here now—to stay? What brought you back?" said the smile.

"A gulet I fell in love with and have decided to buy." Connie saw the surprise.

"Ouh, that's ambitious!" said Bea, but stopped herself as if there had been something more she had wanted to tell her thought Connie, Bea saying instead only, "I wish you all the success! What can I get you to drink?"

"Two *Efes*," said Omer. "The boat's a good investment, Bea. It can't help but make money," he added as, their *Efes* drunk, they rose to face another busy day, Omer reassured her.

"Come back when you have more time."

"I will, Bea, promise!" Connie said as she rose. If only she were a mind-reader and could know what Bea had decided to *not* say, she thought.

Omer's silver stand was just across the narrow strip of park then midway down the deserted quay before which the unattended swimming boats in their wintry sleep were moored. Many of the cafes too were closed. "In here, Connie:" Omer leading her by the hand.

She counted possibly ten stands, five on either side separated by an interlocking mosaic of cast concrete stone. Omer's was the third stand on the right: closed and padlocked by plywood doors. Omer undid the padlock and as he drew the two doors apart Connie discovered a deep slanting shelf at the center displaying all kinds of jewellery from earrings to rings and necklaces. The plywood doors when spread wide, formed wings with additional displays, and drawer space beneath.

Behind the display, backing it, was a continuous mirror. Connie began to look through the jewellery, reaching for a piece here, there. Mostly it was only junk she was examining. "You don't have pierced ears, Connie, do you?"

"No—why?" She could see her Omer begin opening drawers, rummaging for something.

"I don't know why I didn't think of these. See if you like them, Connie. They're good ones—sterling. Try them on."

Earrings! Concave, rectangular in shape, they resembled miniature shields: something Spanish knights might have carried into battle back in the Middle Ages! They had that look of quality, she thought fastening them to her ears, admiring their elegance before the mirror.

"They're gorgeous, Omer!"

"Then they're yours, my *Schatz!*" he said and drew her to him. "Happier now?"

Their car papers arrived at Traffic Police that afternoon and next morning they left for Finike, Connie driving while Omer sat rapt, smiling beside her. From the pocket of his jeans she heard music and she glanced over to see him dug for his *handy*—there was always somebody calling him:

"Afendim?..."

She listened. It was a short conversation, all in Turkish. "Captain Ali sends his greetings, Connie," said Omer as he pushed the phone back into his pocket.

"He knows we're on our way—?"

"Of course, *Schatz.*"

Her thoughts turned back to his silver stand. "What I fail to understand, Omer, is what made you want to buy the stand?"

"I didn't buy it, Connie. It was given to me."

"By whom? When?"

"After I had my accident."

"Diving, you mean?"

"Yes, at the mosque during Friday afternoon prayers. I was telling this one businessman about what happened. I don't know how much property he owns but he has to be one of the richest Turks in Fethiye. Connie, he oozes money!"

She guessed she must have known from the start that he wasn't a disbeliever. But when she saw for the first time on that lovely afternoon, when they had climbed together up to the ruins, that his pubic hair had been shaven, she should have realized then what she did now. "So you attend the mosque!"

"Just sometimes, Connie—it's where you go to conduct business."

"You're saying that mosques are to Islam what golf courses are to the *West*—?" She saw his thoughtful look.

"I never considered at it that way since I don't play golf, Connie. But *why not?* Here if you're somebody important you go to Friday prayers. Why I went."

"And while at *Friday prayers* somebody gave you his silver stand—?"

"After I told him about getting the bends and not being able to dive. He wanted to be rid of it anyway, Connie. It belonged to one of his renters.

But the renter had a bad season and couldn't pay him the rent he owed. So he offered Suleyman (that's the landlord) his silver stand instead. Suleyman I don't think wanted it—not with his money!—but he took it anyway since it was all the poor bastard had left to his name."

"So this landlord with *nothing but money* accepted what quickly became an Albatross which he then transferred to around your neck," mused Connie.

"What's an albatross?"

"A bird—I don't know its Turkish name. But it's famous because of a poem: *The Rhyme of the Ancient Mariner* by Coleridge." But she could sense his disinterest.

"A head's the roundabout. You want to stay right, Connie, and follow the Antalya sign. That other way leads into the mountains."

Now and again she had glimpsed snow. It was another sunny clear day—a perfect day to drive and look at the sun-lit peaks, their snow in the late afternoon appearing soft and creamy, like whipping cream from a distance, she thought. Even so, her lingering concerns were over the mosque; something besides making or inheriting money must have drawn him there and even if he didn't show it, Omer must be somewhat religious—though not to the point of it becoming a problem, Connie decided. In fact, so free of religion had he appeared to her initially that she had had to ask, Are you a Muslim *really,* until that night when he had stopped in the middle of their lovemaking to remove the Koran.

She supposed, thinking back, she had been misled because of his German upbringing, and the fact that he had fought with his fundamentalist father who in the end had kicked him out for being disrespectful and for breaking Muslim taboos. That and his insistence on being not Turkish at all but an outcast—a Yanko! Curious, she asked him finally, "Then why are you still Muslim?"

"We all have to believe in something, Connie."

"No we don't. I don't for one. Religious doctrine is riddled with contradiction, and to know that all you have to do is apply a bit of Aristotelian logic."

"Who's that?"

"You don't know who Aristotle is?" She saw his headshake. "A famous Greek philosopher who taught us deductive logic. The syllogism: how, from two knowns you can deduce other secondary truths and expose lies. For example, if we say that God is '*good*'—"

"We don't. *We* say, 'God is great!'"

"'Great' then—okay. But supposing we're in a mosque praying and there's an earthquake. The mosque is destroyed and the people inside killed. If God is so 'great' we have to ask, then why did He allow the earthquake to happen if, supposedly, He is all-powerful? There can be only two possible answers and, if we're to avoid contradiction, we have to choose between them." She glanced across and though his eyes bore a smile, they seemed to be looking at something in the distance. "You're not following!"

"No I was thinking."

"Omer! I want you to listen. Remember that afternoon when I left the Koran in the bedroom by mistake? Why can't you have sex in the same room with the Koran is what I still want to know. Well, *why?*"

"Just because...Allah might see."

"You're saying He disapproves of sex or *what?*"

"I don't know, Connie, if he doesn't or does."

"Another thing—" she could see his agitation, "Why are you supposed to shave your balls before entering a mosque? Does Allah dislike pubic hair too?"

"I don't know, Connie, the reason. All I know is that you're supposed to shave—not just down there but your armpits too."

"How about facial hair?"

"No, you can have hair on your face."

"So explain for me that logic! The Koran and Bible both say that God made us, that we're His creation, His children. Only He's offended by that creation because it has hair in the wrong places. Is it fair to ask, just *what* is God's problem?"

"Connie, don't go around saying any of this to Turks because it can get you in trouble! You can to me and it's all right because I know you don't understand. You're a Christian."

"There you're wrong! And I resent it when people automatically assume I am. My father was a nonbeliever and so am I! He was a good man; kind, considerate. Not once did he raise his voice or ever mistreat me." *Omer what are you doing?* She could feel his fingers trying to find their way between her legs and she relaxed her thighs to help him.

Chapter 5

AFTER KAS, THE ROAD CLIMBED steeply inland and for a time left the sea. Despite the intense heat of summer, the terrain was surprisingly green, thought Connie, up-and-down rolling country like Scotland, except that the hillsides here were steeper and frequently broken by rocky extrusions, the lustreless green of the canopy occasionally infused with the blue grey of olive tree branches. They were approaching Demre, ancient Mira in Roman times, Omer had started to say. But they were interrupted by music coming again from his pocket. He removed his hand and she watched him dig for his phone. *"Afendim?"* he said into it but immediately switched to a different language.

German, she thought as she listened. "Who was that?" she asked as he finished: "You weren't speaking Turkish."

"No, Connie, she's German."

"She—?"

"Just somebody I knew. There are almost as many Germans living in Fethiye as English. I'm sure you don't know her, she's elderly. Look down, Connie!"

They were descending a long, winding curve with the Mediterranean again visible in the distance. Immediately below she saw hothouses, endless hothouses! They were mostly for tomatoes, Omer told her. Turkey, at least along the coast, seemed an endless vista of orange trees followed immediately by more hothouses. The fruits and vegetables you bought here at roadside stands from farmers and in town square markets tasted ever so much better than they did in cold, sunless England! As they entered Demre Omer pointed to the road sign ahead. "Do you want to see Santa Claus, Connie—at least his church? It's still there." The sign, brown and in the shape of an arrow, pointed and as they drove past it Connie read 'Baba Noel,' *Father Christmas.*

Finike was just twelve kilometres. But the road narrowed, and became winding and twisty as it followed the sea—sometimes right beside it. Then the road twisted sharply upward, climbing, and she could look down again, see the sea break onto the rocks below. Close in it had a turquoise iridescence, but further out it was blue and sparkled in the sunlight.

She saw something closer in: a long filmy slick of unclean matter floating on the surface. The road twisted and turned back on itself again, and when they emerged, they were hugging the edge of a cliff and she could look down, spot yet another of those repulsive slicks. "Omer," she pointed: "are those what I think they are?"

"They are, *Schatz.*"

"And we're supposed to swim in that!"

In the distance Finike appeared, a band of whiteness against the curve of the sea and looking pretty enough as they entered! Its broad main street, split and with a row of shady palm trees down the middle, ran beside a sandy beach while, looking left, the buildings facing the sea were all freshly painted and clean— a rare sight in Turkey where, due to the high humidity, paint weathers and begins to flake often in just one winter. The yacht marina was to their right and Connie could see sailboat masts— a small forest of masts as Omer again dug for his handy and dialled: *Ali?*— she wished she could understand his calls!

"You want to go in *there*, Connie," said Omer, pointing as he slipped the phone back into his pocket. "Follow *that* sign to the harbour office."

"And that's where we're meeting Captain Ali?"

"No, Connie, at the Marina Restaurant—I'll tell you where to turn."

"Exactly how much is Ali asking, has he decided?"

"That's what we have to discuss, Connie. We'll start out by offering him sixty-five thousand, if he'll go that low, *Schatz.* — There's the restaurant! "The large A-framed structure; she had seen it. "So once we agree to a price, then what? We take Ali with us to the bank?"

"Wish it was that simple, *Schatz.* There's Ali!"

Like most Mediterranean peoples do, Turks greet one another in public by hugs or sometimes a kiss. Hardly had Connie stepped from their car before Ali had reached for her fingers and brought them up to his face, first to kiss the back of her hand, and then, bowing, touch the hand to his forehead. Connie had never been kissed that way before and found it puzzling. She wanted to see the *Gul* now, but it was late and day was already turning to dusk as they sat in the restaurant and made plans for tomorrow, Ali drinking tea while she and Omer had *Efes*; and afterward, after they had risen and paid, alone again in the parking lot she asked Omer about the kiss.

That was how Turks kissed older people, Omer responded. It was a show of respect.

Older? "I'm not that old!" she objected. Just the implication left her feeling as though she had been unexpectedly struck. It was a topic she did not want to go near!

The next thing would be to find a hotel. Ali had suggested his: the *2000* which they had passed coming in. It sat high up on a hill and from its rooftop restaurant you could look down on the marina with its sailboats and yachts from all over the Mediterranean, and beyond. There they could have dinner together while they discussed business.

Small, owned by a middle-aged couple, it turned out to be a pleasant hotel with a large comfortable room, balcony overlooking the sea, and a huge king-sized bed that she fell immediately in love with. She could hardly wait to try it! *Omer, are we thinking the same thing?* She tried to catch his eye, but he was lost in conversation with the landlady who, like him, had been raised in Germany and also spoke fluent German. *Omer!*

It was a splendid little hotel! she thought as, arms linked, they climbed the crimson carpeting to the restaurant above where they were joined by Captain Ali. The landlady was also the cook and after Omer conferred with her in German, he announced he would order for Connie too: German dumplings and bratwurst. Connie had never eaten German food before. She had seen a wine rack at the entrance to the dining room and suggested he pick something. But Omer ordered the landlady to choose for them, just so long as it was good; the price didn't matter! "In fact, bring the best you've got in the house!" Clearly, he was in a joyous mood—she could see it by his eyes!

The wine turned out only mediocre, at least to Connie's pallet, though Omer and Ali both praised it and the landlady was more than pleased when Omer immediately ordered a second bottle. Connie had begun to notice that not just the Turks, but the English living here too, drank cheap Turkish wines with the same relish they would something of more quality. Could they not distinguish?

Over dinner she watched the two talk, and sometimes argue, she thought—but wasn't sure, not understanding more than a few words. All she knew with certainty was that it concerned her because they kept glancing over to her. "Sorry, Connie, if it sounds like we're trying to leave you out," Omer said apologetically, "but Ali's English isn't very good." It had sounded quite good to her on the *Gul*, she remembered.

She rose and wandered across to the large windows facing the sea, the marina below with its myriad gleam of lights in cabin windows and from portholes. There were the green and red running lights, and lights at the top of masts too, that cast quivering reflections upon the sea's surrounding darkness. The sky above her glittered and there was a fragile moon floating amid the profusion of stars and she knew she loved it here with Omer, but she couldn't help it—she felt so vulnerable!

As Connie stood by the window looking down to the harbour and out at the night, Omer and Ali decided between them on a price for the gulet. Ali had wanted eighty thousand but Omer argued, "It's an old boat, Ali, and with what you make on the deal you can buy that thirty-three meter one like you want. We can't just strip her of everything!" And when he refused still, Omer had used his only remaining threat:

"I'm not going to let her pay that much, Ali. Now if somebody else wants the boat, fine! Or maybe you know some rich English woman…?" He saw Ali's gesture of slow resignation.

"We agreed on a price, Connie," said Omer as they returned holding each other to their room: "Seventy-five."

"Thousand *pounds?* And he wouldn't go any lower?"

"No-o, *Schatz*, the *Gul's* too good a boat. He could always sell it to someone else, don't forget. The only reason he's letting us have it for that is because he likes you."

"Does he!"

"But I told him, I made it quite clear, *you're mine, Schatzi!*"

She felt his squeeze and squeezed back, hard! "So do we get the money for him tomorrow morning?"

"No, my *Schatz.* Other things come first. First the boat needs to be inspected. Ali knows a certified inspector and is trying to get him for tomorrow morning."

"Omer, can we go too? Watch the boat get inspected?" She hadn't seen the *Gul* since last summer and in two days' time it would be *theirs!* "Omer, let's!"

The repair yard was a square of concrete perhaps the size of a football field and filled with boats of all descriptions resting on their keels on the cement she saw, while to the rear were some low buildings, an engine repair shop, carpenter shop, and the yard office where Captain Ali waited with the inspector.

They met there and, after introducing the inspector, Ali led them through the row of hulls braced upright by lengths of timber shoring, finally to the *Gul*. Out of the water and set in with other similar craft, Connie did not immediately recognize her. "It's that one, Connie," said Omer, and pointed. She would have walked past but there across her squared stern above those two pirate ship windows she liked and to the right of the gangplank that stood straight out, Connie read:

Gull II
Marmaris

"Why Marmaris, Omer?"

"That's its home port, Connie. It's where I used to live," he revealed before thinking better of it.

"Is that where you had the accident and now you can't dive?" And when she saw his head shake, "So when did you live in Marmaris then? Omer, you don't tell me anything!"

"I didn't think you were interested, Connie.—Anyway, *Schatz,* aren't you as happy as I am seeing our gulet again!"

She was and kissed him in thanks. Hand in hand they strolled beside the hull toward a ladder which leaned against the side of the ship and which Ali and the inspector had just gone up, to the deck above. It was a beautiful ship except, she noticed, in places the paint looked old and worn, its colour washed thin. "Does it need painting, Omer?"

"Not for a long time yet. The boat's only four years old," he said as they lingered beside the smoothness of its hull.

"What's the *Gul* made of, Omer—fiberglass? It looks so smooth."

"No, Connie, all Turkish boats are wood. Pine mostly—it's what the *Gul* is made from."

"Then why don't I see any seams?"

"Because the hull is coated in something called 'marja' which is a little like yogurt."

"I thought they had to calk boats—?"

"It's only calked once, on the inside when it's new. You cover the outside of the hull with marja to seal it, and that's what makes it so smooth.—Want to climb the ladder?"

It was of wood and very high, its top rungs resting against the deck where the swimming ladder normally would hang; that ladder she had lowered herself down to fall safe and secure into Omer's waiting arms that lovely summer! "Yes." But with each precarious step she took, the ladder would wobble beneath her. Holding onto every rung as if for her life, she forced herself to continue. Omer was just below her she knew, but she dared not glance down. Finally, she could reach and touch the handrail stanchions and pull herself up onto the deck beside the wheelhouse and look about.

At first the *Gul* seemed exactly as Connie remembered save that the sun mattresses and shade-awning had been removed. But then she noticed something different about the deck. The long narrow lengths of teak separated by thin veins of black calking no longer had their clean grey look but appeared to be coated with a greenish *something*. "I don't recall the deck ever like this, Omer. Look!" she said, sensing him now beside her. "That almost looks like slime!"

"It is, *Schatz*. That's what happens when it rains. Ali needs to wash the deck."

"Or I can. What do you use on it—a good detergent?"

"No, Connie, salt water. Rainwater is the worst thing there is for any boat, but sea water protects it. Once the *Gul* is back floating, you get a pail and tie a length of rope to it. You bring up pailfuls of sea water and pour them over the deck, then scrub. Keep doing that and the green comes off."

"Really? I can do that! Just find me the pail and rope."

"Yes, *Schatz*, that can be your job."

"I'll make that deck perfect!..Omer—"

"Yes, *Schatz?*"

Hold me! "And you know those two back bedrooms with the pirate ship windows—" She was acting like a young girl, she knew: "Let's make one of them ours!"

"You mean when we can't rent them out? We'll see. Let's go find Ali and the inspector."

She followed him aft where she discovered the big captain's table had been wrapped in visqueen. The seat cushions across the stern had also been taken up and the finished wood beneath covered in the same protective plastic. They walked past the ship's wheel to the stair leading into the salon below where, to her surprise, she found in place of carpet a deep hole down into the darkness of the ship, lit by a bulb that shone feebly from somewhere and cast long thick shadows over pipes, and boxes stacked against the sides of the hull. They were ship's stores, said Omer, stacked in against the water and sewage tanks, and around the bilge pump and the seacock. That was where the ship's engine was, and where Ali and the inspector were, checking it over and making sure while they were at it that the ship's ribs were sound, said Omer. He hollered something down. "Choke eeee!" she heard a voice from somewhere underneath her reply: *Very good!* They were among the handful of word-sounds in Turkish she could now recognize.

Heads appeared below her in the dimness, Ali's, then the inspector's. Omer led her back from the open hatch toward the companionway that led on-deck. Ali and the inspector soon followed. The ribs were all still good, the hull showed no sign of any leak. The inspection was over, and he could have the report signed and ready for the Harbour Master by that afternoon announced the inspector. Omer started to lead her up the companionway steps:

"Omer, stop!"

"Yes *Schatzi?*"

"I want to look at those two back cabins with the big windows once more," she said, pulling at his arm as she led him first to the cabin on her left then, after appraising it, to its twin on her right. "Which one do you like the best, Omer?"

"They're both the same, Connie—why?"

"Pick the one you think should be ours."

The agreed-to plan was for them to meet the next day in front of the Harbour Master's office where she would pay the inspection fee first. The inspector asked to be paid not in Turkish lire but in English pounds and Ali also said he preferred the money in pounds. Anticipating exactly this, before visiting the *Gul* Omer had suggested they first locate the local branch of their bank to have most of her money transferred in advance. Pounds, euros, and US dollars the bank usually kept on hand, but in small quantities. The seventy-five thousand pounds could be ordered, said the manager, but it would be far easier to transfer the money directly—if Ali operated the boat as a business, he had to have an account somewhere. So how many pounds should she draw out? Connie had asked. Using the back side of a bank advertisement on interest rates, Omer thoughtfully made a list: three thousand pounds to the notary—that was just for the taxes—plus whatever fee he might charge for actually writing up the sale, then there was the harbour master's fee for preparing the boat's registration papers that listed Omer as the *Gul's* new owner; then the inspector, of course, and finally, whatever last minute repairs might have been required for the boat to pass inspection (for repairs the yard charged ten dollars per square meter of boat plus materials, Omer interjected). "Ali might have said something about the engine needing some work come to think of it."

"What work? You didn't tell me anything about that—I thought you said the boat was practically new!"

"It is—I wouldn't lie to you! But boats are no different than cars, Connie. Even new cars need repair sometimes—I know, I've had one!"

"So how much do you want me to get out, Omer?"

"We might be able to pay the harbour master and notary using the Visa Card, but I don't know. To be on the safe side, *Schatz,* why don't we take out three thousand pounds and change all but five hundred of it to lira (since we know the inspector wants alone three hundred). And if it's too much, we can always put the money back."

Three hundred seemed to Connie an exorbitant amount to pay for an inspection that had taken less than two hours but given no choice, she dutifully drew the money. "And better hand over the lira to me, Connie, since I'm familiar with it and you're not. But you can pay the inspector, *Schatz.*"

Just as with buying their Toyota, her presence she discovered was not needed. Omer and Ali did all the talking and this time no one, not the harbour master, not the notary, even looked her direction. She may as well not have been there she thought watching Omer reach for his roll of banknotes to occasionally peel some of them off. At first, she tried to count what was being paid out, but that too was impossible she found due to the number of zeros on Turkish bills. A one milliard banknote was equal to five thousand English pounds *or was it five hundred?* She could only watch. A certain degree of fear was normal and justified, she told herself—anxiety attacks were nothing new or strange, telling herself that if buying the *Gul* contained risk, then risk had to be taken even if the English tabloids were filled with stories of heedless British women being easy prey for Turks. And—she couldn't help it—the image had stayed with her of Maureen sitting in Bea's Bar at ten in the morning not yet recovered from last night but already having her first glass of that horrid wine, trying to control her shaking.

They had managed to conclude their business at the notary late that afternoon but still in time to reach the bank and transfer the seventy-five thousand pounds from her account into Ali's and finalize the sale if they hurried. Connie watched her bankbook being sucked into the mouth of a machine on the manager's desk and swallowed, then she heard a crackly buzz that called to memory electricity being forced through a long glass tube in the old black and white Frankenstein film she remembered from her father before the bankbook was spat back for the bank manager to sign and return. Connie did not have to read the row of new numbers to know that most of her money had been taken as she folded the bankbook and slipped it back into her purse.

They rose and all shook hands with the bank manager. Ali's part too was finished. The *Gul* theirs and all that remained to be done was to rush the signed bill-of-sale plus receipt that showed the taxes had been paid back to harbour master since he would need to verify them before the new papers for the *Gul* could be drawn up. "How long do you think the papers will take?" she had asked Omer.

"A few days maybe. It's hard to know—*Schatz*, you live in Turkey!" He cast her a pleasing smile. "Happy, my love? I am and think we should celebrate, *Schatz*. I think it's time for the *bubbly!*"

Never had she seen him more elated than now at this moment. *I just hope you appreciate it, Omer!* She did not know what, if any, prearrangement had been made between the two but Ali rode into Finike with them, to the central shopping district where, after pointing out to them a good supermarket, he said goodbye and disappeared as Omer led her inside the market. "Come on, *Schatz,* help me find the champagne. And didn't you want a can of whipping cream?" he said, catching her with his enigmatic dark eyes as he squeezed her hand.

"If *you* want it, you mean," she said, squeezing back. "You do know that pleasing you is what gives me pleasure, Omer. Omer—"

"Yes, *meine schone Liebe?*"

"Sure you love me?"

"You keep asking me, *Schatz.* I've never known any other woman that compares with you!"

"You're sure of that?" she said, squeezing harder.

"By all I hold sacred, Connie, and Omer doesn't lie—not to you. The wine aisle is down this way."

The champagnes were next to the white wines. Omer looked through their labels. "This Kavaklidere brut is supposed to be good. Better take four, don't you think? "But she saw the price: "Omer, that's expensive even in England!"

"Owners of the *Gul II, Schatz,* can certainly afford to buy bubbly if they want it!"

The sun was close to down as they arrived back at the hotel. There was a small refrigerator in their room, and by removing the shelves Omer managed to fit three champagne bottles inside it. The fourth they opened. The room felt cold but the air conditioning could be reversed. Omer turned the thermostat up to its highest and they stepped out onto the balcony with their champagne. The sun was a pulsating orange ball just above the sea: the sea all but motionless and cast in pinks and crimson reds. Beautiful beyond description! she thought as she pressed against her man wrapped in his arms and felt his hand on her buttocks, his finger exploring her cute little tail bone. "Do you know what I want, Omer? To be able to stay here like this forever."

"Do you, *Schatz?* Then finish your champagne so we can go in."

How toasty the room was! Connie pulled back the bed cover. It was the biggest bed she had ever laid on she thought as wide as it was long and the perfect place on which to tumble and roll about! She saw him unbutton his jeans and she reached for her own zipper. She loved watching him undress before her; loved looking at him. "You have a handsome figure, Omer. Do you recall where I first told you that?"

"I do, *Liebe!* You also called me your organ grinder."

"But I'll bet this you didn't know you have bedroom eyes, Omer. Eyes like that can make any girl behave."

She could see the can of whipping cream there on the table near where he stood and, as if drawn there by her eyes, he turned, and she saw him reach for it. Watched him pull the top from the can and unlock the nozzle, "Should I put it on, Connie?"

No, she wanted to! "Let me, Omer!" She loved to fuss over him and she took the can from his hand.

"Now tell me how do you want me, *Schatz?*"

"Not standing up, silly! Lay down on the bed first," she ordered as if she were back in her classroom.

"Like this —flat?"

She could see at once that that wasn't going to work very well. "No, you're going to have to sit up a bit...*Yes!*" Then she was crawling across the bed, the whipping cream can in her hand, until she hovered over him. Holding its base, she sprayed and sprayed. Then she began to lick, like a child might her ice cream. "Connie likes ihm's *sik,*" she said in her prettiest voice, repeating one of the Turkish words he had taught her during their lovemaking. "And ihm's *dashak,*" she said kissing both, feeling his body shiver in tremors of pleasure that she knew both at that instant felt, she because he did; and her heart overflowed in the joy of shared love.

The room was entirely engulfed in darkness now. She could feel his body lying beside hers, spent, while with her finger she drew slow circles through the wavy-soft hairs of his thigh. She had a thought: "Omer—!"

"Yes, *mein sex Katzchen?*"

"When it's time to rent out the gulet, I will go with you—on the boat, I mean?"

"Naturlich." He paused, "Unless you don't want to."

"Of course I do, Omer. I'm sure I can find something to do to help. Not the cooking, of course, but I can take care of the passengers. The boat is half mine!" She could picture the sun sparkle on the water, its blue blues, and the whiteness of the bow- splash. And mooring in some beautiful cove or tiny bay for the night and their brief swim in the last pink light, and having dinner seated around the captain's table in the light of the stars. "Omer— I'm starting to get hungry I just realized. When does the restaurant close?"

"Ten maybe? There's still some champagne."

"If I drank any more of that I'll be sick tomorrow. I think we should make an effort to go eat….Omer—"

"What, Connie?"

"When did you first know you loved me?"

"When? When I held you in the lagoon?"

"But what if we'd never met? Where would you be?"

"I know where I'd be. Still with Charles. Just the idea gives me gooseflesh. And nor would you have the *Gul* right now, or that Toyota…Omer—"

"What is it now, *Schatz?*"

"You said you owned a new car when you lived in Marmaris. When was that?"

"Maybe three years ago. I didn't actually own it. It belonged to some woman I knew."

"Turkish? Or was she German?"

"English.—Connie, if we still want to eat something, we have to go right now."

The restaurant was about to close, its tables empty, and the landlady wheeling inside the wine display rack from where it stood at the entrance. Seeing them, she announced she would stay open and would they like that same wine again? "Yok!" said Connie—it was one of perhaps a half dozen words of Turkish she knew to use: *No!*

"I think we should have just one bottle, Connie."

She couldn't bluntly refuse him. They waited while the landlady went for it.

"So what was her name, the English woman's, and how did you meet her?"

"Connie, I don't see why any of this is important to you."

"You don't think I want to find out as much as I can about the man I'm going to spend the rest of my life with?"

"...Angela. And I met her in a bar."

"Like you met me—?"

"Connie, okay. But I told you about my unhappy first marriage. How the aunties accused me of doing things to my own child and how no one would believe me. I had to leave! I had to go someplace! So I did and met

Angela, and we hit it off. I mean, I was on the rebound anyway—it was like you and Charles, Connie exactly!

Their wine had arrived. She watched as Omer filled the two glasses. Connie hadn't wanted any more wine but forced herself to take just sips to keep him talking.

"It was Angela's bar. She'd leased it, Connie: her along with this Turk who was bartender (because she couldn't be, Connie— if the police ever caught her behind the bar they would have kicked her out of the country!). But she was losing a lot of money and didn't know where so she turned to me for help...

"See, Connie, if there's one thing I do understand, it's how the Turkish mind works. Not only was that bartender a lush, he was stealing from her—he and his friends. I told her just kick him out (it was all her money, not his—he didn't have any!). But she was afraid to—she was just that kind of person. I suggested to her we hire a security guard to keep watch over the place at night."

"So they were stealing from her at night?"

"Well it wasn't happening in the daytime because I was there. Whoever it was had a key—that I was sure of. So I found a security guard for her thinking that would put a stop to it. But it didn't."

"What were they stealing—liquor?"

"Liquor. Money when they could find any. Angela had a really expensive music system installed—the whole bar was wired and I was afraid that would be stolen next! So I decided it was time I checked on that security guard. I let myself in one night, and guess what! He was sound asleep—you could have taken anything right from under his nose! So I decided to remove the stereo system, just see if he would wake up."

Their food was arriving. They waited while the landlady set their plates before them. "And did he?"

"Angela always opened the bar at ten. Anyway, I get a call on my *handy*. It's Angela and she's hysterical: the stereo's been stolen! No, it hasn't, I said, I'll be down in five minutes to explain.

I did, I explained to her who was doing the stealing. Named names. Well, the bartender came in usually by eleven, and when he did, I accused him of being the thief right there to his face. And to make the story short, Connie, he denied it and she believed *him* not me! Turns out she'd been fucking him all the time she was leading me on. You know what they say, Connie, about love being blind..."

"You were in love with her then—?"

"I thought I was. But face it, she was using me! That was when my life reached its lowest, when I lost even the will to live. I even considered suicide, because *why live—for what?* Then you came along, to give me hope, that day I saw you walk into Bea's. My lucky day! I'm not very good at words, Connie, and I don't expect you to believe me but..."

Were they held-back tears she saw glisten in those dark, injured eyes?

"You've given me the reason to live. And though you don't know it, Connie, my life is in your hands."

"Never mind," she said reaching for his hand. She gripped it hard. "We have each other now."

Chapter 6

AT FINIKE IT WAS AS if Connie were riding the crest of a wave. But waves break and had her romantic mind not blocked her vision, she might have seen the beach ahead. Untrue to Turkish form, the *Gul's* new papers were completed a day early. After collecting them from the harbour office and saying goodbye to the *Gul* still resting on concrete, and to Ali who remained for present her captain, Connie and Omer returned to the hotel to pack and request the bill. All the extras had yet to be tallied and that took the owner some time but finally their total bill was ready. Connie was shocked when she read it. The cost per day of their room was only eighty lira (if you ignored the six zeros— which Connie now did). Multiplied by four, the figure came to three hundred and twenty lira, or one hundred fifty English pounds. Why then was their bill more than double that! Connie started down the itemized list and was surprised at some of the prices, particularly what she was being charged for a bottle of wine. "Omer, look at this!" she said and pointed as the hotel's owner watched her from behind the reception desk. The woman said something to Omer in Turkish—something to do with Connie—which Omer briefly answered before saying in English, "Connie, it's okay. Just pay."

But she could sense he was miffed over something and after they had loaded the car, after they had exchanged parting hugs with the owner, after she had insisted on splashing lemon-scented Turkish cologne on the hands and wrists of each and Connie had driven off, she said as she turned the car toward home, "Did you see what she was charging for just one bottle of wine!"

"Connie, please don't embarrass me like that again!"

She was taken back. "I don't understand, Omer. How is that embarrassing?"

"Just is. Can you imagine what she must be thinking right now! That here's two people with money enough to be able to buy a gulet questioning the price of a bottle of wine."

"So?"

"It makes us look small, Connie. We're not beggars in the street, you know!"

Since they would arrive home too late to cook dinner, Connie had suggested they stop off in Kas. How deserted the town looked! The harbour was empty of all but small open craft used by locals to fish, or ferry tourists to close-by beaches, and day swimming boats that made the trip to Kekova and back in summer. Most of the restaurants too were closed, but Omer thought Colette might be open. Colette's was a French restaurant in one of the little backstreets behind the Square and opposite Yilmaz's bar. Yilmaz was one of the town's more interesting characters, said Omer. A New York Turk, Yilmaz had driven a cab in Manhattan for years and some said, even spoke Turkish with a New Yorker accent. He was said to have perhaps the finest collection of jazz in Turkey. Stop in, order a beer, and ask to hear just about anything you could think of by just about any jazz great, and chances were Yilmaz had it! said Omer as he led her into a street no wider than an alley.

Yilmaz looked closed for the season, but Colette's nearby was open. Colette was an aging French ex-pat from Paris with an eroding face but alert blue eyes, Connie discovered as their hostess brought them menus.

Connie's was in French with the English translations beneath.

With some difficulty she started reading.

"Oh look, Connie: wild boar!" said Omer, holding up his menu and pointing.

Omer's menu was in Turkish, Connie saw. Now how did Colette know to bring her a French menu and Omer the Turkish? "Is the wild boar good?" Connie decided to ask.

"Oui, o'ees very good, Madam!"

"Then I'll have that," said Connie, convinced by the owner's immediate smile.

"Think I will too, to try," said Omer. "And a bottle of *this!*": pointing at the wine list.

While they sipped their wine waiting for the food to come, Connie asked, "What happens to the *Gul* now?" It was one of the items she knew they had to discuss. Leaving it in Finike for now would be cheaper Omer said, but she would miss it! "Omer, why can't we have it closer?"

"Like Kas, you mean?"

"Or why not Fethiye?" she said.

"Do you know what that would cost, Connie? Moorage fees for one, and don't forget the *Gul's* not a small boat. Her tank takes three hundred litres of diesel just to get up here and at the moment it's empty."

That was something she had failed to consider. But she still wished it were in Fethiye if only to be able to touch it, to go below and curl up like a like a kitten beside him in that cabin at the stern she had picked out, *their love nest* her mind called it. "No, Omer, given my choice I still want the *Gul* where I can see it!"

"Okay *Schatzi,* I can call Ali, see if he'll sail her up. But we have to pay him don't forget or find ourselves a new captain— and captains don't come cheap, Connie."

She'd overlooked that part. "Why can't you be the captain, Omer?"

"I'd have to go to classes first and captain's school gets expensive!"

They were all things that still needed to be researched, she saw: "How much are we paying Ali to be captain?"

"A thousand five hundred pounds."

"A month!"

"Connie, that's cheap. You go out and find me a captain for less than two thousand pounds a month! The only reason Ali's willing to do it for that little is because he likes you, *Schatz"*

"So when do I pay him? (I know the *Gul* has to have a captain)?"

"I've paid him for this month, Connie."

"So you two have already worked it out! You didn't tell me any of this, Omer. Why—don't you think I'm interested? I am a part of this, you know—or don't I count!"

"Of course you count, *Schatz.* I think Colette's bringing our food."

Deliberately or not, she was being manipulated. Why could he not be open with her—it was as though he kept a distance between them. She had not expected him to just shut her out even if it was unintentional— that was not why she was here. It was to be drawn into his life and made part of it—that was why she had come; why she had sacrificed so much. When they arrived back in Fethiye it was dark and late. How icy cold the apartment was! She shivered as they walked through the rooms turning on electric space heaters. Turks said you didn't need heating. But once cold, stone walls and stone floors stayed cold, and winter had only begun!

That next morning Omer went across to the small corner store for newly baked bread plus fresh eggs and some tomatoes and as he fixed their breakfast he thought, it did not matter to him where his ship slept out the winter. In fact there was an advantage to having the *Gul* here since caring for it would give Connie something to do to occupy her time, and over breakfast he announced, "Connie, I've been thinking it over and you're right. I'll text message Ali as soon as we finish eating and tell him you want the *Gul* up here, if you're sure you want me to?"

"Omer, *yes!*"

"Everything I do, I do for you, Connie." He could see joy in her face, "Because *Schatz,* I was also thinking. The *Gul* will need work done on her anyway if she's to be cleaned up and made pretty again before tourist season. All I have to tell Ali is to get the *Gul* back in the water *ja?* And to find out how much money we'll need to send him.

"Money for *what?*"

"Fuel. The *Gul* can't leave Finike without a tank full of diesel, *Schatz.* Plus we still owe the harbour office for moorage and whatever repair bills. Finike won't let the boat leave, Connie, before everything has been paid."

So that was something else to be concerned over! She listened in each time she heard the now familiar Mozart come from Omer's pocket, just wishing she understood Turkish. It took two days for Ali's reply to come back. Connie knew it was Ali because Omer kept looking at her as they talked.

"How much will he need, Omer?" she asked as he closed the phone and slipped it back into his pocket.

"Two thousand should be enough to cover it, Connie."

"*Pounds!* For what?"

"Harbour taxes and fees. Insurance. Fuel—the *Gul* don't forget needs diesel, Connie. Plus there was some work they found they had to do on her. Turns out—maybe I forgot to mention this to you—one of the ribs was soft after all."

"But it was just inspected!" She saw his resigned shrug: "That's what I said too."

"I think we should drive down there!"

"Why, Connie? It would just be a waste of more money. I trust Ali with my life."

"Well make sure we get an itemized statement of *everything*. Tell Ali. And I want to see the receipts!"

"Ali's a businessman—he knows all that." But her sudden change of tone irritated him. "I know, *Schatz*," he said as he drew her to him and forced a kiss. "Now let's get dressed so we can go to Finance Bank."

"Why is it always my bank we use and never yours! You still have that fifteen thousand pounds I sent—*or do you?*"

"Most of it, *Schatz*. I've had to spend a little of it, here, there."

"On what?"

"I pay Ali's salary. Now next month the rent starts again, plus I'm still paying off all those new clothes you bought. And don't forget I have to pay the water bill each month. Don't you trust me, Connie? Well don't you? You should know by now that I don't lie to you. Do you want to see inside my bankbook, Connie? *Do you?*"

That was how Cliff had controlled her, she remembered. "No," she said firmly.

"Then what is it you want, Connie? Tell Omer," he said, his voice tender—cajoling.

"I don't know. I just feel sometimes..frightened." She could feel tears collect, "Sometimes I need a little reassurance is all." *Love me!*

After transferring the money to Ali's account, they had shopped at Tansas for the food they would need. The lamb chops looked meaty for a change, and Connie picked out a roast she thought might be good. She hoped it wouldn't prove another disappointment; so much of the meat in Turkey was tough! Also, you learned soon enough not to trust pre-ground hamburger which was mostly waste fat. To get lean hamburger you had to buy a roast and have it specially ground, watching to make sure the butcher first cleaned the remaining ground fat from the machine. Afterward they had driven to the Ana Bar for a beer on the promenade before returning to their apartment to start dinner. She watched Omer wash and prepared the roast before sliding it into the oven, reading from those scintillating dark glances he cast what was to follow. She loved their showers together, and afterward, loved hearing him whisper to her as she clung so close, *"Du, I love you so much, mein Schatz! More than my poor English knows how to say!"*—loved the feel of him! But tonight after dinner he announced instead, "I'm going to have to go out for a few hours, Connie. See some friends I haven't seen— okay?"

"Who?"

"Just some Turks—you don't know them."

She couldn't stop him, only appeal, "Try not to be too late."

He had not intended to be. Earlier, Mehmet had phoned to suggest they meet somewhere, say *eightish*? It had been quite some while since he had spent a night out drinking and chatting with his old friends, not since Connie's arrival. At first all his energies had been focused on his new love; making her feel secure, finding an adequate place for them to live, and finally, making sure her money was safely under his control if not in his actual hands. Now, with those aims having been realized, he needed some time away from her; she monopolized him and, the novelty of having her starting to wear thin, he was growing a little tired of her constant demands. And so he had agreed to meet Mehmet at the Scarlet Bar for beers and a chat.

Word of his having bought Ali's gulet had spread like happy fire through the boating community and he found himself the sudden focus of much attention. In fact, had he picked all eight numbers of the New Year's lottery, he could not have been more of a celebrity than he found himself at this moment. Not just Mehmet was in the Scarlet Bar waiting, but Ahmed, hearing Omer would be there, had also decided to come and soon after his arrival another of his friends and a fellow diver, Mustafa, showed; all bombarding him with a flurry of the same questions. What were his plans? Did they include the English woman? Was she going into business with him? Did he plan to stay with her and what was she like?

Until now Omer had guarded her and kept her to himself so that very few in the Scarlet Bar had even seen her, and then only from a distance. Omer knew he was the object of no small amount of envy as he responded to their questions by avoiding some and only half answering the others, just enough to stir their curiosity.

"I don't know who has the most luck—you or Sali," said Mustafa to him as ten o'clock came and passed unnoticed.

At a little before eleven Ahmed suggested a game of cards just for old times! And that was another thing he's had to give up for Connie, his poker nights. Earlier they had turned from beer to drinking raki. His wallet fat with new Turkish banknotes drawn from his even fatter bank account earlier that day, Omer had ordered a bottle of *Yeni Raki* and was now feeling its effects. Not ever had he allowed anyone to control his life in the past, not Angela, not even his father. He'd begged in the streets rather than buckle to his father's authority. He certainly was not going to let Connie run his life now! Digging into his pocket for the *handy*, Omer switched it off. "*Tamam*, let's go play some poker!"

He could always fuck Connie but he couldn't always play poker, he thought as, half drunk, he led the three friends to his car.

Mustafa shared a flat down behind the harbour and it was there they went. The roommate, whom Omer knew slightly, had moved in for now with a woman he had met in Bea's and the flat stood empty—perfect for poker since there would be no one to interrupt their game. Omer carried a new bottle of raki he had purchased from the corner store upstairs. The flat was like an ice box but nobody seemed to notice. Mustafa turned on the space heater which soon glowed a bright orange.

Then he and Ahmed disappeared into the kitchen for raki glasses and a jug of ice water he always kept in the refrigerator for occasions such as this. From a drawer someone produced a poker deck and chips. One night—his lucky night and he had never forgotten it!—Omer had won close to a thousand lira playing blackjack and five card draw.

Tonight started out in just such a way with Omer winning his opening three hands.

Besides card playing, poker nights provided an opportunity for Omer to catch up on what of importance had happened in Fethiye. "Anybody hear anything about Ibrahim's divorce?" he asked as he drew in his winnings then reached for the raki bottle and ice water jug.

"She still won't give it to him, is what I heard," said Mehmet. "Even after putting her in a wheel chair!—who's turn to deal?"

"Yours. She says she'll die before she gives him one now," Mehmet continued.

"From what I hear, he beat her up pretty bad," Ahmed interjected. "Are you going to deal, Omer?"

"Sorry. Just how old was she, does anyone know?"

"I heard eighty," Mustafa had said.

"Seventy-nine. But you know who I blame," said Mehmet as Omer dealt out five cards face down to each. "I blame his village. They already picked out a girl they wanted him to marry and they kept pressuring him to get rid of the old woman any way he could. —Who opens?"

"Omer again."

That was how the night had begun, but then his luck changed. His double stack of chips went down to one, which dwindled further until he was forced to buy more—twice! The problem was his mind just wasn't on the game—it was too busy trying to follow the talk.

"I still can't believe that Sali really threw Doreen out," said Mehmet.

"That's what he told me," Mustafa, studying his cards, said to the table. "I need two cards."

"What's her name, anybody know?"

"Jean. Just how or where he found out about her I don't know—he won't say. All I know is, she's supposed to be loaded. He said she flew in two days ago and he was there to pick her up. When I asked him what she looked like, know what he said?"

They waited, listening.

"Said, 'If you think Doreen looked bad, wait till you see the new one. She looks like she was dug up!'" Omer saw their laughs and headshakes.

"How does he do it!" Ahmed said.

"Ahmed, if you're dealing, deal and let's get this game over with!" said Mustafa.

And so the night had gone. He had been quite drunk and had lost quite a bit of money he discovered when he woke that next morning in Mustafa's flat. How Mehmet and Ahmed had found their way home, Omer never did find out. He knew only that Connie wasn't going to be pleased.

"Why didn't you at least answer my calls?" were her first words.

"You called? Don't tell me my phone was shut off too!"

Chapter 7

LATE THE FOLLOWING AFTERNOON WITH a low, settling sun already touching the tops of her masts, the *Gul II* appeared in the main channel to the left side of Shovalye Island with its fortress ruins which had stood since Hellenistic times like a sentinel guarding Fethiye Bay. Omer had been tracking Ali's progress on his *handy* and as the *Gul* made her appearance, he and Connie were already waiting to meet her. "There it is!" said Omer, squinting into the sun over the harbour.

Connie watched the gulet slow in the water and begin to turn around, and she again marvelled at the *Gul's* elegant lines, her prettiness as Ali, alone on the quarterdeck, continued to bring the ship about. Then he disappeared forward and Connie heard the familiar rattle of the anchor chain being let out before he reappeared to back the ship in while Omer waited to receive the two stern lines that Ali, momentarily abandoning the wheel, would run back to throw. Connie had wanted to catch one of them but Omer had too little trust in her. "Just stand out of the way, Connie!"

Because he lived in Kas when he wasn't sailing the *Gul* in Kekova Sound, Ali had had to stay with them that night, sleeping on the made-up couch, until they could drive him home after breakfast the next morning. Connie decided to go along, just for the ride. The two men talked continuously though Connie scarcely listened—not because she understood only an occasional word in Turkish, but because more and more her thoughts were on their finances. They were going through their money far too quickly and that had to stop!

She approached him on the subject that night as they lay beside each other in bed. "Omer.—"

"Yes, my sex kitten?"

"We have to cut our expenses down. We're living far too high on the hog." She waited for a response and when none came, she added a warning. "If we don't, we could run out before May."

"And you don't have more still in England?"

She had decided not to tell him anything of that remaining two thousand pounds. "No, I thought I made it quite plain, Omer."

"Well let's not think about it, *Schatz*. We can go see the *Gul* in the morning."

She lay tied up not far from the Marina Restaurant where Alice had taken her and Charles for dinner on their first night here. The gangplank had been left raised a bit to discourage those passing by from going on board. Gripping the two ropes that raised or lowered the gangplank, Omer pulled himself up and, once on, lowered the gangplank for her. One glance around was enough to tell both of the neglectful way in which Ali had treated the ship. The teak decks were still green, as were most of the copper and brass fittings along it. If salt water was good for the deck, said Omer, it was equally bad for copper or brass which it would turn green and over time pit. "Write down *b r a s o*!" he said to Connie who was keeping a shopping list of things the *Gul* would need. Only with Brasso and plenty of *elbow grease* Omer said could the metal be made pretty again. That was her job! Connie thought to herself as she followed Omer down into the ship.

The bedding had all been stripped from the mattresses they saw and inside one of the cabins toward the middle, they found a pile of sheets and pillowcases to be washed. The highly finished walls and cabinetry showed scratches and scuff marks, especially at the corners. Connie added furniture polish to the list. Also, the carpeting both inside the cabins and in the passageway between showed old dirt and stains. "We'll have to take it up and have it cleaned," she said to him. And they would also need something to clean the toilet bowls and sinks. There was easily enough work to do to keep both busy for the next three months until the *Gul* could earn money again she thought as they left the ship, Omer raising the gangplank behind, and drove to a hardware store he knew. So what would be tomorrow's schedule? she had asked him at dinner, though she already knew.

Work! Start cleaning up the *Gul* to have her ready by the start of tourist season at the end of April, or even by mid April if they could! For that Connie needed no urging. The boat, theirs at last, her only concern now remained money, though she could not seem to convince Omer of its seriousness. How with such an attitude, she wondered, had he survived all these years? Perhaps it and not his diving accident accounted for why he had acquired so little—just a silver stand. And that property, which was supposed to be his, but which a cousin or some relative had cheated him out of…"Omer," she asked as she lay close and cozy beside him in the dark, "what about the property? I guess the lawyer still doesn't know anything or you would have heard—?"

"I just talked with him as a matter of fact, yesterday."

"And?"

"Things just take time here. This isn't Germany don't forget, *Schatz*. This is Turkey!"

"Where is the property? And how'd you find out—who told you?"

"Nobody. I heard about it just by luck."

"*Luck?*"

"Yes, Connie. It was hot and I decided to stop and drink a beer out in Chiflik (which is close to here) one afternoon. There were four or five locals at the other end of the bar talking and I hear my name. I think, 'Why would people I don't know, strangers, be talking about me?—I must be mistaken'. But I keep listening and, sure enough, they're talking about me, or someone with my name. So I walk down and start to listen. 'Who are you?' I tell them and at first they don't believe me. So I show them my *kimlik*."

"What's a *kimlik*?" said Connie.

"A card Turks need to carry—it's like an identification. Anyway, so finally they believe me. 'Your aunt's been looking all over for you!' one of them says. 'Me—why?' Then they tell me about my grandfather's will he left, and about how my great aunt had been trying to find me to sign some paper that my father was supposed to have, to give me title to land that had actually been my great grandmother's that she'd inherited after her brother said he didn't want it, thinking it was worthless.

"See, here's what happened: Before the tourists came, land next to the sea was considered worthless. But Turkey is a Muslim country, and the Koran says that property goes to the male heir—and that, only after he's taken what he wants and if there's anything left over, can the female have it. (That's why some of the most valuable property here is now owned by elderly women.) But back to the story. So they take me to meet my great aunt—who doesn't believe me at first either, not even when I show her my *kimlik*. It's only when I describe my past life, being born and raised in Germany and the fact that I'm not really Turkish but German, that she does and sends me to see her lawyer."

"Have you ever seen the property?"

"I have and it's beautiful! It's filled with orange trees right now but just as soon as I win my lawsuit, that's where I plan to build. Do you want to look at it, Connie?"

"Can I?"

"Of course, *Schatz!* Some afternoon, I promise. You can help me pick where to build the house. There are two sites, and I can't make up my mind on which. Both would have a view of the sea. In addition to a swimming pool, Connie, we'll even have our own beach! You can help me design the house. I'm going to use only the best materials—no cheap Turkish crap. I'm going to have everything brought from Germany: parquet floors, good German roof tiles, and did I mention swimming pool? You can design it too if you want."

"Can we go look at it—the property?"

"One afternoon, Connie. As I say, it's just got orange trees now."

"Let's go to sleep, *Schatz,* if we want to get to the harbour early. Start to work on our *Gul,*" and as he spoke, she could feel his hand on her thigh move slowly upward, finally to her mound and feel his finger search the hair for her opening. "Does 'ihm love Conniekins?" she whispered back, "Does 'ihm?"

"Yes, Connie."

"Promise?"

"Yes, Connie."

"For ever and ever?"

By the time they finished breakfast and were ready to leave that next morning, it was already eleven. Omer drove to the harbour, parked, and they began carrying cleaning supplies up the gangplank. But with so much to do, where even to start? Since it was a nice day and warm, why not clean the main deck first! Omer found the bucket Ali used and, lowering it, drew up sea water then set about showing her how to scrub the main deck. For those areas where the green didn't want to come off, she could try some fine sandpaper. With Connie put to work, Omer announced he would leave; there were a number of stops he must make, things to be done. At the harbour office he could find out how much they must pay to keep the *Gul* here until May, and ask for the electricity to be turned on if they wanted to avoid having to use their battery each time they needed lights or start the bilge pump if you had to, or pump the waste ashore since you couldn't just dump it. Also, if they wanted to use city water, he would need to visit the *Belediyesi*, said Omer: "I don't know what it is in English, Connie, but in German it's called the *Stadtverwaltung*."

"Town council?–And find out while you're at it about becoming a captain," she said looking up at him from where she sat kneeling against the deck.

"I know."

"And the cost!" she called after him.

"That too. I won't be gone long, promise!"

But he was, though at first she hadn't missed him. All her thoughts were directed at removing the green that discoloured the *Gul's* deck and made it unsightly. But scrubbing was hard work she soon realized as the strength in her arms and fingers began to go. Finally, she set the brush aside and rose. How stripped bare the ship looked without her sun mattresses and awnings. The mattresses were stacked inside the salon and she went below to get one which she carried up to the sunroof.

She laid down on it. The sky above her was soft blue, the sun soon warming and she thought, *How unreal it all was being here.* Had anyone told her that she would do such a thing one day, she would have laughed at the thought.

Not missing Manchester, she rarely thought of it, only her daughter, which made her feel guilty. What would Alice say if she could know that her mother had bought a gulet? Would her daughter applaud her for what she had done and forgive her? Or would she condemn her even more than she in all likelihood already had? And what of Charles? Or the police— were they now searching for her? She was afraid to go near any Internet café to read Alice's emails. The temptation though, had never left, and it was just fortunate that their apartment had no phone line. If things ever got desperate enough she could sell her laptop—there had to be ex-pats out there who would buy it. No, first she would have to erase everything on it including the hard- drive. She wouldn't begin to know how though Omer might— or could find somebody who knew. She thought she heard someone coming up the gangplank: *Omer?* She rose and went to look. Then she saw his broadly grinning face. "It is you, Omer?"

"Jawohl! Just leave everything and let's go. That's an order from your captain!"

"You're not!" she cried out feeling her heart leap at the thought.

"*Schatz*, let's go home. But I want to stop off at Tansas first and buy a bottle of whiskey."

He was in almost a euphoric state, she saw as she followed him down the gangplank and they walked to Tansas where he reached for a bottle of *JB*. "So what are we celebrating?" She knew he couldn't have been made captain.

"All in good time, Connie. All in good time," he said as he drove. They were home it seemed in minutes, unlocking the heavy steel downstairs door and letting themselves inside, to the cold dank stairwell. "So tell me, don't keep me guessing."

"It's been a good day, a very good day, Connie. Do we still have ice?" She thought they had. *Yes.* She watched him drag down two water glasses and she began to fill both with ice. "No, don't put any in my glass," he said, "I'll drink mine straight. It's been a good day, Connie."

She watched him start to pour. He wasn't going to fill the entire glass was he? "Omer, stop!...and don't tease me, tell me what happened."

"Well first, *Schatz,* At the Belediyesi I got us a card so we can use the city's water. Then I drove to the harbour office and you'll like what they said. To keep the *Gul* where it is won't cost us anything for the present. Also, *also* they agreed to let us have electricity (though that we'll have to pay for, unfortunately). She watched him raise his nearly full glass of scotch and clink it against hers, "Cheers!"

"Cheers! and now what about becoming captain?"

It would take him four to five months and the classes were right here in Fethiye, though one of the three tests he had to take was only given in Izmir—that was the bad news he told her. "The good news is, there's a new class just starting and I'm signed up! We'll just have to go down to Finance Bank and take out enough to pay the tuition."

"How much, Omer?"

"The tuition? Not too bad. Not as much as I was afraid it might be."

"Which is *what?*

"Just four thousand lira is all."

"Omer, I don't have it to give. You have all the money now!"

"*Don't have it?*"

With angry fingers she searched through her purse for the bankbook. "Here! Maybe you can find more. I keep telling you it's all we have—this and what is left of that fifteen thousand."

"You sure you don't have anything left in England?"

"You have the fifteen thousand I sent over and that's it! When it's gone, I don't know. Move into the street? Maybe you want to sell the car. Or you might try selling that silver stand!"

"I have tried!" he said holding his anger. "Just take it easy, *Schatz*... Thing is, I signed up for those classes thinking that's what you wanted."

She knew the classes were important—they couldn't just go on paying Captain Ali. But she had no solution. "How much of that fifteen thousand is left, did you say?"

"Enough, Connie, to get us through. So don't worry about it— I've been in these situations before. Tamam?" He kissed her then, but her lips were unresponsive and though he tried to revive the evening, its festive mood was gone. Even the JB failed to bring it back. Nor did she reach down for him in bed that night as normally she would. It had taken him forever before he could fall asleep; his head filled with so many thoughts. In a way, since he had her, he didn't quite know now what to do with her.

He hadn't overcharged Connie! If anything, he'd been easy on her— more so than if she had been just another English woman there for the taking. He really had felt something special for her; she demanded a respect! Of course, they all told you the same thing in the end: how they loved you—and not just English women but the German ones too. The problem was, sooner or later they all tried to get at you—though he still preferred them to Turkish girls because they were more fun to be with. They thought thoughts. They were freer, their minds more open. Turkish girls had never been anywhere to have thoughts—other than village thoughts. No, they bored him to death and besides village girls often smelled. So he preferred western women, Connie, except for the schoolteacher part of her which could rub at him. Rebellious, he'd fought school and so was also afraid of her. All those demands—they were worse even than Angela's— he saw as restrictions, threats to his liberty, and in the end always because of money! He had dreamt of being rich all his life. Only with wealth could he ever be entirely free. That was why he'd wanted the gulet with Connie. But he feared entrapment. He was still the monkey, and for Connie to be the organ grinder was more than he could accept. All his life he had resisted authority. He preferred freedom over duty, chance to planning. He had little patience for the intricacies of Western thought or systems of logic. He lived not by planning or by any ordered structure—but rather by chance, by *Inschallah*—"if God be willing" and if He wasn't now, there always remained the hope of *next time*.

Chapter 8

THE CLASSES SHE HOPED WOULD make Omer a captain began
two days later and marked still another turning in their relations even
though she was unaware of it at first as, each morning, they would return
to the *Gul.* There was still much to be done if the gulet was to be ready in
time for the season. One afternoon Connie pulled up all of the carpets by
herself, and the next morning Omer drove them out to be shampooed at
a place he knew of in Gunlukbashi. What an unpronounceable name for
a place! thought Connie. At lunch sometimes she would walk along the
quay as far as the park. But, instead of crossing it to Bea's, she would turn
right to the post office. Across from it was a restaurant everyone called
the 'beer garden' and from there Connie would return with hot *doners:*
freshly sliced roast lamb from the spit rolled with lettuce, tomato and the
meat juices inside a thin, white, special bread like a Mexican tortilla. Then
after lunch he would go off to class and leave her alone with the ship. She
didn't object. With eight cabins plus the salon to be gotten ready it was a
tediously slow process, trying to make old scars less visible and scratches
disappear under repeated rubbing with furniture polish. Then, after the
sun had dropped below the headland and the chill of night came on, he
would return to take her home.

That was at first. Then one evening he didn't. Instead, he phoned and
said he was being detained at the school—something about a change in
his class hours—and could she take a *dolmush* home this once? Dolmushes
were privately owned busses the size of a small van, ran more frequently
than the city bus, and were very inexpensive. She had and within a half
hour she was back in Chalis Beach, walking through the apartment to turn
on the space heaters, pouring herself a glass of red wine. Then a second
as she waited.

Anybody can be delayed and at first, she was not suspicious.

She knew she couldn't monopolize all his time—that he did have friends. It was ten when finally he came home. Having finished most of the bottle of wine, she felt tipsy—girlish even—as she rushed to kiss him. "Where were you, Omer? I don't like it here when you're not with me."

"My class time got switched, Connie." How's that possible? she thought.

"You didn't have any trouble taking the dolmush, did you?" And when she shook her head, "See I knew you wouldn't."

Thereafter, on those nights when he didn't come home except for very late, he would phone before it got too dark and tell her she must take the dolmush again. When she pressed him *why?* his answers varied. Once there had been a glitch in the school's computers—or something. On another occasion when he failed to come home before morning, he text-messaged to her that the boat he had had to go out on had developed an engine problem. What boat? Until then she'd had no idea his training also took place on the water—he told her so very little of what he actually did. "The school has to have a training ship, Connie. You can see it out in the bay sometimes."

She'd never seen it. "Where do they keep it?"

"The school? Well, you know where the boat yard is, don't you? It's somewhere over past there. If you want, we can go see it sometime when I know it's not out. It's just an old beat up gulet—not like the *Gul.* Not worth even looking at, Connie."

At first she had believed him, telling herself that once May arrived and they were back sailing in Kekova Sound, the two of them, things would change back to what they were before, as she continued the slow work of refurbishing the gulet, cabin by cabin, to make her spotless again, literally shine! Because, though she could not have said exactly what, or what had caused it, something of fundamental importance between them had altered. It was as if the centre of his focus had shifted elsewhere. She didn't think it had to do with their age difference—she still looked fairly young. Sometimes, when her feelings of depression began to come on, when she felt herself at the most risk, alone in a land that did not even speak her tongue, she would first raise the gangplank to make sure no one came up it. Then, going below, she would curl herself up onto the bed in one of the large rear cabins with the pirate ship windows and lie there gazing out wishing it could be blue sea and the ship's white wake she were looking at and not the grey concrete below. Sometimes, lying there, she would phone him and when he did not answer, she would leave a message: "Just wondering what you're doing is all. Love you! Miss you!" At times he would text message back, "Love u 2, Schatz!!" He usually text-messaged her now, like Alice had done when she did not want to be reached. One evening she asked him *why?*

"Teacher banned handies from the classroom, Connie. They disrupt his class."

That made sense. Sometimes in the late afternoon, tired of being left to herself, Connie would go for a stroll along the quay, repeating "Merhaba" and "Nasilsinez," hello, how are you?— to faces she now knew who greeted her the same way. Occasionally she would stop off to visit the closed padlocked silver stand. *Omer, why don't you try harder to see if you can't sell this?* Then she would continue on toward the park which she would then cross, to Bea's.

Since their return from Finike, Connie had never felt entirely comfortable in Bea's. Word of her buying the *Gul* had spread through the ex-pat community—though how, she still didn't know.

"Constance!" Eric had said, discovering her upon her return one afternoon as she moved amid the tables searching for Bea's face, "we heard how you bought a bloody gulet for that *beloved* of yours! When, dear lady, are we to be allowed to see it? I propose a boat-warming party in which I supply the drink. We can go out in the bay some evening, have a rousing time out there! You know, water sport and frolic. Be inventive, dear lady, little *jigi-jigi?*"

Eric, stay out of my life! She had discovered Bea signalling to her and she turned her face away from Eric and his gang—critical eyes looking up at her perhaps in amusement as she pushed past. Thereafter, whenever she returned to the *Gul* from Bea's, Connie would leave the gangplank raised behind her.

"So you did it then?" said Bea, her old eyes regarding her with a sort of curious kindness.

And as Connie nodded, "How much did it set you back (or perhaps I shouldn't ask)?"

"Seventy-five thousand."

"Pounds?"

"Now, if I tell you I'm broke, you know why…but we just have to make it through to May and we should be alright—Omer knows boats and says the *Gul* can't help but make money."

"What made you decide to do something like this, Connie?"

She'd told Bea then what, in retrospect, must have been a confusing story of how a pubescent crush on her cousin in Scotland had led to her nearly drowning and a fear of water ever since and how, because of a Spanish teacher she had known— well, *more* than just known—she'd dreamt of coming here. How finally, because of concerns for her daughter, she had met Omer. And now, because of him, she had lost at last her fear of the water.

For a time Bea remained silent. "I hope you have some proof you paid for that gulet," she said finally.

"I don't, Bea—though it passed through my mind… but I trust Omer."

Bea gazed at her for another long moment. "We all hope for the best."

There were hands waving then, and shouts for more beer from several of the tables. Bea rose. On Bea's side away from Connie sat another of her regular customers: Joy. For as many afternoons as Connie had been coming, Joy could always be found sitting if not beside Bea, at least at the same table where Connie occasionally had engaged her in bits of conversation. How old was Joy? *Old!* was all; loose folds of splotchy flesh hung from her face and her white hair was thin so that one could see through it in places skull. Her eyes, Connie observed, were a faded blue and looked watery.

"So how did it happen, dearie, that he taught you how to swim?" said Joy, "Did you ask him to?"

"Not exactly, it was more the other way. But I knew he was good at it, having been a diver."

"He told you about his accident I guess."

"Well *yes*—why?"

"I just thought he must have."

What is this old woman implying? she thought, "Do you know him then?"

"Never personally. I just know of him."

"Know what of him?" Connie saw her turn hesitant. "*What* of him?"

"Just, reputations get around. It's probably all right and I'm sure he'd be a nice bloke to be with, dearie."

"What reputation, Joy?"

"He likes the women is all. Did he ask you to marry him yet?"

"Should he?" said Connie, suspiciously.

"Lot of the Turks marry women your age just so they can get their English visa. They all think they can make big money if they go there—but what can they do, dearie? Most of those mixed marriages don't work out anyway, Connie, and before long the Turkish bloke can't wait to get back. Mind you, I'm not saying yours would be like that. Here comes Bea."

To where the anger was directed Connie had not taken the time to think out. She rose and turned to leave.

"Constance, I was serious about having the boat warming. We need to celebrate this momentous event in your life."

She paused only long enough to take in the splotchy cheeks, the thin upper lip with its moustache hardly more than the thickness of a pencil line, before rushing into the street.

"Connie, come back!"

Bea's voice, but she didn't give her friend even a glance back as she crossed the park to the quay and returned along it to the *Gul* where, back aboard, she raised the gangplank behind her. Why did people like that spread foundationless rumours? Just to talk and because they had nothing better to do with their meaningless lives! Connie dug for her handy and tried calling Omer but his phone was shut off, so she went below and from the salon turned into the rear passageway that led to her favourite cabin. In her mind she saw it as *their cabin*; but as she opened the door into the head, she caught her face in the mirror above the washstand. How old it looked to her and how unhappy!

Returning to the cabin, she climbed onto the bed where she curled herself up before the window and began by examining a rather ugly blemish on her arm she had discovered, squeezing it to watch the welt form—trying to decide. She did not want to remain on the *Gul* waiting for Omer in case he should come for her. She really felt like she wanted to forget her cares for once in her life, and just get drunk. She reached for her handbag to check her money and discovered she would need some, so she decided to walk past the bank on her way to catch the dolmush.

There was an entire back side to the town just filled with little cafes and bars that she had yet to visit. For today, though, she would limit herself to Chalis Beach. The *Meri Bar* where Omer sometimes went when he wasn't in school was a place she could try.

First, she stopped at the apartment, found it just as they had left it, looking cold, and with the morning's dishes still standing. The days were slowly warming so that now it was actually more comfortable outside.

Most of the two hundred lira she had just drawn from her dwindling savings she decided to leave behind in her drawer.

Twenty would be enough, she thought though to be safe she transferred a second bill to the small purse she used whenever they went out. Sooner or later she would be forced to send for the last of her money, close out the account in England and though she did not like to dwell on the inevitability of what it might mean, its eventuality never was very far from her thoughts as February became March. She wondered how much Omer still had of the fifteen thousand? Now that she had figured out how to read a Turkish bankbook, she searched Omer's drawer for his. But it wasn't anywhere to be found.

The *Meri Bar* was a block away from the water near an intersection where the two principle roads through Chalis crossed to mark the center of the town proper. On one corner as you stood facing the mountains was an Indian restaurant and a bit further down the block a second, smaller place that served Turkish food. Sandwiched between them was the bar Connie had decided upon, set back from the street to allow perhaps half a dozen tables before a glass front with two sliding doors which were left open in all but the worst weather. The outside tables were completely filled with a mix of Turks and English, she saw. But as she drew close a couple rose freeing one, which Connie quickly claimed. At the table closest sat three English women. Two, Connie estimated, were in their sixties, the third looked younger by…*ten years?* and was thin with a narrow, inflamed red face. Of the other two, one was large and obese, her skin floppy, hanging in places. Her face was heavily made-up, like a geisha's almost, and in the folds of her neck and chin faint cracks showed, like the lines that sometimes appear then spread on cheap ceramic dishware. The third appeared well-kept and cared for—though her face upon a closer look revealed a myriad pattern of fine wrinkles. As Connie sat down, she brushed up against the younger one. "Sorry," she said.

"We're no big thing, luv. Don't think we seen you here. You must be new."

"Yes. I'm Connie."

"I'm May," the one with the reddened face responded. "Doreen (*little Dori* we call her) is the one drinking brandy, and that's Jane with the vodka tonic."

"Just another of the many Janes!" Jane—the one with the more cared-for face—said to her.

"You staying or you just on holiday?"

"No, I've been living here for more than two months now," said Connie.

"Have you! Why don't you come over, join us, luv?" May said. Connie slid her chair over.

"So where you living?" asked Jane. "Not very far from here, in Chalis."

"I used to live in Chalis. But me landlord kept raising the rent every six months—it were because of me dog. I had enough and I finally told Fati, 'Fati, get up off your ass and go find us another place!', and I made him. But he's so lazy. All he wants to ever do is play cards all night and sleep all day."

"Who's Fati?" said Connie.

"The one she wants to marry even though we keep telling her *not to!*" said May. "Or if she's going to anyway, she should at least wait until after he's through with the Army."

"How old is he?" said Connie.

"Twenty-eight. By right he should be in and out already. But he finds excuses not to go. Fati's problem is, he's got it too soft. She just spoils the shit out of him. Bought him that car. And now she's talking about buying a house because 'Fati wants a house'. If she don't watch herself, she'll wind up just like poor Dori here!"

"Do you want another *Efes,* Connie?" Jane interrupted. "No thanks."

"Barish," Jane called inside to the bartender, "bring us three more of the same, duk!"

"But it weren't the fault of Sali. It were that bitch Jean who got her claws in him!" said Doreen.

"She's still in love with him, after all he done to her," explained May to Connie. "—Dori, you've got to forget him, luv!"

"But I know he prefers me! He told me so."

"When did he tell you that?" countered May suspiciously.

"Yesterday. He said I could have him back. All I have to do is sell me cottage in England."

"Dori, don't be daft. You're not!" said Jane, "Dori's got a heart that's softer than shit, that's her whole problem!"

"But I know he needs the money. What's going to happen to Sali if I don't!—Ooh, I have to visit the *loo*. If I don't, I'll pee meself."

It was not until Doreen rose staggeringly and made her uncertain way inside that Connie realized how drunk she must be. All three watched, wondering if she could make it.

"I better go with her," said Jane.

They watched her leave. "So how long have you been here?" Connie asked.

"Three years almost. We came on holiday and Len liked it so much he wanted to stay. Len's me husband but he died last year."

"Sorry to hear," said Connie.

"Yah, Len liked it here and didn't want to go back. But he died."

"So is he buried here, or did you take him back?"

"He's out in Fethiye Bay. That were his wish—to have his ashes dumped out there."

"You had him cremated—?"

"In England—they don't permit that here because it's a Muslim country. So I had it done in England and brought the ashes back. Took them out on Muhammad's boat. Made a real afternoon of it. Boat was crammed up to the gunnels with people."

"So the whole English community turned out?"

"No, Turks too! Len had a lot of friends. Dunno how many cases of beer we went through, I lost count."

"So is it hard being by yourself here, I suppose?"

"No, I go out. Go with the girls quite a bit. We usually come here." May reached for her vodka: "Shouldn't 've though last night. Uuh, did I get drunk! It were so bad I couldn't walk."

Connie waited. "And so who took you home—the girls?" she asked finally.

"No, Jane had to go home to make Fati his supper and feed the dog. Said she could take me if I wanted, but I didn't. To make a story short, I wound up with a Turkish bloke in the end. 'Ee drove me. Don't remember much of it though—if 'ee undressed me or I did. Remember 'ee felt heavy. I'd had so much *Efes* in me, and wine. Then 'ee began buying me brandies. All that motion, plus the weight, made me have to upchuck. I told 'im it were urgent, to get off me, and I just did barely make it to the *loo*. Came back, he climbs on me, and it happens again. I finally told him he had to go, that I couldn't do it tonight. Wanted to know if he couldn't come back later."

I still don't believe I'm hearing this, Connie thought: "What did you say—did you let him?"

"Dunno. I still can't remember who he were, luv."

Jane's face appeared in the sliding glass entrance: "May, you better come! Dori fell down inside the *loo* and I can't get her up!"

"Oh, shit!" Jane jumped up. "You guard the drinks, luv!"

What was she doing here with these people! Connie thought half in tears as she dropped two lira on the table and left. Her whole life was a mistake, even being in Turkey a mistake.

She needed reassuring and only Omer could provide that. Omer was the centre of her life, her support, as she hurried back through the gathering dark and cold to her empty apartment.

Only it wasn't. Lights inside burned! She saw him coming from the kitchen to greet her and she fell into his arms. "What a horrid, horrid day!" she told him with a tearful voice.

"Why, Connie, what happened?" he said, freeing himself. He led her into the kitchen. Pointed, "Try a little of *that*—that will make you forget, mein *Schatz*!"

She could see the unfinished raki bottle on the table, the ice cubes and water beside it. "Oh yes, please!" seeing him pour the raki first, then add the ice and water, watching as the raki slowly moved upward in the glass like creamy thick strands, to mix. He handed it to her and she drank, tasting the hot strong licorice taste.

"Now tell Omer!"

She had, starting with having been badgered by Eric, and forced to listen to that old woman's insinuations. Then, after she had been unable to reach him, sitting listening to the three elderly English women talk about their gigolos—seeing Omer's expression change from one of amusement to concern. "You sat with *them?* Connie, why waste your time with a bunch of old women? Half of what you hear is just lies—stories they make up because they got nothing better to do!"

"But you wouldn't answer! I tried phoning you I don't know how many times."

"Connie, I couldn't. My phone was out of contours and there was no place I could buy a phone card. Poor *Schatzi,*" he added, stroking her back and buttocks in that caressing way he had. During supper and for the rest of the evening he was very tender and supportive—it was as if the Omer she knew and loved had returned. But then she noticed in the unused spare room his suitcase laying open. "Omer, what's this?"

"I was about to tell you, Connie. I need to go to Izmir."

"Izmir—why?"

"It's where I have to go if I want to take my captain's test."

He had said something to her about that, it was true. "How long will you be gone?"

"Maybe four days. Could be more, but it could also be less. Connie, it's what you wanted. We can't just go on paying Ali, you said so yourself. It's not that I want to go, *Schatz.* I'd rather stay here with you, naturally. And once summer comes, we'll be together all the time!"

If it had to be, then he must. She would just have to resign herself. "Will you at least phone me from there?"

"Twice a day at least, I promise!"

After supper and after relaxing in front of the TV for a time, he had carried the suitcase into their bedroom to pack. She watched him pack just about everything of his that was in the closet, even his suit. She'd never seen him wear it. "Omer, why are you taking that?"

"I might need it, Connie. In case there's a graduation ceremony."

That night in bed he was at his most caring, his hands continually caressing her as he held himself back waiting for her. "Omer, do you love me?" she whispered to his ear: "...well , do you?"

"You know the answer to that, *Schatz.*"

In the morning she asked him how he would go to Izmir—by bus? She could drive him to the bus station.

"Think I'll take the car, Connie."

"Why not leave it here with me?"

"Connie, why? You know you can't drive it anyway—it's in my name."

"I drove it to Finike and back."

"Yes, but that's only because I was in the car."

She remembered money. "Can you transfer some money into my account before you leave?" she asked and saw his surprise. He would only be gone a week at the outside and, if she had to, couldn't she use the credit card? Saying nothing deliberately, she had reached into her purse for the bankbook which she opened, seeing his forehead wrinkle as he read it. Finally, he dug for his wallet and she watched him search through it for twenties, which he then counted before handing to her. "Here. Five hundred should tide you over until I get back and we can decide then. I won't be gone a week, Connie. You'll be alright—you have enough I hope to keep you busy?"

More than enough! During rainy spells she had had to wash down those teak decks with salt water daily and each time she returned to Tansas for more cleaning supplies she would now buy not one but five bottles of furniture polish! Though resigned to the need at present of spending her afternoons and evenings alone, she could look forward to that fast-approaching time when those classes would end, and he would be entirely hers again but what had he meant by *decide?* His suitcase stowed in the boot, Omer stopped to let her off as he always did opposite the *Gul.* Then that long parting kiss as his hand moved slowly down her saying *goodbye* before he got back in behind the wheel and she watched the Toyota vanish from sight.

That afternoon, as promised, Omer phoned to say that he had arrived safely, had found the school, and would start preparing for the test that afternoon. Now finally she would have something positive to tell when she crossed to Bea's; that when Omer returned, it would be as her captain on the *Gul.* And for the next two days he phoned her each afternoon just as he had said.

But then he missed a day. Then two. Worried, she called him but his phone was shut off. She left a frantic message: Omer, has something happened! Can you at least phone? Finally, he had.

"Well, which do you want first, *Schatz?* The good news or the bad?"

"Omer, don't tease me. Just tell me."

"I failed the test. *But* (this is the good part) since I missed it by so little, they'll let me retake it again next week. Only thing is, I'm stuck here, Connie."

"Just pass the test and come back to me!"

"Connie, I will, I promise. You know how much I miss being there with you, *Schatz.*"

Just to be told was enough to raise her spirits and keep her happy. But then Eric stopped her as she passed his table two days later to ask, "Isn't that a practically new white Toyota four door that you bought for your *betrothed*, dear lady?"

"Yes, I did buy a Toyota—?"

"I saw it, yesterday."

"You couldn't have!" said Connie: "It's in Izmir."

"Then it has an exact twin, because I looked at it thinking it was yours."

She didn't believe him. "Where?"

"Do you know where the *Car Cemetery Bar* is? Or *Bananas*—the night club? It was on one of those streets. I walked right by it, Connie."

She knew where *Bananas* was, but it wasn't possible! Nevertheless, she approached Bea. "Bea, tell me, what did Omer do before I met him?"

She could sense her friend's uneasiness: "There were others before me, right?" Connie saw the nod. "Even when he was a diver?"

"He never had any trouble getting women, before and after— that part made no difference. I nearly told you, several times."

"Then why didn't you?"

"Figured you would find out (if you didn't already know). Plus, I had no way of knowing how serious you were. Then it was too late—you'd already bought him the gulet."

But I told you before and you could have stopped me! she thought.

No she couldn't! Could or couldn't—Connie wasn't at all sure, only that her stomach felt uncomfortably bloated and sick as she walked to catch the dolmush.

The thought crossed her mind to go look where Eric said he had seen the Toyota. No, even if it had been hers as Eric thought, it wouldn't still be there and besides Eric enjoyed nothing more than to find all her hidden vulnerable places in which to stick his barbs.

As she waited for the next dolmush, she again tried phoning Omer but, just as before, his handy was shut off. Her dolmush came and within a half hour she was home, letting herself in through the heavy steel street door that was more like the door in a prison movie, Connie thought as she climbed the dank stairwell to her floor where she found, pinned onto her door, a note in Turkish but with *300* written. She text-messaged the note to Omer, waited, and this time he phoned her:

"I forgot all about it—the rent's due. Just pretend you didn't get his note. Or tell him I'll take care of it when I get back. He won't throw you out—he knows you're with me."

"Alright. Anyway, that's the least of my worries. When are you coming back?"

"Soon, Connie, I hope. They set my test back again until Thursday now. I miss you so much."

"Yes, I know how much!" she said and closed the phone on him.

Not wanting to cook for just herself, Connie had dinner on the seafront before returning to their apartment. How empty and bare it felt to her being on her own; *how cold!* she thought as she went through the rooms turning on the space heaters. In the kitchen she opened herself a bottle of wine which she quickly drank through to quell her anxieties. Towards midnight she went to bed, but slept poorly, waking frequently to discover herself in a cold bed, on a mattress too large for the heat from her inadequate body to warm; and in the morning she felt still tired—achy, as if she had not slept.

From the small corner store Connie brought freshly baked French bread and still warm eggs, one of which she poached and carefully lifted out to place atop a toasted slice of the bread. Then she made herself tea. Perhaps she would not go to the *Gul* today, she thought as she went for her bankbooks, both the English and Turkish and while she waited for the tea to steep, she examined them. Though she had tried her best to forestall the inevitable, she could no longer do so and, following breakfast, took the dolmush into Fethiye. But instead of going directly to the harbour, she turned onto Ataturk Boulevard and walked first to Western Union where she wired her bank in England to send the rest of the money. Then she continued on to Finance Bank where she drew out the remainder of her available savings, leaving only enough in her account to keep it from closing.

Emerging, she paused to decide. By crossing Ataturk and proceeding, she would come out at the harbour. Instead, she turned left toward the Roman Amphitheatre, scanning the parked cars as she went. While she did not for a moment think she would find *it*, the question nagged: and though she thought she could see beneath Eric's cynical public schoolboy surface a cruel desire to inflict hurt upon her at each chance, how could he have made up such a story? As far as she knew, he had never seen her Toyota; she had never showed it to him. She tried to have as little as possible to do with him. If she saw him approaching in the street and there was time, she would turn around, find a different way. So how could he know what kind of car they had bought? But somehow, he did, he knew everything. You couldn't hide anything here in Fethiye no matter how hard you tried, it seemed. Word of what you did travelled, as it were, on the very air you had to breathe.

There were no white cars. She turned at the roundabout before the Amphitheatre, entered the back streets. Soon she found herself on the very one they had walked arm-in-arm on her first day here. Memories of that day and the nights preceding and following it were forever in her consciousness, as the happiest moments of her life. Ahead was the *Bananas* where they had danced. *Where are you right now and what are you doing, Omer?* Digging down into her purse for the handy, she called, found his phone as usual shut off. He might be taking his test even as she phoned *in which case it would be shut off.* She decided to send him a text-message:

> Omer, what are you doing right now? Good luck on your
> test. And I love you so much!

Bananas was closed as she knew it would be. She stood at the centre of where four narrow streets intersected. Opposite her on the right was the old *hamam* where Omer had promised to take her for a real Turkish bath but hadn't. Behind it was another street that backed against the steep hillside beneath the ruined Crusader Castle; and it was in this direction she turned.

The street quickly ended at a *T,* the top of which bent to follow the curvature of the hillside behind. Along its back side stood an irregular row of two and three storied structures: balconies with flimsy wooden railings from which Turkish carpets occasionally hung. Connie looked right from the top of the *T*, saw what must be a café-bar because there were tables extending out into the street—empty, while to her left stood in the middle distance the *Car Cemetery Bar*. Connie had never walked this street before and had never seen the *Car Cemetery Bar* but she knew it was at once by the front end of an old car that hung precariously over the entrance. *I just hope it doesn't decide to fall down on my head!* she thought as she passed under it. She had had no idea of what to expect inside: what her curious eyes might find there.

Nothing at first, darkness, then dim shapes of chairs and tables, all appearing to her as worn and rather dirty. She heard loud rock and roll coming from speakers somewhere above her head and a few even louder English voices that came from the tables and bar at the back. There were no more than a half dozen customers; a table with just men engaged in what sounded like shouting and paying little attention otherwise two more at separate tables. The one at the table nearest looked up at her, then immediately back at his *Efes*. As Connie advanced further and more detail assembled in her vision, she noticed a row of booths along the wall to her right, only in place of wooden benches there were old car seats and in one a couple.

The light was too dim to make out the woman's features only that she had flowing red hair and was attractive—though the face was still too far away to actually see. There was a bottle of wine on the table between them, Connie saw, and she held her glass as if to drink—but didn't, caught, mesmerized by what her companion said and though his back remained to her, Connie knew from the way his hands moved, his head when he gestured, and the way in which his dark thick hair was combed back, his identity. With her wild, pounding heart she knew as she crept ever closer, to listen:

"..and instead of staying, instead of fighting back to clear my good name, I ran away—I'm not proud of it—to Antalya. Then that terrible bus accident. Three-thirty in the morning, we were going from Antalya to Marmaris. It was head-on. Here is the newspaper photo of my little daughter dying in my arms *here*. The impact pitched her out of my..."

It was the woman who had first discovered her and stopped listening to look up. Then Omer and she saw his face redden as, for the first time, speech failed him. She could see him staring helplessly at her, trying to regain presence-of-mind—while his pretty companion looked from one to the other in surprise and confusion. Finally, he said:

"Connie, this is…this is—"

"Kathy."

"Kathy."

With slow suffocating rage she stared into his upturned face, the black eyes alive but with the astonishment of their discovery she saw as she tried to think, decide *what to say or do?*

"When are you going to bring my car back?" she heard herself then, the voice sounding thin and about to break, aware too of the girl's equally astonished eyes moving from her face to Omer's then back. "Cat got your tongue, Omer?" she said watching both, conscious of her words—they were the ones her father had liked to use. "I've never known you speechless before!"

"I'll remove the rest of what I've still got stored from your apartment by tonight, I promise. I'll explain then," he added, addressing her as if they were but chance friends, or two people who had entered into some sort of formal agreement.

Then she was turning, rushing—she couldn't help it—amid the sudden quiet of the bar (even the rock and roll had stopped), into the street beyond feeling the tears wet her face as she half ran, she scarcely knew to where.

Back to her boat. To the *Gul* where she had left the gangplank raised about a foot off the concrete. With the tide at its highest, the angle of the gangplank up to the transom was perhaps thirty degrees. She climbed it to the quarterdeck where she turned and raised the gangplank, this time as high as she could, before going below to her cabin. Collecting extra blankets from the adjoining cabin, she hurriedly made up her own bed and burrowed herself in where she began to cry. She cried and cried—shaking.

Chapter 9

AFTER A TIME—SHE DID NOT know exactly how long she had lain wrapped inside the secure warmth of her covers—she became aware of the cabin's gloom as she stared unseeing up into the polished crossbeams of the deck just above her. Where had the sun gone? Had it crossed the sky already? *How long have you been down here?* She rose to retrieve her watch. Two! That explained how gloomy it had gotten, plus her sudden awareness that she was now hungry also, that she must use the toilet. On her way to the head she had to pass by the mirror. How puffed and red her face appeared in it, especially her eyes with their exposed crow's-feet, she thought, thinking *How sad and unappealing your face looks!* She could understand Omer not wanting it as she turned back into the cabin remembering she also needed to eat.

She was hungry but there was little aboard the *Gul* for her, just that bag of potato chips Omer had brought in that last time they had made love down here. The open sack was still where he had left it, on the marble counter beside the wash basin though, because of the high humidity, the chips no longer were good. There was still some cold *Efes* in the refrigerator up on deck near the steps that led into the salon, but little else. Returning briefly to the bathroom, Connie washed her face first and applied cream to hide the ugly lines, then some lipstick. Finally, she gave her hair a quick brush in an effort to out distance her depression before setting out for the 'beer garden' to bring back a fresh lamb doner. But as she approached the park along the quay, she thought of Bea's.

Could she face going back to Bea's knowing what they must be thinking and saying—Eric and his bunch especially. She'd been beaten up badly enough! Even so, she couldn't help but wonder what all they knew of her situation that she herself did not? The one thing clear to all was that she had been very foolish indeed!—and while you could excuse an eighteen-year-old perhaps, or even someone twenty-one, you certainly could not excuse a forty-year-old woman twice married. For that piece of stupidity she had only herself to blame as she returned to the ship with her lunch, stopping briefly to buy more wine at *Tansas.*

Then Connie continued back to the ship which was now her home, or *home substitute,* she thought because she was now as homeless as a bag-lady—wondering idly who first had coined those words. She felt centreless with neither a purpose nor a direction; that was what frightened her. *Home?* No, in the end she would lose the *Gul* too—this lovely thing more like a dream for which she had traded away all!

No, because what was *all?* Charles? A life she had abhorred? She could see him still, pulling at that ear. What he had received was no more than what he had deserved. Only, in the process of enacting her revenge, she had decided her own fate too since sooner or later Omer would come, bringing as her replacement that redhead he apparently had picked up—Kathy. Where had he found her…Izmir? No, it must have been here, and now was he going to move in with her next? The question was, did he even go to Izmir? Bea might know, she thought as she carried the wine and her doner into the salon. But did it matter he had taken from her all that he had had any use for and, having taken it, wanted her no more. That was the part that hurt so badly.

Inside a galley drawer she found the wine opener. Then she proceeded on deck with the now opened bottle, glass, and her doner. *Where do you want to eat?* Somewhere in front, she thought as she made her way along the side of the salon and wheelhouse, then sunroof over the forward cabins, to the bow where she sat down upon the deck she had spent so many hours making spotless and with her back resting up against the sloping front of the forward cabins, Connie poured herself first the wine. Then she peeled back the paper in which the doner was wrapped and bit at the end tasting its greasy lamb flavour. She must decide and decide *now* what to do!

She could not and did not want to stay in that cold place now that he was moving out. Just the way he had announced to her, *I'll come and get the rest of what I left stored.* And from *your* apartment!—like they were barely more than strangers, like it had never been his. Again she felt tears, felt her stomach going to be sick as she rose dropping the doner and rushed to the side feeling the chewed food wanting to come up. Then it had as she leaned into the ship's dangerously low handrail and felt its thin steel cable cut painfully into the flesh above her knees as she pressed against it and waited for the retching to stop. How easy it would be to let herself fall, she thought gazing down at the water.

Finally, when it was safe to do so, she returned to where she had been sitting on the deck with her back against the superstructure, and slowly reintroduced the wine to her mouth. When did he say he would come for his remaining clothes? *By tonight.* Because the rent remained unpaid, she wanted to be out first. Yes, that would be the first thing she must do. Now.

The sun had dropped behind the seafront and the uneven buildings facing it resembled, in silhouette, a row of teeth badly in need of fixing, she thought as she walked the last block to their apartment and let herself in. How alien and cold the rooms felt to her. Connie shivered. She could not have made herself stay here even a single night now because not just the rooms, the walls, but the objects too were filled with despair and what had been the location of her most intense happiness was now the source of her pain as Connie carried suitcases from the storage room onto their bed and began to pack, drawer by drawer. Omer's, she saw, had been emptied and the last of his things taken from their closet! Did that mean he had already moved in with the redhead? Kathy. Bea said he never had had trouble picking up women. What Connie still had not come to terms with was not just the skill and ease with which he could lie—but that she had been so Completely deceived! She could never have done a thing like that—not even to her enemy let alone someone she loved, Connie told herself as she finished the packing.

Last to go in was her laptop which she had to force then she zipped the suitcase shut. Carrying both to the door, she debated on where to leave the key, downstairs in the mailbox? And if the landlord shouldn't think to look there—? That was the least of her problems—and anyway, he would no doubt ask Omer and Omer would find her: *Connie, where did you hide the key?* It was completely dark and both of her arms ached as she finally arrived back at the gangplank. She managed to lug both suitcases up it one at a time, and to raise the gangplank behind her as high as it could go but then, reconsidering, she lowered it back down to within a foot of the concrete before dragging the suitcases the remaining distance to the salon below deck. Though hungry, she was too tired and upset to think about food.

Instead, she opened the remaining bottle of wine. It was cold on the *Gul* and she began to shiver. So she burrowed down amid the piled bed covers—in that bed where they had made love last. But she couldn't get warm. She'd lain there beneath the pile of blankets and shook as if she were sick with fever—she couldn't stop. Then, finally, she slept.

It was the isolation she feared. That next morning, after having had tea and French bread with honey and cherry jam in one of the cafes along *Ataturk*, Connie had returned to the *Gul* to sort her life out. She thought as she began unloading items she would need over the next few days from her suitcases: blouses, skirts, and her underwear went into the drawers beneath her bed, her cosmetics she lined up inside the specially protected shelves above the head. Since there was nowhere for her dresses, those she laid out atop the bed in the adjoining cabin. Then there was her laptop. What to do with it?

She wondered if Alice still emailed? Or Charles? He had no doubt discovered that his stock certificates had been sold and by now had gone to the police. She hoped Alice's year at Leeds hadn't been too spoiled by what she had done. What would she say if she could know her mother had bought her lover a gulet and that the lover had then dumped her for a younger, prettier woman? No, because she had run out of money! In a sense, and though the thought left her only sad, it was better that Alice wouldn't find out.

She could sell the laptop, but first all the emails must be erased from it and she wasn't sure how. Or how to remove her name from the Internet. First, she would have to find somebody with a phone line. Bea—but Bea would want to know why so she would have to think up a story. Just tell Bea it was for sale—that she needed the money. Bea would understand that much. So after checking with the bank to see if the last of her money had come, Connie crossed the park to Bea's bar and entered seeing their faces. Upon discovering her some, she saw, stopped talking and stared but to her relief she could not locate Eric's face among them, anywhere, as she moved past them toward Bea's table.

Then she saw Bea's face, saw its initial surprise change, become something else as the only one Connie sensed she could trust rose smiling to greet her. "I was wondering when you'd decide to show. I would have come looking for you if you'd left me even your handy number. Where are you staying and why didn't you come earlier!"

"Guess I felt too humiliated to."

"He's a typical Turk, Connie. Here, sit down," said Bea, drawing a chair for her. "I'll bring you some tea."

Connie watched her friend disappear, to appear moments later carrying two steamy mugs. "What do you take in yours, milk? Sugar?"

"Just a little milk, please."

Bea returned with a milk carton and sat down across from her. "And the thing about it is, they can be so convincing! You're not the first western woman it happened to and you won't be the last, I can guarantee."

Connie felt her warm faded old eyes gaze back at her as Bea sipped at her tea—deliberating.

"And I'm speaking from personal experience. Mine was named Ali. One of the many and I was so convinced he loved me."

"*You!*"

"He helped me to open this bar, in fact—with my money. I was about your age—this was about nineteen years ago now. I had just gone through a difficult divorce—"

"This was in England?"

"Of course, and wound up here somehow, where I met this most handsome Turk whom I was convinced loved me... but if you're a Muslim, you can have but one love it says in the Koran. Allah!"

Connie watched as she reached for her tea, again sipped. "So you're saying, the same thing happened to you?" She saw Bea's nod.

"We'd had the bar for about a year. I decided to go back to England for a month—my son wanted me to come, as did my sister. So I said *yes* and left the bar in Ali's capable hands (I thought). And to make the story short, he totally cleaned me out."

"Robbed you!"

"Of my car. The liquor supply. Whatever else he could find (he even sold some of the tables). Fortunately for me, he couldn't get at my money."

"What did you do?"

"Started all over again—what else could I do?"

"But what made you decide to stay?"

"I like Fethiye. Besides, my son was married and didn't want a mother hanging around. There was nothing left for me in England. So where are you living now? You know, I would have come to see you."

"Temporarily on the *Gul*. It was the only place I could think of. He's going to run me off it sooner or later, I know. What am I going to do, Bea?"

"Do you have any money?"

"Two thousand pounds—it just arrived... *After that?* I can't go back to my husband (even if I wanted to!). And I can't work here, *can I?*" She could feel her tears start. She fought them back. "Not legally, though they do. In bars and restaurants, or sometimes on the boats. Some squeeze by selling clothes on the Tuesday market, and in shops. But to do that you need to hook up with another..."

"Turk?" But she saw Bea's attention was now drawn to something directly behind her.

"Dear lady..."

She would know that English public school boy voice anywhere: Connie spun about. "Eric!" He was trying to give her a piece of paper.

"We all know what happened and are genuinely sorry. You remain one of us, after all. So do take *this.*"

The torn sheet of notepad paper. "What's it for?"

"Name and address of my solicitor. I've taken the liberty of mentioning you to him so he is expecting you. Do go see him, dear lady, he speaks English. I would urge you not to take this lying down (no pun intended). And the consultation is free."

"I would," said Bea, adding her voice.

It had been their kindness and support that had made her decide in the end and that next morning she set out in search of Eric's lawyer. His offices were on the second floor, in a rather shabby alley, reached only by an outside stair. The door was of heavy dark wood and, in place of the handle, was a brass knob that would not turn, and button below which she pushed, then waited. Finally the door opened and she saw a young and pretty face smiling at her enquiringly. "I'm Connie Cullingsworth, to see Murat? I think Eric sent me."

"Please," said the girl, opening the door wide for her, upon what appeared a suite of offices tastefully, even opulently, furnished, Connie saw at once. The girl, either a receptionist or secretary, motioned for her to sit as she proceeded with business- like steps in skirt and heels to her desk where she reached for the phone and said something into it in Turkish.

Then a door behind the secretary opened and a man in a brown business suit appeared, *thirtyish* but what struck Connie was not the smile inviting her inside, but the eyes—their blueness! "I am Murat Arslan," he said, extending his hand as he ushered her into his office, to a dark overstuffed chair before a huge desk. Her eyes took in the surroundings. On the wall behind where he sat were framed documents and photos while leather-bound books adorned the wall opposite.

"And you are Missus Cullingsworth who have bought a gulet, I believe. Sit down and welcome! You must tell me first how you buy this gulet. Was it a gift to this Omer? But first, do you like some tea?"

"Only if you're going to have a glass," said Connie. No matter what you did, or where in Turkey, you got offered tea, she thought. In the bank you were handed a glass. Shop owners invited you in for tea. Should she drown—if she fell overboard— even as they lowered her into the ground the Turks would serve tea! The door opened and the pretty secretary appeared with the tea tray.

"Sugar? Milk?" inquired Murat.

Just milk she had answered and watched as the lawyer dropped three sugar cubes into his glass and carefully stirred. "Now, Madam," he said finally, "Say me how you bought this gulet. Was it a present?"

But there had been little more that she could add to what the lawyer knew already—what Eric apparently had told him. Just the actual sums, dates, and place names were missing. The lawyer asked to see her bankbook, which he then went to photocopy. Returning, leaned toward her with his hands spread wide upon the brightly polished desktop. Without a single doubt there had been a crime, he said. It was people like Omer who were giving Turkey its bad name, and so—she could rest completely certain— the courts, the judges, would see her in a sympathetic light. "But the one problem," he said, pausing as though he were reviewing the page in a book "is the *Gul's* papers."

The lawyer again stopped, this time to contemplate the ceiling. "Of course," he went on, "it could be proven that she had paid for the *Gul II.* The unfortunate part was that the papers had had to be in Omer's name because the boat couldn't be hers—and while the situation wasn't impossible, it was complicated. What they would have to prove in order to retrieve any of the seventy-five thousand pounds was that she had been deliberately misled—and much would depend on Captain Ali's account. In fact, should he agree to take the case, that would be the first thing he would do!

"What?" asked Connie.

"Take Ali's deposition. That's the first thing. The second—"

But again they were interrupted by the secretary bringing in more tea.

"Care for another?" the lawyer asked as his secretary set the two fresh glasses onto his desk.

"No thanks." She watched him drop in the sugar cubes, then stir with that tiny spoon made specially for Turkish tea glasses which are equally small and shaped like an inverted bell. "You started to say there was a second thing."

"Marmaris. I was coming to that. I like to find out just what Omer was really doing in Marmaris. You mentioned a woman."

"Angie, she was English and had a bar with this Turk who apparently worked as her bartender. Omer got to know her quite well—enough to make her tell him she suspected she was being robbed."

"Of money?"

"And liquor, which kept disappearing. Anyway, to clear his own name Omer set a trap one night and caught the night bartender in the act, he said. But she refused to believe him."

"You mean *he* could be the thief!" said Murat.

"I hadn't thought of it in that respect," said Connie.

"Interesting," said the lawyer. "Depending on what we find out, it could swing the case in our favour, if we can show a pattern."

"How?" she asked. "We hire detective."

"Oh, I don't know. How much would that cost me?"

"Not so much maybe."

"Do you already have somebody?"

"Mohammed. He was with Traffic Police but he is now retired. He is good detective, and I would say you not expensive. I always use Mohammed in these cases."

Connie felt herself hesitating. "So just how good is my case do you think"

"Very good, I would say. And if we don't win with the first time, always I appeal."

Now she was afraid. "So how much is this going to cost me?"

"Not so much. Five hundred pounds to start. Enough to file your case. Take depositions."

She had never felt very confident when it came to gambling. "I need to think about it," she said.

"Seventy-five thousand, Missus Cullingsworth, is much money," the lawyer reminded her.

"I know. But I still have to think about it," she repeated, and rose.

As Connie returned to the *Gul* she weighed out her chances. She never had had much luck gambling—she supposed it was because, to win, you needed first confidence. How long had Omer's litigation over his disputed inheritance been going on and Omer was a Turk. So what possible chance could a forty-one-year-old English woman who had completely lost her common sense, who had acted so foolishly, have, she thought as she climbed the gangplank to the quarterdeck of her ship pretty as a dream that never had been hers! None in this world: and now she only could wait for whatever or whoever came. Omer sooner or later *must*!

But it was not until the afternoon of the next day that he reluctantly decided to come searching for her because he feared the harm she could do to his relationship with Sylvia who was a prize too good to lose! Though he was careful to conceal it from Connie, Omer had returned to Fethiye three days before after having taken the test in Izmir on the same day he had text- messaged Connie telling her he had failed and must stay to retake the exam. In fact, he had passed it and had driven to the waterfront promenade lined with its bars and restaurants to celebrate success. There, quite by luck, he had run across two English girls still in their twenties, evocatively dressed in expensive-looking clothes, and staying in a four-star hotel near the beach. What had begun as dinner together in a rather posh restaurant he showed them ended with expensive champagne in one of the rooms where he had fucked both for two days and might have stayed a third had he not insisted on picking up their tab! So in the end he'd had no choice but return to Fethiye and Connie.

What had surprised him, being away from her that long, was how little he missed her. Now, as he approached Fethiye, he really did not want to return to her. In the initial phase sex had seemed all-important. He had enjoyed possessing her solely, enjoyed the envy of friends, and had looked forward with aroused feelings to the time spent with her in bed just as now it was getting drunk with his friends that he missed, and nights spent gambling. What did she want from him? There were barriers separating them, and to cross through them he knew he could not, on a level more basic than he thought.

The first thing she would demand from him would be to account for his time. And then, of course, there was always the matter of how much money he had spent. She would probably want to see his bankbook! Well he was not going to put up with being humiliated by any female in front of his friends and he did not care how *good* she thought she was—she was still just a woman! Omer dug for his handy, dialled, then waited. "Ahmed, this is Omer...Tamam! Yah, I'm just coming back from Izmir. Say, Ahmed, you don't have a woman staying there at the moment?...Good, because I need a place to stay for a few days...Yah, she's been giving me problems. I'll explain when I get there. Right now I'm on the Antalya Road and about fifteen minutes away...Tamam!"

Omer was still undecided on what to do about Connie as he parked his Toyota before the curb, then climbed the two flights of stairs to his friend's apartment. It made no sense to dump her for now, so he had text-messaged her again to say that the exam had been postponed once more, to give him more time. He stayed well away from his gulet and from Bea's and began frequenting places he believed she would not think to go such as the Car Cemetery Bar where she had surprised them. She could have ruined things with Kathy for him, and almost had!

Omer had found her sitting in one of the tiny outdoor backstreet cafes as you walked toward the Roman Amphitheatre and, on their second meeting, he had coaxed her into going with him to the Car Cemetery Bar where Connie never came. Should she, the dingy darkness of its cavernous interior would hide him. But despite his precautions she had found them and now he was forced to act; do something before Kathy found out too much. He did not know yet exactly how much his new girlfriend was worth, the actual amount in pounds sterling, but he sensed it was enough certainly to go after.

Finding where Connie had fled to, where she was hiding, was quite easy; he had only to ask around. The owner of a boat moored close to the *Gul* told him what he needed to know and though surprised that she would move her possessions onto the ship, he viewed the matter calmly. Ordinarily her staying aboard the *Gul* would pose no problem for now, he thought as he approached the gangplank since he had no plans to move the *Gul* for the next three weeks, and by then she surely would have gone back to England. But with Kathy that had changed and though he did not enjoy having to get rough with women—he was not a Turk after all, he was German!—now he would be forced to run her off, scare her into going back to where she had come from.

The quarterdeck looked empty and bare, but as he started down the companionway to the saloun he discovered an empty wine bottle, she had to be living down here. The evidence was everywhere: unwashed dishes stacked around the sink in the galley; plastic shopping sacks and food wrappers lying about, more empty wine bottles. He turned into the rear passageway, to the aft starboard cabin where she liked to have sex. Sure enough, she had turned it into a bedroom. He listened for her sound but the ship lay silent. Perhaps she had gone ashore, he thought as he returned on deck and started forward along the wheelhouse. Then he discovered her sitting with her back to him, near the edge of the deck up in the bow above the port anchor: a wine glass beside her idle hand as she gazed motionless out at the sea thinking thoughts.

He did not care what her thoughts were—he was not even curious. To the contrary, he knew he had to keep a careful distance from her. She was English and he knew what she wanted. She was no different than the others before her, like Angie. He would remain firm but he could still be pleasant. Before another two weeks were up, chances were that she would get tired of the *Gul* and leave on her own. The only danger she posed was if the two women should accidentally run into each other. That was the one threat. Kathy was coming along too well to risk anything now. Sooner or later she would insist on being taken aboard the *Gul* and he would run out of reasons *why not*. Or worse still, what if the two women should meet alone in the street! "Hello, Connie, I've been looking all over Fethiye for you."

She started up, snapped from her daydream by his voice and the resurgent joy hearing it brought as she leapt to her feet. He was standing near the foremast but something she saw in his eyes—their hard glitter—struck a chord of fear in her as she struggled to find words. "I suppose you came to tell me to leave!" she said, afraid—she couldn't help it.

"No not, I…didn't know you're here, that's the truth. I've been busy, I had to go back to Izmir. For my papers."

"*Papers*—is that what you call her? Your new girlfriend— what *is* her name? Oh, Kathy!"

He had considered making up a new story but saw at once the pointlessness. He had come, after all, to run her off. "You didn't tell me you were moving out. I asked everybody I could think of if they knew where you'd gone… so how long have you been hiding here?" And when she only stared back at him, he announced, "You can stay a few days more if you want—I'm not moving the *Gul* for another week." The anguish in her eyes began to make him uncomfortable. "If you can't find anywhere to stay you like, I can find you a place. Do you want me to look for a place, Connie?" he said watching her carefully, like you would a somewhat dangerous animal.

His black eyes shone blankly, glinting as she drew closer to that face she had loved. "Why did you do it to me, Omer? Because she was younger and prettier? Or because she has money! Well? Don't you think I deserve an answer?" He took a step back but her eyes continued to hold him fast. "What's the matter, Omer, can't you speak? Cat still got your tongue?"

Backing slightly away from her, finally he spoke the words scarcely above a whisper:

"I have to live, Connie."

"*You* have to live!"—the words breaking inside her hurting terribly. "You! And so you destroy me! All I ever wanted to do was to love you." She could feel her voice exploding and she began beating at him, pummelling his chest with her fists, until his hands caught at her wrists and held her, helplessly. She struggled against him. Then he released her with a shove that sent her backward into the ship's railing, the backs of her knees striking it as she struggled for her balance. His hands caught her, "Be careful, *Schatz.*"

He pulled her away from the railing by both wrists to the centre of the deck where he released her. He did not want to fight her, that was not why he had come. Once a woman turned emotional; she became uncontrollable. There was little point in trying to reason with them then, thought Omer as he turned his back on her and started to walk aft trying to decide what his next move ought to be. But he'd had enough of her and as he reached the wheelhouse he turned and faced her for a last time.

"I want you off!" His voice was level—threatening. "I'm not going to Kas. I'm taking the *Gul* to Marmaris for the season. We're leaving Monday. That's five days from now. I don't care where you go but you've got to be off this boat…I can get someone to help with the suitcases."

For a time she sat silent as a figurehead, her legs extended, feet hanging over the slanting anchor chain, and gazed mutely out at the harbour. *Five days.* She knew in the end that something would happen; knew she must do something *but what?* She liked to sit here on the deck where nobody came bothering her, where she could learn to tolerate her wretchedness, a little like one learns to manage a persistent toothache.

She enjoyed watching the mist rise from the water early in the morning, like steam does, with the appearance of an orange red sun. Cool at first, it would gain heat and intensity as the day progressed.

It was perfect weather—in Manchester it would be cold and rainy. *Where was Alice, was she happy at Leeds?* She did not like to leave the *Gul* and did so only when it was necessary. She would look about the boat each day to see what it needed. Not tea—the galley was loaded. Some more wine and another chicken which Connie discovered she could purchase still warm from the spit. Then in the evening after the sun had set (she liked to watch the sun as it set), she would hurry through town avoiding faces, spending as little time as possible there before returning to her *Gul*.

At first she left the gangplank lowered behind her until the thought occurred, *what if those she knew from Bea's should come looking for her!* She did not want to see anyone, Eric above all— she had had enough of them. So she rose and walked aft to the gangplank which she then raised to keep them all away. Then she went below and opened herself another bottle of wine which she carried forward to her place in the bow above the anchor chain which extended in a long sloping curve far out into the bay. She could trace its shadow over the water until the two met and the chain disappeared.

How different the water appeared out beyond the anchor chain. How pretty, with the sea like a reflective mirror over which, as a wind came up, the sunlight danced. How lovely it was to just sit and gaze out at it. But closer in, beneath her in the shadow of the ship, the water was foul with scum, and she could not see what lay beneath. The sheen of oil coated its surface while tendrils extended like moving fingers down into the darkness. What would she find down there? she thought as she rose and climbed over the ship's railing, that low steel cable tautly strung through a row of stanchions and tried to peer down into that darkness; see what she knew she could not. The edge of the deck beyond the railing was like a narrow ledge over which she leaned unsteadily far above the water as her hands, feeling back, found the steel cable that prevented her from falling while she stared down at the water as if trying to know it: resolve something that was urgent inside her. *He was no Yanko and could never be,* she knew.

She felt so isolated and exposed as all her mistakes, her suppositions, her need to believe in something—in him—came flooding back. Why *him?*—because of those alive black eyes with which he had promised her so much? And that she had foolishly believed as though from inside a dream, almost as if she had lived most of her life by proxy. "But we live as we dream," she told herself aloud as she suddenly recalled that fragment of line her mind equated with despair. *No, Omer is no Yanko.* If anyone was, *she* was, thought Connie as she leaned out over the water knowing only the crooks of her index fingers curled about the steel cable behind held her. *But is it just aloneness that is down there, Mr Conrad—is that really all?*

There was only that one way to find out. She leaned forward still more, until she feared even her two fingers could not hold her. But she remembered something else he had said. If you're a swimmer it's not so easy to drown yourself.

"Mother, is that you up there? Get down before you fall, you know you can't swim!"

"Alice!" She turned. It was her! Slowly Connie stepped back over the cable to the safety of the deck.

"Whatever possessed you to climb out there!? I can't believe it. Now come let me aboard this thing!"

In her joy to see her daughter Connie put aside all thoughts of her disgrace and rushed to drop the gangplank. It was the same Alice, same *be sensible, mother* smile, and the eyes were quick, intelligent like she remembered even if the face looked paler than when she had delivered her daughter to Leeds. But then, English were white. They hugged and hugged—Connie really had begun to think she would not see Alice again. Her daughter would need a chair! was her first thought. "Wait while I go get some wine, Alice, it's up at the bow. No, follow me and see the ship. You can tell me what you think."

"Mum, I can see it's beautiful! But why did you do such a stupid thing? Never mind, I already know. Bea told me just about everything."

Including where she was hiding! Connie had shown Alice the gulet first as they walked forward for the wine that stood opened up near the bow. Then from the salon she had taken a second chair which she placed beside hers before the captain's table. Finally she brought glasses up from the galley. Poured.

"So how did you find me?" asked Connie. "Let me guess. From Bea or Omer—it had to be one of the two."

"No, Mum, I couldn't locate Bea's number. But I knew you had to be here—where else could you be!"

"You tried emailing me, I suppose."

"Both of you, numerous times. I figured you wouldn't answer, but I thought Omer might."

"And Charles?"

"He tried his best to track you—through your bank account. But you'd already closed that, and you weren't sending emails. It was a pretty good escape, Mum."

"Are the police looking for me?"

"No. And for that you have only me to thank. It was a pretty devastating blow to him, whether you realize it or not."

"So he didn't go to the police?"

"He wanted to. But I managed to dissuade him by playing up to his weaknesses (he's a very vain man and I still say, he would make good subject matter for someone's case study.). Anyway, I kept pressing the point: 'Think of the scandal it would create, Charles. What would it do to your reputation at the School Authority? Will they even renew your contract? And what will your employees at *Computer Operations* say? Think about it, Charles!' I kept hammering the message home and in the end it worked. So here I am. I've come to collect you, Mother."

"You mean he wants me back?" Connie reached automatically for the wine glass.

"I'm not sure 'wants' isn't too strong a word, but *yes.*"

Connie wasn't certain at that instant what she felt—mute shock, surprise, a slight twinge of fear even—as she emptied her glass, then refilled both. "But he doesn't know anything about my buying this gullet—how could he?"

"Not yet. And I think, Mum, I would avoid telling him." She watched Alice reach for her wine and pause a moment, to reflect. "Mother, why did you do such a stupid thing! But you don't have to answer me, I already know. Even Don Juan could learn a few pointers from *him.* Tell me this much: when you two met at Bea's the first time—*or was it the second time maybe?*— he asked if he could show you his diving boat. And you went— yes?"

She felt herself go pale, "Yes."

"And he took you below, didn't he!"

"How do you know that?" She was going to be ill.

"Mother, for just this once, try opening your eyes."

Retribution

Chapter 1

I SUPPOSE IT'S RAINING SHE said to herself, sitting before the tiny window of the aircraft looking out at nothing: a shroud of white muslin. Two evenings prior they had collected her clothes and personal effects into two suitcases and her vanity which they then carried to the taxi stand nearest the *Gul.* It had been but a short ride to Alice's hotel somewhere in the back streets behind Bea's where they had eaten Turkish food in one of the cheap cafeteria- style restaurants where tourists would never think to go. Then they had purchased several bottles of wine to take up to Alice's room. The room had twin beds and after several glasses of wine Connie had laid down and in the middle of their conversation, she must have fallen asleep.

Because she felt someone pulling at her arm, jerking at it, and she opened her eyes to discover Alice fully dressed and wearing her coat saying: "Mum, wake up!"

It must have been all that wine, plus the fact that she hadn't slept in the last few nights—she couldn't. She could see the ceiling light burning over her head: "What time is it?"

"I don't know—four o'clock."

"In the morning?"

"Yes. Now get up!"

"Where are we going?"

"Dalaman Airport."

"You didn't tell me anything about buying tickets."

"Mother, get dressed! Ahmed the cab driver—you might remember him—is downstairs waiting. We have to leave *this instant!*"

"Mum," said Alice from the next seat, "are you alright?"

"Perfectly." The pressure in her ears had told her that the aircraft was beginning its descent and she saw tiny beads of water appear now on the outside of her window. She felt Alice's hand.

"Mum, things will work out...By the way —"

"*What?*"

"You still haven't told me what you did with that laptop of yours. Charles turned the house upside down searching for it. That's how I knew you had it. You do know there were messages from me on it. And from Charles. When he tried to track you down, the internet was the first place he looked."

"It's now at the bottom of Fethiye bay," said Connie. She had carried it up to the bow and from the *Gul's* bowsprit let it drop watching it strike the water and sink, swirl downward, disappearing in seconds down into the unknowable darkness below.

"That's one of the few smart things you did, Mum."

"I know...I can't help being nervous about this, Alice."

"Mum, you'll be alright," said her daughter. "You just have to be a little careful is all. Ask him about his computers. Say you like his new job title. Pump up his ego—he enjoys that."

"If that's all that's required...I suppose he still pulls at that ear."

She glanced down at her watch, then back up at her daughter. How unapproachable was that face beside her, how different they were in the way each thought. And while she did not understand Alice at all—her apparent detachment—Connie was glad for her in one respect.

Her own lifestyle had been just the opposite, and for that she had paid. Alice seemed more focused—complete. Yet she remained secretive too. There were so many things Connie wanted to know about her daughter but had been afraid to ask sensing that Alice did not want her life to be looked at, at least not by her mother! Also, she would be exposing something of herself, thought Connie, things perhaps best left hidden. "Tell me this... "

"Tell you *what*, Mother?"

"I take it Omer must have showed you that same *sort-of* cabin at the front of the diving boat and that's where, according to him, you spent a night or two. He let you, he said. Did he stay on the boat with you?" she asked, and read her daughter's surprised glance:

"It's not the end of the world, Mother. Mum, I already knew what he was."

"Beforehand?"

"Yes, by keeping my ears open. Mum, what do you think those middle-aged English women find to talk about all day long? So I was in no danger of falling for him if that's what you were afraid of."

The *bong* sounded. Looking up, Connie saw the seatbelt sign had come on.

"Buckle up, Mum."

"So what's going to happen now? Am I taking you back to Leeds tonight?"

"No, it's the Easter break. So I can stay with you a couple of nights, if that helps."

"Do you like Leeds?"

"It's alright."

"What are you taking—journalism?"

"Yah, but I'm thinking of changing maybe to anthropology (if I decide to go on, that is). One of my profs started me reading Margaret Mead. She's sort of cool."

"*Go on?* You're not thinking of quitting already! I thought sure you would want to go to graduate school when the time comes."

"That's a long way into the future. Probably, but how can I know what I'll be like four years from now? Mum, I really don't know what I want yet."

"*Yet*—why?"

"I don't know, Mum, except there are so many things to choose from. And while some are interesting in certain ways, nothing stands out over the rest...sometimes I think the world is just filled with dead things."

The flight attendant came toward them to see if their seatbelts were fastened, their seats upright. Connie glanced at her watch. "I suppose Charles must be getting on the M-56 about now...I wonder what my status will be when we get there—different, I know that much."

"You're listed as missing for one thing. Charles wanted to go to the police and report that you'd absconded with his stocks but, as you know, I talked him out of it. So he listed you as a missing person. Officially, Mother, you don't exist."

It was a very severe-faced Charles who waited for them as they emerged out onto the rain-wet pavement from the terminal. Was it hate she read in those cold blue eyes? She averted her own, to the wetness of the street. "Where we parked, Charles?" said Alice, her mouth automatically forming to the shape of a smile—its facsimile, Connie thought. "Second floor," came the perfunctory response. There was no greeting in it, none even intended as if she were witnessing a random exchange between two passers-by, the one in one in need of information, on a street corner. Her daughter lugging the two suitcases as Charles led, they crossed to the parking garage through a steadily falling rain, and to the car. Connie did not wait but slipped first into the back seat forcing the choice of where to sit upon her daughter. Alice then slid in next to her.

She could see the back of Charles' head before her and each time he looked left she saw his distended ear. It looked if anything more swollen and ugly, she thought as Charles drove the M-56 toward Stockport, this winding band of concrete and asphalt she had seen so many times, the last a meagre two months before, from a taxi and for the final time she'd thought *how untrustworthy were all such hopes and plans—things you thought inviolable, that you foolishly built hope itself around. But they weren't and you lived to be deceived.* Then they were exiting the M-56 as she soon found herself amid familiar streets and houses, and she remembered looking at what would become their house for the first time—all those hopes for a secure future she had projected into these four brick walls and roof.

It was an attractive enough house seen from the outside—the front yard presentable. But hardly was Connie inside before she sensed the change. While nothing appeared untidy or out of place—everything was in its exact, correct order—there was a stale, unlived odor that she could only associate with rooms used to store objects that are no longer of any use or spaces like closets where the permeating smell is of mothballs. Then the correct answer dawned. It was the seediness of a recluse!

Before her bookshelves in the living room she stopped. All her novels and old college texts she had decided to save had been replaced by more books on computers, or by Charles' catalogues. "Where are all my books, Charles?" she asked.

"In Alice's room. They were in the way, and I didn't know what to do with them…I also considered giving them away."

Conversation stopped and a silence filled with awkwardness, perhaps misgiving, ensued as Connie searched for a neutral response. "Mum, I think you could use a bath after being cooped up—not the right adverb I know but why don't we get you unpacked?"

"Yes," said Connie, conscious of Charles' awakened interest in them. Of his eyes on her back as she followed Alice to the stairs.

Her bedroom too had appeared the same as when she had left it, until she began opening her drawers. Items she had not had room to take and so had left behind lay crumpled and mixed. He could only have done that while he was searching for her computer. It took both an effort but soon the items of clothing were refolded and neatly laid out, the drawers like before, her face creams and cosmetics back to their proper locations on the vanity. "Now you can take your bath," said Alice, "And while you do, I can run to Tesco, buy something good for dinner. How about steaks, or some nice chops if I see any, especially after having to eat Turkish meat which half the time you can't chew anyway."

"Won't Charles object?"

"Mother, why cater to him!"

"Wait—won't you need money?" Connie called after her.

"No, and Mum, I would advise you to hide the rest of that money. Depending on his terms, it may become the only thing separating you and a bag lady!"

Terms? Connie watched her daughter disappear along the landing before turning into the en suite bath. It too was as when she had left. Lined up in the corner beneath the mirror in an order that never varied were his toilet articles: shaving tools, soap, the mug for his shaving brush, finally his Listerine. When they first were married and she would unintentionally mix his toilet things up, often when she returned, she would find each of the items lined back up again in their original order. 'You're Mr Clean!' Alice had called him and whenever her daughter played with his shaving things, deliberately reversing their order; it was she herself who heard about it Connie remembered.

The bath would feel good, she thought, after being forced to make do with the *Gul's* cramped little head where the shower hose was attached to a pipe over the toilet. On her last day aboard there had been no water at all to her sudden and unexplained surprise—until it occurred to her that Omer must have gone to the water department to have the water shut off. So she soaked herself for a long time then towelled and changed into fresh clothes. Then she started along the landing to the stairs but stopped before Alice's room where her books now were.

As she entered, she saw first Alice's unmade bed. Her daughter had always been a messy child, Connie remembered as she took in the room. There was no hint that Scraggles had ever even slept in this room and where his food and water bowls had been the bookshelves now stood. They were Charles' original shelves from his bachelor apartment now stuffed full with her old books she saw as she crossed to them and glanced at some of the titles. *Heart of Darkness. The Waves.* She had more of Virginia Woolf than just *that* she thought as she turned out of the room to find Alice.

Her daughter was in the kitchen starting dinner for the two, working around Charles who was preparing his quorn. On a plate near the gas burners Connie saw two rib steaks and she glanced quickly to Charles; she could sense his irritation.

For as long as Alice stayed with them and slept in her own bed, her presence served as a kind of protection, thought Connie—a barrier that kept Charles away. Only at night was she left defenceless, forced to lay beside him conscious of the narrow strip of bed sheet that kept them apart, his body on one side of the imaginary line, hers on the other. "What did your daughter mean when she said you were 'cooped up'?" she heard him ask in the dark.

"I don't think anything, Charles. My apartment I would think."

"So you stayed in an apartment. *Yours?*"

"Yes, Charles."

"Why?"

Was there no way she could lie herself out of *this?* "Charles, it's been a long exhausting trip and I just need some peace. I know you deserve an answer. Please, Charles, right now I just need to sleep...and besides I have a bad headache." She wanted to turn her back to him, draw far away, but she was so close to the edge of the bed.

"You always have bad headaches. Or so you *say,* but I wonder. You're an educated woman, so you know what larceny is. You understand the meaning of the term."—his voice calm and controlled, each word selected, precise, and delivered with just a hint of threat, as if he were admonishing a class that had badly misbehaved.

"Yes, Charles. "She could feel him beside her and was afraid.

"You're quite a fortunate woman. Quite fortunate! Do you know why?"

She chose silence.

"You know the meaning of the word. Also, that you cleaned me out. Is there anything left at this point? Well, is there?"

"No."

"Yes, quite fortunate. Because if I weren't so forgiving, you wouldn't be sleeping in a nice comfortable bed and living in a nice comfortable house. You know where you'd be, don't you?"

She said nothing.

"So what are you going to do about it?"

"... try and make amends," she answered surprised to hear her little girl's voice. She had not chosen it—not consciously.

"How?" said Charles calmly and evenly—almost with warmth. "Take your time. Think about it first. I'll give you two days."

He was just playing with her, Connie told herself, perhaps waiting for Alice to leave. She was also aware that she could not keep the truth back from him forever. She considered confessing just the part about the Toyota, hoping that that would satisfy him. But she knew it wouldn't. You couldn't spend a hundred thousand pounds even if you bought a new Mercedes. Alice's last whispered warning before leaving Fethiye had been, "Mum, whatever *you* do don't tell him about buying that gulet for Omer."

How? Alice had had no answer either. After having dropped their daughter back at school that next morning, on the return drive Charles broke the silence. Reaching for that ear, he had said, "You do know I can't afford to take time off like this, especially someone in my position of trust. You have no idea all the grief you caused me!"

Then why did you want me back, Charles! "I could have driven her." He was repulsive to her, physically; she now only wanted to keep a separating distance between them.

After dropping her off before their house, Charles returned to his office at Computer Operations Management. Connie spent that afternoon cleaning and tidying the house as she knew Charles wanted, first the downstairs starting at the utility room where she loaded the washing machine with her own soiled clothes and whatever she could find of Charles' before returning through the garage where her car stood just as when she had left, not driven except for on those rare occasions when Charles had allowed Alice to borrow it in their search for her whereabouts.

Her daughter had wanted to buy it she said, but Charles had been unwilling to come down in the price. Now it sat.

Connie turned her attention to the rest of the house, passing as she did Charles' key rack in the hallway. Her car keys weren't there, the peg from which they normally hung was empty. She went upstairs. After cleaning and tidying her own bedroom and bath, Connie turned to Alice's room where the bed remained just as when her daughter had left it that morning.

Connie gathered up the bed sheets to take down and wash. Then she turned to the bookshelves. Her books had been just shoved in by Charles in his haste. All needed dusting and arranging, she saw. So she took them all out and began putting them back one-by-one. There were titles she had even forgotten she still had such as the *Forsythe Saga* from her grandfather-uncle's house on Loch Fyne that she had absconded with.

She thought back then on Loch Fyne and her girlhood in Scotland with almost a longing, remembering her father, their solitary walks, her cousin John, and the day he had saved her from drowning. John whom she had had such a crush on. He had been so good looking!

The most handsome boy in her tiny world and how jealous she had become when John had introduced his bride-to-be! Was he still alive—John? Probably, though Connie did not know. She had cut all ties to her Scottish side even though she had always thought of herself as more Scottish than English she remembered as she dusted and returned the *Forsythe Saga* then reached for the next. *Lady Chatterley's Lover*, an illegal copy printed while the novel was still banned. At least she had been told by the owner of the secondhand shop in which she had found it, and which had made it, at the time, irresistible. Lawrence had named his heroine Connie *too* she thought as she set the volume back.

The next book her hand touched was *The Waves*. Curiously, Virginia Woolf must have had a similar attraction to the sea and what it symbolized. Connie had been drawn to this particular work because of the title. But as she opened it and began to thumb, stopping at a paragraph here, there, she remembered how difficult the book had turned out to be and how in the end, losing interest, she had finally laid it aside. Though aside, though depressing, *To the Lighthouse* was the easier novel. *Yes,* it was still here. Connie lifted it out, opened.

She did not recall having marked it up, but she had, lines or sometimes entire paragraphs, using a green *highlighter.* This line on page 158 for example: *a soul reft of body, hesitating on some windy pinnacle and exposed without protection to all the blasts of doubt.*

Or these words on page 172, *until at last one seemed to be on a narrow plank, perfectly alone, over the sea.* With a tremor Connie thought of the *Gul* and what she had halfway wanted to do. What Virginia Woolf actually had but in that terrible way, with rocks to weight her down. Connie set the book back and turned from the room, turning downstairs. That must have taken some courage—more than she herself would ever find.

She thought as she reached the bottom of the stairs just how untenable her situation here was. What was she going to do? Perhaps if she could get her old teaching job back, that might help her over the difficult part at least. In the past work had always provided her a way to avoid difficult or painful situations. She would suggest the idea to Charles that evening over dinner and from the refrigerator she began selecting foods she knew he would like, then from the wine stock a nice bottle of chardonnay which she set in to chill. But when he entered that evening, she knew from his face that something must have happened. "Charles, should I start tea? What's wrong?"

"The system's down!" He turned immediately upstairs.

She followed him as far as the door to his computer room. "Can I put the dinner on, Charles?" But when he only looked back at her annoyed, she said, "Can I bring you a cold glass of wine then?" Not waiting for his reply, she returned with the wine. "I'm going to start your lasagna anyway. You need to eat, Charles," she added, appealing to him. She put out the food the way he would want then waited for as long as she could before re-climbing the stairs to announce a little timidly that the food was soon on the table. He came without objection. But from the tiny amount he ate, and the haste with which he chewed then swallowed, she knew now was not the time to announce her decision. The meal finished, Charles poured himself more wine and disappeared with it upstairs. He always worked at his computers while she cleaned the kitchen and put on the dishwasher.

He was still at work when Connie went to bed. She laid there not knowing which to do, try to get to sleep or wait for him. Finally she heard him come and called out, "You can turn on the light, I'm not asleep."

He had and she watched him undress. How underdeveloped his body looked, she thought. His stomach protruded almost as if he were pregnant, his legs, hairless, were smooth and white. "Did you figure out the problem, Charles?"

"Fortunately! I'm going in the shower now. I'll turn the light back off."

She waited, hearing first the rush and splashing of water. Then, after a period of nothing, the sound of him gargling and rinsing his mouth. She waited to snap on her bed light until the bathroom door at last opened and she saw him. How different the two males appeared *there,* she thought as she watched him cross to the bed. The head of Omer's was round while Charles had none, the skin tapered down to just a small hole. "So the computers are all working again," she said, watching him climb into bed.

She waited until he was settled into position: "Charles, I've been thinking—"

"You can't imagine the pressure I'm under. The weight of the responsibility that are on *these* shoulders and only *these!* How hard I work just to be able to provide us with a comfortable income, and a lifestyle that's the envy of not just a few, I can assure you! So are you ready to talk? "

"Tomorrow, you said. It's late, Charles, and you need to sleep."

Only she couldn't, she laid in the wondering what she would say. She wished she still had some sleeping pills, or her Valium! But that would mean a trip to Dr. Collins who was bound to ask questions.

"Charles, how's your quorn?" she asked at dinner that next evening.

"Good, since I made it. That's something you will need to learn, how to make quorn."

She had drunk most of a bottle of wine over the course of the afternoon—enough to help her become aggressive. "I was thinking, Charles. We can use two incomes." Now she had his attention. "It's time I go back to work, don't you think?"

He laid his fork aside. "Work *where?* You're still a missing person."

She still did not know quite what to do about that detail— what removing herself from, she supposed, a police list would entail. "See if I can get my job back. And if I can't, then I can always work as a substitute for the remainder of the term."

"No!" he said at once: "You've done me enough harm! Dragging my name in the dirt, making me a laughingstock. Almost costing me my job?

No again, and you stay well away from that school *or else!*"—his manner, like his voice, harsh— unforgiving. She watched as he cast his serviette aside and rose. Or else *what?* she thought. But there was little chance he would change his mind—and, she was forced to concede, not without reason.

"If I don't go near the school—if I go where nobody knows me and get a job as a sales lady for instance, would that be alright, Charles?" she had asked him in bed that night, in her most reasonable voice. "Or am I a prisoner here?" She sensed he was having trouble deciding and added, "I know what I did is inexcusable."

"'Inexcusable' is a rather mild term for grand larceny, wouldn't you say? And you still haven't told me how you spent all that money! Well—?"

"I just did. I bought the car."

"A Toyota I think you said. And so what happened to it?"

"It's with Bea. Bea is trying to sell it for me," she lied.

"You don't spend a hundred thousand pounds on any car. So how did you squander the rest, Connie?"

"Bought a business."

"I see. So now you own a business, do you? In Turkey!"

"...no."

"Then what happened to it?"

"… I lost it."

"Ho-ow? "

"You have to be a resident. I didn't know that."

"I see. What kind of business?"

" …."

"What kind of business?" he repeated sharply. "I made a big mistake. Does it matter, Charles?"

"What kind of business?"

"I bought a boat." She was going to be sick.

"A boat! What for? I suppose next you'll tell me you were going to teach yourself to swim with it! Whose boat! Do I know it?"

"... Ali's." She felt him bolt up in bed. "Captain *Ali's that I was on?*"

" —that you were on."

For an instant he seemed unable to speak. She could only lay there.

"What made you do something so stupid is what I want to know!"

"Because Ali owed money and was going to lose it, I could get it at a good price. And I…guess I thought it would be a good investment. Like stocks," she thought to add.

"You were set up!"

"I was stupid! Now can we leave it? You wanted to know and I told you the truth. You can call me any name you like (and I'm sure you already have!). Can't we just go to sleep? You have to be at work in the morning. And I have to use the little girl's room before I bust. Please, Charles," she pleaded.

But he wouldn't leave her alone, even for one day. Over dinner that next evening he started grilling her again. "I've been thinking about it and parts of what you said can't be. You didn't just go over on a spur of the moment holiday—a *lark*, taking with you a hundred thousand of my money—so don't lie to me. You were meeting someone—who?….I said *who?* It was that Omer, wasn't it? Answer me!"

"…yes."

"See, telling the truth wasn't so hard after all, was it?" he said, smiling— it was not a warm or friendly smile. "So they put their heads together and set you up. Simple as that and you're supposed to be an intelligent woman. Which one did you give my money to, Omer or Ali?"

"Ali. It was transferred into his bank account if you must know."

"So there was no change of ownership even. Figures!"

Her hands trembled so that her fingers could hardly grip the knife and fork. "Please, Charles, I promise I'll make restitution. I'll try and pay as much of it back as I can."

"*How?*"

"I said I'd work…If I just worked as a substitute, Charles?"

"Don't you dare go near that school now!"

She had to do something didn't he see? and occupy herself somehow, if only to prevent herself from going stare-crazy! she thought, watching him pick up his knife and fork and continue eating.

But he stopped, and casting knife and fork aside said, "Pretty clever the way you did that: copying the stock certificates and leaving me the forgeries thinking I wouldn't notice. Who did you plan it with?"

She said nothing, feeling her heart beating inside her chest.

"It wouldn't have been with Ali. So it had to be Omer. That's who you nearly bankrupted me for! Isn't it?…I asked you a question!"

She could feel his eyes, their cold intent. "...yes," she confessed hoping that would satisfy him.

But it hadn't. That night as she lay in bed, her back turned trying to sleep, he suddenly said:

"I suppose you fucked him….did you? "

Whatever she said would make him only more enraged.

"Don't pretend you're asleep when I know you're not. I asked a civil question and I demand a civil answer. Did You Fuck Him?"

"... yes, Charles, *I fucked him!*" feeling the anger erupt in her half-whispered words.

"Yes, I thought as much."

"Now leave me alone. *Please, Charles?*" she pleaded as she tried to move away from him. But she was already crowding the edge of the bed.

Over dinner the following evening Charles remained hostile and withdrawn, scarcely exchanging five words with her as he ate hastily then retreated back upstairs. He was still with his computers when she crept past his door on her way to bed in the hope of falling asleep. But without sleeping pills or her Valium, she could not. She could only lie there with her eyes closed, unable to stop herself from thinking, remembering odd or random moments from the past; lying curled up beside her father and smelling his slightly musky odor. Hear Alice say, 'Mother whatever did you see in him? You had a perfectly good husband!' Or remember Omer's laughing look of boyish delight as she sprayed the whipping cream *Omer why did you do it to me when I would have done anything for you? I even stole for you and it still wasn't enough!*

That particular night she was still awake, still thinking thoughts, when he came to bed. She listened to him for a time in the bathroom, saw inside her closed lids the light extinguish and heard the pad of his feet across the carpet; then felt as the mattress dipped.

He lay unmoving beside her for the longest time and, when he still said nothing, she began to think their fighting was over, and to think of ways she might coax herself to sleep, take repeated deep breaths and try to hold them.

"Why I ever listened to that daughter of yours is beyond me. You know where you would be right now if I hadn't, don't you?... Don't you! I said—"

"Yes, Charles," she whispered back.

"You're no better than my first wife!"

"I already know what I am, Charles. I live with it every day," she said—it was no more than a whisper. But he wasn't listening, he rushed on.

"If Marilyn was a slut, you're even a viler slut and you know that too, don't you! I suppose you even gave him a blowjob while you were at it—some dirty unwashed Turk who you don't even know from Adam, and on my money! You're no better than some common whore you pay for on the street—and that's what it boils down to!" he said, his hands grabbing for her.

But she freed herself and, falling, slid off the bed. Half stumbling, she ran across the carpet to the door and down the darkened landing to Alice's room, which she entered slamming the door shut behind. But there was no way to lock it and she crossed to Alice's bed and crawled under the covers where she hid, hoping he would let her be.

But he hadn't. She heard the door and sensed him approach like you sense a swiftly moving shadow before she felt him over her, felt his hot breath then on her face:

"So what made some Turk's cock so special that you gave him my money for it? Was it bigger than mine? Is that why you ran all that way to Turkey just to hand him my money? Is it? Answer me!"

She thought later, until that moment she had not realized that sex wasn't just about love, it was about hate and the need to hurt! At the beginning she had tried to fight him off as he pulled her nightgown violently up, feeling his knee force her clamped thighs apart. "No *please*, I'll make restitutions, Charles," she pleaded. But he had not listened and since she couldn't stop him, force him off her, she could only abandon her body finally as if it were some dead thing and not her. She lay like dead— unresponsive to each punishing thrust, trying to leave herself and that body which had been her betrayer. But there were details she remembered later; how at one point she had even aided him in the act— hating herself. Yet she felt nothing. Her mind, now blank, was elsewhere and she was a little girl lying cuddled in her father's lap feeling his fingers move lovingly through her hair as they listened to his music, and she felt his kiss before the image stopped in her mind with the abruptness of a window blind being drawn down suddenly.

She had lain pinned beneath him and felt his anger subside, there in the tense dark. His fury spent, he released her then. "Now come back to bed," he whispered, his breath hard beside her.

"No"—except had she actually said the word aloud or just thought it?

She felt the mattress dip; then, freed of his weight, spring back and she was alone again in total darkness unable to alter or slow the rush of her thoughts, thinking *You should never have let Alice talk you into coming back. You knew, didn't you, it would turn out like this.*

"Yes, but what else could I have done?" she heard herself say. *You should have jumped that day from the Gul like you'd wanted.*

"Yes."

As she waited there in the dark, her mind too active—tense— to sleep, she tried to think of a way out. Perhaps Charles was right, and she merely deserved all that she had ever gotten. It would have been best never to have lived! she thought as she lay there wired, feeling herself silently cry. Why had he agreed to take her back? Because he still had had hopes of seeing at least some of his money returned? Yes, perhaps that too, but there was more. *What?* The true answer then came to her, because, like Marilyn before her, she had shown him what she was, a vile street whore who deserved to be punished. And that was why to this day he had never forgotten Marilyn, why he still kept that dirty old couch of hers. Not because she had cheated on him, but because she had escaped! Connie knew she could not stay either, she must leave *now*, take with her only what she would miss, what was still dear. Some clothes, her father's ashes. Just go— *where?* That she didn't know was of little concern. What was, were her car keys. *I wonder where you put them?* she thought as she waited for first light.

But she must have fallen asleep then. Because, when she next opened her eyes it was to see light, the gray light of a Manchester morning. She sat up— listening. The house was quite as a mausoleum. Charles must have already left for work, she thought as she rose and entered the landing. Their bedroom door at the end stood open and she approached tentative as a wary cat.

The bed stood empty, the top sheet and blankets crumpled up in a clump. She could smell him too amid odors of castoff socks and underwear, lingering human smells that she could associate with his close presence as, entering, she crossed to the window to peer down at the driveway, then out at the street that was grey and wet. It had rained during the night. What time was it? *Nine?* She turned and, slipping into her house shoes, went downstairs.

On the kitchen counter next to the sink she saw Charles' empty teacup and saucer, beside his bowl of scarcely touched porridge which she first emptied down the garbage disposal, then together with his cup and saucer placed in the sink before preparing her own tea. As she waited for the water to heat, she began searching about for something she might eat: toast and marmalade or perhaps a soft-boiled egg. Charles of course didn't eat eggs or cheese, but Alice had bought both and there should be an egg or two still, she thought as she walked to the refrigerator, *yes*. In fact, there were three. She set them on the counter while from the dishwasher she removed a pot and partly filled it with cold water into which she laid all three eggs since she no longer intended to be here past today and so would have no further need for food, she knew as she lit the burner under the pot. Then she reached for a teabag.

She put two slices of bread into the toaster and found the marmalade. The tea steeped, she carried it on a tray together with two soft boiled eggs, the toast, marmalade, and remaining cheese into the dining room where she broke the top of the egg and began to eat though she found she didn't want to and had forcibly to make herself chew each mouthful. The first thing she must do, she thought, would be to locate her old car keys. *Where did you put them, Charles?*

Most likely they were somewhere in the computer room, though they could be mixed in with his clothes in a drawer—that was another possibility. Leaving her dishes and food on the table, she climbed the stairs to his computer room but found it locked. *Locked?* At some point during her absence he had replaced the former door handle with this new one he could lock. So the room was now off limits to her. The key, she had no doubt, was with him, perhaps on the house-key ring. So her future he had already worked out, down to which rooms she was permitted into, and which she was not! With a sickening feeling she continued on to their bedroom, though it was unlikely she would find the keys hidden in a drawer. Still, she had found things there before, she recalled as she dug down amid socks and underwear, remembering for a fleeting instant the odd memorabilia she had discovered in Omer's drawer that day she had gone hunting for his bankbook. Connie searched beneath the folded stacks of clothing: *nothing.* In a sudden flare of anger she began pulling out handfuls of underwear and flinging them onto the floor. That drawer was clean!

She opened the next and dug in, flinging out items of his clothing, hurling them, but this drawer too contained nothing. In defeat she retreated from the room, stopping again before the door to his computers. Again she tried the handle. She put her weight against the door then trying to force it. But it would not budge. Hopelessly she returned downstairs and started through the empty house. Of course the key could be anywhere! Mechanically she began to wander, out through the kitchen, to the garage where, in the gloom, she saw her car standing mired in a coating of dust. On the bonnet she drew an eight with her index finger to measure the thickness of the dust. The car was locked. Back when she still taught, she had always intended to have an extra ignition key cut, and to hide it under the car somewhere in case she should lose her keys and be stranded.

Connie turned back toward the kitchen. To her right she could see the utility room door, partly open. She entered snapping on the light, and her eyes fell upon the workbench. On the wall behind it garden tools hung from pegs and there was long shelf above, empty save for the odd box of weed poison or garden fertilizer.

She could tell by their cobwebs they had not been used. Beneath the bench top were cupboards. Approaching, she began to open each door. The shelves inside were mostly bare. She could see a box of *Weed and Feed,* like the shelves coated with dust nothing had been touched. Then she saw something else shoved well back into a corner and reached in through the cobwebs for it. Scraggles' water bowl. So that was where *he* had put it! She felt tears form as she pressed the bowl to her breast: it was in here where Scraggles spent perhaps his last moments!

Setting the bowl gently aside, Connie returned to the house in need of a glass of wine. She knew where there were two bottles of *shiraz* and she opened one, poured, and carried the glass to the living room. *What are you going to do?* the voice said. More than likely her keys were hidden in the computer room and that was why the door was locked. *Yes.*

Then another thought occurred: Alice had been allowed to drive the car. She might have had a spare set made—it was possible. Connie rose and crossed to the phone. From her address log she located Alice's number and dialled. Then waited. It was a house phone, located out in the landing, and if there were no students about to hear it, the phone would just ring and ring.

Connie hung up for now and returned to her wine. What else had he taken of hers and hidden just to have his revenge? She had left nothing behind for him to hurt her with, not anymore. Her father's ashes but he wouldn't throw those out, *would he?* On the other hand, after she had disappeared, thinking she was gone forever, or dead, why would he not— they were of no interest or value to him!

Connie set her wine glass aside and rushed upstairs to their bedroom. She'd slid the urn with her father's ashes onto the shelf above the clothes at her end of the closet, pushed well back from view, after Charles had complained about having to look at it in the dining room. No, it was still where she had put it! Relieved, she lifted it down and, after wiping the dust from it using a towel in the bathroom, carried it downstairs and placed it on the coffee table before her. How she had missed him! Connie reached for her wine, then rose to try Alice again. This time after just two rings someone answered, a student who knew where Alice's room was and who agreed to leave a note under the door saying Call—it was urgent!

Refilling her wine glass, she sat back down to wait for Alice's return call. But if Alice were in class, which was likely, she might not get the message in time. Besides, it was unlikely that Alice would have made a key. Connie still had the two thousand pounds of Charles hidden and the thought occurred, *What if he should find it!* She was now afraid of him, physically, and she thought, *even if you have to take a cab, do it!* But she still had her English driving license, why couldn't she rent a car—nothing prevented her?

She rose and, taking her glass and the wine bottle, went upstairs to collect what she would need in clothing. Sweaters. Warm slacks and, of course, her raincoat. Also, in one of her old purses were family photos of her father and mother on their wedding: one of her father when he was very young and also his baby picture which she had always adored. Her mother's was there too, and there was another, she remembered, of her Scottish aunts and uncles all gathered before her Uncle Jim's house on Loch Fyne. Her cousin John was in that. She recalled her crush on him and that moment of humiliation! The purse was stuffed in one of the drawers of her dressing table. She found it and carried it to the bed which she had smoothed. Then she began going through her underwear drawer, to select what she would take, singling out items Omer had liked seeing her in, when the phone rang. *Alice!*

She dropped the clothing and picked up the phone. Only it was Charles' voice she heard say *Connie?*

"What do you want, Charles?"

"Just thought I'd check see how you are…" When she said nothing, "And I've been thinking. Maybe you should try looking for work. If that's what you want. What do you think?"

And when she still refused to speak:

"We can decide tonight. I took our dinner out to thaw. It's in the bottom of the fridge. You may want to look at it later and if it's not thawed, you'll just have to take it out, okay?"

As if the voice were from a great distance away, or as if she were carrying on a second conversation with another at that same moment, she had difficulty focusing on the words.

Finally, she said, "Yes, I see. What time will you be home, Charles?"

"I'll try to be there by six latest."

"Six!": her voice echoing the word. She set the phone back and looked over at the digital clock on the nightstand, she still had the afternoon to sort herself out.

She began laying out what she would take on the bed, trying to decide what best to do, leave in a cab, or go first to the car rental? She could wait up until three for Alice should she phone—though it was unlikely Alice had had an extra key made. Or would know where Charles kept hers. The clothing she had decided to take (most of what was in the closet, her skirts and summer dresses plus tank-tops and her blouses, items which she had no use for now, she would leave) she placed on the bed together with a few cosmetics she would need, and other items such as photographs, and articles Alice had written back when she was editor or the school newspaper and that Connie had kept, including the one on Charles. Making a mental list of things cherished lest she overlook something, she inventoried the items before her. Everything she could possibly think of was there save for the two novels of Virginia Woolf in Alice's room, and of course her father's ashes.

The items assembled, Connie walked to the stairs. The suitcases would be in the garage and there was a question of which to take. Her small overnighter would be sufficient, she thought, since there was that other question, one she had yet to face: where and how would she dispose of it?

The suitcases were stored in an overhead loft at the rear of the garage. She could see her overnighter just above her head and by standing on her tiptoes on the stepladder and reaching, she could nudge it with her with her fingers until she finally managed to coax it down. It had been one of the pieces of luggage she had taken with her to Omer in Fethiye. *Anyone foolish and gullible as you has only herself to blame for it!* a voice of stern reprimand reminded her.

"You think I don't know? "

She heard the phone and, dropping the suitcase, rushed to the living room and snatched the receiver from its cradle: "Alice?"

"Mum, sorry I didn't phone but I just got in. What's happened? Is it to do with Charles?"

She felt herself break, she couldn't help it, she began to cry into the phone.

"Mum, what has he done?"

She could hear the concern in Alice's voice and fought to regain her self control in the phone. Haltingly, she began telling her daughter some of what had transpired.

He's an asshole! Mum, you've got to get out of there. Pack the car and leave!"

"But Charles has my keys," she sobbed back.

"Mum, I made you an extra—didn't I tell you?"

"I don't think so."

"Mum, I know I did. Right when we walked into the house.

"Don't tell me you didn't hear?"

That was another of her faults, not paying attention when she should. Listening instead to those things that would only trap her!

"Mother, go in my bedroom. At the head of the bed near the wall lift the mattress. I taped the key under it."

As if she had just been saved from something too frightening even to contemplate, joy surged. "Oh, thank you, Alice!" She could again feel tears, only this time they were happy!

"So pack and just get out—you still have the two thousand, don't you?"

"That I kept well hidden."

"Do you know where you will go?"

"No. Maybe to see Virginia."

"Who's *Virginia?*"

"Did I say— Mandy, I meant."

"I thought you said she's living in London? "

"She does. Maybe I'll surprise her."

"Are you sure? Mum, you can always come here to Leeds."

"Yes, I know Alice, and—"

"Yes? "

"Try not to think too badly of me. I know I've made some terrible mistakes. But I always acted in what I thought at the time was your best interest."

"I know that, Mum. So when are you coming? "

"I don't know. I'll probably just stay in a hotel tonight."

"Tomorrow I'll be gone until quite late. But I can leave my room key with somebody."

"No, I promised Mandy."

"Well…phone."

"Yes. Goodbye. Love you!" said Connie, thinking as she then rushed upstairs trying to locate the key. *But what would you have done at your daughter's—you've caused her enough problems.*

Chapter 2

THE M-6, WHICH BYPASSED PLACES Connie remembered as a child and was the route most took now driving to Scotland, had not existed when she was growing up. Only the A-6 which passed through Stockport on its way north had and near the entrance to it there was a *BP* station where Connie stopped to fill the petrol tank, put air in the tires, and wash the car's windows. Then, her overnight case behind and her father's ashes resting on the passenger's seat beside her, Connie pulled onto the A-6. Glancing down, she read the time on the digital clock: Charles could be walking in the door in as little as an hour or an hour and a half. She pictured him wandering about the deserted house from room to room, perhaps calling out her name. Finally, he would go into the garage and realize only then that she was gone, vanished as completely and finally as if she had never been. What would he think? Do? She didn't care.

The sky through her windscreen was broken by scudding clouds that sometimes hid the sun while at others revealed it either to one side or directly in front of her vision forcing her to squint with half-closed eyes, depending on the meander of the motorway as it followed the contour of the moor, up and down, in and out of towns with their rows of terrace houses, the same walls of weathered brick and roofs the colour of coal that she had seen all her life, and so knew without knowing, or having to see, just as she knew without having to remember the last time she had travelled this stretch. It had been with her father and mother. She squeezed in back together with household goods and personal effects, whatever could be gotten in—believing that she had said goodbye to Scotland forever.

Overtaken by darkness and rain, they had pulled off the A-6 at Preston to stay the night. Ahead Connie could see the exit sign and slowed. Then, on her right, she could make out the hotel, the *Tickled Trout,* and glimpse the river as it wound beside it seemingly without motion, like a gray sluggish snake.

But she thought as she drew closer and failed to recognize it, it could be any hotel that was long and not very high. She couldn't recall it being white, for example. Nor were the lobby and reception area at all familiar, they were too modern and airy for one thing. The *Tickled Trout* she knew and thought she would remember had been old, she reflected as she approached the reception desk, the clerk behind watching her as she said, Do you have any singles?"

Had she a reservation? he asked. No—she had been driving past and decided to stop, was all. It didn't matter—the hotel wasn't full, said the clerk smilingly.

"And can I have one facing the river?" she asked.

The bellboy had accompanied her back to her car for the suitcase. She slipped on the raincoat as a way to carry it, working the urn with her father's ashes into a pocket (the fit being tight, she found), and followed the bellboy to the lift, her room was on the second floor.

It was a rather small room she saw, though it had been recently painted and so was clean. A not unpleasant room, she decided as she tried the bed, found the mattress firm though not hard. She rose and turned to the window to look out. The river was quite wide here, she discovered: she could see a piece of something—*wood?*—being carried slowly by the current. *Was that the sort of river in which Virginia Woolf, her pocket weighted with rocks, ended her life?*

The bellboy had left Connie's overnight case on the luggage stand near the door. She crossed, unsnapped the locks, and opened. The two novels lay on top. Connie carried them to the bed for now, returned, and reached down into the suitcase, to feel for the other bottle of *shiraz*. She carried it to the small table and chair beside the window in the corner. The wine opener she had dropped into her purse last as she left behind that house of pain. The bottle uncorked, Connie walked into the bathroom and returned with a water glass. Pouring, she tasted the wine slowly, savouring its flavours. Then she reached for the novels.

The Waves she remembered buying after she had gone back to school. She had always been fond of reading. As a child, in Scotland, it had been her main escape. But it was while she was studying to become a teacher that her tastes became more focused. In the student cafeteria before tables cluttered not just with plates of food half consumed and stained tea cups, but with books and binders containing lecture notes, was where she would listen in on arguments and discussions over this point or that in *Heart of Darkness* or D.H. Lawrence, listening to classmates or sometimes strangers, all with the same high hopes, the same dreamy goals during that all too brief spell where one is freed from the past but not yet shackled to a future. Her mistake was easy enough to see in hindsight: she should never have believed Joyce, or, worse still, competed. What Joyce set out to get what she had to have, starting with the man. Her mistake had been in believing that if you were satisfied with each other in bed, the rest would be there too like parts of an attractive package deal: money for a nice house, cars, a holiday in Spain. Respect, you radiated in his success, and in the belief that you were looked up to and envied by others who had made, for whatever reason, the wrong choice. That was why it was all up to Alice now, not to make her mother's mistakes.

Connie sipped her wine. She started to reach for one of the novels, but the room was turning dusky. What time was it? Eight, possibly. She thought of eating, putting something in her stomach before the restaurant closed whenever that would be. So she rose to leave, but paused in the bathroom before the mirror, to run a comb through her hair first. How plain was the face looking back at her! And how it had aged; thinking of how all her cosmetics, the face creams and skin reconditioners she had used could not hide the fact, and all the while Omer must have seen that. *How could you have been so blind!* she thought pinching her arm, feeling it welt.

There were but a few customers in the dining room. Connie selected a table where she would be alone and ordered first a bottle of wine. Then the *chef's special of the day* which turned out to be roast beef and a Yorkshire pudding. It was of no matter. She cut the roast beef into pieces and began to chew. But the meat was dried out. Never mind, she wanted only to be finished and go back. When she had had enough, she signalled the waiter over, she would take the remainder of the wine upstairs. Should she pay now?

If she wished. Or he could charge it to her room number. Here, Connie decided. With cash or credit card? "Cash." She carried on her person almost two thousand pounds and *what to do* with it presented a dilemma.

She took the lift up, discovered her room completely dark, the river beyond her window gone as though dissolved by the darkness. Connie snapped on the ceiling light above her but found the energy-saver bulb cast the room in somber shades. She turned on both nightstand lamps then the small night light attached to the headboard above the pillows *she* had stacked to lie against. Then she filled her water glass to the edge with red wine and, placing it on the nightstand, laid back against the pillows, her hand feeling for the two Virginia Woolfs: *To the Lighthouse* which she had read while she was still married to Cliff, and *The Waves* which she had been unable to get into. What had interested her most in Virginia Woolf was not even the suicide as such (though the manner in which it was done stirred her curiosity). *Why* when her life had been a success? Connie had asked herself but found no acceptable answer. Besides her gift with words, she'd had a good husband. Dissimilar though they were, she felt a closeness and sympathy for Virginia Woolf, as if she were her twin. Connie's copy of *To the Lighthouse* was a hardcover, and on the inside of the dust jacket there was a portrait of Virginia Woolf when she was young and said to have been beautiful. The old black-and-white photo showed a strikingly handsome face, long like Connie's, with a thin, aristocratic nose, and eyes cast in thoughtful reflection. But there was something pensive too in that look, Connie saw as she examined the photo. Virginia Woolf had been tall and slender also. But there the resemblance ended Connie knew as she opened the novel and began to thumb through its pages.

She'd forgotten just how many places she had underscored words, or sometimes whole passages, using a highlighter, starting on page 18 with these five words she had highlighted in green: *her own inadequacy, her insignificance.* Then on page 40, the word *unworthiness* was underscored, this time in pink.

None of this did she recall marking up as she continued turning pages. On page 83 Connie had highlighted *She could not understand how she had ever felt any emotion or affection for him.* And under it were her own scrawled words, in pencil across the bottom of the page, "Such basic things as food made him uncomfortable and, because of that, she had married this odious man who pulled at his ear!"

She wrote that! Connie reached for her wine and took several swallows, before turning back to the book curious to see what else she might have written. But she hadn't, there were only a few lines more that she had taken the time to mark, one a repeat. On page 167 Connie had highlighted over *"We perished, each alone."* Then, near the very end she found the line again and it made her think of that other line, from Conrad, *"We live as we dream—alone,"* and for an instant she saw herself back on the *Gul* standing leaned out over the anchor chain above the water trying to see what really was down there when Alice had discovered what she was up to.

Connie laid *To the Lighthouse* aside and reached again for her wine. The glass was empty and she rose to refill it. Returned, she reached this time for *The Waves* which she opened. Deciding to skip the introduction, she began leafing through pages, but there were no highlighted sentences or notes in the margins, nothing to make her remember why she had laid the book aside. No, here was something. She had scrawled in pen at the bottom of a page: Is Rhoda V.W.?? The lines above were being said by Rhoda. Connie read, her eye skipping through them, *"One sails alone. That is my ship. It sails into icy caverns where the sea-bear barks and stalactites swing green chains."* It was a beautiful line! V.W.'s but it could also encapsulate her feeling.

She moved on more rapidly, skipping pages until toward the end, she slowed. In the past, whenever she abandoned a novel, she would first read its end trying to discover what she would miss by shutting the book? Here, near the bottom of the next to last paragraph she read, *"We may sink and settle on the waves. The sea will drum in my ears. Rolling me over the waves will shoulder me under. Everything falls in a tremendous shower, dissolving me."*

In what year was *The Waves* written? She turned back to the front. There, opposite the Table of Contents, was the copyright, 1931. And in what year had she drowned herself? Connie turned to the introduction, March 28, 1941. Ten years later! Had it taken her those ten years to build up the courage?

After having her breakfast in the hotel restaurant—tea and two soft boiled eggs, slowly ingesting them with toast dipped in their yoke—Connie returned upstairs to pack. What should she do with her father's ashes? Leave them in the raincoat pocket even though they made one side of the coat heavy and lopsided to walk in? It wasn't her father's remains that weighted the coat down, it was the urn. She could fit it into her overnight case; there was room. No, leave it until she got to her car.

Connie glanced out the window at the sky. It was clouded over, the river below grey—angry. It would be raining where she went.

Her room bill came to fifty pounds. Cash or credit card? The clerk had inquired. "Cash," she replied and saw a look of surprised curiosity appear on the face across the counter as she drew from her purse the envelope stuffed with pound notes of various denominations. Before the watching eyes of the clerk, Connie sifted through them for two twenties, then the ten.

She laid the raincoat folded on the seat next to her. Then she was back on the A-6, following it to a destination her hands and even the toes of her feet seemed already to know and so need not be told as she mindlessly drove, her thoughts again freed. Virginia Woolf apparently had heard voices—how, what kind? According to friends who knew her, she'd suffered from madness. Nobody was diagnosed with madness in the Twentieth Century!

When did Freud die—before Virginia Woolf, or after? But did it even matter? By 1941 there must have been qualified psychiatrists all over London. So why did she not go?

Connie saw the first splatter of drops strike the windscreen as she approached the Scottish border. It always rained here, just like in Manchester. Hadrian's Wall was somewhere close, she recalled her father stopping to show it to her—what year was it? 1973 perhaps, or 74 when they left Glasgow for a new life? What would her life be like now had her father not been made redundant and they had stayed in Glasgow? Ahead was a junction and signs. Here she had to be careful if she was to avoid Glasgow. It was a sprawling place and she was sure to become lost if she were not watchful, even though it had been home for the first thirteen years of her life. Mostly happy years, she reflected back, despite having had only herself for company. Long solitary walks on hillsides of heather when the weather permitted and when it did not, hiding herself in her grandfather-uncle's library where she had been a bookworm to avoid her Scottish aunts and uncles with their insinuations.

Ahead she saw the signs for Paisley and for the airport which she remembered passing from years before. She had only to continue north, following the motorway as it fish hooked. Or she could turn west and take the ferry across. No, that way she would get lost. What time was it? Past three. It must stay light until nine anyway this time of year, she thought.

Not finding the turn-off in the failing light was one of her concerns. Getting to a bank before it closed was the other, more immediate, one.

There were many towns to choose from along the A-85 as it wound north and at Lochearnhead, before the motorway made its abrupt turn west, Connie decided to stop. There must be several banks, and the post office. She found a pub where she ordered a glass of red wine, *your last,* said the voice inside, she thinking trying to arrange in her mind, what it was she would do and the order in which she must do it. She chose a table near the stained front windows for light and drew the envelope of money from her handbag to count. She still had about one thousand eight hundred pounds she thought, most of it in a hundred-pound notes though she could find fifties and twenties mixed in. The money counted, she drew one of the twenties which she then folded and began to stuff inside her purse, stopping in the act as her mind tried to tally to the exact number her remaining needs. She had totally forgotten petrol! There might be about a half tank—she thought so. But why had she not thought until now to look? The last thing she wanted was to find herself stranded somewhere and people forced to look for and find her. *But if you no longer exist?* She unfolded the twenty and laid it back in the stack and hunted until she found a fifty which she similarly folded and placed in her purse before returning the bulk of her money to its safe location inside the handbag. Next, she dug for and found the clean sheet of stationary which she'd brought from *The Tickled Trout* for just this purpose. But, pen in hand, her will reneged. What could she say that would not hurt Alice more? All the apologies she might offer would not make the slightest difference now. She could hear Alice saying, "Mother, why ever did you marry *him!* when you had a perfectly good husband in my father?

And when she told Alice about Omer, "Mother, and let me guess, the first thing he did in Bea's was offer to show you his diving boat. Mother, when are you going to learn!"

So what should she write: *Please, Alice, don't make the same mistakes!* No, Alice was far too intelligent for that. Connie ordered a second glass of the red wine. She had not eaten since breakfast back at the hotel and was beginning to feel the alcohol work, give her courage, the needed boost to write a single line, one simply saying that she would not need the money and so wanted Alice, who did, to have it. *Dear Alice, I am sending you this bank draft as a sort of peace-offering, and because I know you cannot turn to Charles for anything.* After reading the thought over in her mind Connie struck out *peace-offering* and wrote in its place "because you will be needing it."

No that wasn't what she had wanted to say. *Never mind* she thought as she folded the sheet of stationary and slipped into an envelope she had also taken from the *Tickled Trout.* She began feeling for the money at the bottom of the handbag but stopped. If she sealed the envelope now she would only have to tear it opened at the bank, so she instead dropped the unsealed envelope into her handbag and rose to pay for her wine. The next thing would be to locate the bank.

But why not just mail the money and skip buying the bank check since, if she mailed her a bank draft, then Alice would guess something was wrong! Best mail the money with the note saying she wanted her daughter to have it is all. But what if the letter became lost? Or the money stolen out of it! No: either way it would not make a difference since Alice wouldn't receive the letter anyway and so couldn't know anything was wrong.

She was in front of a bank now trying to decide. If the money were stolen that would be the end of it, while if the bank draft were made out in her daughter's name only, she could cash it Connie remembered, and entered the bank. But when she got to the teller's window she couldn't locate the money—it was nowhere inside her bag! She must have left it in the pub! she thought and started to panic when an elderly customer behind her in line touched her and said, "It's right there in your handbag, dearie—I can see it from here. It couldn't plainer if it bit you!"

Connie thanked the elderly lady profusely. The check purchased, Connie then dropped it and the unsealed envelope into her handbag and started back toward the car, thinking she would see a mailbox on the way to a Mark and Spencer food store she had earlier passed, and which was coming again into sight. Entering, she walked to the wines, and had started to reach for a red when she saw the *amontillados.* Harvey's had been her father's favourite and she reached for a bottle. Also, she had eaten nothing since leaving the hotel and her stomach was beginning to complain. There was a small deli section and in it were some pre-made sandwiches. Connie reached for the closest, tore open the wrapper and began to eat. But she found she did not want food and returned the half sandwich to its wrapper and paid using the fifty pound note she had kept aside. *You still haven't passed a mailbox* she thought arriving back at the car. But there was still time, she thought as she dug into her handbag searching for Alice's letter which she slid into the folds of her raincoat beneath the urn containing her father's ashes, there beside her on the seat. She best leave now if she were to avoid driving that narrow winding road in the dark, she thought as she returned to the A-85.

She did not recognize any of the landmarks as she had hoped, or even the road itself as it twisted. Fighting back the fear that she was horribly lost, she continued on telling herself that there was only one road and that she could not possibly have strayed from it. In a sky the colour of sorrow there was no sign of any sun by which she could track her change of direction. Still, she had left Lochearnhead driving north and now it seemed to her that she was headed west, or southwest, that her uncle's house would be on her left. What time was it now? Past four. But there would still be light enough to see by even at nine this time of year, without a sun. She could glimpse Alice's letter still not mailed on the empty seat beside her and she debated, trying to decide in herself, which was better: simply vanish *and it would be as if you never had been…*or do as she was about to? And if there were no money involved? No, she would have to leave something—an apology. Did it come from Shakespeare, that line: To be cruel is to be kind —? *Is that what you were being, Omer, that day on the deck of the Gul?*

Ahead she saw road signs, and the name of a town: Cladich! A typical Scottish name, she played its sound over slowly in her mind: *Kladickh!* spoken harshly, gutturally like German, she thought as what must have been its main street took form in her vision, one and two storied structures. Facades of mostly gray stone, thick to keep out the cold of Scottish winters. Ahead she spotted a space beside the curb and pulled in. The post office would be somewhere close, she thought, reaching for the letter.

But as she closed the car door it slipped from her fingers, fell to the gutter. She reached down and snatched! She had to snatch twice as a man on the street stopped to watch her clumsy attempts. "Do you know where there's a post office?" she said trying to hide her awkwardness as she rose.

"Och i, in the next street up, be on this side…you all right, lassie?" he had responded in that thick brogue she had not heard since her father's death.

"Yes! No, do you know how I get to Fyne from here?"

"The sea loch?"

"Yes."

"Turn left just up *there*." He pointed. "Sure you're alright?"

"Yes!" She hurried away from him. The post office was near the corner. But as she drew up before the mail drop her hands began to shake and she had to control them. Force herself to lift the handle. Trembling, she made her fingers release the letter.

There, *gone!*

The Scotsman was still observing her as she returned, climbed back into her car. Through the window she gave him a little wave and smile of thanks, *You see, I'm perfectly alright.*

But she knew she wasn't, that her life had been a lie. A mistake she'd tried to hide. But was it her fault that she had only been used, lied to by those males she had trusted most? Only her father had been true, kind and good. How she missed him. She saw herself as a little girl curled up close beside him to share their warmth. But then he had died. In Manchester where they'd been so unhappy. Was that why? because of the way he spoke, and so made him seem different, 'Alan, you must try to learn English if you're going to live in this country!" had said Aunt Isabel who disliked both of them. Her father had died from a tumour in the end; he had always been a heavy smoker. Connie felt for his urn on the seat beside her. Not her first husband, plus all the Omers and Juans, had ever made up for his loss. *Never!* she remembered that afternoon in the hospital corridor, being stopped by the doctor, "Your father is dying, Connie." Then he had, and for weeks after she had had the same dream of standing before a door watching it slowly open upon nothing, a void filled with the voiceless terror of her being alone.

She found herself on a single-track asphalted road that occasionally widened, then narrowed, climbing, then dipping as it wound as though lost. The road to nowhere, she remembered it had been called. To her right, below the crown of the road stood a croft, abandoned, just the four exterior walls of bleak and unpainted stone, the roof having since collapsed in, while hillsides of purplish pink heather rose before her wandering eyes. Further up the slopes she saw stands of trees, Scottish pine, or fir and below their dark mass were thickets of bramble, wild raspberries and nettles she remembered from her girlhood walks so long ago. The sudden singing of tires passing over a cattle- guard, vibrated upward so that she could feel it through the steering wheel, alerting a memory: somewhere just beyond the narrow bridge she now crossed, and the stream below, would be the village where in summer her aunts and uncles would come to buy odd items—bread, maybe eggs, or sometimes a pound of butter—and just after it a road went off, to her left as she drove toward her uncle's house.

The uncle was dead, of course, and she had no idea or interest in the subsequent fate of the house as she passed that less-than village of drab stone. It was the road she was determined to find and follow if she were to reach her destination, the boat ramp, before dark whenever that came, it was seven now.

She drove on not knowing, not even sure this was the road, all appeared unrecognizable, not new exactly but confused. She was in an old gully or creek bottom and on either side of the road were small trees, their branches scraping against the sides of the car at times. She didn't recall the road being so grown in like this. Perhaps she picked the wrong road! If so, where did it lead? She thought of stopping long enough to find the bottle of sherry; how she wished at that moment it were her father driving. Then she would be safe, her life secure again.

Ahead the trees parted, and in place of them she saw grey sky, and a flat area for parking. There should be the stone walls of what had been a croft if this was the right place. But as she opened the car door, she saw none. The sky was dark, the air itself damp, thick as if with minute particles of fine cold spray. It was a chilling cold. Shivering, she slipped into her raincoat feeling it weigh to one side. From the back seat she drew the bottle of sherry, opened and drank. Warm and not sweet exactly, she felt it heat and cheer her insides as it went through her. Finished for the moment, she forced the sherry bottle into her other pocket, the weight evened. Suddenly she was being attacked by insects blackly swarming at her face, *midgies!* With her hands she batted at them. On their long-ago walks, her father and even her mother, who didn't smoke, kept lit cigarettes to stop the midgies from biting. Connie had forgotten that. But never mind, she thought, trying to walk out of their swarm, you had to keep moving. She looked over at the wood, the trees and brush. What were the trees—*weeping willows?* There were also nettles and then she could see what might be a wall. It was only partially visible, overgrown by Scotch Broom. To escape the midgies she walked toward it.

Yes, this is where it had been, only she didn't remember it as being anything like what she saw, the walls overgrown this way like up in the Sunken City where they'd gone to escape the sun's full heat. *You'd found shade beneath the eucalyptus trees growing out of the foundations, out of the walls themselves, where you made the bed of leaves. Then you stripped down your bikini in front of him watching his black eyes for their response. That spot where he caught you by total surprise when he said he was like Yanko.*

"You're not, you're the reverse!"

Yet she had trusted him, believed in those eyes and wanted their attention, from the first when she discovered him looking at her that way in Bea's. Believed true what he said to her in the water, and on the *Gul* when he took her ashore and they walked together up to the ruins. Her happiest day and all the time he was only manipulating her. Cold bloodedly just for the money—that was the part that still hurt.

She turned away, back to the road, to where it continued ill- defined toward the beach. But there was a steep slope and she could not see what lay at the bottom. She thought it would be the boat ramp. But it wasn't, there were just the stones of the beach, the road ending at them. Had she driven the wrong road?

No, it looked like the place she thought she remembered, all except for the paving stones of the boat ramp—they were missing.

Still, the more she examined the beach and inlet, the more convinced she became that it was from here they had launched the boat that morning, backing it down over the flagstones into the water. Just around the point to her left was the fishing spot where she had almost drowned—would have had John now gotten her out. *Why, why John, did you have to save me? Why didn't you let me!*

She continued down the pebbly beach to the water. How cold it looked! She shivered. It was motionless and flat, like an inky black mirror. The shingle of the beach continued at a slant as if into shallows, but she knew the picture deceptive, that the darkness of the water obscured its danger. After a meter, or perhaps two, it went down without warning. In one moment you would be wading over stones then you wouldn't; you would be falling through icy darkness and soon lose consciousness.

She was shaking, trembling with cold and discomfort beside the water. She fished down into her raincoat pocket to retrieve the sherry bottle, then drank, swallowing it in large gulps not taking time to taste it feeling it burn as it went making her feel somewhat better. She hoped it would make her drunk! The bottle at last emptied, she bent over at the edge of the loch and held the bottle under, feeling it refill. Then she reset the cork and placed the bottle back into her pocket to correct the balance while Virginia waited. But she felt ill and dizzy then and had to sit down at the edge of the water. *"Mother get down from there before you fall! You know you can't swim."* But would she have jumped if Alice hadn't come? It still wasn't clear—she'd wanted to. *And if you had then you wouldn't be here now and it would already be as if you'd never existed and so you'd no longer have to explain to Alice why you did all those senseless things.* But would she have drowned? The Mediterranean was such a different place, the water warm and salty—it held you in its caress. No, here was not the same; the waters as unlike as were the two countries. The midgies were back to remind her of what she had returned here to do—what she had been unable to that day on the *Gul. You can't back out this time* the voice reminded her. *Had she wanted all that much?*

The midgies swarmed stinging at her face as she sat frozen before the frigid black water where she could hear her friend calling for her.

Epilogue

THE FACT THAT SHE'D HAD that key all along proved just how scheming and *deceitful!* that mother of hers, whom he had married in honest good faith Charles said, was. But where she had gone Charles could only guess. There was that *Mandy person* whom he never had trusted, said Charles. *Whine some more, Charles!* thought Alice as she watched him pull at his ear.

She believed she knew where her mother might be following the arrival in Leeds of the letter containing just money and that cryptic, frightening note which was to make her miss a week of class. The letter had been postmarked from somewhere in Scotland. As a girl her mother had nearly drowned there—Alice remembered her describing it so she had rented a car and had set out in what proved a fruitless search. Then yesterday after class Alice had returned to her room at the student residence. As usual, she opened her laptop first to find that she had received an email from Bea. *So that's where you went!* Alice thought and for an instant her hope soared, until she thought: *No, you're not stupid enough to go back after what happened.* The email read:

Dear Alice:

How are you? I don't have your mother's email address but feel confident that you will forward what I am about to relate to her in the hope that it gives her consolation at least. And at some sense of closure (correct me if I am wrong but isn't that the word people like to use for it nowadays).

But what I heard is that the *Gul II* sank while it was tied up to the dock on the very same night you and your mother left.

The next day they sent a diver down to find out why, and guess what!

Somebody had deliberately opened the sea cock. I found out about it that very next morning when Omer came to me looking for your mother. He is convinced Connie did it because who else would have a motive? And besides, how many people would know how even if they wanted to?

Alice paused to muse. There is a pipe three or perhaps four inches in diameter that comes out of the ship's hull near the bottom with something attached at the top. Alice could not remember what Omer had called it that day on the diving boat, but whatever the red steel thing was, it had a handle and it did not require much in the way of intelligence to turn a handle ninety degrees, or—once it was turned—to know to get the hell out of there before the water caught you, thought Alice smiling, and continued to read:

You would know if she did it or not, I don't. Anyway he had all his friends out looking for her and I am so glad they didn't find her. Omer has been known to beat women up in the past. If your mother has any plan to come back, tell her from me don't! even though, following the sinking, she has become something of a folk hero with ones like Eric, who doesn't really like Turks to start out with.

In the closure department there is more your mother will surely appreciate. It looks like Omer may lose the Gul. It was raised the next day by the local tugboat operator who is claiming the gulet is his after the insurance company refused to pay the cost of salvage. Apparently, the former owner, Ali I think, let the boat's insurance run out. Or Omer was supposed to pick it up but didn't.

Now they are pointing fingers at each other, and trading accusations while the tugboat owner takes Omer to court claiming the *Gul* is his. And tell your mother that from what I hear, Omer is as broke as he was when he met her. I guess that new girlfriend left him fast after that, also tell your mother.

I know that while all this may come as good news to her, it does not begin to make up for her loss. for which I feel partly responsible. Tell her I think of her and wonder what has happened in her life since. We all wish her the best, even Eric though I know how he liked to rub her the wrong way. And tell her to email me, that I want to stay in contact. After all she was, and is still, one of us.

"I will, Bea," Alice typed back, "and I am sure she will be pleased." Alice closed the notebook by saying to herself as she had many times, *Mum, bringing you back here maybe wasn't a good decision—okay. But where was the choice?*

END

How I Came to Write this Book

I PERSONALLY HOLD HOMER TO blame. Why? Because he composed the first great book of the West about 800 BC by best estimate.

While it may not always be the case now, when I was in school history was taught starting with the Trojan War made famous as every schoolboy knows by the words of the world's first great poet Homer.

The story of that war, as told in Homer's great epic involves the abduction of the Greek queen Helen, said to be the world's most beautiful woman. Hers was the face that "launched a thousand ships" manned, as Greek legend tells us, by angry and vengeful Greeks intent on taking her back. And so the Greek army attacks Troy, and only after long and bitter ten-year struggle are the Greeks able to enter the city to sack and burn it by the trick of a wooden horse.

In 2000 Helga and I flew to Turkey to see Troy for ourselves, and wound staying 16 years, in a pretty little seaport on the Aegean Sea called Fethiye which led to the writing of this book. To tell you why, I must describe Fethiye.

Fethiye had a population of about eighty thousand at the time, roughly ten percent of which were English. There were also Germans and Dutch living there; people in search sun and sea and, yes, sometimes sex. They would arrive and quicky make friends with the Turks and, in the end, would simply not leave.

Helga and I became close friends with many of the English especially. Calis Beach where we lived was a lively place of drinking and partying where the Turks and English fraternized freely. Many of the English who came and stayed were single (and married) women looking for more perhaps than just sun and sea, romance and sex, which the Turks needless to say, were more than willing to provide!

It was a situation that would appeal instantly to any writer and when one of the English women had her novel picked up by a London agent, I decided it was time I try.

No sooner had I let it be known around Calis Beach that I intended to write a novel set in the beach than I received all sorts of valuable advice and support from the expatriates, many of whom are in the novel (with fictitious names of course). Help came from all quarters. There was one elderly Scottish expatriate who helped me with writing Scottish brogue, for example; she proofed much of the novel. There were Turks too who were helpful. One in particular critiqued the novel and gave me his input. He was more than glad to help out providing, he said, "my name doesn't appear in Wikipedia!"

To all of those people without whose help I could not have written this book, I send my thanks and gratitude.

Thomas Lawrence